A MARBLE WOMAN

A MARBLE WOMAN

unknown thrillers of

LOUISA MAY ALCOTT

*Edited and with an
Introduction by*

MADELEINE STERN

(ORIGINALLY PUBLISHED IN HARDCOVER AS *PLOTS AND COUNTERPLOTS*)

AVON BOOKS ◆ NEW YORK

Originally published in hardcover as *Plots and Counterplots*

AVON BOOKS
A division of
The Hearst Corporation
1350 Avenue of the Americas
New York, New York 10019

Copyright © 1976 by Madeleine B. Stern
Cover art by Jeff K. Potter
Published by arrangement with William Morrow and Company, Inc.
Library of Congress Catalog Card Number: 76-3578
ISBN: 0-380-72677-7

First Avon Books Trade Printing: September 1995

AVON TRADEMARK REG. U.S. PAT. OFF. AND IN OTHER COUNTRIES, MARCA REGISTRADA, HECHO EN U.S.A.

Printed in the U.S.A.

OPM 10 9 8 7 6 5 4 3 2 1

❧ *Contents* ❧

❧ *Introduction* ❧

BY MADELEINE STERN

[Jo March] took to writing sensation stories, for in those dark ages, even all-perfect America read rubbish. She told no one, but concocted a "thrilling tale," and boldly carried it herself to . . . [the] editor of the Weekly Volcano. . . .

. . . Jo rashly took a plunge into the frothy sea of sensational literature.[1]

When Louisa Alcott adopted the name of Jo March for her own role in *Little Women,* she was not writing "behind a mask." The creation is as vital as the creator and many of the episodes in the life of this flesh-and-blood character are autobiographical. The author herself once listed the "facts in the stories that are true, though often changed as to time and place," and that list included "Jo's literary . . . experiences."[2]

The exact nature of Louisa's clandestine "literary experiences"—the discovery of her pseudonym, the identification of her Gothic effusions—was all revealed in *Behind a Mask.*[3] There four of her thrillers were reprinted, suspenseful stories that for over a century had lain unrecognized and unread in the yellowing pages of once gaudy journals. Now the remaining sensational narratives written by Jo March's prototype have been assembled in a companion volume. Again readers may revel in more stories by an L. M. Alcott masked in anonymity or in pseudonymity. From the garret where the author wrote in a vortex flowed the tales emblazoned in flashy weeklies circulated to campfire and hearthstone in the 1860's. Now they can be devoured again—these suspenseful cliff-hangers which are also extraordinary revelations of a writer who turns out to be not simply "The Children's Friend" but a delver in darkness familiar with the passions of the mind.

As a professional who could suit the demands of diverse tastes, Louisa Alcott disdained a precise duplication of her themes and characters. Her repetitions are repetitions with variations. Her heroines—those *femmes fatales* who could manipulate whole families—are in this second volume *femmes fatales* with a difference. Motivated still by jealousy or thwarted love, ambition or innate cruelty, they now take on the texture of marble beneath whose cold white surface the fires of passion flame or are banked. Louisa Alcott's marble women have their variants too: sometimes they have encased themselves in marble the better to execute their purposes; sometimes an attempt is made by a demonic character to transform them into marble. Whatever the nature of their seeming frigidity, they are all extraordinary actresses, mistresses of the arts of disguise who use their props—their bracelets or ebony caskets, their miniatures and keys or bloodstained slippers—with histrionic skill. In one of the narratives of *A Marble Woman*, Alcott's most evil heroine has been painted, the dancer Virginie Varens of "V. V.," a creature seductive, viperish, manipulating, who with a lovely bit of irony wins even as she loses in the end.

Here too will be found themes that go beyond the tamer shockers of *Behind a Mask*: the child-bride theme, which had a strange lure for the creator of *Little Women*, stemming perhaps from her early disastrous experience as a domestic in the service of the elderly James Richardson of Dedham; the theme of murder, which appears here in gory splendor; the theme of insanity, which is traced through many variations from a hereditary curse to an attempt at manipulated insanity, a black plot to madden a benighted heroine. The whole psychology of manipulation is presented with singular power in these tales, the drive of one dark mind to shape another, the Pygmalion theme in a somber setting. Finally, in addition to the lure of evil and violence, mental aberrations and mind control, *A Marble Woman* will offer to devotees of "The Children's Friend" another sinister theme—drug addiction and experimentation. The creator of Jo March was skilled not only in the wholesome delights of apples and ginger cookies but in the more macabre delights of opium and hashish.

Like the stories presented in *Behind a Mask*, these narratives with their purple passages and their scarlet motifs had their sources not only in the gaudy Gothics which their author devoured but also in the life she had led, the observations she had made, the fantasies she had dreamed. Louisa Alcott was to some extent the Jo March who "like most young scribblers . . . went abroad for her characters and scenery; and banditti, counts, gypsies, nuns, and duchesses appeared upon her stage. . . .

"As thrills could not be produced except by harrowing up the souls of the readers, history and romance, land and sea, science and art, police records and lunatic asylums, had to be ransacked for the purpose. . . . Eager to find material for stories, and bent on making them original in plot, if not masterly in execution, she searched newspapers for accidents, incidents, and crimes; she excited the suspicions of public librarians by asking for works on poisons; she studied faces in the street, and characters, good, bad, and indifferent, all about her; she delved in the dust of ancient times for facts or fictions . . . and introduced herself to folly, sin, and misery." [4]

She delved also into her own "ancient times," dredging up especially the ingredients of those "Comic Tragedies" she had penned as a girl with her sister Anna and produced on the stage of the Hillside barn in Concord.[5] Love scenes and direful lines, dramatic confrontations and disguises, desertions and suicides, magic herbs, love potions and death phials that had been the staples of "The Unloved Wife" or "The Captive of Castile" could be introduced again with alterations. If they had once chilled the blood of an audience of illustrious neighbors, now, having undergone a subtle sea change, they could chill the blood of subscribers to flamboyant weeklies.

Other episodes in Louisa Alcott's past could be served up to readers of sensational stories. In 1858, after her sister Lizzie's death, she had seen a light mist rise from the body. Seven years later a misty apparition would arise from a fictional Alcott grave. Before the Civil War, Louisa had heard tales of Jonathan Walker, whose hand had been branded with the letters S.S. for "Slave Stealer." For the prototype of Jo March's *Blarneystone Banner* or *Weekly Volcano* the initials *V. V.* would be tattooed upon an imaginary wrist. A short period during the summer of 1860, when Louisa had cared for "a young friend during a temporary fit of insanity," would be put to use for lurid excursions into nightmarish derangements.[6]

Louisa Alcott's service as a Civil War nurse in the Union Hotel Hospital, Georgetown, was followed by an illness that provided her with one of the most interesting sources for her tales of violence and revenge. After some six weeks of nursing she succumbed to typhoid pneumonia, a severe attack of which she wrote, "I was never ill before this time, and never well afterward." The bout was accompanied by sinister dreams from which the patient would awaken unrefreshed. Since those dreams, that fevered delirium, would be interwoven into the fabric of her blood-and-thunders, they merit an attention less medical than literary.

> *The most vivid and enduring was the conviction that I had married a stout, handsome Spaniard, dressed in black velvet, with very soft hands, and a voice that was continually saying, "Lie still, my dear!" This was Mother, I suspect; but with all the comfort I often found in her presence, there was blended an awful fear of the Spanish spouse who was always coming after me, appearing out of closets, in at windows, or threatening me dreadfully all night long. . . .*
>
> *A mob at Baltimore breaking down the door to get me, being hung for a witch, burned, stoned, and otherwise maltreated, were some of my fancies. Also being tempted to join Dr. W. and two of the nurses in worshipping the Devil. Also tending millions of rich men who never died or got well.*

After three weeks of delirium "the old fancies still lingered, seeming so real I believed in them, and deluded Mother and May with the most absurd stories, so soberly told that they thought them true." As her father reported in a letter to Anna in January, 1863, Louisa "asked me to sit near her bedside, and tell her the adventures of our fearful journey home [from Georgetown] . . . and enjoyed the story, laughing over the plot and catastrophe, as if it were a tale of her imagining." [7]

The tales of her imagining would still pay the family bills. The economic necessity that had prompted the stories in *Behind a Mask* prompted those in *A Marble Woman*. At times the only breadwinner of the family, Louisa Alcott set about liberating that family from debt with her thrillers, and in so doing she achieved a psychological catharsis that liberated her own mind from its phantasmagorias. Her father had observed in "the elements of your temperament" both the "Spaniard" and the "Saxon." [8] The "Spanish" elements were surely in the ascendancy when she reeled off her " 'thrilling' tales, and mess up my work in a queer but interesting way." She was at this time a compulsive writer, dashing off her narratives "like a thinking machine in full operation." Stories simmered in her brain demanding to be written. "My pen," she despaired, "will not keep in order, and ink has a tendency to splash when used copiously and with rapidity." Once she wrote, "Liberty is a better husband than love to many of us," and often she "longed for a crust in a garret with freedom and a pen." [9]

It was to the office of the *Weekly Volcano* that Jo March boldly ventured with a thrilling tale and "bravely climbed two pairs of dark and dirty stairs to find herself in a disorderly room, a cloud of cigar smoke, and the presence of three gentlemen, sitting with their heels rather higher than their hats." [10] If "Louisa Alcott" is read for "Jo March," then *The Flag of Our Union* may be read for the *Weekly Volcano,* and for the three gentlemen in a cloud of cigar smoke, the three colorful Boston publishers, Messrs. Elliott, Thomes and Talbot, whose "disorderly room" was part of the Journal Building at 118 Washington Street.

Louisa Alcott's first contribution to *The Flag of Our Union* was also the story that flaunted her most unregenerate heroine. "V. V.: or, Plots and Counterplots" "By a Well Known Author" [11] appeared in February, 1865, to titillate readers and divert them from news of the war that would end two months later. A shocker it was, with its heady ingredients—poison in an opal, footprints left by a murderess, drugged coffee, a feigned pistol duel, theatrical props against sketchy theatrical backgrounds of a fancied Spain or India, Paris or Scottish estate. But it is less for its plots and counterplots moving relentlessly on to the "éclat" of a "grand *dénouement*" that "V. V." becomes a fascinating narrative. It is, as in most of the Alcott thrillers, the nature of the heroine that captures the intense interest of the reader.

Virginie Varens is no Jo March. All Spanish, she bears no traces of her author's "Saxon" elements. "A sylph she seemed" in the greenroom of a Paris theater, a seventeen-year-old dancer "costumed in fleecy white and gold . . . flushed and panting, but radiant with the triumphs of the hour." Her cousin and dancing partner, that sinewy, animated flame of fire, Victor, has set his mark upon her—two dark letters "tattooed on the white flesh" of her wrist, the monogram *V. V.*, which she conceals by means of a bracelet fastened with a golden padlock. Virginie is already a *fille* if not a *femme fatale* with many suitors, including a viscount who offers her an establishment and infamy, and the Scot Allan Douglas who offers her an honorable name and a home. "Mercenary, vain, and hollow-hearted" as well as conniving and ambitious, Virginie accepts the latter. Thereupon the "fiery and fierce" Victor, enraged with jealousy, "reckless of life or limb," takes "the short road to his revenge," and "with the bound of a wounded tiger" stabs the bridegroom. As for the heroine, one "night of love, and sin, and death" has transformed her into wife, widow, and, as it turns out, mother too.

So the curtain rises upon a melodrama of deceit and death. Because she is motivated primarily by social ambition, Virginie Varens appears more innately evil than her competitors—those powerful and passionate

Alcott heroines urged on by the more primitive force of jealousy. The
remainder of the narrative is set in the Scottish estate of Lady Lennox,
where V. V. determines to win Allan Douglas's cousin, a noble Scot also
named Douglas who looks like Allan's twin. For this mercenary purpose
Virginie assumes several theatrical disguises and perpetrates sins both
venial and venal, ranging from peccadillo to crime. Posing as Mrs. Vane—
she has been Colonel Vane's mistress in India, not his wife—she capti-
vates every Scot but her target, Cousin Douglas, who astutely detects
in her "gliding gait" and "brilliant eyes" the hint of "a little green viper."

The "viper" is accompanied by a deaf-and-dumb servant named
Jitomar, supposedly one of Colonel Vane's Indian retainers, actually, of
course, the treacherous Victor in Eastern disguise. With his help Virginie
lays her plot and spins her counterplots. Her pawn is the lovely Diana
Stuart, betrothed to Douglas, who must be eliminated. This V. V. pro-
ceeds to accomplish, feigning, lying, conniving, manipulating. To
Douglas this female Iago confides that Diana may be the victim of a
hereditary curse; to Diana she "proves" that Douglas is already married.

These viperish machinations and the plots they generate are imple-
mented by a succession of fascinating props that recall performances in
the Hillside barn: an ancient iron seal ring; a satin slipper with a dull
red stain; a bit of black lace. But the most potent dea ex machina is, of
course, the heroine herself. She is an exciting *femme fatale*. She has
some feminist inclinations although they stem primarily from a basic
misanthropy. To Diana she observes, "A man's honor is not tarnished in
his eyes by treachery to a woman, and he believes that a woman's peace
will not be marred by the knowledge that in God's sight she is not his
wife, although she may be in the eyes of the world." Virginie has "the
nerves of a man, the quick wit of a woman, and presence of mind enough
for . . . all." She has also the malignancy of a Satan and the conniving
skills of a Machiavelli. She has both the power and the will to inveigle
her rival, Diana, to a loathsome death.

Since crime must in some way, however subtle, be followed by punishment, the counterplots spin on. A surprisingly modern, pre-Sherlock-
ian detective, M. Duprès, is introduced for the purpose—a man who
"adore[s] mystery; to fathom a secret, trace a lie, discover a disguise,
is my delight . . . this brain of mine is fertile in inventions, and by
morning will have been inspired with a design which will enchant you
by its daring, its acuteness, its romance."

Against such an agent Virginie, adopting a variety of disguises, continues to weave her deceitful web until, in the "éclat" of the "grand dé-

nouement," that web is broken and the spinner brought to judgment. "A hunted creature driven to bay," she is arrogant, audacious, and conniving to the end. In a final confrontation Douglas condemns her: "Your treachery, your craft, your sin deserve nothing but the heavy retribution you have brought upon yourself." Her disguises—her "artifices of costume, cosmetics, and consummate acting"—have all been penetrated. Her plots and counterplots have been unraveled. "Virginie, this night your long punishment begins"—a punishment intolerable to contemplate, a punishment from which "escape is impossible," but from which, in her ultimate triumph, Virginié Varens, the most Mephistophelian of Louisa Alcott's heroines, does in her way escape.

This was doubtless one of the tales the author had in mind when, in January, 1865, she recorded in her journal: "Fell back on rubbishy tales, for they pay best, and I can't afford to starve on praise, when sensation stories are written in half the time and keep the family cosey." [12] As for Jo March, "She . . . began to feel herself a power in the house, for by the magic of a pen, her 'rubbish' turned into comforts for them all. *The Duke's Daughter* paid the butcher's bill, *A Phantom Hand* put down a new carpet, and the *Curse of the Coventrys* proved the blessing of the Marches in the way of groceries and gowns." [13]

If "V. V.: or, Plots and Counterplots" is "rubbish," then it is superb rubbish. Though the heart of the heroine may be molded of marble, she is a creature of flesh and blood who, in the very act of appalling, enchants. The plots and counterplots, though derivative, are inventive enough to lure the reader on. As star of this page-turner, Virginie Varens merits a lead position in the Alcott gallery of *femmes fatales*.

The first of the Alcott contributions to *The Flag of Our Union* was by no means the last. The delighted editor James R. Elliott assured his new author that he "should be pleased to have you write me some stories for the Flag, of about 25 to 40 pages of such Ms. as 'V. V.'" [14] Using the pseudonym of A. M. Barnard, she obliged; and three months after "V. V.'s" bow, "A Marble Woman: or, The Mysterious Model" appeared in the pages of Elliott's weekly.

Richmond had been taken in April, and Louisa had gone to Boston "and enjoyed the grand jollification. Saw Booth again in Hamlet." [15] Less than a week after Appomattox came news of Lincoln's assassination. Despite, or perhaps because of, the crisis and grief of the Union, the story papers churned out their narratives for avid readers in search of escape. On May 20, *The Flag of Our Union* carried the first installment of "A Marble Woman: or, The Mysterious Model. A Novel of Absorbing Interest. By A. M. Barnard, Author of 'V. V.: or, Plots and Counterplots.' " [16]

Into this remarkable tale the author injected a delectable combination of themes, including the Pygmalion-Galatea motif, the concept of the child-bride, a hint at incest, and a brief but intriguing bout with opium addiction. Add to these the enigma of the "mysterious model," a masquerade, a chase at sea, and a satisfactory dénouement, and the result is a story as varied in its episodes as it is absorbing in its totality.

Of all the themes used by A. M. Barnard one of the most interesting is her variation on the Pygmalion and Galatea motif—her depiction of the woman who is molded into marble by a sculptor whose clay is flesh and blood. The "marble woman" first appears on stage as a twelve-year-old orphan, Cecilia Bazil Stein, whose dying mother has selected as her guardian a former lover, the genius sculptor Bazil Yorke. Against a Gothic background replete with ancient furniture, dark window hangings, gloomy pictures, a great dog on a "tawny tiger skin," and a spiral staircase leading to Bazil's tower studio, the child and her artist guardian interact. Bazil Yorke bears "traces of deep suffering, latent passion, and a strange wistfulness, as if the lonely eyes were forever seeking something they had lost." To crush his rising affection for the child of the woman he once loved and lost, the sculptor attempts to stifle her warmth and remold her into marble. "If I had power to kill the savage beast, skill to subdue the fierce dog, surely I can mold the child as I will, and make the daughter pay the mother's debt." Bazil's ruthless purpose is complicated by the third actor in this melodrama, who appears at first as a face at a window—"a strange, uncanny face, half concealed by a black beard that made the pallor of the upper part more striking'—the face of the hidden watcher or mysterious model, whose identity is suspensefully withheld until an appropriate time.

In the tower studio Yorke models from a handful of clay. The long large room is "filled with busts, statues, uncut blocks, tools, dust, and disorder." Young Cecil—for so Yorke calls her—learns the art of modeling, and there is no doubt that A. M. Barnard borrowed for the sequences in the tower studio the knowledge of art that Louisa Alcott had acquired from observing her artist sister May. Indeed, Dr. William Rimmer, May's anatomical drawing teacher, was one day to be incorporated into the character of Professor Bhaer in Little Women.[17]

Meanwhile, five years pass and a different kind of modeling is attempted by the sculptor in flesh and blood. Cecil, dressed in white from neck to ankle, has no companions but marble men and women. She is cautioned to live without love. "Be what I would have you," Yorke commands, to which she replies, "A marble woman like your Psyche, with no heart to love you, only grace and beauty to please your eye and bring you honor. . . ."

"Yes," says Yorke, "I would have you beautiful and passionless as Psyche. . . . I am done with love."

The experiment all but succeeds. As Yorke's wife in name only, Cecil becomes "Yorke's statue," "his best work." Yorke has married "one of his marble goddesses. . . . He fell in love with her beauty, and is as proud of it as if he had carved the fine curves of her figure and cut the clear outline of her face." But the snow image is not marble yet. Out of her unsatisfied human desires arises one of the most interesting episodes in the Alcott blood-and-thunders, an episode concerned with drug addiction. The theme engrossed A. M. Barnard, who would return to it, with fascinating variations, later on.

As narrated in "A Marble Woman," Yorke gives the sleepless Cecil a bitter, dark liquid that will bring her "deep and dreamless sleep." She recalls that her mother had taken laudanum for pain and that she herself has "often tasted it." After the unconsummated marriage with her sculptor Cecil develops a growing taciturnity, takes short unexplained flights, and ventures upon mysterious errands. She appears "dreamy, yet intense, blissfully calm, yet full of a mysterious brightness that made her face strangely beautiful." An unnatural inner excitement is followed by "an unconquerable drowsiness" that overpowers her. A "restless sleep" deepens into a "deathlike immobility; the feverish flush was gone, and violet shadows gave her closed eyes a sunken look; through her pale lips slow breaths came and went." A physician recognizes immediately that Cecil has taken an overdose of laudanum and that she has survived the overdose because she is addicted.

"Your wife eats opium, I suspect."

The suspicion is verified. For a year Cecil has had the habit, which "grew upon me unconsciously, and became so fascinating I could not resist it." She eats her opium in the form of little comfits that leave traces of "grayish crumbs" and an "acrid odor." Her need for this "dangerous comforter" is clearly traced to the secluded life forced upon her as the teen-age virgin bride of a thirty-eight-year-old recluse. She has found it too "hard to tame myself to the quiet, lonely life you wish me to lead."

The opium episode is pivotal to the plot of "A Marble Woman" and its dénouement. But its interest is not literary alone. As the concoction of the future author of *Little Women* it raises the eyebrows. The fact

that Louisa May Alcott concerned herself with drug addiction is a
shocker which, today especially, requires some analysis and investigation.

Bazil Yorke's library—and doubtless Louisa Alcott's—contained a
copy of De Quincey's *Confessions of an Opium-Eater*. But the opium
poppy, *Papaver somniferum*, played a less bookish part in many nineteenth-century American lives.[18] Indeed, some of the great New England
fortunes accrued from the shipping industry in which opium trade with
China was often involved. A. M. Barnard's publisher, William Henry
Thomes of Elliott, Thomes & Talbot, had sailed aboard an opium
smuggler that plied between China and California.[19] Little more than
a month after "A Marble Woman" completed its run in his paper, Louisa
Alcott would go abroad as companion to a young woman whose father,
William Fletcher Weld, owned a fleet of ships that flew the Black
Horse flag to Hong Kong and Manila.[20] Obviously the opium trade
was familiar to her.

Laudanum—tincture of opium—was part of the pharmacopoeia of
every nineteenth-century physician except those who eschewed medicine
of every kind. It was freely prescribed for coughs and digestive disorders,
arthritis and rheumatism, and despite the Alcott preference for homeo-
pathic medicine, there is a strong possibility that at some stage of
Louisa's typhoid pneumonia some derivative of the opium poppy had
been administered to her. During her brief but disastrous period as a
nurse in the Civil War, she had certainly observed the use of morphine
as a narcotic for wounded soldiers and was perforce aware of the morphine addiction that sometimes followed and was known as "soldier's
disease." With the influx of Chinese laborers on expanding American
railways, tales of Oriental opium dens in the West provided grist for
the mill of sensation writers in the East.

And so for A. M. Barnard laudanum or opium was not merely sur-
cease from pain but a useful narrative device. She applied it skillfully
in "A Marble Woman," in which Cecil's addiction softens and trans-
forms Yorke into a human being who can react to love. The inevitable
Alcott masquerade party; a mad chase in a storm at sea against a back-
drop of buffeting gusts, torrential rain, and thick mists; the identification
of the mysterious model and the hint of incestuous love this entails—all
lead to a satisfactory conclusion. By curtainfall the marble has been re-
converted into very human clay and, as her publisher assured her, "my
friends think the 'Marble Woman' is just splendid; & I think no author
of novels need be ashamed to own it for a bantling."[21]

The conclusion of "A Marble Woman" by A. M. Barnard appeared
in *The Flag of Our Union* on June 10, 1865. On July 19, Louisa M.

Alcott, traveling companion, sailed aboard the *China* bound for Liverpool and her first journey abroad. Her travels were productive for they yielded a partial prototype for Laurie in *Little Women* as well as romantic backgrounds for Gothic tales—castles and towers, gardens and lighthouses on moon-shaped bays. They produced also an urgent compulsion to write, for her mother had borrowed money to keep the traveler in London after she had left her charge. According to her father, Mr. Weld had complacently remarked, "Miss Alcott can easily pay all her travelling expenses by contributing to some newspapers." [22] Shortly after her return she "fell to work on some stories, for things were, as I expected, behindhand when the money-maker was away. Found plenty to do, as orders from E. . . . and several other offers waited for me." [23]

One of the stories she produced at this time for "E." (James R. Elliott) was a short but dramatic narrative in which the heroine is a self-made marble woman. She is also, it develops, a woman of noble character, and so Louisa M. Alcott allowed her name to appear as the author of *The Skeleton in the Closet* [24] when Elliott, Thomes & Talbot issued it in November, 1867. It is, like most of the Alcott thrillers, a page-turner. It is also of more than ordinary interest for its variation on the marble-woman theme and for its description of a mind unhinged.

Mme. Mathilde Arnheim, "the loveliest widow in all France," graces a château which, although she "desires no Adam," she has converted into an Eden. With its "airy balconies" and "inviting apartments," its "rare pictures" and "graceful statues," its "light draperies" swaying before "open casements" and "leafy shadows" flickering on a marble floor, Madame's château was surely based upon some villa the scribbling traveling companion had seen on her recent journey. As for Madame herself, she is slender and white-robed, wearing a black lace scarf in the Spanish style, an Italian greyhound tripping daintily beside her. She seems "a marble image, beautiful and cold, though there are rare flashes of warmth that win, a softness that enchants, which make her doubly dangerous." Her eyes are lustrous, dark, "filled with the soft gloom of a patient grief." She calls herself a widow. Like V. V. she wears a steel bracelet clasped by a golden lock, the key of which hangs by a golden chain. But unlike V. V., Mme. Arnheim is an *involuntary femme fatale* who lives in seclusion guarding her secret—the skeleton in her closet.

Despite the isolation of this "loveliest spot in France," Madame attracts a lover. Gustave Novaire's jealousy is aroused when he glimpses an apparent rival whose arm encircles "her graceful neck," whose hand plays "idly with a tress of sunny hair." Gustave spies his beloved "pacing to and fro with clasped hands and streaming eyes, as if full of some passionate despair." He sees her "strike her fettered arm" upon the balcony and knows that the bracelet binds her to a dire fate. The mystery is at length revealed—"the secret anguish of my life, the haunting specter of my home, the stern fate which makes all love a bitter mockery, and leaves me desolate." At sixteen—again the child-bride theme—Mathilde was married to the victim of a "fearful malady," "a hereditary curse"—a "wreck of manhood" afflicted with a weakened brain. Having learned of her plan to commit suicide to escape this "marriage mockery," Reinhold Arnheim suffers further mental derangement until he becomes an imbecile mouthing senseless words, smiling a vacant smile.

Now Mathilde is "bound by a tie which death alone can sever; till then I wear this fetter, placed here by a husband's hand nine years ago; it is a symbol of my life, a mute monitor of duty. . . . I have thrown away the key, and its place is here till this arm lies powerless, or is stretched free and fetterless."

After the passage of three years and the machinations of two artful villains, Mathilde's loathsome tie is broken and the steel bracelet is replaced by a slender chain of gold. The heroine has been faithful unto death, and so the author's sally into the nightmare of mental aberration could be acknowledged.

Several years before, Louisa Alcott had ventured more boldly into a similar region of the mind. Six months after her prize story, "Pauline's Passion and Punishment," [25] had appeared in *Frank Leslie's Illustrated Newspaper*, Prize Story No. 17—the anonymous "A Whisper in the Dark" [26]—was emblazoned in the columns of that gaudy weekly. The narrative goes far beyond the effort at mind control that provides the basis for the plot of "A Marble Woman." Here the reader is regaled with the lowest form of psychological manipulation—an attempt, for mercenary purposes, to drive the heiress heroine insane so that her inheritance will be denied her. Interwoven in this black fabric are several scarlet threads: suicidal thoughts and chemical experiments, sleepwalking and the hint of sexual attraction between a forty-five-year-old adopted uncle-guardian and the heroine, Sybil, who is not quite eighteen. With an unusual last will and testament, a large measure of maternal love, and a house of horrors for background, "A Whisper in the Dark" becomes not only an engrossing gruesome Gothic but an interesting foray into the disorders of the mind.

The teen-age orphan Sybil is thrust almost immediately into the clutches of her so-called uncle, who "regarded me mutely for an instant, then, holding me fast, deliberately returned my salute on lips,

cheeks, and forehead, with such warmth that I turned scarlet and struggled to free myself, while he laughed that mirthless laugh of his till my
shame turned to anger, and I imperiously commanded him to let me go.

"'Not yet, young lady. You came here for your own pleasure, but
shall stay for mine, till I tame you as I see you must be tamed. . . . Chut!
What a little fury it is!'

"I was just then; for exasperated at his coolness . . . I had suddenly stooped and bitten the . . . hand that held both my own. I had
better have submitted; for . . . it had an influence on my afterlife. . . ."

Although Sybil is betrothed to her adopted uncle's son, Guy, she is
at first not averse to trying her "power over them both." Before the plot
advances she sits on "Uncle's" knee and smokes "a cigarette of his own
offering . . . then I slept on his arm an hour, and he was fatherly
kind."

"Uncle's" fatherly kindness is soon exposed for the dastardly mercenary sham it is. When Sybil refuses the role of child-bride and rejects
her "uncle"—"I had rather die than marry you!"—her fate is sealed.

Now, with the aid of the "stealthy, sallow-faced Spaniard," Dr.
Karnac, "Uncle" resorts to mind control. If he can unhinge Sybil's mind,
he—not she—will receive the inheritance. And so the horrors accumulate.
Spirited away in a drugged sleep to a nightmarish domain "twenty miles
from the Moors," she is placed in a dreary room, its door locked, its
window grated. "An ominous foreboding thrilled cold through nerves
and blood, as, for the first time, I felt the paralyzing touch of fear." A
great hound guards the room above where a mysterious occupant paces,
a ghostly hand emerges, a whisper sounds through a keyhole. Sybil walks
in her sleep through the haunted house. Since "madness seemed [her]
inevitable fate," she resolves to commit suicide. Instead, she elucidates
the mystery of the room above, learning that if she is "not already mad,
[she] will be . . . [she was] sent here to be made so; for the air is poison,
the solitude is fatal, and Karnac remorseless in his mania for prying into
the mysteries of human minds."

Despite the terrors of this dark plot, "A Whisper in the Dark" has
moral overtones, thanks to which Louisa Alcott eventually found it possible to acknowledge its authorship. Twenty-five years after its initial
appearance she agreed to reprint "A Whisper in the Dark" with a new
edition of her *Modern Mephistopheles*.

Only by means of initials did Louisa acknowledge authorship of
the final story in *A Marble Woman*. "Perilous Play" [27] by "L. M. A."

appeared not in *Frank Leslie's Illustrated Newspaper* but in another of
Leslie's expanding chain of periodicals. Issued in February, 1869, shortly
after she had completed the second part of her perennial best seller
Little Women, it was the last of Jo March's necessity stories.

In January, 1865, Louisa had written in her journal: "L. asked me
to be a regular contributor to his new paper, and I agreed if he'd pay
beforehand; he said he would, and bespoke two tales at once, $50 each
. . . Alcott brains seem in demand, whereat I sing 'Hallyluyer' and fill
up my inkstand." [28]

Frank Leslie's "new paper" was actually his present mistress's and
future wife's new paper. *Frank Leslie's Chimney Corner* [29] had been
started, planned, and edited by that *femme fatale* of real life Miriam
Squier, who assembled its corps of writers and defined its purpose. It
was conceived as a family paper that would appeal to every member of
the American home, an illustrated fireside friend in which the mother
would find a domestic story, the daughter a romance of love, the son a
dramatic escapade, the youngsters adventures and fairy tales. Miriam
Squier's flowery prospectus rivaled some of Louisa Alcott's purple passages: "We present herewith, just as the aurora of peace irradiates the
horizon, the first number of The Chimney Corner . . . which shall be
a welcome messenger of instruction and amusement to the young and
old, in the family and by the fireside—that altar around which cluster
our holiest and most cherished recollections." The astute editor selected
for her "welcome messenger" articles less holy than titillating—sketches
of Chinese gamblers or insane monarchs, the original Bluebeard or the
werewolf of Dole—along with such stories of engaging violence as "The
Queen of the Stranglers" and "The Phantom Hand." "We give," she
boasted, "a story a day . . . some to touch by their tragic power, some
to thrill with love's vicissitudes, some to hold in suspense with dramatic
interest."

"Perilous Play" by L. M. A. could be assigned to this last category
when it was run in 1869 in that "Great Family Paper of America." The
last, the shortest of the Alcott thrillers, it is also in a way the most
dramatic shocker of all, for it is devoted in its entirety to an experiment
with hashish.

As usual the now extremely skillful author sketches her dramatis
personae with broad brushstrokes, presenting the familiar Alcott heroine,
daughter of a Spanish mother and an English father (the "Spanish" and
"Saxon" elements are here combined). Rose St. Just is "pale, and yet
brilliant" with magnificent "Southern eyes," "clear olive cheeks," "lips
like a pomegranate flower." She is attired in an "airy burnoose" and she

wears a bracelet of Arabian coins. She reads the legend of "The Lotus Eaters."

To while away a long afternoon for Rose St. Just and others of the party, Dr. Meredith produces his "little box of tortoiseshell and gold" containing "that Indian stuff which brings one fantastic visions" and is called hashish. The clever and ingenious twist that L. M. A. gives to this experiment results in a story of delicate charm that is also a page-turner. But it is the experiment itself that transcends the interest of the plot, for in "Perilous Play" the twentieth-century reader familiar with marijuana can be introduced to the nineteenth-century attitude toward hashish.

Although *Cannabis sativa,* the source of hashish and marijuana, is one of the oldest drugs known to man, it has been stated that "the only account of the use of this drug in the United States prior to the twentieth century" is an autobiographical work by Fitz Hugh Ludlow entitled *The Hasheesh Eater: Being Passages from the Life of a Pythagorean,* published anonymously in New York in 1857.[30]

Now another nineteenth-century account of the drug has been unearthed—authored by "The Children's Friend"! Had Louisa Alcott ever used hashish? It was freely available at six cents a stick. Had Louisa Alcott ever heard of the Hashish Club of writers and artists modeled in the 1850's upon the French Club des Hashishins? Had she pondered upon the "joy-giver" of the Hindu sages, Rabelais's "Herb Pantagruelion" that induced "cerebral excitation"?

Her description of the effects of hashish in "Perilous Play" certainly suggests either an incomparable imagination or a familiarity with the drug. According to Dr. Meredith, "Six ["comfits"] can do no harm. . . . I take twenty before I can enjoy myself. . . . I've tried many experiments, both on the sick and the well, and nothing ever happened amiss, though the demonstrations were immensely interesting. . . . A heavenly drowsiness comes over one, in which they move as if on air. Everything is calm and lovely to them: no pain, no care, no fear of anything, and while it lasts one feels like an angel half asleep." The trance comes on "about three hours after you take your dose. . . . Your pulse will rise, heart beat quickly, eyes darken and dilate, and an uplifted sensation will pervade you generally. Then these symptoms change, and the bliss begins. I've seen people sit or lie in one position for hours, rapt in a delicious dream, and wake from it as tranquil as if they had not a nerve in their bodies." As for an overdose, that is "not so pleasant, unless one likes phantoms, frenzies, and a touch of nightmare, which seems to last a thousand years."

And so the experiment is made. Rose St. Just is offered "a taste of Elysium," which she secretly accepts. Her lover, Mark Done, is maddened by both love and hashish, and the two are caught not only in a gathering storm at sea but in the unnatural and wild excitement induced by *Cannabis sativa*. "Every nerve was overstrained, every pulse beating like a trip-hammer, and everything . . . was intensified and exaggerated with awful power. The thundershower seemed a wild hurricane, the quaint room a wilderness peopled with tormenting phantoms." All night Mark "lay motionless, with staring eyes, feverish lips, and a mind on the rack, for the delicate machinery which had been tampered with revenged the wrong by torturing the foolish experimenter." Nevertheless, thanks to the author's ingenuity, the hashish folly ends happily and the Perilous Players can exclaim at curtainfall, "Heaven bless hashish, if its dreams end like this!"

With "Perilous Play" most of Louisa May Alcott's nightmarish dreams—or at least their literary applications—ended. The publication of Part II of *Little Women* in April, 1869, brought her the fame and fortune she coveted and set her on the path of sweetness and light from which she seldom strayed.

Astute and sometimes piratical publishers, however, did not hesitate to reprint the Alcott forays into the realms of darkness and from time to time, without her knowledge, her thrillers reappeared. "Perilous Play," for example, was lifted out of *Frank Leslie's Chimney Corner* and run in November, 1876, in *Frank Leslie's Popular Monthly*. "V. V.: or, Plots and Counterplots" reemerged around 1870 in an altogether new dress, as a *Ten Cent Novelette* by A. M. Barnard. Both *The Mysterious Key, and What It Opened*[31] and *The Skeleton in the Closet* had been issued by Elliott, Thomes & Talbot of Boston in their series of *Ten Cent Novelettes* by *Standard American Authors*—the latter as the trailer of *The Foundling* by Perley Parker. Now, as the new decade of the 1870's began, the firm—restyled Thomes & Talbot—reprinted *V. V.* under the authorship of A. M. Barnard as No. 80 in that series. The pseudonymous thriller, bound in blue wrappers, took its place in the literature of the dime novel and is today one of the rarest and most desirable of those ephemeral pamphlets thumbed to death in the nineteenth century, treasured in the twentieth.

The dime novel, introduced by the New York firm of Beadle in 1860, caught on. A. M. Barnard's publishers, Elliott, Thomes & Talbot, entered into competition, issuing their first *Ten Cent Novelette* in 1863—*The Golden Eagle* by Sylvanus Cobb, Jr., an author scorned by Louisa Alcott's illustrious neighbor Ralph Waldo Emerson. The *Ten Cent*

Novelettes[32] issued by Elliott, Thomes & Talbot were described as the handsomest and largest ten-cent books ever published. A new one appeared on the last Monday of every month, bound in pink, later in blue paper, and for one dollar subscribers could receive twelve complete choice novels a year. For a country from whose borders romantic adventure was fast disappearing, these stories offered the lure of the distant in time and space, the excitement of conquest and exploration, the color of the gun-toting West, not to mention the lurid delights of *The Black Adder* or *The Dwarf Fiend*.

From their new address at 63 Congress Street, Boston, Thomes & Talbot reissued A. M. Barnard's effusion *V. V.*, and unbeknownst to Louisa May Alcott the violent and elaborate plots and counterplots she had abandoned were again made available to the public. Between the blue wrappers of a dime novel, the Spanish temptress Virginie Varens still danced, still wove her malignant web, still escaped her punishment. That paperback is remarkable indeed, for it tells a tale not only of a Spanish dancer but of a writer from New England whose variety was all but infinite.

Unlike V. V., who embodied corruption, the heroine of "A Whisper in the Dark" was the victim, not the perpetrator, of evil. Partly for this reason Louisa Alcott, toward the end of her life, permitted her publishers to reprint that story under her own name as a trailer to *A Modern Mephistopheles*. On May 7, 1887, she wrote to Thomas Niles, of Roberts Brothers, who had made the suggestion: "'A Whisper' is rather a lurid tale, but might do if I add a few lines to the preface of 'Modern Mephistopheles,' saying that this is put in to fill the volume, or to give a sample of Jo March's necessity stories, which many girls have asked for."[33]

It was eminently fitting to reprint "A Whisper in the Dark" with *A Modern Mephistopheles*. When in 1877 her publishers had proposed that the author of *Little Women* provide an anonymous book for their "No Name Series," Louisa Alcott had dipped her pen into A. M. Barnard's lurid ink and written a novel dreamed by A. M. Barnard's ghost. In *A Modern Mephistopheles*[34] she had reverted to the Gothic technique, incorporating in her novel the Mephistophelian sybarite Jasper Helwyze, who manipulates his victim, Felix Canaris; Gladys, beguiled out of "her tranquil girlhood"; and the familiar lush heroine, Olivia, "a woman in the midsummer of her life, brilliant, strong, and stately . . . passion slept in the Southern eyes . . . and will curved the closely folded lips of vivid red."

In her room at the Bellevue Hotel in Boston the erstwhile contributor to *The Flag of Our Union* rose from the past, dredging up themes once woven through "A Marble Woman," "A Whisper in the Dark," and "Perilous Play": mind control and the lure of drugs. Again she analyzed the "psychological curiosity" that penetrates and violates "the mysterious mechanism of human nature." And again she described an elaborate experiment with hashish.

Jasper Helwyze's "little bonbonnière of tortoiseshell and silver" contained "white comfits"—the "Indian drug," which "made the face of Coleridge shine." Hashish is given to Gladys who, like Rose St. Just, experiences "inward excitement . . . a strange chill . . . through her blood. Everything seemed vast and awful; every sense grew painfully acute; and she walked as in a dream. . . . Her identity was doubled" until she floated into "the unconscious stage of the hasheesh dream."

Interspersed though it is with metaphysical borrowings from Goethe and Hawthorne, *A Modern Mephistopheles* is an A. M. Barnard thriller in which the now celebrated Louisa May Alcott indulged her "natural ambition . . . for the lurid" [35] and enjoyed a psychological and literary catharsis. When it was first published as an anonymous full-length novel in 1877, the author wrote in her journal: " 'M.M.' appears and causes much guessing. It is praised and criticised, and I enjoy the fun, especially when friends say, 'I know *you* didn't write it, for you can't hide your peculiar style.' " [36]

For some time she hid it successfully, reviewers asking, "Who wrote this story? Whose hand painted these marvellous pictures of the angel and the demon striving for the mastery in every human soul?" [37] A decade after its appearance in the "No Name Series," when the author was paying the penalty of years of overwork and suffering with the cancer that would soon prove fatal, she agreed to the reprinting of *A Modern Mephistopheles and A Whisper in the Dark*. The combined volume that embodied the techniques and preoccupations of her salad days was published posthumously in 1889.

Now "A Whisper in the Dark" has been reprinted once again for the twentieth-century audience that still clamors for more stories by Louisa May Alcott. With "V. V.: or, Plots and Counterplots," "A Marble Woman: or, The Mysterious Model," "The Skeleton in the Closet" and "Perilous Play," it forms a collection that rounds out the stories introduced in *Behind a Mask*. Always there may be a lingering suspicion that Louisa Alcott had other masks, that in the brittle pages of sensational nineteenth-century weeklies lurk more of her anonymous and pseudonymous shockers awaiting excited discovery. The lingering suspicion is really but a persistent hope, for the appetite grows with what it feeds on. The flamboyant thrillers of *A Marble Woman*—narratives delving into violence, mind control, drug experimentation—present in still another, wilder guise the many-sided author of *Little Women*.

The corpus of Louisa Alcott's excursions into the gruesome horrors of the mind has now been completed. The Concord Scheherazade emerges full-face from behind her mask.

Mr

Old Terms

THE AMERICAN UNION.
Two Dollars a Year.

THE FLAG OF OUR UNION.
Two Dollars a Year.

THE NOVELETTE.
$2 a Year—Four Copies, $6.

THE DOLLAR MONTHLY.
$1 a Year—Six Copies, $5.

OFFICE OF

ELLIOTT, THOMES & TALBOT'S

PUBLICATIONS,

JOURNAL BUILDING, 118 WASHINGTON STREET.

BOSTON, MASS.

J. R. ELLIOTT.   WM. H. THOMES.   NEWTON TALBOT.

We will combine our publications on the following terms:
The Dollar Monthly Magazine and The Novelette, together, for $2 50
The Novelette and The Flag of our Union, together, for 3 25
The American Union and Dollar Monthly, together, for 2 50
The Flag of our Union and Dollar Monthly, together, for 2 50
The American Union and Flag of our Union, together, for 3 50

Jan. 5. 1865.

Louisa M. Alcott,

    Dear Madam,

        I forward you
this evening the 3 first copies of the
"Flag" in its new form.

    I think it is now a
literary paper that none
need to blush for, and
a credit to contribute
to its columns, rather
than otherwise.

Now I have a proposition
to make you, I want

to publish your story "Y. Y." in it, in place of publishing it as a Novelette in cheap style. as I had intended, and will give you $25. more for the story provided I can publish it under your own name. Please look the "Flag" over & let me know as early as Saturday & oblige

Very Truly Yours

Elliott Thompson
J. R. Elliott
Ed...

THE AMERICAN UNION.
Two Dollars a Year.

THE FLAG OF OUR UNION.
Two Dollars a Year.

THE NOVELETTE.
$2 a Year—Four Copies, $6.

THE DOLLAR MONTHLY.
$1 a Year—Six Copies, $5.

OFFICE OF
ELLIOTT, THOMES & TALBOT'S
PUBLICATIONS,
JOURNAL BUILDING, 118 WASHINGTON STREET.
BOSTON, MASS.

J. R. ELLIOTT.   WM. H. THOMES.   NEWTON TALBOT.

☞ We will combine our publications on the following terms:
The Dollar Monthly Magazine and The Novelette, together, for ... $2 50
The Novelette and The Flag of our Union, together, for 3 25
The American Union and Dollar Monthly, together, for 2 50
The Flag of our Union and Dollar Monthly, together, for 2 50
The American Union and Flag of our Union, together, for 3 50

Jan. 7 1865.

Dear Miss Alcott,

I should be pleased to have you write me some stories for the Flag, of about 25 to 40 pages of such Ms. as "V. V." I want them over your own name of course, & will give you $2.00 a column (short columns you will notice) for them. That rate will be fully equal to $16.00 for a first page story in the "American Union"

which paper I think you
contributed to while it was
under the management
of Messrs. Graves & Weston.
Will you not contribute
a poem or two for the
"Flag" also? I do not know
as that is in your line,
if it is I shall be glad
to receive poems from —
your pen. I have entered
your name on our gratis
list, & you will receive
the "Flag" regularly.
Very truly Yours
J. R. Elliott

P.S. I will purchase another
Novelette of you at any time
you may wish to dispose
of one. "R.V." will be com-
menced in No. 5, about two
weeks. What title would

you suggest in place of
"V. Y?" Or what for a second
title? Please answer at
your earliest convenience
R.W.E.

AMERICAN UNION.
Three Dollars a year.
FLAG OF OUR UNION.
Four Dollars a year.
MONTHLY NOVELETTE.
Two Dollars a year.
DOLLAR MONTHLY,
$1.50 a year.

OFFICE OF **Elliott, Thomes & Talbot's Publications,**

63 CONGRESS STREET,

Boston, June 15 1865

Dear Miss Alcott,

Have you written anything in the novel line you would like to have me publish by A. M. Barnard, author of "V. V." "The Marble Woman" &c. &c.? If not can you furnish me with a sensation story of about 145 to 150 pages such MS. as you used last "The Marble Woman" so that I can have it by the middle of July? I don't care about even any particular name. if you prefer any other nom de plume for this one

Story, use it, as it is for
one of my Cheap Novelettes.

I will give you
$50. for such a story, &
don't want it to exceed
150 pages of MSS the size
of "The Marble Woman," 140
pages will answer, oo
145 will be better.

By the way my friends
think the "Marble Woman" is
just splendid; & I think
no author of novels need
be ashamed to own it for
a last thing. I am sorry
you should have had
any feeling in regard
to the nom de plume. I
am sure that I have not
given currency to the idea

that "A. M. Barnard" & yourself were identical.

Please let me hear from you by return mail, if possible, in regard to the short novel.

Very Truly Yours

J. R. Elliott

TEN CENT NOVELETTES.

By A. M. BARNARD

COMPLETE

STANDARD AMERICAN AUTHORS

THOMES & TALBOT,
63 Congress St., Boston.

A MARBLE WOMAN

V. V.:

or,

PLOTS
AND COUNTERPLOTS

❧ *Chapter I* ❧

WON AND LOST

IN the greenroom of a Parisian theater a young man was pacing to and fro, evidently waiting with impatience for some expected arrival.

The room was empty, for the last performance of a Grand Spectacle was going on, and the entire strength of the company in demand. Frequent bursts of barbaric music had filled the air; but now a brief lull had fallen, broken only by the soft melody of flutes and horns. Standing motionless, the young man listened with a sudden smile, an involuntary motion of the head, as if in fancy he saw and followed some object of delight. A storm of applause broke in on the last notes of the air. Again and again was it repeated, and when at length it died away, trumpet, clarion, and drum resumed their martial din, and the enchanting episode seemed over.

Suddenly, framed in the dark doorway, upon which the young man's eyes were fixed, appeared an apparition well worth waiting for. A sylph she seemed, costumed in fleecy white and gold; the star that glittered on her forehead was less brilliant than her eyes; the flowers that filled her graceful arms were outrivaled by the blooming face that smiled above them; the ornaments she wore were forgotten in admiration of the long blond tresses that crowned her spirited little head; and when the young man welcomed her she crossed the room as if borne by the shining wings upon her shoulders.

"My Virginie, how long they kept you," began the lover, as this beautiful girl leaned against him, flushed and panting, but radiant with the triumphs of the hour.

"Yes, for they recalled me many times; and see—not one bouquet without a *billet-doux* or gift attached!"

"I have much to say, Virginie, and you give me no time but this. Where is Victor?"

"Safe for many minutes; he is in the 'Pas des Enfers,' and then we are together in the 'Pas des Déesses.' Behold! Another offer from the viscount. Shall I accept?"

While speaking she had been rifling the flowers of their attractive burdens, and now held up a delicately scented note with an air half serious, half gay. Her lover crushed the paper in his hand and answered hotly, "You will refuse, or I shall make the viscount a different sort of offer. His devotion is an insult, for you are mine!"

"Not yet, monsieur. Victor has the first claim. And see, he has set his mark upon me."

Pushing up a bracelet, she showed two dark letters stamped or tattooed on the white flesh.

"And you permitted him to disfigure you? When, Virginie, and why?"

"Ah, that was years ago when I cared nothing for beauty, and clung to Victor as my only friend, letting him do what he would, quite content to please him, for he was very kind, and I, poor child, was nothing but a burden. A year ago we were betrothed, and next year he hopes to marry—for we do well now, and I shall then be eighteen."

"You will not marry him. Then why deceive him, Virginie?"

"Yes, but I may if no one else will offer me a name as he does. I do not love him, but he is useful; he guards me like a dragon, works for me, cherishes me, and keeps me right when from mere youth and gaiety of heart I might go astray. What then? I care nothing for lovers; they are false and vain, they annoy me, waste my time, keep Victor savage, and but for the éclat it gives me, I would banish all but—" She finished the sentence with a caress more eloquent than any words and, before he could speak, added half tenderly, half reproachfully, while the flowers strayed down upon the ground, "Not one of all these came from you. I thought you would remember me on this last night."

Passionately kissing the red lips so near his own, the lover answered, "I did remember you, but kept my gift to offer when we were alone."

"That is so like you! A thousand thanks. Now give it to me."

With a pretty gesture of entreaty she held out her little hand, and the young man put his own into it, saying earnestly, "I offer this in all sincerity, and ask you to be my wife."

A brilliant smile flashed over her face, and something like triumph shone in her eyes as she clasped the hand in both her own, exclaiming with mingled delight and incredulity, "You ask that of me, the *danseuse,* friendless, poor and humble? Do you mean it, Allan? Shall I go with you to Scotland, be 'my lady' by-and-by? *Ciel!* It is incredible."

"Yes, I mean it. Passion has conquered pride, and for love's sake I can forgive, forget anything but degradation. That you shall never know; and I thank Victor that his jealous vigilance has kept you innocent through all the temptation of a life like yours. The viscount offers you an establishment and infamy; I offer you an honorable name and a home with my whole heart. Which shall it be, Virginie?"

She looked at him keenly—saw a young and comely face, now flushed and kindled with the ardor of a first love. She had seen many such waiting for her smile; but beyond this she saw truth in the honest eyes, read a pride on the forehead that no dishonor could stain, and knew that she might trust one whose promises were never broken. With a little cry of joy and gratitude she laid her face down on the generous hand that gave so much, and thanked heaven that the desire of her life was won. Gathering her close, Allan whispered, with a soft cheek against his own, "My darling, we must be married at once, or Victor will discover and betray us. All is arranged, and this very night we may quit Paris for a happy honeymoon in Italy. Say yes, and leave the rest to me."

"It is impossible! I cannot leave my possessions behind me; I must prepare a little. Wait till tomorrow, and give me time to think."

She spoke resolutely; the young man saw that his project would fail unless he yielded the point, and controlling his impatience, he modified his plan and won her by the ease of that concession.

"I will not hurry you, but, Virginie, we must be married tonight, because all is prepared, and delay may ruin us. Once mine, Victor has no control over you, and my friends will have no power to part us. Grant me this boon, and you shall leave Paris when you will."

She smiled and agreed to it, but did not confess that the chief reason of her reluctance to depart so suddenly was a desire to secure the salary which on the morrow would be paid her for a most successful but laborious season. Mercenary, vain, and hollow-hearted as she was, there was something so genuine in the perfect confidence, the ardent affection of her lover, that it won her respect and seemed to gift the rank which she aspired to attain with a redoubled charm.

"Now tell me your plan, and tell me rapidly, lest Victor should divine that we are plotting and disturb us," she said, with the look of exultation still gleaming in her eyes.

"It is this. Your engagement ends tonight, and you have made no new one. You have spoken of going into the country to rest, and when you vanish people will believe that you have gone suddenly to rusticate. Victor is too proud to complain, and we will leave a penitent confession behind us to appease him."

"He will be terrible, Allan."

"You have a right to choose, I to protect you. Have no fear; we shall be far beyond his reach when he discovers his mistake. I asked you of him honorably once, and he refused with anger."

"He never told me that. We are requited, so let him rave. What next?"

"When your last dance is over, change your dress quickly, and instead of waiting here for your cousin, as usual, slip out by the private door. I shall be there with a carriage, and while Victor is detained searching for you, we will be married, and I shall take you home to gather up those precious possessions of yours. You will do this, Virginie?"

"Yes."

"Your courage will not fail when I am gone, and some fear of Victor keep you?"

"Bah! I fear nothing now."

"Then I am sure of you, and I swear you never shall regret your confidence; for as soon as my peace is made at home, you shall be received there as my honored wife."

"Are you very sure that you *will* be forgiven?" she asked anxiously, as if weighing possibilities even then.

"I *am* sure of pardon after the first anger is over, for they love me too much to disinherit or banish me, and they need only see you to be won at once."

"This marriage, Allan—it will be a true one? You will not deceive me; for if I leave Victor I shall have no friend in the wide world but you."

The most disloyal lover could not have withstood the pleading look, the gesture of appeal which accompanied her words, and this one, who harbored no treachery, assured her with solemn protestations and the most binding vows.

A few moments were spent in maturing their plan, and Virginie was just leaving him with the word "Tomorrow" on her lips when an animated flame of fire seemed to dart into the room. It was a youth whose scarlet-and-silver costume glowed and glittered in the light, as with one marvelous bound he crossed the room and stood before them. Supple, sinewy, and slight was the threatening figure which they saw; dark and defiant the face, with fierce black eyes, frowning brows, and the gleam of set teeth between lips parted by a muttered malediction. Lovely as the other apparition had been, this was far more striking, for it seemed full of the strong grace and beauty of the fallen angel whom it represented. The pose was magnificent; a flaming crown shone in the dark hair, and filmy pinions of scarlet flecked with silver drooped from shoulder to heel. So fiery and fierce he looked, it was little wonder that one lover drew back and the other uttered an exclamation of surprise. Instantly recovering herself, however, Virginie broke into a blithe laugh, and airily twirled away beyond the reach of Victor's outstretched hand.

"It is late; you are not dressed—you will be disgraced by a failure. Go!" he said, with an air of command.

"*Au revoir, monsieur;* I leave Paris with you." And as she uttered the words with a glance that pointed their double meaning, Virginie vanished.

Turning to the long mirror behind him, the young gentleman replaced his hat, resettled in his buttonhole the flower just given him, tranquilly drew on his gloves, saying, as he strolled toward the door, "I shall return to my box to witness this famous 'Pas des Déesses.' Virginie, Lucille, and Clotilde, upon my word, Paris, you will find it difficult to decide upon which of the three goddesses to bestow the golden apple."

Not a word spoke Victor, till the sounds of steps died away. Then he departed to his dressing room, moodily muttering as he went, "Tomorrow, she said. They intend to meet somewhere. Good! I will prevent *that.* There has been enough of this—it must end, and Virginie shall keep her promise. I will stand guard tonight and watch them well tomorrow."

Three hours later, breathless and pale with fatigue and rage, Victor sprang up the steps leading to his cousin's chamber in the old house by the Seine. A lamp burned in a niche beside her door; a glass of wine and a plate of fruit stood there also, waiting as usual for him. As his eye fell upon these objects a long sigh of relief escaped him.

"Thank heaven, she has come home then. Yet hold! It may be but a ruse to prevent my discovering her absence. Virginie! Cousin! Are you there?"

He struck upon the door, lightly at first, then vehemently, and to his great joy a soft, sleepy voice replied, "Who calls?"

"It is Victor. I missed you, searched for you, and grew anxious when I found you gone. Why did you not wait, as usual?"

"Mlle. Clotilde offered me a seat in her carriage, and I gladly accepted it. She was set down first, and it is a long distance there and back, you know. Now let me rest; I am very tired."

"Good night, my heart," answered Victor, adding, in a tone of pain

and tenderness, as he turned away, "*mon Dieu!* How I love that girl,
and how she tortures me! Rest well, my cousin; I shall guard your sleep."

Hour after hour passed, and still a solitary figure paced to and fro
with noiseless feet along the narrow terrace that lay between the ancient
house and the neglected garden sloping to the river. Dawn was slowly
breaking in the east when the window of Virginie's chamber opened
cautiously, and her charming head appeared. The light was very dim,
and shadows still lay dark upon the house; but Victor, coming from the
water gate whither he had been drawn by the sound of a passing boat,
heard the soft movement, glided behind a group of shrubs, and eyed
the window keenly, remembering that now it was "tomorrow." For a
moment the lovely face leaned out, looking anxiously across terrace,
street, and garden. The morning air seemed to strike cold on her uncovered shoulders, and with a shiver she was drawing back when a man's
hand laid a light cloak about her, and a man's head appeared beside her
own.

"Imprudent! Go quickly, or Victor will be stirring. At noon I shall
be ready," she said half aloud, and as she withdrew the curtain fell.

With the bound of a wounded tiger, Victor reached the terrace, and
reckless of life or limb, took the short road to his revenge. The barred
shutters of a lower window, the carved ornaments upon the wall, and
the balcony that hung above, all offered foot- and handhold for an agile
climber like himself, as, creeping upward like a stealthy shadow, he
peered in with a face that would have appalled the lovers had they seen
it. They did not, for standing near the half-opened door, they were
parting as Romeo and Juliet parted, heart to heart, cheek to cheek, and
neither saw nor heard the impending doom until the swift stroke fell.
So sure, so sudden was it that Virginie knew nothing, till, with a stifled
cry, her lover started, swayed backward from her arms, and dyeing her
garments with his blood, fell at her feet stabbed through the heart.

An awful silence followed, for Virginie uttered no cry of alarm,
made no gesture of flight, showed no sign of guilt; but stood white and
motionless as if turned to stone.

Soon Victor grasped her arm and hissed into her ear, "Traitress!
I could find it in my heart to lay you there beside him. But no; you
shall live to atone for your falsehood to me and mourn your lover."

Something in the words or tone seemed to recall her scattered senses
and rouse her to a passionate abhorrence of him and of his deed. She
wrenched herself from his hold, saying vehemently, though instinctively
below her breath, "No; it is you who shall atone! He was my husband,
not my lover. Look if I lie!"

He did look as a trembling hand was stretched toward him over that dead form. On it he saw a wedding ring, and in it the record of the marriage which in a single night had made her wife and widow. With an ejaculation of despair he snatched the paper as if to tear and scatter it; but some sudden thought flashed into his mind, and putting the record in his bosom, he turned to Virginie with an expression that chilled her by its ominous resolve.

"Listen," he said, "and save yourself while you may; for I swear, if you raise your voice, lift your hand against me, or refuse to obey me now, that I will denounce you as the murderer of that man. You were last seen with him, were missed by others besides me last night. There lies his purse; here is the only proof of your accursed marriage; and if I call in witnesses, which of us looks most like an assassin, you or I?"

She listened with a terror-stricken face, glanced at her bloody garments, knew that she was in the power of a relentless man, and clasped her hands with a gesture of mute supplication and submission.

"You are wise," he said. "Apart, we are both in danger; together we may be strong and safe. I have a plan—hear it and help me to execute it, for time is life now. You have spoken to many of going into the country; it shall be so, but we will give our departure the appearance of a sudden thought, a lover's flight. Leave everything behind you but money and jewels. That purse will more than pay you the sum you cannot claim. While I go to fling this body into the river, to tell no tales till we are safe, destroy all traces of the deed, prepare yourself for traveling, and guard the room in silence until I come. Remember! One sign of treachery, one cry for help, and I denounce you where my word will have much weight and yours none."

She gave him her hand upon the dark bargain, and covering up her face to hide the tragic spectacle, she heard Victor leave the room with his awful burden.

When he returned, she was nearly ready, for though moving like one in a ghastly dream, bewildered by the sudden loss of the long coveted, just won prize, and daunted by the crime whose retribution a word might bring upon herself, she still clung to life and its delights with the tenacity of a selfish nature, a shallow heart. While she finished her hasty preparations, Victor set the room in order, saw that the red witnesses of the crime were burnt, and dashed off a gay note to a friend, enclosing money for all obligations, explaining their sudden flight as an innocent ruse to escape congratulations on their hasty marriage, and promising to send soon for such possessions as were left behind. Then, leaving the quiet room to be forever haunted by the memory of a night of love, and sin, and death, like two pale ghosts they vanished in the dimness of the dawn.

⧽ *Chapter II* ⧼

EARL'S MYSTERY

FOUR ladies sat in the luxurious privacy of Lady Lennox's boudoir, whiling away the listless hour before dinner with social chat. Dusk was deepening, but firelight filled the room with its warm glow, flickering on mirrors, marbles, rich hues, and graceful forms, and bathing the four faces with unwonted bloom.

Stately Diana Stuart leaned on the high back of the chair in which sat her aunt and chaperon, the Honorable Mrs. Berkeley. On the opposite side of the wide hearth a slender figure lounged in the deep corner of a couch, with a graceful abandon which no Englishwoman could hope to imitate. The face was hidden by a hand-screen, but a pair of ravishing feet were visible, and a shower of golden hair shone against the velvet pillow. Directly before the fire sat Lady Lennox, a comely, hospitable matron who was never so content as when she could gather her female guests about her and refresh herself with a little good-natured gossip. She had evidently been discussing some subject which interested her hearers, for all were intently listening, and all looked eager for more, when she said, with a significant nod:

"Yes, I assure you there is a mystery in that family. Lady Carrick has known them all her life, and from what she has dropped from time to time, I quite agree with her in believing that something has gone wrong."

"Dear Lady Lennox, pray go on! There is nothing so charming as a family mystery when the narrator can give a clue to her audience, as I am sure you can," exclaimed the lady on the couch, in a persuasive voice which had a curious ring to it despite its melody.

"That is just what I cannot do, Mrs. Vane. However, I will gladly tell you all I know. This is in strict confidence, you understand."

"Certainly!" "Upon my honor!" "Not a word shall pass my lips!" murmured the three listeners, drawing nearer, as Lady Lennox fixed her eyes upon the fire and lowered her voice.

"It is the custom in ancient Scottish families for the piper of the house, when dying, to put the pipes into the hand of the heir to name or title. Well, when old Dougal lay on his deathbed, he called for Earl, the fourth son—"

"What a peculiar name!" interrupted Mrs. Berkeley.

"It was not his proper name, but they called him so because of his strong resemblance to the pictures of the great earl, Black Douglass. They continued to call him so to this day, and I really don't know whether his name is Allan, Archie, or Alex, for they are all family names, and one cannot remember which belongs to whom. Now the eldest son was Robert, and Dougal should have called for him, because the title and the fortune always go to the eldest son of the eldest son. But no, Earl must come; and into his hands the pipes were put, with a strange prophecy that no heir would enjoy the title but a year until it came to him."

"Was the prediction fulfilled?" asked Diana.

"To the letter. This was five or six years ago, and not one year has passed without a death, till now a single feeble life is all that stands between Earl and the title. Nor was this all. When his father died, though he had lain insensible for days, he rose up in his bed at the last and put upon Earl's hand the iron ring which is their most precious heirloom, because it belonged to the ancient earl. This, too, should have gone to Robert; but the same gift of second sight seemed given to the father as to the servant, and these strange things made a deep impression upon the family, as you may suppose."

"That is the mystery, then?" said Mrs. Vane, with an accent of disappointment in her voice.

"Only a part of it. I am not superstitious, so the prediction and all the rest of it don't trouble me much, but what occurred afterward does. When Earl was one-and-twenty he went abroad, was gone a year, and came home so utterly and strangely changed that everyone was amazed at the alteration. The death of a cousin just then drew people's attention from him, and when that stir was over the family seemed to be reconciled to the sad change in him. Nothing was said, nothing ever transpired to clear up the matter; and to this day he has remained a cold, grave, peculiar man, instead of the frank, gay fellow he once was."

"He met with some loss in an affair of the heart, doubtless. Such little tragedies often mar a young man's peace for years—perhaps for life."

As Mrs. Vane spoke she lowered her screen, showing a pair of wonderfully keen and brilliant eyes fixed full upon Diana. The young lady was unconscious of this searching glance as she intently regarded Lady Lennox, who said:

"That is my opinion, though Lady Carrick never would confirm it, being hampered by some promise to the family, I suspect, for they are almost as high and haughty now as in the olden time. There was a vague rumor of some serious entanglement at Paris, but it was hushed up at once, and few gave it credence. Still, as year after year passed, and Earl remains unmarried, I really begin to fear there was some truth in what I fancied an idle report."

Something in this speech seemed to ruffle Mrs. Berkeley; a look of intelligence passed between her and her niece as she drew herself up, and before Diana could speak, the elder lady exclaimed, with an air of mystery, "Your ladyship does Mr. Douglas great injustice, and a few months, weeks, perhaps, will quite change your opinion. We saw a good deal of him last season before my poor brother's death took us from town, and I assure you that he is free to address any lady in England. More I am not at liberty to say at present."

Lady Lennox looked politely incredulous, but Diana's eyes fell and a sudden color bathed her face in a still deeper bloom than that which the firelight shed over it. A slight frown contracted Mrs. Vane's beautiful brows as she watched the proud girl's efforts to conceal the secret of her heart. But the frown faded to a smile of intelligent compassion as she said, with a significant glance that stung Diana like an insult, "Dear Miss Stuart, pray take my screen. This glowing fire is ruining your complexion."

"Thank you, I need no screens of any sort."

There was a slight emphasis upon the "I," and a smile of equal significance curled her lips. If any taunt was intended it missed its mark, for Mrs. Vane only assumed a more graceful pose, saying with a provoking little air of superior wisdom, "There you are wrong, for our faces are such traitors, that unless we have learned the art of self-control, it is not best for us to scorn such harmless aids as fans, screens, and veils. Emotions are not well-bred, and their demonstrations are often as embarrassing to others as to ourselves."

"That, doubtless, is the reason why you half conceal your face behind a cloud of curls. It certainly is a most effectual mask at times," replied Diana, pushing back her own smooth bands of hair.

"Thanks for the suggestion. I wonder it never occurred to me before," sweetly answered Mrs. Vane, adding, as she gathered up the disheveled locks, "my poor hair is called a great ornament, but indeed it is a trial both to Gabrielle and to myself."

Lady Lennox touched a long tress that rolled down the pillow, saying with motherly admiration, "My dear, I promised Mrs. Berkeley she should see this wonderful hair of yours, for she could not believe my account of it. The dressing bell will ring directly, so you may gratify us without making more work for Gabrielle."

"Willingly, dear Lady Lennox; anything for you!"

As she spoke with affectionate goodwill, Mrs. Vane rose, drew out a comb or two, and a stream of golden hair rippled far below her knee. Mrs. Berkeley exclaimed, and Diana praised, while watching with a very natural touch of envy the charming picture the firelight showed her. In its full glow stood Mrs. Vane; against the deep purple of her dress glittered the golden mass, and a pair of lovely hands parted the shining veil from a face whose beauty was as peculiar and alluring as the mingled spirit and sweetness of her smile.

"A thousand pardons! I thought your ladyship was alone." A deep voice broke the momentary silence, and a tall figure paused upon the threshold of the softly opened door. All started, and with a little cry of pleasure and surprise, Lady Lennox hurried forward to greet her guest.

"My dear Earl, this is a most inhospitable welcome. George should have apprised me of your arrival."

"He is a lazy fellow, as he bade me find you here. I tapped, but receiving no reply, fancied the room empty and peeped to make sure. Pray accept my apologies, and put me out if I intrude."

The voice of Mr. Douglas was remarkably calm, his manner stately yet cordial, and his dark eyes went rapidly from face to face with a glance that seemed to comprehend the scene at once.

"Not in the least," said Lady Lennox heartily. "Let me present you to Mrs. Berkeley, Miss Stuart, and—why, where is she? The poor little woman has run away in confusion, and must receive your apologies by-and-by."

"We must run away also, for it is quite time to dress." And with a most gracious smile Mrs. Berkeley led her niece away before the gentleman should have time to note her flushed face and telltale eyes.

"You did not mention the presence of those ladies in your ladyship's letter," began Douglas, as his hostess sat down and motioned him to do likewise.

"They came unexpectedly, and you have met before, it seems. You never mentioned that fact, Earl," said Lady Lennox, with a sharp glance.

"Why should I? We only met a few times last winter, and I quite forgot that you knew them. But pray tell me who was the fair one with golden locks, whom I frightened away?"

"The widow of Colonel Vane."

"My dear lady, do you mean to tell me that child is a widow?"

"Yes; and a very lovely one, I assure you. I invited you here expressly to fall in love with her, for George and Harry are too young."

"Thank you. Now be so kind as to tell me all about her, for I knew Vane before he went to India."

"I can only tell you that he married this lady when she was very young, took her to India, and in a year she returned a widow."

"I remember hearing something of an engagement, but fancied it was broken off. Who was the wife?"

"A Montmorenci; noble but poor, you know. The family lost everything in the revolution, and never regained their former grandeur. But one can see at a glance that she is of high birth—high enough to suit even a Douglas."

"Ah, you know our weakness, and I must acknowledge that the best blood in France is not to be despised by the best blood in Scotland. How long have you known her?"

"Only a few months; that charming Countess Camareena brought her from Paris, and left her when she returned. Mrs. Vane seemed lonely for so young a thing; her family are all gone, and she made herself so agreeable, seemed so grateful for any friendship, that I asked her here. She went into very little society in London, and was really suffering for change and care."

"Poor young lady! I will do my best to aid your friendly purpose—for Vane's sake, if not for her own," said Douglas, evidently continuing the subject, lest her ladyship should revert to the former one.

"That reminds me to give you one warning: Never speak to her or before her of the colonel. He died three or four years ago; but when I mentioned him, she implored me to spare her all allusion to that unhappy past, and I have done so. It is my belief that he was not all she believed him to be, and she may have suffered what she is too generous to complain of or confess."

"I doubt that; for when I knew him, though weak on some points, Vane was an excellent fellow. She wears no weeds, I observe."

"You have a quick eye, to discover that in such an instant," replied Lady Lennox, smiling.

"I could scarcely help looking longest at the most striking figure of the group."

"I forgive you for it. She left off her weeds by my advice, for the somber colors seemed to oppress and sadden her. Three or four years are long enough to mourn one whom she did not wholly love, and she is too young to shroud herself in sables for a lifetime."

"Has she fortune?"

"The colonel left her something handsome, I suspect, for she keeps both man and maid, and lives as becomes her rank. I ask no questions, but I feel deeply for the poor child, and do my best for her. Now tell me about home, and your dear mother."

Earl obeyed, and entertained his hostess till the dressing bell rang.

❧ *Chapter III* ❧

THE IRON RING

WHEN Douglas entered the drawing rooms, he was instantly seized upon by Major Mansfield, and while he stood listening with apparent interest to that gentleman's communications, he took a survey of the party before him. The elder ladies were not yet down; Harry Lennox was worshiping Diana with all the frank admiration of a lad of eighteen, and Mrs. Vane was pacing up and down the rooms on the arm of George Lennox, the young master of the house. Few little women would have appeared to advantage beside the tall guardsman; but Mrs. Vane moved with a dignity that seemed to add many inches to her almost fairylike stature, and make her a fit companion for her martial escort. Everything about her was peculiar and piquant. Her dress was of that vivid silvery green which is so ruinous to any but the purest complexion, so ravishing when worn by one whose bloom defies all hues. The skirt swept long behind her, and the Pompadour waist, with its flowing sleeves, displayed a neck and arms of dazzling fairness, half concealed by a film of costly lace. No jewels but an antique opal ring, attached by a slender chain to a singular bracelet, or wide band of enchased gold. A single deep-hued flower glowed on her bosom, and in that wonderful hair of hers a chaplet of delicate ferns seemed to gather back the cloud of curls, and encircle coil upon coil of glossy hair, that looked as if it burdened her small head.

The young man watched her so intently that the major soon observed his preoccupation, and paused in the middle of his account of a review to ask good-naturedly, "Well, what do you think of the bewitching widow?"

"She reminds me of a little green viper," replied Douglas coolly.

"The deuce she does! What put such an odd fancy into your head?" asked the major.

"The color of her gown, her gliding gait, her brilliant eyes, and poor George's evident fascination."

"Faith! I see the resemblance, and you've expressed my feeling exactly. Do you know I've tried to fall in love with that woman, and, upon my soul, I can't do it!"

"She does not care to fascinate you, perhaps."

"Neither does she care to charm George, as I happen to know; yet you see what a deuce of a state he's getting into."

"His youth prevents his seeing the danger before it is too late; and there you have the advantage, Major."

"We shall see how you will prosper, Douglas; for you are not a lad of twenty, like George, or an old fellow of forty, like me, and, if rumor does not lie, you have had 'experiences,' and understand womankind."

Though he spoke in a tone of raillery, the major fixed a curious eye upon his companion's countenance. But the dark handsome face remained inscrutably calm, and the only answer he received was a low—

"Hush! they are coming. Present me, and I'll see what I can make of her."

Now Douglas was undoubtedly the best *parti* of the season, and he knew it. He was not a vain man, but an intensely proud one—proud of his ancient name, his honorable race, his ancestral home, his princely fortune; and he received the homage of both men and women as his due. Great, therefore, was his surprise at the little scene which presently occurred, and very visible was his haughty displeasure.

Lennox and his fair companion approached, the one bending his tall head to listen ardently, the other looking up with a most tempting face, as she talked rapidly, after softening a hard English phrase by an entrancing accent. The major presented his friend with much *empressement,* and Douglas was prepared to receive the gracious greeting which women seldom failed to give him. But scarcely pausing in her progress, Mrs. Vane merely glanced at him, as his name was mentioned, returned his bow with a slight inclination, and rustled on as if quite oblivious that a direct descendant of the great Scotch earl had been presented to her.

The major stifled an irrepressible laugh at this unexpected rebuff, and took a malicious pleasure in watching his friend's eye kindle, his attitude become more stately as he talked on, and deigned to take no notice of an act which evidently much annoyed and amazed him. Just then Lady Lennox entered, and dinner was announced. George beckoned, and Douglas reluctantly joined him.

"As host, I am obliged to take Mrs. Berkeley down; Harry has monopolized Miss Stuart, and the major belongs to my mother—so I must reluctantly relinquish Mrs. Vane to you."

Being a well-bred man, Douglas could only bow, and offer his arm. Mrs. Vane made George happy by a smile, as he left her, then turned to Douglas with a "May I trouble you?" as she gave him her fan and handkerchief to hold, while she gathered up her train and took his arm, as unconcernedly as if he had been a footman. Though rather piqued by her nonchalance, Douglas found something half amusing, half captivating in her demeanor; for, much as he had been courted and admired, few women were quite at ease with the highborn gentleman, whose manners were so coldly charming, whose heart seemed so invulnerable. It was a new sensation to be treated like other men, and set to serve an imperious lady, who leaned upon his arm as if she needed its support, and tranquilly expected the small courtesies which hitherto had been left to his own goodwill and pleasure to offer.

Whatever the secret of his past might be, and however well he might conceal his real self behind a grave demeanor, Douglas had not yet lost his passion for beautiful women, and though no word was spoken during the short transit from drawing room to dinner table, the power of loveliness and womanhood made itself felt beyond a doubt. The touch of a fair hand upon his arm, the dazzle of white shoulders at his side, the soft scent of violets shaken from the folds of lace and cambric which he held, the glimpse of a dainty foot, and the glance of a vivacious eye, all made the little journey memorable. When they took their places, the hauteur had melted from his manner, the coldness from his face, and with his courtliest air he began a conversation which soon became absorbing—for Mrs. Vane talked with the grace of a French woman, and the intelligence of an English woman.

When the gentlemen rejoined the ladies, they were found examining some antique jewels, which Lady Lennox had been prevailed upon to show.

"How well those diamonds look in Diana's dark hair. Ah, my dear, a coronet becomes you vastly. Does it not?" said Mrs. Berkeley, appealing to Douglas, who was approaching.

"So well that I hope you will soon see one rightfully there, madam," he answered, with a glance that made Diana's eyes fall, and Mrs. Berkeley look radiant.

Mrs. Vane saw the look, divined its meaning, and smiled a strange smile, as she looked down upon the jewels that strewed her lap.

Mrs. Berkeley mistook her attitude for one of admiration and envy, and said, "You wear no ornaments but flowers, I observe; from choice, doubtless, for, as you are the last of your race, you must possess many of the family relics."

Mrs. Vane looked up, and answered with an indescribable mixture of simplicity and dignity, "I wear flowers because I have no other ornaments. My family paid the price of loyalty with both life and fortune; but I possess one jewel which I value above all these—a noble name."

A banished princess might have so looked, so spoken, as, gathering up the glittering mass in her white hands, she let it fall again, with an air of gentle pride. Douglas gave her a glance of genuine admiration, and Diana took the diamonds from her hair, as if they burdened her. Mrs. Berkeley saw that her shot had failed, but tried again, only to be more decidedly defeated.

"Very prettily done, my dear; but I really thought you were going to say that your most valuable jewel was the peculiar bracelet you wear. Is there any charming legend or mystery concerning it? I fancied so, because you never take it off, however out of taste it may be; and otherwise your dress is always perfect."

"I wear it in fulfillment of a vow, and the beauty of the ring atones for the ugliness of the bracelet. Does it not?"

As she spoke, Mrs. Vane extended an exquisitely molded arm and hand to Douglas, who answered with most unusual gallantry, "The beauty of the arm would render any fetter an ornament."

He bent to examine the jewel as he spoke, and Mrs. Vane whispered, below her breath, "You have offended Diana; pray make your peace. I should be desolated to think my poor arm had estranged you, even for an hour."

So entirely was he thrown off his guard by this abrupt address, that he whispered eagerly, "Do my actions interest her? Have I any cause for hope? Does she—"

There he paused, recovered his self-possession, but not his countenance—for an angry flush stained his dark cheek, and he fixed a look upon Mrs. Vane that would have daunted any other woman. She did not seem to see it, for her head drooped till her face was hidden, and she sat absently playing with the little chain that shone against her hand. George Lennox looked fiercely jealous; Diana turned pale; Mrs. Berkeley frowned; and good, unconscious Lady Lennox said blandly, "Apropos to heirlooms and relics, I was telling these ladies about your famous iron ring, Earl. I wish you had it here to show them."

"I am happy to be able to gratify your ladyship's wish. I never leave without it, for I use it as my seal. I will ring for it."

Mrs. Vane lifted her head with an air of interest as Douglas gave an order, and his servant presently put a small steel-bound case into his hand. Opening this with a key that hung upon his watch guard, he displayed the famous relic. Antique, rusty, and massive it was, and on its shield the boar's head and the motto of the house.

"You say you use this as a signet ring; why do you not have your arms cut on some jewel, and set in a more graceful setting? This device is almost effaced, and the great ring anything but ornamental to one's hand or chatelaine," said Mrs. Vane, curiously examining the ring as it was passed to her.

"Because I am superstitious and believe that an especial virtue lies in this ancient bit of iron. The legend goes that no harm can befall its possessor, and as I have gone scatheless so far, I hold fast to the old faith."

As Douglas turned to hear and answer Mrs. Vane's question, Harry Lennox, with the freedom of a boy, had thrown back the lid of the case, which had been opened with peculiar care, and, lifting several worn papers, disclosed two objects that drew exclamations of surprise from several of the party. A satin slipper, of fairylike proportions, with a dull red stain upon its sole, and what looked like a ring of massive gold, till the lad lifted it, when coil after coil unwound, till a long curl of human hair touched the ground.

"My faith! That is the souvenir of the beautiful *danseuse* Virginie Varens, about whom you bored me with questions when you showed me that several years ago," said the major, staring with all his eyes.

Mrs. Vane had exclaimed with the rest, but her color faded perceptibly, her eye grew troubled, and when Harry leaned toward her to compare the long tress with her own, she shrank back with a shudder. Diana caught a muttered ejaculation from Douglas, saw Mrs. Vane's discomposure, and fixed a scrutinizing gaze upon her. But in a moment those obedient features resumed their former calm, and, with a little gesture of contrition, Mrs. Vane laid the long curl beside one of her own, saying tranquilly:

"Pardon, that I betrayed an instinctive shrinking from anything plebeian. The hair of the dancer is lighter than mine, you see; for this is pure gold, and mine is fast deepening to brown. Let me atone for my rudeness thus; and believe me, I can sympathize, for I, too, have loved and lost."

While speaking, she had refolded the lock, and, tying it together with a little knot of ribbon from her dress, she laid it back into its owner's hand, with a soft glance and a delicate dropping of the voice at the last words.

If it was a bit of acting, it was marvelously well done, and all believed it to be a genuine touch of nature. Diana looked consumed with curiosity, and Douglas answered hastily, "Thanks for the pity, but I need none. I never saw this girl, and as for love—"

He paused there, as if words unfit for time and place were about to pass his lips. His eye grew fierce, and his black brows lowered heavily, leaving no doubt on the mind of any observer that hate, not love, was the sentiment with which he now regarded the mysterious *danseuse*. An uncomfortable pause followed as Douglas relocked the case and put it in his pocket, forgetting, in his haste, the ring he had slipped upon his finger.

Feeling that some unpleasant theme had been touched upon, Lady Lennox asked for music. Diana coldly declined, but Mrs. Vane readily turned to the piano. The two elder ladies and the major went to chat by the fire; Lennox took his brother aside to administer a reproof; and Douglas, after a moment of moody thoughtfulness, placed himself beside Diana on the couch which stood just behind Mrs. Vane. She had begun with a brilliant overture, but suddenly passed to a softer movement, and filled the room with the whispering melody of a Venetian barcarole. This seeming caprice was caused by an intense desire to overhear the words of the pair behind her. But though she strained her keen ear to the utmost, she caught only broken fragments of their low-toned conversation, and these fragments filled her with disquiet.

"Why so cold, Miss Stuart? One would think you had forgotten me."

"I fancied the forgetfulness was yours."

"I never shall forget the happiest hours of my life. May I hope that you recall those days with pleasure?"

There was no answer, and a backward glance showed Mrs. Vane Diana's head bent low, and Douglas watching the deepening color on her half-averted cheek with an eager, ardent glance. More softly murmured the boat song, and scarcely audible was the whispered entreaty:

"I have much to say; you will hear me tomorrow, early, in the park?"

A mute assent was given, and, with the air of a happy lover, Douglas left her, as if fearing to say more, lest their faces should betray them. Then the barcarole ended as suddenly as it had begun, and Mrs. Vane resumed the stormy overture, playing as if inspired by a musical frenzy. So pale was she when she left the instrument that no one doubted the fact of her needing rest, as, pleading weariness, she sank into a deep chair, and leaning her head upon her hand, sat silent for an hour.

As they separated for the night, and Douglas stood listening to his young host's arrangements for the morrow, a singular-looking man appeared at the door of an anteroom and, seeing them, paused where he stood, as if waiting for them to precede him.

"Who is that, George? What does he want?" said Douglas, drawing his friend's attention to the dark figure, whose gleaming eyes belied his almost servile posture of humility and respect.

"Oh, that is Mrs. Vane's man, Jitomar. He was one of the colonel's Indian servants, I believe. Deaf and dumb, but harmless, devoted, and invaluable—*she* says. A treacherous-looking devil, to my mind," replied Lennox.

"He looks more like an Italian than an Indian, in spite of his Eastern costume and long hair. What is he after now?" asked Earl.

"Going to receive the orders of his mistress. I would gladly change places with him, heathen as he is, for the privilege of serving her. Good night."

As George spoke, they parted, and while the dark servant watched Douglas going up the wide oaken stairs, he shook his clenched hand after the retreating figure, and his lips moved as if he muttered something low between his teeth.

A few moments afterward, as Earl sat musing over his fire, there came a tap at his door. Having vainly bidden the knocker to enter, he answered the summons, and saw Jitomar obsequiously offering a handkerchief. Douglas examined it, found the major's name, and, pointing out that gentleman's room, farther down the corridor, he returned the lost article with a nod of thanks and dismissal. While he had been turning the square of cambric in his hands, the man's keen eyes had explored every corner of the room. Nothing seemed to escape them, from the ashes on the hearth, to a flower which Diana had worn, now carefully preserved in water; and once a gleam of satisfaction glittered in them, as if some desired object had met their gaze. Making a low obeisance, he retired, and Douglas went to bed, to dream waking dreams till far into the night.

The great hall clock had just struck one, and sleep was beginning to conquer love, when something startled him wide awake. What it was he could not tell, but every sense warned him of impending danger. Sitting up in his bed, he pushed back the curtains and looked out. The night lamp burned low, the fire had faded, and the room was full of dusky shadows. There were three doors: one led to the dressing room, one to the corridor, and the third was locked on the outside. He knew that it opened upon a flight of narrow stairs that communicated with the library, having been built for the convenience of a studious Lennox long ago.

As he gazed about him, to his great amazement the door was seen to move. Slowly, noiselessly it opened, with no click of lock, no creak of hinge. Almost sure of seeing some ghostly visitant enter, he waited mute and motionless. A muffled hand and arm appeared and, stretching to their utmost, seemed to take something from the writing table that stood near this door. It was a human hand, and with a single leap Douglas was halfway across the room. But the door closed rapidly, and as he laid his hand upon it, the key turned in the lock. He demanded who was there, but not a sound replied; he shook the door, but the lock held fast; he examined the table, but nothing seemed gone, till, with an ominous thrill, he missed the iron ring. On reaching his chamber, he had taken it off, meaning to restore it to its place; had laid it down, to put Diana's rose in water; had forgotten it, and now it was gone!

Flinging on dressing gown and slippers, and taking a pistol from his traveling case, he left his room. The house was quiet as a tomb, the library empty, and no sign of intruders visible, till, coming to the door itself, he found that the rusty lock had been newly oiled, for the rusty key turned noiselessly, and the hinges worked smoothly, though the dust that lay thickly everywhere showed that this passage was still unused. Stepping into his room, Douglas gave a searching glance about him, and in an instant an expression of utter bewilderment fell upon his face, for there, on the exact spot which had been empty five minutes ago, there lay the iron ring!

❧ *Chapter IV* ❧

A SHRED OF LACE

LONG before any of the other guests were down, Diana stole into the garden on her way to the park. Hope shone in her eyes, smiles sat on her lips, and her heart sang for joy. She had long loved in secret; had believed and despaired alternately; and now her desire was about to be fulfilled, her happiness assured by a lover's voice. Hurrying through the wilderness of autumn flowers, she reached the shrubbery that divided park and garden. Pausing an instant to see if anyone awaited her beyond, she gave a great start, and looked as if she had encountered a ghost.

It was only Mrs. Vane; she often took early strolls in the park, followed by her man; Diana knew this, but had forgotten it in her new bliss. She was alone now, and as she seemed unconscious of her presence, Diana would have noiselessly withdrawn, if a glimpse of Mrs. Vane's face had not arrested and detained her. As if she had thrown herself down in a paroxysm of distress, sat Mrs. Vane, with both hands tightly clasped; her white lips were compressed, and in her eyes was a look of mingled pain, grief, and despair. The most careless observer would have detected the presence of some great anxiety or sorrow, and Diana, made generous by the assurance of her own happiness, for the first time felt a touch of pity for the woman of whom she had been both envious and jealous. Forgetting herself, she hastened forward, saying kindly, "Are you suffering, Mrs. Vane? What can I do for you?"

Mrs. Vane started as if she had been shot, sprang to her feet, and putting out her hands as if to keep the other off, cried, almost incoher-

(24)

ently, "Go back! Go back, and save yourself! For me you can do nothing —it is too late!"

"Indeed, I hope not. Tell me your trouble, and let me help you if I can," urged Diana, shocked yet not alarmed by the wildness of Mrs. Vane's look and manner.

But she only clasped her hands before her face, saying despairingly, "You can help both of us—but at what a price!"

"No price will be too costly, if I can honorably pay it. I have been unjust, unkind; forgive it, and confide in me; for indeed, I pity you."

"Ah, if I dared!" sighed Mrs. Vane. "It seems impossible, and yet I ought—for you, not I, will suffer most from my enforced silence."

She paused an instant, seemed to calm herself by strong effort, and, fixing her mournful eyes upon Diana, she said, in a strangely solemn and impressive manner, "Miss Stuart, if ever a woman needed help and pity, it is I. You have misjudged, distrusted, and disliked me; I freely forgive this, and long to save you, as I alone can do. But a sacred promise fetters me—I dare not break it; yet if you will pledge your word to keep this interview secret, I will venture to give you one hint, one warning, which may save you from destroying your peace forever. Will you give me this assurance?"

Diana shrank back, disturbed and dismayed by the appeal and the requirement. Mrs. Vane saw her hesitation, and wrung her hands together in an agony of impotent regret.

"I knew it—I feared it. You will not trust me—you will not let me ease my conscience by trying to save another woman from the fate that darkens all my life. Go your way, then, and when the bitter hour comes, remember that I tried to save you from it, and you would not hear me."

"Stay, Mrs. Vane! I do trust you—I will listen; and I give you my word that I will conceal this interview. Speak quickly—I must go," cried Diana, won to compliance even against her wishes.

"Stoop to me—not even the air must hear what I breathe. Ask Allan Douglas the mystery of his life before you marry him, else you will rue the hour that you became his wife."

"Allan Douglas! You know his name? You know the secret of his past?" exclaimed Diana, lost in wonder.

"My husband knew him, and I— Hush! Someone is coming. Quick! Escape into the park, or your face will betray you. I can command myself; I will meet and accost whoever comes."

Before the rapid whisper ended, Diana was gone, and when Douglas came hastening to his tryst, he too found Mrs. Vane alone—and he too paused a moment, surprised to see her there. But the picture he saw was

a very different one from that which arrested Diana. Great indeed must
have been Mrs. Vane's command of countenance, for no trace of agitation was visible, and never had she looked more lovely than now, as she
stood with a handful of flowers in the white skirt of her dress, her bright
hair blowing in the wind, her soft eyes fixed on vacancy, while a tranquil smile proved that her thoughts were happy ones.

So young, so innocent, so blithe she looked that Douglas involuntarily thought, with a touch of self-reproach: "Pretty creature! What
injustice my ungallant smile did her last night! I ask her pardon." Then
aloud, as he approached, "Good morning, Mrs. Vane. I am off for an
early stroll."

With the shy grace, the artless glance of a child, she looked up at
him, offering a flower, and saying, as she smilingly moved on, "May it be
a pleasant one."

It was not a pleasant one, however; and perhaps Mrs. Vane's wish
had been sweetly ironical. Diana greeted her lover coldly, listened to his
avowal with an air of proud reserve, that contrasted strangely with the
involuntary betrayals of love and joy that escaped her. Entirely laying
aside the chilly gravity, the lofty manner, which was habitual to him,
Douglas proved that he could woo ardently, and forget the pride of the
man in the passion of the lover. But when he sued for a verbal answer
to his prayer, although he thought he read the assent in the crimson
cheek half turned away, the downcast eyes, that would not meet his
own, and the quick flutter of the heart that beat under his hand, he
was thunderstruck at the change which passed over Diana. She suddenly
grew colorless and calm as any statue, and freeing herself from his hold,
fixed a searching look upon him, while she said slowly and distinctly,
"When you have told me the mystery of your life, I will give my answer
to your love—not before."

"The mystery of my life!" he echoed, falling back a step or two,
with such violent discomposure in face and manner that Diana's heart
sank within her, though she answered steadily:

"Yes; I must know it, before I link my fate with yours."

"Who told you that I had one?" he demanded.

"Lady Lennox. I had heard the rumor before, but never gave it
thought till she confirmed it. Now I wait for your explanation."

"It is impossible to give it; but I swear to you, Diana, that I am innocent of any act that could dishonor my name, or mar your peace, if it
were known. The secret is not mine to tell; I have promised to keep it,
and I cannot forfeit my word, even for your sake. Be generous; do not

let mere curiosity or pique destroy my hopes, and make you cruel when you should be kind."

So earnestly he spoke, so tenderly he pleaded, that Diana's purpose wavered, and would have failed her, had not the memory of Mrs. Vane's strange warning returned to her, bringing with it other memories of other mysterious looks, hints, and acts which had transpired since Douglas came. These recollections hardened her heart, confirmed her resolution, and gave her power to appear inexorable to the last.

"You mistake my motive, sir. Neither curiosity nor pique influenced me, but a just and natural desire to assure myself that in trusting my happiness to your keeping, I am not entailing regret upon myself, remorse upon you. I must know all your past, before I endanger my future; clear yourself from the suspicions which have long clung to you, and I am yours; remain silent, and we are nothing to each other from this day forth."

Her coldness chilled his passion, her distrust irritated his pride; all the old hauteur returned fourfold, his eye grew hard, his voice bitter, and his whole manner showed that his will was as inflexible as hers.

"Are you resolved on making this unjust, ungenerous test of my affection, Miss Stuart?"

"I am."

"You have no faith in my honor, then? No consideration for the hard strait in which my promise places me? No compassion for the loss I must sustain in losing the love, respect, and confidence of the woman dearest to me?"

"Assure me that you are worthy of love, respect, confidence, and I gladly accord them to you."

"I cannot, in the way you demand. Will nothing else satisfy you?"

"Nothing!"

"Then, in your words, we are nothing to one another from this day forth. Farewell, Diana!"

With an involuntary impulse, she put out her hand to detain him as he turned away. He took it, and bending, kissed it, with a lingering fondness that nearly conquered her. The act, the look that accompanied it, the tremor of the lips that performed it, touched the poor girl's heart, and words of free acceptance were rising to her lips, when, as he bent, a miniature, suspended by a chain of mingled hair and gold, swung forward from its hiding place in his breast, and though she saw no face, the haste with which he replaced it roused all her suspicions again, and redoubled all her doubts. Scorning herself for her momentary weakness, the gesture of recall was changed to one of dismissal, as she withdrew her hand, and turned from him, with a quiet "Farewell, then, forever!"

"One moment," he pleaded. "Do not let us destroy the peace of both our lives by an unhappy secret which in no way but this can do us harm. Bear with me for a few days, Diana; think over this interview, remember my great love for you, let your own generous nature appeal to your pride, and perhaps time may show you that it is possible to love, trust, and pardon me."

Glad of any delay which should spare her the pain of an immediate separation, she hesitated a moment, and then, with feigned reluctance, answered, "My visit was to have ended with the coming week; I will not shorten it, but give you till then to reconsider your decision, and by a full confession secure your happiness and my own."

Then they parted—not with the lingering adieus of happy lovers, but coldly, silently, like estranged friends—and each took a different way back, instead of walking blissfully together, as they had thought to do.

"Why so *triste*, Diana? One would think you had seen a ghost in the night, you look so pale and solemn. And, upon my word, Mr. Douglas looks as if he had seen one also," said Mrs. Berkeley, as they all gathered about the breakfast table two hours later.

"I did see one," answered Douglas, generously distracting general attention from Diana, who could ill sustain it.

"Last night?" exclaimed Mrs. Berkeley, full of interest at once.

"Yes, madam—at one o'clock last night."

"How charming! Tell us all about it; I dote upon ghosts, yet never saw one," said Mrs. Vane.

Douglas narrated his adventure. The elder ladies looked disturbed, Diana incredulous; and Mrs. Vane filled the room with her silvery laughter, as Harry protested that no ghost belonged to the house, and George explained the mystery as being the nightmare.

"I never have it; neither do I walk in my sleep, and seldom dream," replied Douglas. "I perfectly remember rising, partially dressing, and going down to the library, up the private stairs, and examining the door. This may be proved by the key, now changed to my side of the lock, and the train of wax which dropped from my candle as I hurried along."

"What woke you?" asked Mrs. Vane.

"I cannot tell; some slight sound, probably, although I do not remember hearing any, and fancy it was an instinctive sense of danger."

"That door could not have been opened without much noise, for the key was rusted in the lock. We tried to turn it the other day, and could not, so were forced to go round by the great gallery to reach that room."

Diana spoke, and for the first time since they parted in the park, Douglas looked at and addressed her.

"You have explored the private passage then, and tried the door? May I ask when?"

"Harry was showing us the house; anything mysterious pleased us, so we went up, tried the rusty key, and finding it immovable, we came down again."

"Of whom was the party composed?"

"My aunt, Mrs. Vane, and myself, accompanied by Harry."

"Then I must accuse Harry of the prank, for both key and lock have been newly oiled, and the door opens easily and noiselessly, as you may prove if you like. He must have had an accomplice among the housemaids, for it was a woman's hand that took the ring. She doubtless passed it to him, and while I was preparing to sally forth, both ran away —one to hide, the other to wait till I left my room, when he slipped in and restored the ring. Was that it, Hal?"

As Douglas spoke, all looked at Harry; but the boy shook his head, and triumphantly replied to his brother:

"George will tell you that your accusation is entirely unjust; and as he sat up till dawn, writing poetry, I could not have left him without his knowledge."

"True, Hal—you had nothing to do with it, I know. Did you distinctly see the hand that purloined your ring, Earl?" asked Lennox, anxious to divert attention from the revelation of his poetical amusements.

"No; the room was dusky, and the hand muffled in something dark. But it was no ghostly hand, for as it was hastily withdrawn when I sprang up, the wrapper slipped aside, and I saw white human flesh, and the outlines of a woman's arm."

"Was it a beautiful arm?" asked Lennox, with his eyes upon Mrs. Vane's, which lay like a piece of sculptured marble against the red velvet cushion of her chair.

"Very beautiful, I should say; for in that hasty glimpse it looked too fair to belong to any servant, and when I found this hanging to the lock, I felt assured that my spirit was a lady, for housemaids do not wear anything like this, I fancy," and Douglas produced a shred of black lace, evidently torn from some costly flounce or scarf.

The ladies put their heads together over the scrap, and all pronounced it quite impossible for any dressing maid to have come honestly by such expensive trimming as this must have been.

"It looks as if it had belonged to a deeply scalloped flounce," said Mrs. Vane. "Who of us wears such? Miss Stuart, you are in black; have I not seen you with a trimming like this?"

"You forget—I wear no trimming but crepe. This never was a part of a flounce. It is the corner of a shawl. You see how unequally rounded the two sides are; and no flounce was ever scalloped so deeply as this," returned Diana.

"How acute you are, Di! It is so, I really believe. See how exactly this bit compares with the corner of my breakfast shawl, made to imitate lace. Who wears a black lace shawl? Neither Di nor myself," said Mrs. Berkeley.

"Mrs. Vane often wears one."

Diana uttered the name with significance, and Douglas stirred a little, as if she put into words some vague idea of his own. Mrs. Vane shrugged her shoulders, sipped her coffee, and answered tranquilly, "So does Lady Lennox; but I will bear all the suspicions of phantom folly, and when I dress for dinner will put on every rag of lace I possess, so that you may compare this bit, and prove me guilty if it gives you pleasure. Though what object I could have in running about in the dark, oiling door locks, stealing rings, and frightening gentlemen is not as clear to me as it appears to be to you—probably because I am not as much interested in the sufferer."

Diana looked embarrassed, Lady Lennox grave, and, as if weary of the subject, Douglas thrust the shred of lace into his waistcoat pocket, and proposed a riding party. Miss Stuart preferred driving her aunt in the pony carriage, but Mrs. Vane accepted the invitation, and made George Lennox wretched by accepting the loan of one of Earl's horses in preference to his own, which she had ridden the day before. When she appeared, ready for the expedition, glances of admiration shone in the eyes of all the gentlemen, even the gloomy Douglas, as he watched her, wondering if the piquant figure before him could be the same that he had seen in the garden, looking like a lovely, dreaming child. Her black habit, with its velvet facings, set off her little lithe figure to a charm; her hair shone like imprisoned sunshine through the scarlet net that held it, and her face looked bewilderingly brilliant and arch in the shadow of a cavalier hat, with its graceful plume.

As Douglas bent to offer his hand in mounting her, she uttered an exclamation of pain, and caught at his arm to keep herself from falling. Involuntarily he sustained her, and for an instant she leaned upon him, with her face hidden in his breast, as if to conceal some convulsion of suffering.

"My dear Mrs. Vane, what is it? Let me take you in—shall I call for help?" began Douglas, much alarmed.

But she interrupted him and, looking up with a faint smile, answered quietly, as she attempted to stand alone, "It is nothing but the cramp in my foot. It will be over in a moment; Gabrielle fastened my boot too tightly—let me sit down, and I will loosen it."

"Allow me; lean on my shoulder; it's but a moment."

Down knelt Douglas; and, with one hand lightly touching his shoulder to steady herself, the other still closely folded, as if not yet out of pain, Mrs. Vane stood glancing from under her long lashes at Diana, who was waiting in the hall for her aunt, and observing the scene in the avenue with ill-concealed anxiety. The string was in a knot, and Douglas set about his little service very leisurely, for the foot and ankle before him were the most perfect he had ever seen. While so employed, Jitomar, Mrs. Vane's man, appeared, and, tossing him the gloves she had taken off, she signed to him to bid her maid bring her another pair, as some slight blemish in these had offended her fastidious taste. He comprehended with difficulty, it seemed, for words were useless to a deaf-mute, and the motions of his mistress's hands appeared at first without meaning to him. The idea came with a flash, and bowing, he bounded into the house, with his white robes streaming, and his scarlet slippers taking him along as if enchanted, while the grooms wondered, and Mrs. Vane laughed.

Jitomar hurried to his lady's room, delivered his message, and while Gabrielle went down with a fresh pair of gloves, he enacted a curious little scene in the deserted chamber. Carefully unfolding the discarded gloves, he took from the inside of one of them the shred of lace that Douglas had put into his waistcoat pocket at the breakfast table. He examined it with a peculiar smile; then going to a tiger-skin rug that lay beside the bed, he lifted it and produced a black lace shawl, which seemed to have been hastily hidden there. One corner was gone; but laying the torn bit in its place, it fitted exactly, and, as if satisfied, Jitomar refolded both, put them in his pocket, glided to his own room, prepared himself for going out, and, unobserved by anyone, took the next train to London. Mrs. Vane meanwhile had effaced the memory of her first failure by mounting her horse alone, with an elasticity and grace that filled her escort with astonishment and admiration. Laughing her enchanting laugh, she settled herself in the saddle, touched her hat to

Lady Lennox, and cantered away with Douglas, while Harry followed far behind, for George had suddenly remembered that an engagement would prevent his joining them, having no mind to see Mrs. Vane absorbed by another.

As they climbed a long hill, Mrs. Vane suddenly paused in her witty badinage, and after a thoughtful moment, and a backward glance at Harry, who followed apparently out of earshot, she said, earnestly yet timidly, "Mr. Douglas, I desire to ask a favor of you—not for myself, but for the sake of one who is dear to both of us."

"Mrs. Vane can ask no favor that I shall not be both proud and happy to grant for her own sake," returned Earl, eyeing her with much surprise.

"Well, then, I shall be most grateful if you will shun me for a few days; ignore my presence as far as possible, and so heal the breach which I fear I may unconsciously have caused between Miss Stuart and yourself."

"I assure you that you are mistaken regarding the cause of the slight coolness between us, and it is impossible to ignore the existence of Mrs. Vane, having once had the happiness of seeing her."

"Ah, you take refuge in evasion and compliments, as I feared you would; but it is my nature to be frank, and I shall compass my end by leaving you no subterfuge and no power to deny me. I met you both this morning, and read a happy secret in your faces; I hoped when next I saw you to find your mutual happiness secured. But no—I found you grave and cold; saw trouble in your eyes, jealousy and pain in Diana's. I have seen the latter sentiment in her eyes before, and could not but think that I was the unhappy cause of this estrangement. She is peculiar; she does not like me, will not let me love her, and wounds me in many ways. I easily forgive her, for she is not happy, and I long to help her, even against her will—therefore I speak to you."

"Again I assure you that you are wrong. Diana is jealous, but not of you alone, and she has placed me in a cruel strait. I, too, will be frank, and confess that she will not listen to me, unless I betray a secret that is not my own."

"You will not do this, having sworn to keep it?"

"Never! A Douglas cannot break his word."

"I comprehend now," said Mrs. Vane. "Diana wishes to test her power, and you rebel. It is not natural in both; yet I beseech you not to try her too much, because at a certain point she will become unmanageable. She comes of an unhappy race, and desperate things have been done in her family. Guard your secret, for honor demands it, but take my warning and shun me, that you may add nothing to the trouble she has brought upon herself."

"I have no wish to do so; but she also must beware of testing her power too severely, for I am neither a patient nor a humble man, and my will is inflexible when once I am resolved. She should see this, should trust me, and let us both be happy."

"Ah, if she truly loved, she would; for then one believes blindly, can think no ill, fear no wrong, desire no confidence that is not freely given. She does not know the bliss of loving with one's whole heart and soul, and asking no happier fate than to live for a man whose affection makes a heaven anywhere."

They had paused on the brow of the hill to wait for Harry, and as she spoke, Mrs. Vane's face kindled with a glow that made it doubly beautiful; for voice, eyes, lips, and gestures all betrayed how well *she* could love. Douglas regarded her with a curious consciousness of attraction and repulsion, feeling that had he met her before he saw and loved Diana, he never should have given his peace into the keeping of that exacting girl. An involuntary sigh escaped him; Mrs. Vane brightened instantly, saying:

"Nay, do not fall back into your gloomy mood again, or I shall think that I have increased, not lessened, your anxiety. I came to cheer you if I could, for though I have done with love myself, it gives me sincerest satisfaction to serve those who are just beginning to know its pleasant pain."

She was smiling as she spoke, but the lovely eyes lifted to her companion's face were full of tears. Remembering her loneliness, her loss, and with a grateful sense of all she desired to do for him, Douglas ungloved and offered her his hand, with an impulsive gesture, saying warmly, "You are very kind; I thank you, and feel already comforted by the thought that though I may have lost a lover, I have gained a friend."

Here Harry came up brimful of curiosity, for he had seen and heard more than they knew. After this they all rode on together, and when Douglas dismounted Mrs. Vane she whispered, "Remember, you are to shun me, no matter how pointedly. I shall forgive you, and she will be happier for our little ruse."

This speech, as well as the first uttered by Mrs. Vane when their serious conversation began, was overheard by Harry, and when Diana carelessly asked him if he had enjoyed his ride, he repeated the two remarks, hoping to gain some explanation of them before he told his brother, whose cause he heartily espoused. He knew nothing of Miss Stuart's love, and made her his confidante without a suspicion of the pang he was inflicting. She bade him forget what he had heard, but could not do so herself, and all that day those two sentences rang through her mind unceasingly.

Pausing that evening in the hall to examine one of the ancient portraits hanging there, Douglas heard a soft rustle, and turning, saw Mrs. Vane entering, as if from a moonlight stroll on the balcony. The night was cool, and over her head was drawn a corner of the black lace shawl that drooped from her shoulders. Her dress of violet silk was trimmed with a profusion of black lace, and wonderingly becoming to white skin and golden hair was the delicate tint and its rich decoration. Douglas went to her, saying, as he offered his hand, "You see how well I keep my word; now let me reward myself by taking you in. But, first, pray tell me if this is a picture of Sir Lionel."

He led her to the portrait that had excited his curiosity, and while she told him some little legend of it, he still lingered, held as much by the charm of the living voice as by the exploits of the dead knight. Standing thus, arm in arm, alone and engrossed in one another, neither, apparently, saw Diana pausing on the threshold of the library with an expression of deep displeasure in her face. Douglas did not see her; Mrs. Vane did, though not a sign betrayed it, except that in an instant her whole expression changed. As Douglas looked up at the picture, she looked up at him with love, grief, pain, and pity visibly contending in her beautiful face; then suddenly withdrawing her arm, she said, "I forgot, we are strangers now. Let me enter alone." And gliding from him with bent head, she passed into the drawing room.

Much amazed at her abrupt flight, Earl looked after her, saw Diana watching him, and inexpressibly annoyed by the contretemps, he started, colored, bowed coldly, and followed Mrs. Vane without a word. For a moment, Diana lingered with her head in her hands, thinking disconsolately: "What secret lies between them? She leaned and looked as if she had a right there. He is already more at ease with her than me, although they met but yesterday. Have they not met before? She asked some favor 'for the sake of one dear to both.' Who is it? He must shun her that someone may be happy, though deceived. Is that me? She knows his mystery, has a part in it, and I am to be kept blind. Wait a little! I too can plot, and watch, and wait. I can read faces, fathom actions, and play a part, though my heart breaks in doing it."

All that evening she watched them; saw that Douglas did not shun Mrs. Vane; also that he feigned unconsciousness of her own keen scrutiny, and seemed endeavoring to chase from her mind the memory of the morning's interview, or the evening's discovery. She saw Mrs.

Vane act surprise, pique, and displeasure at his seeming desertion, and console herself by making her peace with Lennox. To others, Diana appeared unusually animated and carefree, but never had an evening seemed so interminable, and never had she so gladly hailed the hour of separation.

She was standing by Lady Lennox when Mrs. Vane came up to say good night. Her ladyship did not like Diana, and did both love and pity the lonely little widow, who had endeared herself in so many ways. As she swept a curtsy, with the old-fashioned reverence that her hostess liked, Lady Lennox drew her nearer and kissed her with motherly affection, saying playfully as she did so, "No pranks tonight among the spirits, my dear, else these friends will think you and I are witches in good earnest."

"That reminds me, I have kept my promise, and Mr. Douglas can compare his telltale bit with my mother's, and, as you see, very precious in every respect."

Gravely exploring one pocket after another, Earl presently announced, with some chagrin, that the bit was lost, blown away while riding, probably. So nothing could be done, and Mrs. Vane was acquitted of lending her laces to the household ghost. Diana looked disappointed, and taking up a corner of the shawl, said, as she examined it narrowly, "As I remember the shred, it matched this pattern exactly. It is a peculiar one, and I observed it well. I wish the bit was not lost, for if people play such games with your clothes, they may take equal liberties with mine."

Seeing suspicion in her eyes, Mrs. Vane gathered the four corners of the shawl together, and with great care spread each over her violet skirt before Diana. Not a fracture appeared, and when she had done the same with every atom of trimming on her dress, she drew her slender figure up with an air of proud dignity, asking almost sternly, "Am I acquitted of this absurd charge, Miss Stuart?"

Entirely disconcerted by the quickness with which her distrust had been seen and exposed, Diana could only look guilty, apologize, and find herself convicted of an unjust suspicion. Mrs. Vane received her atonement graciously, and wrapping her shawl about her, went away to bed, with a mischievous smile shining in her eyes as she bowed to Douglas, whose glance followed her till the last glimpse of the violet dress disappeared.

↣ *Chapter V* ↢

TREASON

THE week passed gaily enough, externally, but to several of the party it was a very dreary and very memorable week. George Lennox basked in the light of Mrs. Vane's smiles, and his mother began to hope that Douglas would not take her at her word, but leave her son to woo and win the bonny widow, if he could. Earl watched and waited for Diana to relent, pleading with his eyes, though never a word of submission or appeal passed his lips. And poor Diana, hoping to conquer him, silenced the promptings of her reason, and stood firm, when a yielding look, a tender word, would have overcome his pride, and healed the breach. She suffered much, but told no one her pain till the last day came. Then, driven by the thought that a few hours would seal her fate, she resolved to appeal to Mrs. Vane. She knew the mystery; she professed to pity her. She was a woman, and to her this humiliation would not be so hard, this confession so impossible.

Diana haunted the hall and drawing rooms all that morning, hoping to find Mrs. Vane alone. At last, just before lunch, she caught her playing with Earl's spaniel, while she waited for Lennox to bring her hat from the garden seat where she had left it.

"Be so kind as to take a turn with me on the balcony, Mrs. Vane. I wish much to say a few words to you," began Diana, with varying color and anxious eyes, as she met her at the great hall door.

"With pleasure. Give me your arm, and let us have our little chat quite comfortably together. Can I do anything for you, my dear Miss Stuart? Pray speak freely, and, believe me, I desire to be your friend."

So kind, so cordial was the tone, the look, that poor Diana felt comforted at once; and bending her stately head to the bright one at her side, she said, with a sad humility, which proved how entirely her love had subdued her pride, "I hope so, Mrs. Vane, for I need a friend. You, and you alone, can help me. I humble myself to you; I forget not my own misgivings. I endeavor to see in you only a woman younger, yet wiser than myself, who, knowing my sore necessity, will help me by confessing the share she bears in the secret that is destroying my peace."

"I wish I could! I wish I dared! I have thought of it often; have longed to do it at all costs; and then remembering my vow, I have held my peace!"

"Assure me of one thing and I will submit. I will ask Allan to forgive me, and I will be happy in my ignorance, if I can. He told me that this mystery would not stain his honor, or mar my peace if it were known. Mrs. Vane, is this true?" asked Diana solemnly.

"No; a man's honor is not tarnished in his eyes by treachery to a woman, and he believes that a woman's peace will not be marred by the knowledge that in God's sight she is not his wife, although she may be in the eyes of the world."

"Mrs. Vane, I conjure you to tell me what you mean! I have a right to know; it is your duty to save me from sin and sorrow if you can, and I will make any promise you exact to keep eternally secret whatever you may tell me. If you fear Douglas, he shall never know that you have broken your vow, whether I marry or discard him. Have pity upon me, I implore you, for this day must make or mar my life!"

Few women could have withstood the desperate urgency of Diana's prayer; Mrs. Vane did not. A moment she stood, growing paler as some purpose took shape in her mind, then drew her companion onward, saying hurriedly, as George Lennox appeared in the avenue, "Invite me to drive out alone with you after lunch, and then you shall know all. But, O Miss Stuart, remember that you bring the sorrow upon yourself if you urge this disclosure. I cannot think it right to see you give yourself to this man without a protest; but you may curse me for destroying your faith in him, while powerless to kill your love. Go now, and if you retract your wish, be silent; I shall know."

They parted, and when Lennox came up, the balcony was deserted.

"My love, you get so pale and spiritless that I am quite reconciled to our departure; for the air here does not suit you, and we must try the seashore," said Mrs. Berkeley, as they rose from the table after lunch.

"I shall be myself again soon, Aunt. I need more exercise, and if Mrs. Vane will allow me, I should enjoy a long drive with her this afternoon," returned Diana, growing still paler as she spoke.

Mrs. Vane bowed her acceptance, and as she left the room a curious shiver seemed to shake her from head to foot as she pressed her hands together and hurried to her chamber.

The two ladies drove in silence, till Diana said abruptly, "I am ready, Mrs. Vane; tell me all, and spare nothing."

"Your solemn oath first, that living or dying, you will never reveal to any human soul what I shall tell you." And as she spoke, Mrs. Vane extended her hand.

Diana gave her own, and took the oath which the other well knew she would keep inviolate.

"I shall not torture you by suspense," Mrs. Vane began, "but show you at once why I would save you from a greater suffering than the loss of love. Miss Stuart, read that, and learn the mystery of your lover's life."

With a sudden gesture, she took from her bosom a worn paper, and unfolding it, held before the other's eyes the marriage record of Allan Douglas and Virginie Varens.

Not a word passed Diana's lips, but with the moan of a broken heart she covered up her face, and slowly, tremulously, the voice at her side went on, "You see here the date of that mysterious journey to Paris, from which he returned an altered man. There, too, is his private seal. That long lock of hair, that stained slipper, belonged to Virginie; and though he said he had never seen her, the lie cost him an effort, and well it might, for I sat there before him, and I am Virginie."

Diana's hands dropped from her pallid face, as she shrank away from her companion, yet gazed at her like one fascinated by an awful spell.

"Hear my story, and then judge between us," the voice continued, so melancholy, yet so sweet that tears came to the listener's eyes, as the sad story was unfolded. "I am of a noble family, but was left so poor, so friendless, that but for a generous boy I should have perished in the streets of Paris. He was a dancer, his poor earnings could not support us both. I discovered this, and in my innocence, thought no labor degrading that lessened my great debt to him. I, too, had become a dancer. I had youth, beauty, health, and a grateful heart to help me on. I made money. I had many lovers, but Victor kept me safe, for he, too, loved, but in secret, till he was sure I could give him love, not gratitude. Then Allan came, and I forgot the world about me; for I loved as only a girl of seventeen can love the first man who has touched her heart. He offered me his hand and honorable name, for I was as wellborn as himself, and even in my seeming degradation, he respected me. We were married, and for a year I was as happy as an angel. Then my boy was born, and for a time I lost my beauty. That cooled Allan's waning passion. Some fear of consequences, some later regret for his rash act, came over him, and made him very bitter to me when I most needed tenderness. He told me that our marriage had been without witnesses, that our faith was different, and that vows pronounced before a Catholic priest alone were not binding upon him. That he was weary of me, and having been recalled to Scotland, he desired to return as free as he went. If I would promise solemnly to conceal the truth, he would support the boy and me abroad, until I chose to marry; that I must destroy the record of the deed, and never claim him, or he would denounce me as an impostor, and take away the boy. Miss Stuart, I was very ignorant and young; my heart was broken, and I believed myself dying. For the child's sake, I promised all things, and he left me; but remorse haunted him, and his peace was poisoned from that hour."

"And you? You married Colonel Vane?" whispered Diana, holding her breath to listen.

"No, I have never married, for in my eyes that ceremony made me Allan's wife, and I shall be so till I die. When I was most forlorn, Colonel Vane found me. He was Allan's friend; he had seen me with him, and when we met again, he pitied me; and finding that I longed to hide myself from the world, he took me to India under an assumed name, as the widow of a friend. My boy went with me, and for a time I was as happy as a desolate creature could be. Colonel Vane desired to marry me; for, though I kept my promise, he suspected that I had been deceived and cruelly deserted, and longed to atone for his friend's perfidy by his own devotion. I would not marry him; but when he was dying, he begged me to take his name as a shield against a curious world, to take his fortune, and give my son the memory of a father when his own had cast him off. I did so; and no one knew me there except under my false name. It was believed that I had married him too soon after my husband's death to care to own it at once, and when I came to England, no one denied me the place I chose to fill."

"Oh, why did you come?" cried Diana, with a tearless sob.

"I came because I longed to know if Allan had forgotten me, if he had married, and left his poor boy fatherless. I saw him last winter, saw that you loved him, feared that he would love you, and when I learned that both were coming here, I resolved to follow. It was evident that Allan had not forgotten me, that he had suffered as well as I; and perhaps if he could bring himself to brave the pity, curiosity, and criticism of the world, he might yet atone for his deceit, and make me happy. We had met in London; he had told me to remember my vow; had

confessed that he still loved me, but dared not displease his haughty
family by owning me; had seen his boy, and reiterated his promise to
provide for us as long as we were silent. I saw him no more till we met
here, and this explains all that has seemed so strange to you. It was I
who entered his room, but not to juggle with the ring. He invented that
tale to account for the oiled lock, and whatever stir might have been
overheard. I went to implore him to pause before he pledged himself
to you. He would not yield, having gone too far to retract with honor,
he said. Then I was in despair; for well I knew that if ever the knowledge
of this passage in his life should come to you, you would feel as I feel,
and regard that first marriage as sacred in God's eye, whatever the world
might say. I gave him one more opportunity to spare you by the warning
I whispered in the park. That has delayed the wrong, but you would
have yielded had not other things roused suspicion of me. I had decided to say no more, but let you two tangle your fates as you would.
Your appeal this morning conquered me, and I have broken every vow,
dared every danger, to serve and save you. Have I done all this in vain?"

"No; let me think, let me understand—then I will act."

For many minutes they rolled on silently, two pale, stern-faced
women, sitting side by side looking out before them, with fixed eyes
that saw nothing but a hard task performed, a still harder one yet to be
done. Diana spoke first, asking, "Do you intend to proclaim your wrong,
and force your husband to do you justice?"

"No, I shall not ask that of him again, but I shall do my best to
prevent any other woman from blindly sacrificing her happiness by
marrying him, unconscious of my claim. For the boy's sake I have a
right to do this."

"You have. I thank you for sparing me the affliction of discovering
that man's perfidy too late. Where is your boy, Mrs. Douglas?"

Steadily she spoke; and when her lips pronounced the name she
had hoped to make her own, a stern smile passed across her white face,
and left a darker shadow behind. Mrs. Vane touched her lips with a
warning gesture, saying pitifully, yet commandingly: "Never call me that
until he gives me the right to bear it openly. You ask for my boy; will
you come and see him? He is close by; I cannot be parted from him
long, yet must conceal him, for the likeness to his father would betray
him at once, if we were seen together."

Turning down a grassy lane, Mrs. Vane drove on till the way
became too narrow for the carriage. Here they alighted, and climbing a
wooded path, came to a lonely cottage in a dell.

"My faithful Jitomar found this safe nook for me, and brings me tidings of my darling every day," whispered Mrs. Vane, as she stole along the path that wound round the house.

Turning a sharp corner, a green, lawnlike bit of ground appeared. On a vine-covered seat sat an old French *bonne,* knitting as she nodded in the sun. But Diana saw nothing but a little figure tossing buttercups into the air, and catching them as they fell with peals of childish laughter. A three-year-old boy it was, with black curls blowing round a bold bright face, where a healthful color glowed through the dark skin, and brilliant eyes sparkled under a brow so like that other that she could not doubt that this was Allan's son. Just then the boy spied his mother, and with a cry of joy ran to her, to be gathered close, and covered with caresses.

There was no acting here, for genuine mother love transformed Mrs. Vane from her usual inexplicable self into a simple woman, whose heart was bound up in the little creature whom she loved with the passionate fondness of an otherwise cold and superficial nature.

Waving off the old *bonne* when she would have approached, Mrs. Vane turned to Diana, asking, "Are you satisfied?"

"Heaven help me, yes!"

"Is he not like his father? See, the very shape of his small hands, the same curve to his baby mouth. Stay, you shall hear him speak. Darling, who am I?"

"Mamma, my dear mamma," replied the little voice.

"And who is this?" asked Mrs. Vane, showing a miniature of Douglas.

"Oh, Papa! When will he come again?"

"God only knows, my poor baby. Now kiss Mamma, and go and make a pretty daisy chain against I come next time. See, love, here are bonbons and new toys; show them to Babette. Quick, let us slip away, Miss Stuart."

As the boy ran to his nurse the ladies vanished, and in silence regained the carriage. Only one question and answer passed between them, as they drove rapidly homeward.

"Diana, what will you do?"

"Go tomorrow, and in silence. It is all over between us, forever. Mrs. Vane, I envy you, I thank you, and I could almost *hate* you for the kind yet cruel deed you have done this day."

A gloomy darkness settled down on her altered face; despair sat in her eyes, and death itself could not have stricken hope, energy, and vitality out of it more utterly than the bitter truth which she had wrung from her companion.

George Lennox and Douglas were waiting at the door, and both ran down to help them alight. Diana dragged her veil over her face, while Mrs. Vane assumed an anxious, troubled air as the carriage stopped, and both gentlemen offered a hand to Miss Stuart. Putting Earl's aside with what seemed almost rude repugnance, she took George's arm, hurried up the steps, and as her foot touched the threshold of the door, she fell heavily forward in a swoon.

Douglas was springing toward her, when a strong grasp detained him, and Mrs. Vane whispered, as she clung to his arm tremblingly, "Do not touch her; she must not see you; it will kill her."

"Good heavens! What is the cause of this?" he asked, as Lennox carried Diana in, and help came flocking at his call.

"O Mr. Douglas, I have had an awful drive! She terrified me so by her wild conversation, her fierce threats of taking her own life, that I drove home in agony. You saw how she repulsed you, and rushed away to drop exhausted in the hall; imagine what it all means, and spare me the pain of telling you."

She spoke breathlessly, and glanced nervously about her, as if still in fear. Earl listened, half bewilderingly at first, then, as her meaning broke upon him, his dark cheek whitened, and he looked aghast.

"You do not mean that she is mad?" he whispered, recalling her fierce gesture, and the moody silence she had preserved for days.

"No, oh, no, I dare not say that *yet*; but I fear that her mind is unsettled by long brooding over one unhappy thought, and that the hereditary taint may be upon the point of showing itself. Poor girl!"

"Am I the cause of this outbreak? Is our disagreement the unhappy thought that has warped her reason? What shall I, what ought I to do?" Earl asked in great distress, as Diana's senseless body was carried up the stairs, and her aunt stood wringing her hands, while Lady Lennox dispatched a servant for medical help.

"Do nothing but avoid her, for she says your presence tortures her. She will go tomorrow. Let her leave quietly, and when absence has restored her, take any steps toward a reconciliation that you think best. Now I must go to her; do not repeat what I have said. It escaped me in my agitation, and may do her harm if she learns that her strange behavior is known."

Pressing his hand with a sympathizing glance, Mrs. Vane hurried in, and for an hour busied herself about Diana so skillfully that the physician sent all the rest away and gave directions to her alone. When recovered from her faint, Diana lay like one dead, refusing to speak or move, yet taking obediently whatever Mrs. Vane offered her, as if a mutual sorrow linked them together with a secret bond. At dusk she seemed to fall asleep, and leaving Gabrielle to watch beside her, Mrs. Vane went down to join the others at a quiet meal.

≫ *Chapter VI* ≪

A DARK DEATH

THE party separated early. Diana was still sleeping, and leaving her own maid to watch in the dressing room between their chambers, Mrs. Berkeley went to bed. As he passed them down the gallery to his apartment, Earl heard Mrs. Vane say to the maid, "If anything happens in the night, call me." The words made him anxious, and instead of going to bed, he sat up writing letters till very late. It was past midnight when the sound of a closing door broke the long silence that had filled the house. Stepping into the gallery, he listened. All was still, and nothing stirred but the heavy curtain before the long window at the end of the upper hall; this swayed to and fro in the strong current of air that swept in. Fearing that the draft might slam other doors and disturb Diana, he went to close it.

Pausing a moment to view the gloomy scene without, Douglas was startled by an arm flung violently about his neck, lips pressed passionately to his own, and a momentary glimpse of a woman's figure dimly defined on the dark curtain that floated backward from his hand. Silently and suddenly as it came, the phantom went, leaving Douglas so amazed that for an instant he could only stare dumbly before him, half breathless, and wholly bewildered by the ardor of that mysterious embrace. Then he sprang forward to discover who the woman was and whither she had gone. But, as if blown outward by some counterdraft, the heavy curtain wrapped him in its fold, and when he had freed himself, neither ghost nor woman was visible.

Earl was superstitious, and for a moment he fancied the spirit of Diana had appeared to him, foretelling her death. But a second thought assured him that it was a human creature, and no wraith, for the soft arms had no deathly chill in them, the lips were warm, living breath had passed across his face, and on his cheek he felt a tear that must have fallen from human eyes. The light had been too dim to reveal the partially shrouded countenance, or more than a tall and shadowy outline, but with a thrill of fear he thought, "It was Diana, and she is mad!"

Taking his candle, he hurried to the door of the dressing room, tapped softly, and when the sleepy maid appeared, inquired if Miss Stuart still slept.

"Yes, sir, like a child, it does one's heart good to see her."

"You are quite sure she is asleep?"

"Bless me, yes, sir, I've just looked at her, and she hasn't stirred since I looked an hour ago."

"Does she ever walk in her sleep, Mrs. Mason?"

"Dear, no, sir."

"I thought I saw her just now in the upper gallery. I went to shut the great window, lest the wind should disturb her, and someone very like her certainly stood for a moment at my side."

"Lord, sir! You make my blood run cold. It couldn't have been her, for she never left her bed, much less her room."

"Perhaps so; never mind; just look again, and tell me if you see her, then I shall be at ease."

Mrs. Mason knew that her young lady loved the gentleman before her, and never doubted that he loved her, and so considering his anxiety quite natural and proper, she nodded, crept away, and soon returned, saying, with a satisfied air, "She's all right, sir, sleeping beautifully. I didn't speak, for once when I looked at her, she said, quite fierce, 'Go away, and let me be until I call you.' So I've only peeped through the curtain since. I see her lying with her face to the wall, and the coverlet drawn comfortably round her."

"Thank God! She is safe. Excuse my disturbing you, Mrs. Mason, but I was very anxious. Be patient and faithful in your care of her; I shall remember it. Good night."

"Handsome creeter; how fond he is of her, and well he may be, for she dotes on him, and they'll make a splendid couple. Now I'll finish my nap, and then have a cup of tea."

With a knowing look and a chilly shiver, Mrs. Mason resettled herself in a luxurious chair, and was soon dozing.

Douglas meanwhile returned to his room, after a survey of the house, and went to bed, thinking with a smile and frown that if all spirits came in such an amicable fashion, the fate of a ghost seer was not a hard one.

In the dark hour just before the dawn, a long shrill cry rent the silence, and brought every sleeper under that roof out of his bed, trembling and with fright. The cry came from Diana's room, and in a moment the gallery, dressing room, and chamber were filled with pale faces and half-dressed figures, as ladies and gentlemen, men and maids came flocking in, asking breathlessly, "What is it? Oh, what is it?"

Mrs. Berkeley lay on the floor in strong hysterics, and Mrs. Mason, instead of attending to her, was beating her hands distractedly together, and running wildly about the room, as if searching for something she had lost. Diana's bed was empty, with the clothes flung one way and the pillows another, and every sign of strange disorder, but its occupant was nowhere to be seen.

"Where is she?" "What has happened?" "Why don't you speak?" cried the terrified beholders.

A sudden lull fell upon the excited group, as Mrs. Vane, white, resolute, and calm, made her way through the crowd, and laying her hand on Mrs. Mason's shoulder, commanded her to stand still and explain the mystery. The poor soul endeavored to obey, but burst into tears, and dropping on her knees, poured out her story in a passion of penitent despair.

"You left her sleeping, ma'am, and I sat as my lady bid me, going now and then to look at Miss. The last time I drew the curtain, she looked up and said, sharp and short, 'Let me be in peace, and don't disturb me till I call you.' After that, I just peeped through the crack, and she seemed quiet. You know I told you so, sir, when you came to ask, and oh, my goodness me, it wasn't her at all, sir, and she's gone! She's gone!"

"Hush! Stop sobbing, and tell me how you missed her. Gabrielle and Justine, attend to Mrs. Berkeley; Harry, go at once and search the house. Now, Mrs. Mason."

Mrs. Vane's clear, calm voice seemed to act like a spell on the agitation of all about her, and the maids obeyed; Harry, with the menservants, hurried away, and Mrs. Mason more coherently went on:

"Well, ma'am, when Mr. Douglas came to the door asking if Miss was here, thinking he saw her in the hall, I looked again, and thought she lay as I'd left her an hour before. But oh, ma'am, it wasn't her, it was the pillow that she'd fixed like herself, with the coverlet pulled round it, like she'd pulled it round her own head and shoulders when she spoke last. It looked all right, the night lamp being low, and me so sleepy, and I went back to my place, after setting Mr. Douglas's mind ât rest. I fell asleep, and when I woke, I ran in here to make sure she was safe, for I'd had a horrid dream about seeing her laid out, dead and dripping, with weeds in her hair, and her poor feet all covered with red clay, as if she'd fallen into one of them pits over yonder. I ran in here, pulled up the curtain, and was just going to say, 'Thank the Lord,' when, as I stooped down to listen if she slept easy, I saw she wasn't there. The start took my wits away, and I don't know what I did, till my lady came running in, as I was tossing the pillows here and there to find her, and when I told what had happened, my lady gave one dreadful scream, and went off in a fit."

There was a dead silence for a moment, as Mrs. Mason relapsed into convulsive sobbing, and everyone looked into each other's frightened face. Douglas leaned on Lennox, as if all the strength had gone out of him, and George stood aghast. Mrs. Vane alone seemed self-possessed, though an awful anxiety blanched her face, and looked out at her haggard eyes.

"What did you see in the hall?" she asked of Douglas. Briefly he told the incident, and Lady Lennox clasped her hands in despair, exclaiming, "She has destroyed herself, and that was her farewell."

"Your ladyship is mistaken, I hope, for among the wild things she said this afternoon was a longing to go home at once, as every hour here was torture to her. She may have attempted this in her delirium. Look in her wardrobe, Mrs. Mason, and see what clothes are gone. That will help us in our search. Be calm, I beg of you, my lady; I am sure we shall find the poor girl soon."

"It's no use looking, ma'am; she's gone in the clothes she had on, for she wouldn't let me take 'em off her. It was a black silk with crepe trimmings, and her black mantle's gone, and the close crepe bonnet. Here's her gloves just where they dropped when we laid her down in her faint."

"Is her purse gone?" asked Mrs. Vane.

"It's always in her pocket, ma'am; when she drives out, she likes to toss a bit of money to the little lads that open gates, or hold the ponies while she gets flowers, and such like. She was so generous, so kind, poor dear!"

Here Harry came in, saying that no trace of the lost girl was visible in the house. But as he spoke, Jitomar's dark face and glittering eyes looked over his shoulder with an intelligent motion, which his mistress understood, and put into words.

"He says that one of the long windows in the little breakfast room is unfastened and ajar. Go, gentlemen, at once, and take him with you; he is as keen as a hound, and will do good service. It is just possible that she may have remembered the one o'clock mail train, and taken it. Inquire, and if you find any trace of her, let us know without delay."

In an instant they were gone, and the anxious watchers left behind traced their progress by the glimmer of the lantern, which Jitomar carried low, that he might follow the print her flying feet had left here and there in the damp earth.

A long hour passed, then Harry and the Indian returned, bringing the good news that a tall lady in black had been seen at the station alone, had not been recognized, being veiled, and had taken the mail train to London. Douglas and Lennox had at once ordered horses, and gone with all speed to catch an early train that left a neighboring town in an hour or two. They would trace and discover the lost girl, if she was in London.

"There can be no doubt that it was she, no lady would be traveling alone at such an hour, and the station people say that she seemed in great haste. Now let us compose ourselves, hope for the best, and comfort her poor aunt."

As Mrs. Vane spoke, Harry frankly looked his admiration of the cheerful, courageous little woman, and his mother took her arm, saying affectionately, "My dear, what should we do without you? For you have the nerves of a man, the quick wit of a woman, and presence of mind enough for us all."

The dreary day dawned, and slowly wore away. A dull rain fell, and a melancholy wind sighed among the yellowing leaves. All occupations flagged, all failed, except the one absorbing hope. The servants loitered, unreproved, and gossiped freely among themselves about the sad event. The ladies sat in Mrs. Berkeley's room, consoling her distress, while Harry haunted the station, waiting for an arrival or a telegram. At noon the letter came.

"The lady in black not Diana. On another scent now. If that fails, home at night."

No one knew how much they leaned upon this hope, until it failed and all was uncertainty again. Harry searched house, garden, park, and riverside, but found no trace of the lost girl beyond the point where her footprints ended on the hard gravel of the road. So the long afternoon wore on, and at dusk the gentlemen returned, haggard, wet, and weary, bringing no tidings of good cheer. The lady in black proved to be a handsome young governess, called suddenly to town by her father's dangerous illness. The second search was equally fruitless, and nowhere had Diana been seen.

Their despondent story was scarcely ended when the bell rang. Every servant in the house sprang to answer it, and every occupant of the drawing room listened breathlessly. A short parley followed the ring; then an astonished footman showed in a little farmer lad, with a bundle under his arm.

"He wants to see my lady, and would come in," said the man, lingering, as all eyes were fixed on the newcomer.

The boy looked important, excited, and frightened, but when Lady Lennox bade him to do his errand without fear, he spoke up briskly, though his voice shook a little, and he now and then gave a nervous clutch at the bundle under his arm.

"Please, my lady, Mother told me to come up as soon as ever I got home, so I ran off right away, knowing you'd be glad to hear something, even if it weren't good."

"Something about Miss Stuart, you mean?"

"Yes, my lady, I know where she is."

"Where? Speak quickly, you shall be paid for your tidings."

"In that pit, my lady," and the boy began to cry.

"No!"

Douglas spoke, and turned on the lad a face that stopped his crying, and sent the words to his lips faster than he could utter them, so full of mute entreaty was its glance of anguish.

"You see, sir, I was here this noon, and heard about it. Mrs. Mason's dream scared me, because my brother was drowned in the pit. I couldn't help thinking of it all the afternoon, and when work was done, I went home that way. The first thing I saw were tracks in the red clay, coming from the lodge way. The pit has overflowed and made a big pool, but just where it's deepest, the tracks stopped, and there I found these."

With a sudden gesture of the arm, he shook out the bundle; a torn mantle, heavily trimmed, and a crushed crepe bonnet dropped upon the floor. Lady Lennox sank back in her chair, and George covered up his face with a groan; but Earl stood motionless, and Mrs. Vane looked as if the sight of these relics had confirmed some wordless fear.

"Perhaps she is not there, however," she said below her breath. "She may have wandered on and lost herself. Oh, let us look!"

"She *is* there, ma'am, I see her sperrit," and the boy's eyes dilated as they glanced fearfully about him while he spoke. "I was awful scared when I see them things, but she was good to me, and I loved her, so I took 'em up and went on round the pool, meaning to strike off by the great ditch. Just as I got to the bit of brush that grows down by the old clay pits, something flew right up before me, something like a woman, all black but a white face and arms. It gave a strange screech, and seemed to go out of sight all in a minute, like as if it vanished in the pits. I know it warn't a real woman, it flew so, and looked so awful when it wailed, as Granny says the sperrits do."

The boy paused, till Douglas beckoned solemnly, and left the room with the one word "Come."

The brothers went, the lad followed, Mrs. Vane hid her face in Lady Lennox's lap, and neither stirred nor spoke for one long dreadful hour.

"They are coming," whispered Mrs. Vane, when at length her quick ear caught the sound of many approaching feet. Slowly, steadily they came on, across the lawn, up the steps through the hall; then there was a pause.

"Go and see if she is found, I cannot," implored Lady Lennox, spent and trembling with the long suspense.

There was no need to go, for as she spoke, the wail of women's voices filled the air, and Lennox stood in the doorway with a face that made all question needless.

He beckoned, and Mrs. Vane went to him as if her feet could hardly bear her, while her face might have been that of a dead woman, so white and stony had it grown. Drawing her outside, he said, "My mother must not see her yet. Mrs. Mason can do all that is necessary, if you will give her orders, and spare my mother the first sad duties. Douglas bade me come for you, for you are always ready."

"I will come; where is she?"

"In the library. Send the servants away, in pity to poor Earl. Harry can't bear it, and it kills me to see her look so."

"You found her there?"

"Yes, quite underneath the deepest water of the pool. That dream was surely sent by heaven. Are you faint? Can you bear it?"

"I can bear anything. Go on."

Poor Diana! There she lay, a piteous sight, with stained and dripping garments, slimy weeds entangled in her long hair, a look of mortal woe stamped on her dead face, for the blue lips were parted, as if by the passage of the last painful breath, and the glassy eyes seemed fixed imploringly upon some stern specter, darker and more dreadful even than the most desperate death she had sought and found.

A group of awestricken men and sobbing women stood about her. Harry leaned upon the high arm of the couch where they had laid her, with his head down upon his arm, struggling to control himself, for he had loved her with a boy's first love, and the horror of her end un-manned him. Douglas sat at the head of the couch, holding the dead hand, and looking at her with a white tearless anguish, which made his face old and haggard, as with the passage of long and heavy years.

With an air of quiet command, and eyes that never once fell on the dead girl, Mrs. Vane gave a few necessary orders, which cleared the room of all but the gentlemen and herself. Laying her hand softly on Earl's shoulder, she said, in a tone of tenderest compassion, "Come with me, and let my try to comfort you, while George and Harry take the poor girl to her room, that these sad tokens of her end may be removed, and she made beautiful for the eyes of those who loved her."

He heard, but did not answer in words, for waving off the brothers, Earl took his dead love in his arms, and carrying her to her own room, laid her down tenderly, kissed her pale forehead with one lingering kiss, and then without a word shut himself into his own apartment.

Mrs. Vane watched him go with a dark glance, followed him up-stairs, and when his door closed, muttered low to herself, "He loved her better than I knew, but she has made my task easier than I dared to hope it would be, and now I can soon teach him to forget."

A strange smile passed across her face as she spoke, and still, with-out a glance at the dead face, left the chamber for her own, whither Jitomar was soon summoned, and where he long remained.

❧ *Chapter VII* ❧

THE FOOTPRINT
BY THE POOL

THREE sad and solemn days had passed, and now the house was still again. Mr. Berkeley had removed his wife, and the remains of his niece, and Lennox had gone with him. Mrs. Vane devoted herself to her hostess, who had been much affected by the shock, and to Harry, who was almost ill with the excitement and the sorrow. Douglas had hardly been seen except by his own servant, who reported that he was very quiet, but in a stern and bitter mood, which made solitude his best comforter. Only twice had he emerged during those troubled days. Once, when Mrs. Vane's sweet voice came up from below singing a sacred melody in the twilight, he came out and paced to and fro in the long gallery, with a softer expression than his face had worn since the night of Diana's passionate farewell. The second time was in answer to a tap at his door, on opening which he saw Jitomar, who with the graceful reverence of his race, bent on one knee, as with dark eyes full of sympathy, he delivered a lovely bouquet of the flowers Diana most loved, and oftenest wore. The first tears that had been seen there softened Earl's melancholy eyes, as he took the odorous gift, and with a grateful impulse stretched his hand to the giver. But Jitomar drew back with a gesture which signified that his mistress sent the offering, and glided away. Douglas went straight to the drawing room, found Mrs. Vane alone, and inexpressibly touched by her tender thought of him, he thanked her warmly, let her detain him for an hour with her soothing conversation, and left her, feeling that comfort was possible when such an angel administered it.

On the third day, impelled by an unconquerable wish to revisit the lonely spot hereafter, and forever to be haunted by the memory of that tragic death, he stole out, unperceived, and took his way to the pool. It lay there dark and still under a gloomy sky, its banks trampled by many hasty feet; and in one spot the red clay still bore the impress of the pale shape drawn from the water on that memorable night. As he stood there, he remembered the lad's story of the spirit which he believed he had seen. With a dreary smile at the superstition of the boy, he followed his tracks along the bank as they branched off toward the old pits, now half-filled with water by recent rains. Pausing where the boy had passed when the woman's figure sprang up before him with its old-witch cry, Douglas looked keenly all about, wondering if it were possible for any human being to vanish as the lad related. Several yards from the clump of bushes and coarse grass at his feet lay the wide pit; between it and the spot where he stood stretched a smooth bed of clay, unmarked by the impress of any step, as he first thought. A second and more scrutinizing glance showed him the print of a human foot on the very edge of the pit. Stepping lightly forward, he examined it. Not the boy's track, for he had not passed the bushes, but turned and fled in terror, when the phantom seemed to vanish. It was a child's footprint, apparently, or that of a very small woman; probably the latter, for it was a slender, shapely print, cut deep into the yielding clay, as if by the impetus of a desperate spring. But whither had she sprung? Not across the pit, for that was impossible to any but a very active man, or a professional gymnast of either sex. Douglas took the leap, and barely reached the other side, though a tall agile man. Nor did he find any trace of the other leaper, though the grass that grew to the very edge of that side might have concealed a lighter, surer tread than his own.

With a thrill of suspicion and dread, he looked down into the turbid water of the pit, asking himself if it were possible that two women had found their death so near together on that night. The footprint was not Diana's; hers was larger, and utterly unlike; whose was it, then? With a sudden impulse he cut a long, forked pole, and searched the depths of the pit. Nothing was found; again and again he plunged in the pole and drew it carefully up, after sweeping the bottom in all directions. A dead branch, a fallen rod, a heavy stone were all he found.

As he stood pondering over the mysterious mark, having recrossed the pit, some sudden peculiarity in it seemed to give it a familiar aspect. Kneeling down, he examined it minutely, and as he looked, an expression of perplexity came into his face, while he groped for some recollection in the dimness of the past, the gloom of the present.

"Where have I seen a foot like this, so dainty, so slender, yet so strong, for the tread was firm here, the muscles wonderfully elastic to carry this unknown woman over that wide gap? Stay! It was not a foot, but a shoe that makes this mark so familiar. Who wears a shoe with a coquettish heel like this stamped here in the clay? A narrow sole, a fairy-like shape, a slight pressure downward at the top, as if the wearer walked well and lightly, yet danced better than she walked? Good heavens! Can it be? That word 'danced' makes it clear to me—but it is impossible—unless—can she have discovered me, followed me, wrought me fresh harm, and again escaped me? I will be satisfied at all hazards, and if I find her, Virginie shall meet a double vengeance for a double wrong."

Up he sprang, as these thoughts swept through his mind, and like someone bent on some all-absorbing purpose, he dashed homeward through bush and brake, park and garden, till, coming to the lawn, he restrained his impetuosity, but held on his way, turning neither to the right nor the left, till he stood in his own room. Without pausing for breath, he snatched the satin slipper from the case, put it in his breast, and hurried back to the pool. Making sure that no one followed him, he cautiously advanced, and bending, laid the slipper in the mold of that mysterious foot. It fitted exactly! Outline, length, width, even the down-ward pressure at the toe corresponded, and the sole difference was to the depth of heel, as if the walking boot or shoe had been thicker than the slipper.

Bent on assuring himself, Douglas pressed the slipper carefully into the smooth clay beside the other print, and every slight peculiarity was repeated with wonderful accuracy.

"I am satisfied," he muttered, adding, as he carefully effaced both the little tracks, "no one must follow this out but myself. I have sworn to find her and her accomplice, and henceforth it shall be my life business to keep my vow."

A few moments he stood buried in dark thoughts and memories, then putting up the slipper, he bent his steps toward the home of little Wat, the farmer's lad. He was watering horses at the spring, his mother said, and Douglas strolled that way, saying he desired to give the boy something for the intelligence he brought three days before. Wat lounged against the wall, while the tired horses slowly drank their fill, but when he saw the gentleman approaching, he looked troubled, for his young brain had been sadly perplexed by the late events.

"I want to ask you a few questions, Wat; answer me truly, and I will thank you in a way you will like better than words," began Doug-las, as the boy pulled off his hat and stood staring.

"I'm ready; what will I say, sir?" he asked.

"Tell me just what sort of a thing or person the spirit looked like when you saw it by the pit."

"A woman, sir, all black but her face and arms."

"Did she resemble the person we were searching for?"

"No, sir; leastways, I never saw Miss looking so; of course she wouldn't when she was alive, you know."

"Did the spirit look like the lady afterward? When we found her, I mean?"

The boy pondered a minute, seemed perplexed, but answered slowly, as he grew a little pale, "No, sir, then she looked awful, but the spirit seemed scared like, and screamed as any woman would if frightened."

"And she vanished in the pit, you say?"

"She couldn't go nowhere else, sir, 'cause she didn't turn."

"Did you see her go down into the water, Wat?"

"No, sir, I only see her fly up out of the bushes, looking at me over her shoulder, and giving a great leap, as light and easy as if she hadn't no body. But it started me, so that I fell over backward, and when I got up, she was gone."

"I thought so. Now tell me, was the spirit large or small?"

"I didn't mind, but I guess it wasn't very big, or them few bushes wouldn't have hid it from me."

"Was its hair black or light?"

"Don't know, sir, a hood was all over its head, and I only see the face."

"Did you mind the eyes?"

"They looked big and dark, and scared me horridly."

"You said the face was handsome but white, I think?"

"I didn't say anything about handsome, sir; it was too dark to make out much, but it was white, and when she threw up her arms, they looked like snow. I never see any live lady with such white ones."

"You did not go down to the edge of the pit to leap after her, did you?"

"Lord, no, sir. I just scud the other way, and never looked back till I see the lodge."

"Is there any strange lady down at the inn, or staying anywhere in the village?"

"Not as I know, sir. I'm down there every day, and guess I'd hear of it if there was. Do you want to find anyone, sir?"

"No, I thought your spirit might have been some live woman, whom you frightened as much as she did you. Are you quite sure it was not?"

"I shouldn't be sure, if she hadn't flown away so strange, for no woman could go over the pit, and if she'd fell in, I'd have heard the splash."

"So you would. Well, let the spirit go, and keep away from the pit and the pool, lest you see it again. Here is a golden thank-you, my boy, so good-bye."

"Oh, sir, that's a deal too much! I'm heartily obliged. Be you going to leave these parts, please, sir?"

"Not yet; I've much to do before I go."

Satisfied with his inquiries, Douglas went on, and Wat, pulling on his torn hat as the gentleman disappeared, fell to examining the bit of gold that had been dropped into his brown palm.

"Do you want another, my lad?" said a soft voice behind him, and turning quickly, he saw a man leaning over the wall, just below the place where he had lounged a moment before.

The man was evidently a gypsy; long brown hair hung about a brown face with black eyes, a crafty mouth, and glittering teeth. His costume was picturesquely ragged and neglected, and in his hand he held a stout staff. Bending farther over, he eyed the boy with a nod, repeating his words in a smooth low tone, as he held up a second half-sovereign between his thumb and finger.

"Yes, I do," answered Wat sturdily, as he sent his horses trotting homeward with a chirrup and a cut of his long whip.

"Tell me what the gentleman said, and you shall have it," whispered the gypsy.

"You might have heard for yourself, if you'd been where you are a little sooner," returned Wat, edging toward the road—for there was something about the swarthy-faced fellow that he did not like, in spite of his golden offer.

"I was there," said the man with a laugh, "but you spoke so low I couldn't catch it all."

"What do you want to know for?" demanded Wat.

"Why, perhaps I know something about that spirit woman he seemed to be asking about, and if I do, he'd be glad to hear it, wouldn't he? Now I don't want to go and tell him myself, for fear of getting into trouble, but I might tell you, and you could do it. Only I must know what he said, first; perhaps he has found out for himself what I could tell him."

"What are you going to give me that for, then?" asked Wat, much reassured.

"Because you are a clever little chap, and were good to some of my people here once upon a time. I'm rich, though I don't look it, and I'd like to pay for the news you give me. Out with it, and then here's another yellow boy for you."

Wat was entirely conquered by the grateful allusion to a friendly act of his own on the previous day, and willingly related his conversation with Douglas, explaining as he went on. The gypsy questioned and cross-questioned, and finished the interview by saying, with a warning glance, "He's right; you'd better not tell anyone you saw the spirit—it's a bad sign, and if it's known, you'll find it hard to get on in the world. Now here's your money; catch it, and then I'll tell you my story."

The coin came ringing through the air, and fell into the road not far from Wat's feet. He ran to pick it up, and when he turned to thank the man, he was gone as silently and suddenly as he had come. The lad stared in amaze, listened, searched, but no gypsy was heard or seen, and poor bewildered Wat scampered home as fast as his legs could carry him, believing that he was bewitched.

That afternoon Douglas wrote a long letter, directed it to "M. Antoine Duprès, Rue Saint Honoré, Paris," and was about to seal it when a servant came to tell him that Mrs. Vane desired her adieus, as she was leaving for town by the next train. Anxious to atone for his seeming negligence, not having seen her that day, and therefore being in ignorance of her intended departure, he hastily dropped a splash of wax on his important letter, and leaving it upon his table hurried down to see her off. She was already in the hall, having bidden Lady Lennox farewell in her boudoir—for her ladyship was too poorly to come down. Harry was giving directions about the baggage, and Gabrielle chattering her adieus in the housekeeper's room.

"My dear Mrs. Vane, forgive my selfish sorrow; when you are settled in town let me come to thank you for the great kindness you have shown me through these dark days."

Douglas spoke warmly; he pressed the hand she gave him in both his own, and gratitude flushed his pale face with a glow that restored all its lost comeliness.

Mrs. Vane dropped her beautiful eyes, and answered, with a slight quiver of the lips that tried to smile, "I have suffered for you, if not with you, and I need no thanks for the sympathy that was involuntary. Here is my address; come to me when you will, and be assured that you will always find a welcome."

He led her to the carriage, assiduously arranging all things for her comfort, and when she waved a last adieu, he seized the little hand, regardless of Harry, who accompanied her, and kissed it warmly as he said, "I shall not forget, and shall see you soon."

The carriage rolled away, and Douglas watched it, saying to the groom, who was just turning stableward, "Does not Jitomar go with his mistress?"

"No, sir; he's to take some plants my lady gave Mrs. Vane, so he's to go in a later train—and good riddance to the sly devil, I say," added the man, under his breath, as he walked off.

Had he turned his head a moment afterward, he would have been amazed at the strange behavior of the gentleman he had left behind him. Happening to glance downward, Douglas gave a start, stooped suddenly, examining something on the ground, and as he rose, struck his hands together like one in great perplexity or exultation, while his face assumed a singular expression of mingled wonder, pain, and triumph. Well it might, for there, clearly defined in the moist earth, was an exact counterpart of the footprint by the pool.

⊱ *Chapter VIII* ⊰

ON THE TRAIL

THE packet from Havre was just in. It had been a stormy trip, and all the passengers hurried ashore, as if glad to touch English soil. Two gentlemen lingered a moment, before they separated to different quarters of the city. One was a stout, gray-haired Frenchman, perfectly dressed, blandly courteous, and vivaciously grateful, as he held the other's hand, and poured out a stream of compliments, invitations, and thanks. The younger man was evidently a Spaniard, slight, dark, and dignified, with melancholy eyes, a bronzed, bearded face, and a mien as cool and composed as if he had just emerged from some elegant retreat, instead of the cabin of an overcrowded packet, whence he had been tossing about all day.

"It is a thousand pities we do not go on together; but remember I am under many obligations to Señor Arguelles, and I implore that I may be allowed to return them during my stay. I believe you have my card; now *au revoir,* and my respectful compliments to Madame your friend."

"Adieu, Monsieur Dupont—we shall meet again."

The Frenchman waved his hand, the Spaniard raised his hat, and they separated.

Antoine Duprès, for it was he, drove at once to a certain hotel, asked for M. Douglas, sent up his name, and was at once heartily welcomed by his friend, with whom he sat in deep consultation till very late.

Arguelles was set down at the door of a lodging house in a quiet street, and admitting himself by means of a latchkey, he went noiselessly upstairs and looked about him. The scene was certainly a charming one, though somewhat peculiar. A bright fire filled the room with its ruddy light; several lamps added their milder shine; and the chamber was a flush of color, for carpet, chairs, and tables were strewn with brilliant costumes. Wreaths of artificial flowers strewed the floor; mock jewels glittered here and there; a lyre, a silver bow and arrow, a slender wand of many colors, a pair of ebony castanets; a gaily decorated tambourine lay on the couch; little hats, caps, bodices, jackets, skirts, boots, slippers, and clouds of rosy, blue, white, and green tulle were heaped, hung, and scattered everywhere. In the midst of this gay confusion stood a figure in perfect keeping with it. A slight blooming girl of eighteen she looked, evidently an actress—for though busily sorting the contents of two chests that stood before her, she was *en costume,* as if she had been reviewing her wardrobe, and had forgotten to take off the various parts of different suits which she had tried on. A jaunty hat of black velvet, turned up with a white plume, was stuck askew on her blond head; scarlet boots with brass heels adorned her feet; a short white satin skirt was oddly contrasted with a blue-and-silver hussar jacket; and a flame-colored silk domino completed her piquant array.

A smile of tenderest joy and admiration lighted up the man's dark features, as he leaned in, watching the pretty creature purse up her lips and bend her brows, in deep consideration, over a faded pink-and-black Spanish dress, just unfolded.

"Madame, it is I."

He closed the door behind him, as he spoke, and advanced with open arms.

The girl dropped the garment she held, turned sharply, and surveyed the newcomer with little surprise but much amazement, for suddenly clapping her hands, she broke into a peal of laughter, exclaiming, as she examined him, "My faith! You are superb. I admire you thus; the melancholy is becoming, the beard ravishing, and the *tout ensemble* beyond my hopes. I salute you, Señor Arguelles."

"Come, then, and embrace me. So long away, and no tenderer welcome than this, my heart?"

She shrugged her white shoulders, and submitted to be drawn close, kissed, and caressed with ardor, by her husband or lover, asking a multitude of questions the while, and smoothing the petals of a crumpled camellia, quite unmoved by the tender names showered upon her, the almost fierce affection that glowed in her companion's face, and lavished itself in demonstrations of delight at regaining her.

"But tell me, darling, why do I find you at such work? Is it wise or needful?"

"It is pleasant, and I please myself now. I have almost lived here since you have been gone. At my aunt's in the country, they say, at the other place. The rooms there were dull; no one came, and at last I ran away. Once here, the old mania returned; I was mad for the gay life I love, and while I waited, I played at carnival."

"Were you anxious for my return? Did you miss me, *carina?*"

"That I did, for I needed you, my Juan," she answered, with a laugh. "Do you know we must have money? I am deciding which of my properties I will sell, though it breaks my heart to part with them. Mother Ursule will dispose of them, and as I shall never want them again, they must go."

"Why will you never need them again? There may be no course but that in the end."

"My husband will never let me dance, except for my own pleasure," she answered, dropping a half-humble, half-mocking curtsy, and glancing at him with a searching look.

Juan eyed her gloomily, as she waltzed away clinking her brass heels together, and humming a gay measure in time to her graceful steps. He shook his head, threw himself wearily into a chair, and leaned his forehead upon his hand. The girl watched him over her shoulder, paused, shook off her jaunty hat, dropped the red domino, and stealing toward him, perched herself upon his knee, peering under his hand with a captivating air of penitence, as she laid her arm about his neck and whispered in his ear, "I meant you, *mon ami,* and I will keep my promise by-and-by when all is as we would have it. Believe me, and be gay again, because I do not love you when you are grim and grave, like an Englishman."

"Do you ever love me, my—"

She stopped his mouth with a kiss, and answered, as she smoothed the crisp black curls off his forehead, "You shall see how well I love you, by-and-by."

"Ah, it is always 'by-and-by,' never now. I have a feeling that I never shall possess you, even if my long service ends this year. You are so cold, so treacherous, I have no faith in you, though I adore you, and shall until I die."

"Have I ever broken the promise made so long ago?"

"You dare not; you know the penalty of treason is death."

"Death for you, not for me. I am wiser now; I do not fear you, but I need you, and at last I think—I love you."

As she added the last words, the black frown that had darkened the man's face lifted suddenly, and the expression of intense devotion returned to make it beautiful. He turned that other face upward, scanned it with those magnificent eyes of his, now soft and tender, and answered with a sigh, "It would be death to me to find that after all I have suffered, done, and desired for you, there was no reward but falsehood and base ingratitude. It must not be so; and in that thought I will find patience to work on for one whom I try to love for your sake."

A momentary expression of infinite love and longing touched the girl's face, and filled her eyes with tenderness. But it passed, and settling herself more comfortably, she asked, "How have you prospered since you wrote? Well, I know, else I should have read it at the first glance."

"Beyond my hopes. We crossed together; we are friends already, and shall meet as such. It was an inspiration of yours, and has worked like a charm. Monsieur from the country has not yet appeared, has he?"

"He called when I was out. I did not regret it, for I feel safer when you are by, and it is as well to whet his appetite by absence."

"How is this to end? As we last planned?"

"Yes; but not yet. We must be sure, and that we only can be through himself. Leave it to me. I know him well, and he is willing to be led, I fancy. Now I shall feed you, for it occurs to me that you are fasting. See, I am ready for you."

She left him and ran to and fro, preparing a dainty little supper, but on her lips still lay a smile of conscious power, and in the eyes that followed her still lurked a glance of disquiet and distrust.

Mrs. Vane was driving in the park—not in her own carriage, for she kept none—but having won the hearts of several amiable dowagers, their equipages were always at her command. In one of the most elegant of these she was reclining, apparently unconscious of the many glances of curiosity and admiration fixed upon the lovely face enshrined in the little black tulle bonnet, with its frill of transparent lace to heighten her blond beauty.

Two gentlemen were entering the great gate as she passed by for another turn; one of them pronounced her name, and sprang forward. She recognized the voice, ordered the carriage to stop, and when Douglas came up, held out her hand to him, with a smile of welcome. He touched it, expressed his pleasure of meeting her, and added, seeing her glance at his companion, "Permit me to present my friend, M. Dupont, just from Paris, and happy in so soon meeting a countrywoman."

Duprès executed a superb bow, and made his compliments in his mother tongue.

Mrs. Vane listened with an air of pretty perplexity, and answered, in English, while she gave him her most beaming look, "Monsieur must pardon me that I have forgotten my native language so sadly that I dare not venture to use it in his presence. My youth was spent in Spain, and since then England or India has been my home; but to this dear country I must cordially welcome any friend of M. Douglas."

As she turned to Earl, and listened to his tidings of Lady Lennox, Duprès fixed a searching glance upon her. His keen eyes ran over her from head to foot, and nothing seemed to escape his scrutiny. Her figure was concealed by a great mantle of black velvet; her hair waved plainly away under her bonnet; the heavy folds of her dress flowed over her feet; and her delicately gloved hands lay half buried in the deep lace of her handkerchief. She was very pale, her eyes were languid, her lips sad even in smiling, and her voice had lost its lightsome ring. She looked older, graver, more pensive and dignified than when Douglas last saw her.

"You have been ill, I fear?" he said, regarding her with visible solicitude, while his friend looked down, yet marked every word she uttered.

"Yes, quite ill; I have been through so much in the last month that I can hardly help betraying it in my countenance. A heavy cold, with fever, has kept me a prisoner till these few days past, when I have driven out, being still too feeble to walk."

Earl was about to express his sorrow when Duprès cried, "Behold! It is he—the friend who so assuaged the tortures of that tempestuous passage. Let me reward him by a word from M. Douglas, and a smile from Madame. Is it permitted?"

Scarcely waiting for an assent, the vivacious gentleman darted forward and arrested the progress of a gentleman who was bending at the moment to adjust his stirrup. A few hasty words and emphatic gestures prepared the stranger for the interview, and with the courtesy of a Spaniard, he dismounted and advanced bareheaded, to be presented to Madame. It was Arguelles; and even Douglas was struck with his peculiar beauty, and the native pride that was but half veiled by the Southern softness of his manners. He spoke English well, but when Mrs. Vane addressed him in Spanish, he answered with a flash of pleasure that proved how grateful to him was the sound of his own melodious tongue.

Too well-bred to continue the conversation in a language which excluded the others, Mrs. Vane soon broke up the party by inviting Douglas and his friend to call upon her that evening, adding, with a glance toward the Spaniard, "It will gratify me to extend the hospitalities of an English home to Señor Arguelles, if he is a stranger here, and to enjoy again the familiar sound of the language which is dearer to me than my own."

Three hats were lifted, and three grateful gentlemen expressed their thanks with smiles of satisfaction; then the carriage rolled on, the *señor* galloped off, looking very like some knightly figure from a romance, and Douglas turned to his companion with an eager "Tell me, is it she?"

"No; Virginie would be but one-and-twenty, and this woman must be thirty if she is a day, ungallant that I am to say so of the charming creature."

"You have not seen her to advantage, Antoine. Wait till you meet her again tonight in full toilet, and then pronounce. She has been ill; even I perceive the great change this short time has wrought, for we parted only ten days ago," said Douglas, disappointed, yet not convinced.

"It is well; we will go; I will study her, and if it be that lovely devil, we will cast her out, and so avenge the past."

At nine o'clock, a cab left Douglas at the door of a handsome house in a West End square. A servant in livery admitted him, and passing up one flight of stairs, richly carpeted, softly lighted, and decorated with flowers, he entered a wide doorway, hung with curtains of blue damask, and found himself in a charming room. Directly opposite hung a portrait of Colonel Vane, a handsome, soldierly man, with such a smile upon his painted lips that his friend involuntarily smiled in answer and advanced as if to greet him.

"Would that he were here to welcome you."

The voice was at his side, and there stood Mrs. Vane. But not the woman whom he met in Lady Lennox's drawing room; that was a young and blooming creature, festally arrayed—this a pale, sad-eyed widow, in her weeds. Never, surely, had weeds been more becoming, for the black dress, in spite of its nunlike simplicity, had an air of elegance that many a balldress lacks, and the widow's cap was a mere froth of tulle, encircling the fair face, and concealing all the hair but two plain bands upon the forehead. Not an ornament was visible but a tiny pearl brooch which Douglas himself had given his friend long ago, and a wedding ring upon the hand that once had worn the opal also. She, too, was looking upward toward the picture, and for an instant a curious pause fell between them.

The apartment was an entire contrast to the gay and brilliant drawing rooms he had been accustomed to see. Softly lighted by the pale flame of antique lamps, the eye was relieved from the glare of gas, while the graceful blending of blue and silver, in furniture, hangings, and decorations, pleased one as a change from the more garish colors so much in vogue. A few rare pictures leaned from the walls; several statues stood cool and still in remote recesses; from the curtained entrance of another door was blown the odorous breath of flowers; and the rustle of leaves, the drip of falling water, betrayed the existence of a conservatory close at hand.

"No wonder you were glad to leave the country, for a home like this," said Douglas, as she paused.

"Yes, it is pleasant to be here; but I should tell you that it is not my own. My kind friend Lady Leigh is in Rome for the winter, and knowing that I was a homeless little creature, she begged me to stay here, and keep both servants and house in order till she came again. I was very grateful, for I dread the loneliness of lodgings, and having arranged matters to suit my taste, I shall nestle here till spring tempts me to the hills again."

She spoke quite simply, and seemed as thankful for kindness as a solitary child. Despite his suspicions, and all the causes for distrust—nay, even hatred, if his belief was true—Douglas could not resist the wish that she might be proved innocent, and somewhere find the safe home her youth and beauty needed. So potent was the fascination of her presence that when with her his doubts seemed unfounded, and so great was the confusion into which his mind was thrown by these conflicting impressions that his native composure quite deserted him at times.

It did so then, for, leaning nearer, as they sat together on the couch, he asked almost abruptly, "Why do I find you so changed, in all respects, that I scarcely recognize my friend just now?"

"You mean this?" and she touched her dress. "As you have honored me with the name of friend, I will speak frankly, and explain my seeming caprice. At the desire of Lady Lennox, I laid aside my weeds, and found that I could be a gay young girl again. But with that discovery came another, which made me regret the change, and resolve to return to my sad garb."

"You mean that you found that the change made you too beautiful for George's peace? Poor lad—I knew his secret, and now I understand your sacrifice," Earl said, as she paused, too delicate to betray her young lover, who had asked and been denied.

She colored beautifully, and sat silent; but Douglas was possessed by an irresistible desire to probe her heart as deeply as he dared, and quite unconscious that interest lent his voice and manner an unusual warmth, he asked, thinking only of poor George, "Was it not possible to spare both yourself and him? You see I use a friend's privilege to the utmost."

She still looked down, and the color deepened visibly in her smooth cheek as she replied, "It was not possible, nor will it ever be, for him."

"You have not vowed yourself to an eternal widowhood, I trust?"

She looked up suddenly, as if to rebuke the persistent questioner, but something in his eager face changed her own expression of displeasure into one of half-concealed confusion.

"No, it is so sweet to be beloved that I have not the courage to relinquish the hope of retasting the happiness so quickly snatched from me before."

Douglas rose suddenly, and paced down the room, as if attracted by a balmy gust that just then came floating in. But in truth he fled from the siren by his side, for despite the bitter past, the late loss, the present distrust, something softer than pity, warmer than regard, seemed creeping into his heart, and the sight of the beautiful blushing face made his own cheek burn with a glow such as his love for Diana had never kindled. Indignant at his own weakness, he paused halfway down the long room, wheeled about, and came back, saying, with his accustomed tone of command disguised by a touch of pity, "Come and do the honors of your little paradise. I am restless tonight, and the splash of that fountain has a soothing sound that tempts me to draw nearer."

She went with him, and standing by the fountain's brim talked tranquilly of many things, till the sound of voices caused them to look toward the drawing room. Two gentlemen were evidently coming to join them, and Earl said with a smile, "You have not asked why I came alone; yet your invitation included Arguelles and Dupont."

Again the blush rose to her cheek, and she answered hastily, as she advanced to meet her guests, "I forgot them, now I must atone for my rudeness."

Down the green vista came the gentlemen—the stout Frenchman tripping on before, the dark Spaniard walking behind, with a dignity of bearing that made his companion's gait more ludicrous by comparison. Compliments were exchanged, and then, as the guests expressed a desire to linger in the charming spot, Mrs. Vane led them on, doing the honors with her accustomed grace.

Busied in translating the names of remarkable plants into Spanish for Arguelles, they were somewhat in advance of the other pair; and after a sharp glance or two at Douglas, Duprès paused behind a young orange tree, saying, in a low whisper, "You are going fast, Earl. Finish this business soon, or it will be too late for anything but flight."

"No fear; but what can *I* do? I protest I never was so bewildered in my life. Help me, for heaven's sake, and do it at once!" replied Douglas, with a troubled and excited air.

"Chut! You English have no idea of *finesse;* you bungle sadly. See, now, how smoothly I will discover all I wish to know." Then aloud, as he moved on, "I assure you, *mon ami*, it is an orange, not a lemon tree. Madame shall decide the point, and award me yonder fine flower if I am right."

"Monsieur is correct, and here is the prize."

As she spoke, Mrs. Vane lifted her hand to break the flower which grew just above her. As she stretched her arm upward, her sleeve slipped back, and on her white wrist shone the wide bracelet once attached to the opal ring. As if annoyed by its exposure, she shook down her sleeve with a quick gesture, and before either gentleman could assist her, she stepped on a low seat, gathered the azalea, and turned to descend. Her motion was sudden, the seat frail; it broke as she turned, and she would have fallen, had not Arguelles sprung forward and caught her hands. She recovered herself instantly, and apologizing for her awkwardness, presented the flower with a playful speech. To Earl's great surprise, Duprès received it without his usual flow of compliments, and bowing, silently settled it in his buttonhole, with such a curious expression that his friend fancied he had made some unexpected discovery. He had— but not what Douglas imagined, as he lifted his brows inquiringly when Mrs. Vane and her escort walked on.

"Hush!" breathed Duprès in answer. "Ask her where Jitomar is, in some careless way."

"Why?" asked Earl, recollecting the man for the first time.

But his question received no reply, and the entrance of a servant with refreshments offered the desired pretext for the inquiry.

"Where is your handsome Jitomar? His Oriental face and costume would give the finishing touch to this Eastern garden of palms and lotus flowers," said Douglas, as he offered his hostess a glass of wine, when they paused at a rustic table by the fountain.

"Poor Jitomar—I have lost him!" she replied.

"Dead?" exclaimed Earl.

"Oh, no; and I should have said happy Jitomar, for he is on his way home to his own palms and lotus flowers. He dreaded another winter here so much that when a good opportunity offered for his return, I let him go, and have missed him sadly ever since—for he was a faithful servant to me."

"Let us drink the health of the good and faithful servant, and wish him a prosperous voyage to the torrid land where he belongs," cried Duprès, as he touched his glass to that of Arguelles, who looked somewhat bewildered both by the odd name and the new ceremony.

By some mishap, as Duprès turned to replace his glass upon the table, it slipped from his hand and fell into the fountain, with a splash that caused a little wave to break over the basin's edge, and wet Mrs. Vane's foot with an unexpected bath.

"Great heavens—what carelessness! A thousand pardons! Madame, permit me to repair the damage, although it is too great an honor for me, *maladroit* that I am," exclaimed the Frenchman, with a gesture of despair.

Mrs. Vane shook her dress and assured him that no harm was done; but nothing could prevent the distressed gentleman from going down upon his knees, and with his perfumed handkerchief removing several drops of water from the foot of his hostess—during which process he discovered that, being still an invalid, she wore quilted black silk boots, with down about the tops; also that though her foot was a very pretty one, it was by no means as small as that of Virginie Varens.

When this small stir was over, Mrs. Vane led the way back to the saloon, and here Douglas was more than ever mystified by Duprès's behavior. Entirely ignoring Madame's presence, he devoted himself to Arguelles, besetting him with questions regarding Spain, his own family, pursuits, and tastes; on all of which points the Spaniard satisfied him, and accepted his various invitations for the coming days, looking much at their fair hostess the while, who was much engrossed with Douglas, and seemed quite content.

Arguelles was the first to leave, and his departure broke up the party. As Earl and Duprès drove off together, the former exclaimed, in a fever of curiosity, "Are you satisfied?"

"Entirely."

"She is not Virginie, then?"

"On the contrary, she *is* Virginie, I suspect."

"You suspect? I thought you were entirely satisfied."

"On another point, I am. She baffles me somewhat, I confess, with her woman's art in dress. But I shall discover her yet, if you let me conduct the affair in my own way. I adore mystery; to fathom a secret, trace a lie, discover a disguise, is my delight. I should make a superb detective. Apropos to that, promise me that you will not call in the help of your blundering constabulary, police, or whatever you name them, until I give the word. They will destroy the éclat of the *dénouement*, and annoy me by their stupidity."

"I leave all to you, and regret that the absence of this Jitomar should complicate the affair. What deviltry is he engaged in now, do you think? Not traveling to India, of course, though she told it very charmingly."

His companion whispered three words in his ear.

Earl fell back and stared at him, exclaiming presently, "It is impossible!"

"Nothing is impossible to me," returned the other, with an air of conviction. "That point is clear to my mind; one other remains, and being more difficult, I must consider it. But have no fear; this brain of mine is fertile in inventions, and by morning will have been inspired with a design which will enchant you by its daring, its acuteness, its romance."

≈ *Chapter IX* ≈

MIDNIGHT

FOR a week the three gentlemen haunted the house of the widow, and were much together elsewhere. Duprès was still enthusiastic in praise of his new-made friend, but Douglas was far less cordial, and merely courteous when they met. To outside observers this seemed but natural, for the world knew nothing of his relations to Diana, nor the sad secret that existed between himself and Mrs. Vane. And when it was apparent that the Spaniard was desperately in love with that lady, Douglas could not but look coldly upon him as a rival, for according to rumor the latter gentleman was also paying court to the bewitching widow. It was soon evident which was the favored lover, for despite the dark glances and jealous surveillance of Arguelles, Mrs. Vane betrayed, by unmistakable signs, that Douglas possessed a power over her which no other man had ever attained. It was impossible to conceal it, for when the great passion for the first time possessed her heart, all her art was powerless against this touch of nature, and no timid girl could have been more harassed by the alternations of hope and fear, and the effort to hide her passion.

Going to their usual rendezvous somewhat earlier than usual one evening, Duprès stopped a moment in an anteroom to exchange a word with Gabrielle, the coquettish maid, who was apt to be in the way when the Frenchman appeared. Douglas went on to the drawing room, expecting to find Mrs. Vane alone. The apartment was empty, but the murmur of voices was audible in the conservatory, and going to the curtained arch, he was about to lift the drapery that had fallen from its fastening, when through a little crevice in the middle he saw two figures that arrested him, and, in spite of certain honorable scruples, held him motionless where he stood.

Mrs. Vane and the Spaniard were beside the fountain; both looked excited. Arguelles talked vehemently; she listened with a hard, scornful expression, and made brief answers that seemed to chafe and goad him bitterly. Both spoke Spanish, and even if they had not, so low and rapid were their tones that nothing was audible but the varied murmur rising or falling as the voices alternated. From his gestures, the gentleman seemed by turns to reproach, entreat, command; the lady to recriminate, refuse, and defy. Once she evidently announced some determination that filled her companion with despair; then she laughed, and in a paroxysm of speechless wrath he broke from her, hurrying to the farthest limits of the room, as if unconscious whither he went, and marking with scattered leaves and flowers the passage of his reckless steps.

As he turned from her, Mrs. Vane dipped her hands in the basin and laid them on her forehead, as if to cool some fever of the brain, while such a weight of utter weariness came over her that in an instant ten years seemed to be added to her age. Her eyes roved restlessly to and fro, as if longing to discover some method of escape from the danger or the doubt that oppressed her.

A book from which Douglas had read to her lay on the rustic table at her side, and as her eye fell on it, all her face changed beautifully, hope, bloom, and youth returned, as she touched the volume with a lingering touch, and smiled a smile in which love and exultation blended. A rapid step announced the Spaniard's return; she caught her hand away, mused a moment, and when he came back to her, she spoke in a softer tone, while her eyes betrayed that now she pleaded for some boon, and did not plead in vain. Seizing both her hands in a grasp more firm than tender, Arguelles seemed to extort some promise from her with sternest aspect. She gave it reluctantly; he looked but half satisfied, even though she drew his tall head down and sealed her promise with a kiss; and when she bade him go, he left her with a gloomy air, and some dark purpose stamped upon his face.

So rapidly had this scene passed, so suddenly was it ended, that Douglas had barely time to draw a few paces back before the curtain was pushed aside and Arguelles stood in the arch. Unused to the dishonorable practices to which he had lent himself for the completion of a just work, Earl's face betrayed him.

The Spaniard saw that the late interview had not been without a witness, and forgetting that they had spoken in an unknown tongue, for a moment he looked perfectly livid with fear and fury. Some recollection suddenly seemed to reassure him, but the covert purpose just formed appeared to culminate in action, for, with ungovernable hatred flaming up in his eyes, he said, in a suppressed voice that scarcely parted his white lips, "Eavesdropper and spy! I spit upon you!" And advancing one step struck Douglas full in the face.

It had nearly been his last act, for, burning with scorn and detestation, Earl took him by the throat, and was about to execute swift retribution for both the old wrong and the new when Duprès came between them, whispering, as he wrenched Earl's arm away, "Hold! Remember where you are. Come away, señor, I am your friend in this affair. It shall be arranged. Douglas, remain here, I entreat you."

As he spoke, Duprès gave Earl a warning glance, and drew Arguelles swiftly from the house. Controlling a desperate desire to follow, Douglas remembered his promise to let his friend conduct the affair in his own way, and by a strong effort composed himself, though his cheek still tingled with the blow, and his blood burned within him. The whole encounter had passed noiselessly, and when after a brief pause Douglas entered the conservatory, Mrs. Vane still lingered by the fountain, unconscious of the scene which had just transpired. She turned to greet the newcomer with extended hand, and it was with difficulty that he restrained the rash impulse to strike it from him. The very effort to control this desire made the pressure of his own hand almost painful as he took that other, and the strong grasp sent a thrill of joy to Mrs. Vane's heart, as she smiled and glowed under his glance like a flower at the coming of the sun. The inward excitement, which it was impossible to wholly subdue, manifested itself in Earl's countenance and manner more plainly than he knew, and would have excited some of ill in his companion's mind had not love blinded her, and left none but prophecies of good. A little tremble of delight agitated her, and the eyes that once were so coldly bright and penetrating now were seldom lifted to the face that she had studied so carefully, not long ago. After the first greetings, she waited for him to speak, for words would not come at her will when with him; but he stood thoughtfully, dipping his hand into the fountain as she had done, and laying the wet palm against his cheek, lest its indignant color should betray the insult he had just received.

"Did you meet Señor Arguelles as you came in?" she asked presently, as the pause was unbroken.

"He passed me, and went out."

"You do not fancy him, I suspect."

"I confess it, Mrs. Vane."

"And why?"

"Need I tell *you?*"

The words escaped him involuntarily, and had she seen his face just then, her own would have blanched with fear. But she was looking down, and as he spoke the traitorous color rose to her forehead, though she ignored the betrayal by saying, with an accent of indifference, "He will not annoy you long. Tomorrow he fulfills some engagement with a friend in the country, and in the evening will take leave of me."

"He is about to return to Spain, then?"

"I believe so. I did not question him."

"You will not bid him adieu without regret?"

"With the greatest satisfaction, I assure you, for underneath that Spanish dignity of manner lurks fire, and I have no desire to be consumed." And the sigh of relief that accompanied her words was the most sincere expression of feeling that had escaped her for weeks.

Anxious to test his power to the utmost, Douglas pursued the subject, though it was evidently distasteful to her. Assuming an air of loverlike anxiety, he half timidly, half eagerly inquired, "Then when he comes again to say farewell, you will not consent to go with him to occupy the 'castle in Spain' which he has built up for himself during this short week?"

He thought to see some demonstration of pleasure at the jealous fear his words implied, but her color faded suddenly, and she shivered as if a chilly gust had blown over her, while she answered briefly, with a little gesture of the hand as she set the topic decidedly aside, "No, he will go alone."

There was a momentary pause, and in it something like pity knocked at the door of Earl's heart, for with all his faults he was a generous man, and as he saw this woman sitting there, so unconscious of impending danger, so changed and beautiful by one true sentiment, his purpose wavered, a warning word rose to his lips, and with an impetuous gesture he took her hand, and turned away with an abrupt "Pardon me— it is too soon—I will explain hereafter."

The entrance of a servant with coffee seemed to rouse him into sudden spirits and activity, for begging Mrs. Vane to sit and rest, he served her with assiduous care.

"Here is your own cup of violet and gold; you see I know your fancy even in trifles. Is it right? I took such pains to have it as you like it," he said, as he presented the cup with an air of tender solicitude.

"It does not matter, but one thing you have forgotten, I take no sugar," she answered, smiling as she tasted.

"I knew it, yet the line 'Sweets to the sweet' was running in my head, and so I unconsciously spoiled your draft. Let me retrieve the error?"

"By no means. I drink to you." And lifting the tiny cup to her lips, she emptied it with a look which proved that his words had already retrieved the error.

He received the cup with a peculiar smile, looked at his watch, and exclaimed, "It is late, and I should go, yet—"

"No, not yet; stay and finish the lines you began yesterday. I find less beauty in them when I read them to myself," she answered, detaining him.

Glad of an excuse to prolong his stay, Earl brought the book, and sitting near her, lent to the poem the sonorous music of his voice.

The last words came all too soon, and when Douglas rose, Mrs. Vane bade him good night with a dreamy softness in her eyes which caused a gleam of satisfaction to kindle in his own. As he passed through the anteroom, Gabrielle met him with a look of anxious though mute inquiry in her face. He answered it with a significant nod, a warning gesture, and she let him out, wearing an aspect of the deepest mystery.

Douglas hurried to his rooms, and there found Duprès with Major Mansfield, who had been put in possession of the secret, and the part he was expected to play in its unraveling.

"What in heaven's name did you mean by taking the wrong side of the quarrel, and forcing me to submit quietly to such an indignity?" demanded Earl, giving vent to the impatience which had only been curbed till now, that he might perform the portion of the plot allotted to him.

"Tell me first, have you succeeded?" said Duprès.

"I have."

"You are sure?"

"Beyond a doubt."

"It is well; I applaud your dexterity. Behold the major, he knows all, he is perfect in his role. Now hear yours. You will immediately write a challenge."

"It is impossible! Antoine, you are a daft to ask me to meet that man."

"Bah! I ask you to meet, but not to honor him by blowing his brains out. He is a dead shot, and thirsts for your blood, but look you, he will be disappointed. We might arrest him this instant, but he will confess nothing, and that clever creature will escape us. No, my little arrangement suits me better."

"Time flies, Duprès, and so perhaps may this crafty hind that you are about to snare," said the major, whose slow British wits were somewhat confused by the Frenchman's *finesse.*

"It is true; see then, my Earl. In order that our other little affair may come smoothly off without interference from our friend, I propose to return to the *señor,* whom I have lately left writing letters, and amuse myself by keeping him at home to receive your challenge, which the major will bring about twelve. Then we shall arrange the affair to take place at sunrise, in some secluded spot out of town. You will be back here by that time, you will agree to our plans, and present yourself at the appointed time, when the grand *dénouement* will take place with much éclat."

"Am I not to know more?" asked Douglas.

"It would be well to leave all to me, for you will act your part better if you do not know the exact program, because you do not perform so well with Monsieur as with Madame. But if you must know, the major will tell you, while you wait for Hyde and the hour. I have seen him, he has no scruples; I have ensured his safety, and he will not fail us. Now the charming *billet* to the *señor,* and I go to my post."

Douglas wrote the challenge; Duprès departed in buoyant spirits; and while Earl waited for the stranger, Hyde, the major enlightened him upon the grand finale.

The city clocks were striking twelve as two men, masked and cloaked, passed up the steps of Mrs. Vane's house and entered noiselessly. No light beamed in the hall, but scarcely had they closed the door behind them when a glimmer shone from above, and at the stairhead appeared a woman beckoning. Up they stole, as if shod with velvet, and the woman flitted like a shadow before them, till they reached a door to the second story. Opening this, she motioned them to enter, and as they passed in, she glided up another flight, as if to stand guard over her sleeping fellow servants.

One of the men was tall and evidently young, the other a bent and withered little man, whose hands trembled slightly as he adjusted his mask, and peered about him. It was a large still room, lighted by a night lamp, burning behind its shade, richly furnished, and decorated with warm hues, that produced the effect of mingled snow and fire. A luxurious nest it seemed, and a fit inmate of it looked the beautiful woman asleep in the shadow of the crimson-curtained bed. One white arm pillowed her head; from the little cap that should have confined it flowed a mass of golden hair over neck and shoulders; the long lashes lay dark against her cheek; the breath slept upon her lips; and perfect unconsciousness lent its reposeful charm to both face and figure.

Noiselessly advancing, the taller man looked and listened for a moment, as if to assure himself that this deep slumber was not feigned; then he beckoned the other to bring the lamp. It flickered as the old man took it up, but he trimmed the wick, removed the shade, and a clear light shone across the room. Joining his companion, he too looked at the sleeping beauty, shook his gray head, and seemed to deplore some fact that marred the pretty picture in his sight.

"Is there no danger of her waking, sir?" he whispered, as the light fell on her face.

"It is impossible for an hour yet. The bracelet is on that wrist; we must move her, or you cannot reach it," returned the other; and with a gentle touch drew the left arm from underneath her head.

She sighed in her sleep, knit her brows, as if a dream disturbed her, and turning on her pillow, all the bright hair fell about her face, but could not hide the glitter of the chain about her neck. Drawing it forth, the taller man started, uttered an exclamation, dragged from his own bosom a duplicate of the miniature hanging from that chain, and compared the two with trembling intentness. Very like they were, those two young faces, handsome, frank and full of boyish health, courage, and blithesomeness. One might have been taken a year after the other, for the brow was bolder, the mouth graver, the eye more steadfast, but the same charm of expression appeared in both, making the ivory oval more attractive even to a stranger's eye than the costly setting, or the initial letters *A. D.* done in pearls upon the back. A small silver key hung on the chain the woman wore, and as if glad to tear his thoughts from some bitter reminiscence, the man detached this key, and glanced about the room, as if to discover what lock it would be.

His action seemed to remind the other of his own task, for setting down the lamp on the little table where lay a prayer book, a bell, and a rosary, he produced a case of delicate instruments and a bunch of tiny keys, and bending over the bracelet, examined the golden padlock that fastened it. While he carefully tried key after key upon that miniature lock, the chief of this mysterious inspection went to and fro with the silver key, attempting larger locks. Nowhere did it fit, till in passing the toilet table his foot brushed its draperies aside, disclosing a quaint foreign-looking casket of ebony and silver. Quick as thought it was drawn out and opened, for here the key did its work. In the upper tray lay the opal ring in its curiously thick setting, beside it a seal, rudely made from an impression in wax of his own iron ring, and a paper bearing its stamp. The marriage record was in hand, and he longed to keep or destroy it, but restrained the impulse; and lifting the tray, found below two or three relics of his friend Vane, and some childish toys, soiled and broken, but precious still.

"A child! Good God! What have I done?" he said to himself, as the lid fell from his hand.

"Hush, come and look, it is off," whispered the old man, and hastily restoring all things to their former order, the other relocked and replaced the casket, and obeyed the call.

For a moment a mysterious and striking picture might have been seen in that quiet room. Under the crimson canopy lay the fair figure of the sleeping woman, her face half hidden by the golden shadow of her hair, her white arm laid out on the warm-hued coverlet, and bending over it, the two masked men, one holding the lamp nearer, the other pointing to something just above the delicate wrist, now freed from the bracelet, which lay open beside it. Two distinctly traced letters were seen, *V. V.*, and underneath a tiny true-lover's knot, in the same dark lines.

The man who held the lamp examined the brand with minutest care, then making a gesture of satisfaction, he said, "It is enough, I am sure now. Put on the bracelet, and come away; there is nothing more to be done tonight."

The old man skillfully replaced the hand, while the other put back locket and key, placed the lamp where they found it; and with a last look at the sleeper, whose unconscious helplessness appealed to them for mercy, both stole away as noiselessly as they had come. The woman reappeared the instant they left the room, lighted them to the hall door, received some reward that glittered as it passed from hand to hand, and made all fast behind them, pausing a moment in a listening attitude, till the distant roll of a carriage assured her that the maskers were safely gone.

❧ *Chapter X* ❧

IN THE SNARE

THE first rays of the sun fell on a group of five men, standing together on a waste bit of ground in the environs of London. Major Mansfield and Duprès were busily loading pistols, marking off the distance, and conferring together with a great display of interest. Douglas conversed tranquilly with the surgeon in attendance, a quiet, unassuming man, who stood with his hand in his pocket, as if ready to produce his case of instruments at a moment's notice. The Spaniard was alone, and a curious change seemed to have passed over him. The stately calmness of his demeanor was gone, and he paced to and fro with restless steps, like a panther in his cage. A look of almost savage hatred lowered on his swarthy face; desperation and despair alternately glowed and gloomed in his fierce eye; and the whole man wore a look of one who after long restraint yields himself utterly to the dominion of some passion, dauntless and indomitable as death.

Once he paused, drew from his pocket an ill-spelled, rudely written letter, which had been put into his hand by a countryman as he left his hotel, reread the few lines it contained, and thrust it back into his bosom, muttering, "All things favor me; this was the last tie that bound her; now we must stand or fall together."

"Señor, we are prepared," called Duprès, advancing, pistol in hand, to place his principal, adding, as Arguelles dropped hat and cloak, "our custom may be different from yours, but give heed, and at the word 'Three,' fire."

"I comprehend, monsieur," and a dark smile passed across the

Spaniard's face as he took his place and stretched his hand to receive the weapon.

But Duprès drew back a step—and with a sharp metallic click, around that extended wrist snapped a handcuff. A glance showed Arguelles that he was lost, for on his right stood the counterfeit surgeon, with the well-known badge now visible on his blue coat, behind him Major Mansfield, armed, before him Douglas, guarding the nearest outlet of escape, and on his left Duprès, radiant with satisfaction, exclaiming, as he bowed with grace, "A thousand pardons, Monsieur Victor Varens, but this little ruse was inevitable."

Quick as a flash that freed left hand snatched the pistol from Duprès, aimed it at Douglas, and it would have accomplished its work had not the Frenchman struck up the weapon. But the ball was sped, and as the pistol turned in his hand, the bullet lodged in Victor's breast, sparing him the fate he dreaded more than death. In an instant all trace of passion vanished, and with a melancholy dignity that nothing could destroy, he offered his hand to receive the fetter, saying calmly, while his lips whitened, and a red stain dyed the linen on his breast, "I am tired of my life; take it."

They laid him down, for as he spoke, consciousness ebbed away. A glance assured the major that the wound was mortal, and carefully conveying the senseless body to the nearest house, Douglas and the detective remained to tend and guard the prisoner, while the other gentlemen posted to town to bring a genuine surgeon and necessary help, hoping to keep life in the man till his confession had been made.

At nightfall, Mrs. Vane, or Virginie, as we may now call her, grew anxious for the return of Victor, who was to bring her tidings of the child, because she dared not visit him just now herself.

When dressed for the evening, she dismissed Gabrielle, opened the antique casket, and put on the opal ring, carefully attaching the little chain that fastened it securely to her bracelet, for the ring was too large for the delicate hand that wore it. Then with steady feet she went down to the drawing room to meet her lover and her victim.

But some reproachful memory seemed to start up and haunt the present with a vision of the past. She passed her hand across her eyes, as if she saw again the little room, where in the gray dawn she had left her husband lying dead, and she sank into a seat, groaning half aloud, "Oh, if I could forget!"

A bell rang from below, but she did not hear it; steps came through the drawing room, yet she did not heed them; and Douglas stood before her, but she did not see him till he spoke. So great was her surprise, that with all her power of dissimulation she would have found difficulty in concealing it, had not the pale gravity of the newcomer's face afforded a pretext for alarm.

"You startled me at first, and now you look as if you brought ill news," she said, with a vain effort to assume her usual gaiety.

"I do" was the brief reply.

"The señor? Is he with you? I am waiting for him."

"Wait no longer, he will never come."

"Where is he?"

"Quiet in his shroud."

He thought to see her shrink and pale before the blow, but she did neither; she grasped his arm, searched his face, and whispered, with a look of relief, not terror, in her own, "You have killed him?"

"No, his blood is not upon my head; he killed himself."

She covered up her face, and from behind her hands he heard her murmur, "Thank God, he did not come! I am spared that."

While he pondered over the words, vainly trying to comprehend them, she recovered herself, and turning to him said, quite steadily though very pale, "This is awfully sudden; tell me how it came to pass. I am not afraid to hear."

"I will tell you, for you have a right to know. Sit, Mrs. Vane; it is a long tale, and one that will try your courage to the utmost.

"Six years ago I went abroad to meet my cousin Allan," Douglas began, speaking slowly, almost sternly. "He was my senior by a year, but we so closely resembled each other that we were often taken for twin brothers. Alike in person, character, temper, and tastes, we were never so happy as when together, and we loved one another as tenderly as women love. For nearly a year we roamed east and west, then our holiday was over, for we had promised to return. One month more remained; I desired to revisit Switzerland, Allan to remain in Paris, so we parted for a time, each to our own pleasures, appointing to meet on a certain day at a certain place. I never saw him again, for when I reached the spot where he should have met me, I found only a letter, saying that he had been called from Paris suddenly, but that I should receive further intelligence before many days. I waited, but not long. Visiting the Morgue that very week, I found my poor Allan waiting for me there. His body had been taken from the river, and the deep wound in his breast showed that foul play was at the bottom of the mystery. Night and day I labored to clear up the mystery, but labored secretly, lest publicity should warn the culprits, or bring dishonor upon our name, for I soon found that Allan had led a wild life in my absence, and I feared to make some worse discoveries than a young man's follies. I did so; for it appeared that he had been captivated by a singularly beautiful girl, a *danseuse,* had privately married her, and both had disappeared with a young cousin of her own. Her apartments were searched, but all her possessions had been removed, and nothing remained but a plausible letter, which would have turned suspicion from the girl to the cousin, had not the marriage been discovered, and in her room two witnesses against them. The handle of a stiletto, half consumed in the ashes, which fitted the broken blade entangled in the dead man's clothes, and, hidden by the hangings of the bed, a woman's slipper, with a bloodstain on the sole. Ah, you may well shudder, Mrs. Vane; it is an awful tale."

"Horrible! Why tell it?" she asked, pressing her hand upon her eyes, as if to shut out some image too terrible to look upon.

"Because it concerns our friend Arguelles, and explains his death," replied Earl, in the same slow stern voice. She did not look up, but he saw that she listened breathlessly, and grew paler still behind her hand.

"Nothing more was discovered then. My cousin's body was sent home, and none but our two families ever knew the truth. It was believed by the world that he died suddenly of an affection of the heart—poor lad! it was the bitter truth—and whatever rumors were about regarding his death, and the change it wrought in me, were speedily silenced at the time, and have since died away. Over the dead body of my dearest friend, I vowed a solemn vow to find his murderer and avenge his death. I have done both."

"Where? How?"

Her hand dropped, and she looked at him with a face that was positively awful in its unnatural calmness.

"Arguelles was Victor Varens. I suspected, watched, ensnared him, and would have let the law avenge Allan's death, but the murderer escaped by his own hand."

"Well for him it was so. May his sins be forgiven. Now let us go elsewhere, and forget this dark story and its darker end."

She rose as she spoke, and a load seemed lifted off her heart; but it fell again, as Douglas stretched his hand to detain her, saying, "Stay, the end is not yet told. You forget the girl."

"She was innocent—why should she suffer?" returned the other, still standing as if defying both fear and fate.

"She was *not* innocent—for she lured that generous boy to marry her, because she coveted his rank and fortune, not his heart, and, when he lay dead, left him to the mercies of wind and wave, while she fled away to save herself. But that cruel cowardice availed her nothing, for though I have watched and waited long, at length I have found her, and at this moment her life lies in my hand—for you and Virginie are one!"

Like a hunted creature driven to bay, she turned on him with an air of desperate audacity, saying haughtily, "Prove it!"

"I will."

For a moment they looked at one another. In his face she saw pitiless resolve; in hers he read passionate defiance.

"Sit down, Virginie, and hear the story through. Escape is impossible—the house is guarded, Duprès waits in yonder room, and Victor can no longer help you with quick wit or daring hand. Submit quietly, and do not force me to forget that you are my cousin's—wife."

She obeyed him, and as the last words fell from his lips a new hope sprang up within her, the danger seemed less imminent, and she took heart again, remembering the child, who might yet plead for her, if her own eloquence should fail.

"You ask me to prove that fact, and evidently doubt my power to do it; but well as you have laid your plots, carefully as you have erased all traces of your former self, and skillfully as you have played your new part, the truth has come to light, and through many winding ways I have followed you, till my labors end here. When you fled from Paris, Victor, whose mother was a Spaniard, took you to Spain, and there, among his kindred, your boy was born."

"Do you know that, too?" she cried, lost in wonder at the quiet statement of what she believed to be known only to herself, her dead cousin, and those far-distant kindred who had succored her in her need.

"I know everything," Earl answered, with an expression that made her quail; then a daring spirit rose up in her, as she remembered more than one secret, which she now felt to be hers alone.

"Not everything, my cousin; you are keen and subtle, but I excel you, though you win this victory, it seems."

So cool, so calm she seemed, so beautifully audacious she looked, that Earl could only resent the bold speech with a glance, and proceed to prove the truth of his second assertion with the first.

"You suffered the sharpest poverty, but Victor respected your helplessness, forgave your treachery, supplied your wants as far as possible, and when all other means failed, left you there, while he went to earn bread for you and your boy. Virginie, I never can forgive him my cousin's death, but for his faithful, long-suffering devotion to you, I honor him, sinner though he was."

She shrugged her shoulders, with an air of indifference or displeasure, took off the widow's cap, no longer needed for a disguise, and letting loose the cloud of curls that seemed to cluster round her charming face, she lay back in her chair with all her former graceful ease, saying, as she fixed her lustrous eyes upon the man she meant to conquer yet, "I let him love me, and he was content. What more could I do, for I never loved *him?*"

"Better for him that you did not, and better for poor Allan that he never lived to know it was impossible for you to love."

Earl spoke bitterly, but Virginie bent her head till her face was hidden, as she murmured, "Ah, if it were impossible, this hour would be less terrible, the future far less dark."

He heard the soft lament, divined its meaning, but abruptly continued his story, as if he ignored the sorrowful fact which made her punishment heavier from his hand than from any other.

"While Victor was away, you wearied of waiting, you longed for the old life of gaiety and excitement, and, hoping to free yourself from him, you stole away, and for a year were lost to him. Your plan was to reach France, and under another name dance yourself into some other man's heart and home, making him your shield against all danger. You did reach France, but weary, ill, poor, and burdened with the child, you failed to find help, till some evil fortune threw Vane in your way. You had heard of him from Allan, knew his chivalrous nature, his passion for relieving pain or sorrow, at any cost to himself, and you appealed to him for charity. A piteous story of a cruel husband, desertion, suffering, and destitution you told him; he believed it, and being on the point of sailing for India, offered you the place of companion to a lady sailing with him. Your tale was plausible, your youth made it pathetic, your beauty lent it power, and the skill with which you played the part of a sad gentlewoman won all hearts, and served your end successfully. Vane loved you, wished to marry you, and would have done so had not death prevented. He died suddenly; you were with him, and though his last act was to make generous provision for you and the boy, some devil prompted you to proclaim yourself his wife, as soon as he was past denying it. His love for you was well-known among those with whom you lived, and your statement was believed."

"You are a magician," she said suddenly. "I have thought so before; now I am sure of it, for you must have transported yourself to India, to make these discoveries."

"No—India came to me in the person of a Hindoo, and from him I learned these facts," replied Douglas, slow to tell her of Victor's perfidy, lest he should put her on her guard, and perhaps lose some revelation which in her ignorance she might make. Fresh bewilderment seemed to fall upon her, and with intensest interest she listened, as that ruthless voice went on.

"Your plan was this: From Vane you had learned much of Allan's family, and the old desire to be 'my lady' returned more strongly than before. Once in England, you hoped to make your way as Colonel Vane's widow, and if no safe, sure opportunity appeared of claiming your boy's right, you resolved to gain your end by wooing and winning another Douglas. You were on the point of starting with poor Vane's fortune in your power (for he left no will, and you were prepared to produce forged papers, if your possession was questioned in England), when Victor found you. He had traced you with the instinct of a faithful dog, though his heart was nearly broken by your cruel desertion. You saw that he could not serve you; you appeased his anger and silenced his reproaches by renewed promises to be his when the boy was acknowledged, if he would aid you in that project. At the risk of his life, this devoted slave consented, and disguised as an Indian servant came with you to England. On the way, you met and won the good graces of the Countess Camareena; she introduced you to the London world, and you began your career as a lady under the best auspices. Money, beauty, art served you well, and as an unfortunate descendant of the noble house of Montmorenci, you were received by those who would have shrunk from you as you once did from the lock of hair of the plebeian French *danseuse,* found in Allan's bosom."

"I *am* noble," she cried, with an air that proved it, "for though my mother was a peasant, my father was a prince, and better blood than that of the Montmorencis flows in my veins."

He only answered with a slight bow, which might be intended as a mocking obeisance in honor of her questionable nobility, or a grave dismissal of the topic.

"From this point the tale is unavoidably egotistical," he said, "for through Lady Lennox you heard of me, learned that I was the next heir to the title, and began at once to weave the web in which I was to be caught. You easily understood what was the mystery of my life, as it was called among the gossips, and that knowledge was a weapon in your hands, which you did not fail to use. You saw that Diana loved me, soon learned my passion for her, and set yourself to separate us, without one thought of the anguish it would bring us, one fear of the consequences of such wrong to yourself. You bade her ask of me a confession that I could not make, having given my word to Allan's mother that her son's name should not be tarnished by the betrayal of the rash act that cost his life. That parted us; then you told her a tale of skillfully mingled truth and falsehood, showed her the marriage record on which a name and date appeared to convict me, took her to the boy whose likeness to his father, and therefore to myself, completed the cruel deception, and drove that high-hearted girl to madness and to death."

"I did not kill her! On my soul, I never meant it! I was terror-stricken when we missed her, and knew no peace or rest till she was found. Of that deed I am innocent—I swear it to you on my knees."

The haunting horror of that night seemed again to overwhelm her; she fell down upon her knees before him, enforcing her denial with clasped hands, imploring eyes, and trembling voice. But Douglas drew back with a gesture of repugnance that wounded her more deeply than his sharpest word, and from that moment all traces of compassion vanished from his countenance, which wore the relentless aspect of a judge who resolves within himself no longer to temper justice with mercy.

"Stand up," he said. "I will listen to no appeal, believe no oath, let no touch of pity soften my heart, for your treachery, your craft, your sin deserve nothing but the heavy retribution you have brought upon yourself. Diana's death lies at your door, as much as if you had stabbed her with the same dagger that took Allan's life. It may yet be proved that you beguiled her to that fatal pool, for you were seen there, going to remove all traces of her, perhaps. But in your hasty flight you left traces of yourself behind you, as you sprang away with an agility that first suggested to me the suspicion of Virginie's presence. I tried your slipper to the footprint, and it fitted too exactly to leave me in much doubt of the truth of my wild conjecture. I had never seen you. Antoine Duprès knew both Victor and yourself. I sent for him, but before the letter went, Jitomar, your spy, read the address, feared that some peril menaced you both, and took counsel with you how to delude the new-comer, if any secret purpose lurked behind our seeming friendliness. You devised a scheme that would have baffled us, had not accident betrayed Victor. In the guise of Arguelles he met Duprès in Paris, re-turned with him, and played his part so well that the Frenchman was entirely deceived, never dreaming of being sought by the very man who would most desire to shun him. You, too, disguised yourself, with an art that staggered my own senses, and perplexed Duprès, for our mascu-line eye could not fathom the artifices of costume, cosmetics, and con-summate acting. We feared to alarm you by any open step, and resolved to oppose craft to craft, treachery to treachery. Duprès revels in such intricate affairs, and I yielded, against my will, till the charm of success drew me on with increasing eagerness and spirit. The day we first met here, in gathering a flower you would have fallen, had not the Spaniard sprung forward to save you; that involuntary act betrayed him, for the momentary attitude he assumed recalled to Duprès the memory of a certain pose which the dancer Victor often assumed. It was too peculiar to be accidental, too striking to be easily forgotten, and the entire unconsciousness of its actor was a proof that it was so familiar as to be quite natural. From that instant Duprès devoted himself to the Spaniard; this first genuine delusion put Victor off his guard with Antoine; and Antoine's feigned friendship was so adroitly assumed that no suspicion woke in Victor's mind till the moment when, instead of offering him a weapon with which to take my life, he took him prisoner."

"He is not dead, then? You lie to me; you drive me wild with your horrible recitals of the past, and force me to confess against my will. Who told you these things? The dead alone could tell you what passed between Diana and myself."

Still on the ground, as if forgetful of everything but the bewilderment of seeing plot after plot unfolded before her, she had looked up and listened with dilated eyes, lips apart, and both hands holding back the locks that could no longer hide her from his piercing glance. As she spoke, she paled and trembled with a sudden fear that clutched her heart, that Diana was not dead, for even now she clung to her love with a desperate hope that it might save her.

Calm and cold as a man of marble, Douglas looked down upon her, so beautiful in all her abasement, and answered steadily, "You forget Victor. To him all your acts, words, and many of your secret thoughts were told. Did you think his love would endure forever, his patience never tire, his outraged heart never rebel, his wild spirit never turn and rend you? All day I have sat beside him, listening to his painful confessions, painfully but truthfully made, and with his last breath he cursed you as the cause of a wasted life, and ignominious death. Virginie, this night your long punishment begins, and that curse is a part of it."

"Oh, no, no! You will have mercy, remembering how young, how friendless I am? For Allan's sake you will pity me; for his boy's sake you will save me; for your own sake you will hide me from the world's contempt?"

"What mercy did you show poor Diana? What love for Allan? What penitence for your child's sake? What pity for my grief? I tell you, if a word would save you, my lips should not utter it!"

He spoke passionately now, and passionately she replied, clinging to him, though he strove to tear his hands away.

"You have heard Victor's confession, now hear mine. I *have* longed to repent; I did hope to make my life better, for my baby's sake; and oh, I did pity you, till my cold heart softened and grew warm. I should have given up my purpose, repaid Victor's fidelity, and gone away to grow an honest, happy, humble woman, if I had not loved *you*. That made me blind, when I should have been more keen-sighted than ever; that kept me here to be deceived, betrayed, and that should save me now."

"It will not; and the knowledge that I detest and despise you is to add bitterness to your threefold punishment; the memory of Allan, Victor, and Diana is another part of it; and here is the heaviest blow which heaven inflicts as a retribution that will come home to you."

As he spoke, Douglas held to her a crumpled paper, stained with a red stain, and torn with the passage of a bullet that ended Victor's life. She knew the writing, sprang up to seize it, read the few lines, and when the paper fluttered to the ground, the white anguish of her face betrayed that the last blow *had* crushed her as no other could have done. She dropped into a seat, with the wail of tearless woe that breaks from a bereaved mother's heart as she looks on the dead face of the child who has been her idol, and finds no loving answer.

"My baby gone—and I not there to say good-bye! Oh, my darling, I could have borne anything but this!"

So utterly broken did she seem, so wild and woeful did she look, that Douglas had not the heart to add another pang to her sharp grief by any word of explanation or compassion. Silently he poured out a glass of wine and placed it nearer, then resumed his seat and waited till she spoke. Soon she lifted up her head, and showed him the swift and subtle blight that an hour had brought upon her. Life, light, and beauty seemed to have passed away, and a pale shadow of her former self alone remained. Some hope or some resolve had brought her an unnatural calmness, for her eyes were tearless, her face expressionless, her voice tranquil, as if she had done with life, and neither pain nor passion could afflict her now.

"What next?" she said, and laid her hand upon the glass, but did not lift it to her lips, as if the former were too tremulous, or the latter incapable of receiving the draft.

"Only this," he answered, with a touch of pity in his voice. "I will not have my name handed from mouth to mouth, in connection with an infamous history like this. For Allan's sake, and for Diana's, I shall

keep it secret, and take your punishment into my hands. Victor I leave
to a wiser judge than any human one; the innocent child is safe from
shame and sorrow; but you must atone for the past with the loss of
liberty and your whole future. It is a more merciful penalty than the law
would exact, were the truth known, for you are spared public contempt,
allowed time for repentance, and deprived of nothing but the liberty
which you have so cruelly abused."

"I thank you. Where is my prison to be?"

She took the glass into her hand, yet still held it suspended, as she
waited for his answer, with an aspect of stony immobility which troubled
him.

"Far away in Scotland I own a gray old tower, all that now remains
of an ancient stronghold. It is built on the barren rock, where it stands
like a solitary eagle's eyrie, with no life near it but the sound of the wind,
the scream of the gulls, the roll of the sea that foams about it. There
with my faithful old servants you shall live, cut off from all the world,
but not from God, and when death comes to you, may it find you ready
and glad to go, a humble penitent, more fit to meet your little child than
now."

A long slow tremor shook her from head to foot, as word by word
her merciful yet miserable doom was pronounced, leaving no hope, no
help but the submission and repentance which it was not in her nature
to give. For a moment she bowed her head, while her pale lips moved,
and her hands, folded above the glass, were seen to tremble as if some
fear mingled even in her prayers. Then she sat erect, and fixing on him
a glance in which love, despair, and defiance mingled, she said, with
all her former pride and spirit, as she slowly drank the wine, "Death
cannot come too soon; I go to meet it."

Her look, her tone, awed Douglas, and for a moment he regarded
her in silence, as she sat there, leaning her bright head against the dark
velvet of the cushioned chair. Her eyes were on him still brilliant and
brave, in spite of all that had just passed; a disdainful smile curved her
lips, and one fair arm lay half extended on the table, as it fell when
she put the glass away. On this arm the bracelet shone; he pointed to it,
saying, with a meaning glance, "I know that secret, as I know all the
rest."

"Not all; there is one more you have not discovered—yet."

She spoke very slowly, and her lips seemed to move reluctantly,
while a strange pallor fell on her face, and the fire began to die out of
her eyes, leaving them dim, but tender.

"You mean the mystery of the iron ring; but I learned that last

night, when, with an expert companion, I entered your room, where you
lay buried in the deep sleep produced by the drugged coffee which I
gave you. I saw my portrait on your neck, as I wear Allan's, ever since
we gave them to each other, long ago, and beside the miniature, the
silver key that opened your quaint treasure casket. I found the wax
impression of my signet, taken, doubtless, on the night when, as a ghost,
you haunted my room; I found the marriage record, stamped with that
counterfeit seal, to impose upon Diana; I found relics of Vane, and of
your child; and when Hyde called me, I saw and examined the two
letters on your arm, which he had uncovered by removing the bracelet
from it."

He paused there, expecting some demonstration. None appeared;
she leaned and listened, with the same utter stillness of face and figure,
the same fixed look and deathly pallor. He thought her faint and spent
with the excitement of the hour, and hastened to close the interview,
which had been so full of contending emotions to them both.

"Go now, and rest," he said. "I shall make all necessary arrangements here, all proper explanations to Lady Leigh. Gabrielle will prepare
for your departure in the morning; but let me warn you not to attempt
to bribe her, or to deceive me by any new ruse, for now escape is impossible."

"I have escaped!"

The words were scarcely audible, but a glance of exultation flashed
from her eyes, then faded, and the white lids fell, as if sleep weighed
them down. A slight motion of the nerveless hand that lay upon the table
drew Earl's attention, and with a single look those last words were
explained. The opal ring was turned inward on her finger, and some
unsuspected spring had been touched when she laid her hands together;
for now in the deep setting appeared a tiny cavity, which had evidently
contained some deadly poison. The quick and painless death that was
to have been Victor's had fallen to herself, and, unable to endure the
fate prepared for her, she had escaped, when the net seemed most
securely drawn about her. Horror-stricken, Douglas called for help; but
all human aid was useless, and nothing of the fair, false Virginie remained but a beautiful, pale image of repose.

A Marble Woman:

~ or, ~

THE MYSTERIOUS MODEL

❧ *Chapter I* ❧

LITTLE CECIL

"WHAT do you mean by pulling the bell fit to bring the house down?" demanded gruff old Anthony, as he flung the door open and found himself confronted with a large trunk and a small girl holding a letter in her hand.

"It was the coachman, please, sir" was the composed answer.

"Well, what do you want, child?"

"I wish to come in. This is my luggage; I'll help you with it."

The small personage laid hold of one handle with such perfect good faith in her own strength that it produced a chuckle from the old servant as he drew the trunk in with one hand, the child with the other, and shut the door, saying more respectfully, "Now, ma'am, what next?"

Smoothing her disordered dress with dignity, the little girl replied, as if repeating a carefully learned lesson, "You are to give this letter to Mr. Bazil Yorke, and say Miss Stein has come. Then I am to wait till he tells me what to do."

"Are you Miss Stein?" asked Anthony, bewildered by the appearance of a child in that lonely house.

"Yes, sir; and I've come to live here if Mr. Yorke will keep me," said the little girl, glancing wistfully about her as if waiting for a welcome.

"Are you a relation of Master's?" questioned Anthony, still more mystified.

"No, sir. He knew my papa and mamma, but he never saw me. That's all I know about it."

The old man shook his head with an air of resignation as he muttered to himself, "Some whim of Master's; it's just like him." Then aloud, "I'll take up the letter, but you'd better play out here till you're wanted; for when Master gets busy up aloft, it's no use trying to fetch him down before the time."

Leading her through the hall, he opened a glass door and ushered her into a city garden, where a few pale shrubs and vines rustled in the wind. The child glanced listlessly about her as she walked, for nothing was in bloom, and the place had a neglected air. Suddenly a splendid, full-blown rose softly brushed her cheek and fell at her feet. With an exclamation of pleasure she caught it up and looked skyward to see what friendly fairy had divined her wish and granted it.

"Here I am," called a laughing voice, and turning about she saw a boy leaning on the low wall that divided Mr. Yorke's garden from an adjoining one. A rosy, bright-eyed boy about her own age he seemed, full of the pleasant audacity which makes boyhood so charming, and in a neighborly mood just then; for as she looked up wondering, he nodded, smiled, and said merrily, "How are you? Do you like the rose?"

"Oh, yes! Did you mean it for me?"

"I thought you looked as if you needed one, so I tossed it over. It's very dismal down there. Suppose you come up here, and then you can see my garden while we talk a bit. Don't be afraid of me; just give me your hand and there you are."

There was something so winning in voice, face, and gesture that little Miss Stein could not resist the invitation. She gave her hand, and soon sat on the wide coping of the wall, regarding her new friend with a shy yet confiding look as he did the honors of the place with well-bred eagerness. Neither asked the other's name, but making the rose their master of ceremonies, introduced themselves through that pretty medium, and soon forgot that they had been entire strangers five minutes before.

"Do you like my garden?" asked the boy, as the girl smelled her flower and smiled down upon the blooming plot below her.

"Very much; I wish Mr. Yorke would have one like it."

"He don't care for such things; he's odd and busy, and a genius, you know."

"I hope that's nothing bad, because I'm going to live with him. Tell me all about him, for I never saw him in my life."

"He's a sculptor and makes splendid statues up in that tower where nothing but the sun and sparrows can see him. He never shows them, and no one would ever see them if they didn't beg and tease and give him no peace till they do."

"Is he kind and pleasant?" asked the girl.

"He looks precious grim with his long hair and beard, but he's got kind eyes, though his face is dark and strange."

"Has he got a wife and any little children?"

"Oh, dear, no! He lives here with old Tony and Mrs. Hester, the maid. I heard my mother tell a lady that Mr. Yorke had a love trouble and can't bear women, so none dare go near him. He's got a splendid great dog, but he's as fierce as a wolf to everyone but his master and Tony."

"I wish I hadn't come. I don't like odd people, and I'm afraid of dogs," sighed Miss Stein.

"Mr. Yorke will be kind to such a little thing as you, and make old Judas like you, I dare say. Perhaps you won't have to stay long if you don't like it. Is your home far away?"

"I've got no home now. Oh, Mamma! Mamma!" And covering her face with her little black frock, the child broke into such sudden, bitter sobs that the boy was stricken with remorse. Finding words vain, he sprang impetuously off the wall, and filling his hands with his choicest flowers, heaped them into the child's lap with such demonstrations of penitence and goodwill that she could not refuse to be comforted.

Just then Anthony called her, and with a hasty good-bye she turned to obey, but the boy detained her for a moment to say, "Don't forget to ask Mr. Yorke if you may play with me, because you'll be very dull all by yourself, and I should like you for my little sweetheart."

"Alfred! Alfred! It is rather too soon for that," called a smiling lady from a window of the adjoining house, whereat the boy sprang down, laughing at the unexpected publicity of his declaration, and Miss Stein walked away, looking much disturbed by Anthony's chuckles.

"The master will be down to his tea directly, so you can look out a winder and not meddle till he comes," said the old man as he left her.

The memory of the pretty lad warmed the child's heart and seemed to shed a ray of cheerfulness over the somber room. A table was spread with care, and beside one plate lay a book, as if "the master" was in the habit of enlivening his solitary meals with such society as the full shelves about afforded him. The furniture was ancient, the window hangings dark, the pictures weird or gloomy, and the deep silence that reigned through the house oppressed the lonely child. Approaching the table she ventured to examine the book. It proved intelligible and picturesque; so establishing herself in the armchair, she spread the volume before her, and soon became happily forgetful of orphanage and solitude.

So intent was she that a man came to the door unobserved, and

pausing there, scrutinized her from head to foot. Had she looked up she
would have seen a tall, athletic figure and a singularly attractive face,
though it was neither beautiful nor gentle. The dark, neglected hair was
streaked with gray at thirty; the forehead was marked with deep lines,
and under the black brows were magnificent yet melancholy eyes, that
just then looked as if some strong emotion had kindled an unwonted
fire in their depths. The lower part of the face gave flat contradiction
to the upper, for the nose was disdainful, the chin square and grim, the
whole contour of the mouth relentless, in spite of the softening effect
of a becoming beard. Dressed in velvet cap and paletot, and framed in
the dark doorway, he looked like a striking picture of some austere
scholar aged with care or study, not with years; yet searching closer,
one would have seen traces of deep suffering, latent passion, and a
strange wistfulness, as if lonely eyes were forever seeking something
they had lost.

For many minutes Bazil Yorke watched the unconscious child, as if
there was some strong attraction for him in the studious little figure
poring over the book with serious eyes, one hand turning the pictured
pages, the other pushing back the wavy hair from a blooming cheek and
a forehead possessing delicate brows and the harmonious lines about the
temples which artists so love. The man's eyes softened as he looked,
for the child's patient trust made her friendlessness the more pathetic.
He put out his hand as if to draw her to him, then checked the impulse,
and the hard mouth grew grimmer as he swept off the cap, saying coldly,
"Miss Stein, I am ready now."

His guest started, shut the book, slipped down, and went to meet
her host, offering her hand as if anxious to atone for the offense of
meddling.

Like one unused to such acts, Mr. Yorke took the small hand, gave
it a scarcely perceptible pressure, and dropped it without a word. The
action grieved the child, yet nothing betrayed the pang of disappointment it gave her except a slight tremor in the voice that timidly asked,
"Did you get the letter, sir?"

"I did. Your mother wished me to keep you till you were eighteen,
when you were to choose a guardian for yourself. Her family will not
receive you, and your father's family is far away; but your mother and
myself were old friends many years ago, and she hoped I would take you
for a time."

"Will you, sir? I'll try not to be a trouble."

"No, I cannot. This is no place for a child; nor am I a fit guardian if it was. I will find some better home for you tomorrow. But as you will remain here tonight, you may take off your hat and cloak, or whatever it is."

Half pityingly, half impatiently he spoke, and eyed the child as if he longed to yet dared not keep her. The little hat was taken off, but the ribbons of the mantle were in a knot, and after pulling at it for a moment, she turned to her companion for help. As he stooped to give it with a curious reluctance in his manner, she scanned the face so near her own with innocent freedom, and presently murmured, as if to herself, "Yes, the boy was right; his eyes *are* kind."

With a wrench that tore the silk, and caused the child to start, Mr. Yorke broke the knot, and turning away, rang the bell with vehemence.

"What is your name?" he asked, carefully averting his eyes as the little girl sat down.

"Cecilia Bazil Stein."

"What an ominous conjunction!"

She did not understand the scornful exclamation and proceeded to explain.

"Mamma's name was Cecilia, yours is Bazil, and Papa's was Stein. You can call me Celia as Mamma did, if you please, sir."

"No, I shall call you Cecil. I dislike the other name."

Quick tears sprang to the child's eyes, but none fell, and lowering her voice she said, with trembling lips, "Mamma wished me to tell you that she sent her love, and the one precious thing she had as a keepsake, and hoped you'd take it in memory of the happy days when you and she were friends."

Mr. Yorke turned his back upon her for several minutes, then asked abruptly, "Where have you been this last year?"

"Here in America. We were in England before that, because Mamma did not like Germany since Papa died, and we were tired of going about."

"Your father died when you were a baby, I think. Have you been with your mother ever since?" asked Mr. Yorke with a half-smile, as the little creature spoke of these countries as composedly as if they were neighboring towns.

"Yes, I was always with her, and we were very happy staying in all sorts of new and pleasant places. But Mamma wished to save up some money for me, so we came here and lived very plainly in the country till she—"

The child stopped there, for her lips trembled and she did not wish to disgrace herself by crying twice in one hour. He saw that she controlled herself, and the little trait of character pleased him as did the pretty mixture of innocent frankness and good breeding betrayed by her manner and appearance.

"When did she leave you?" he ventured to ask, carefully avoiding the hard word "die."

"Three weeks ago."

"How old are you, Cecil?" he said presently, in order to change the current of her thoughts, although the question was an unnecessary one.

"Nearly twelve, sir."

"Twelve years, twelve long years since I saw her last, and then gave up the world."

He spoke low to himself, and his thoughts seemed to wander from the present to the past, as, bending his head upon his breast, he stood mute and motionless till Anthony announced, "Tea is ready, master."

Looking up with the melancholy shadow gloomier than ever in his eyes, Yorke led the child to the table, filled her cup, put everything within her reach, and opening a book, read more than he ate. Twilight was deepening in the room; the oppressive silence made the meal unsocial, and Cecil's heart was heavy, for she felt doubly forlorn, bereft of the protection she had hoped to find and the familiar name her mother's voice had endeared to her. She ate a few morsels, then leaned back in her chair, looking drearily about and wondering what would happen next. She did not wait long before a somewhat startling incident occurred.

As her eye roved to and fro it was arrested by the sudden appearance of a face at one of the windows. A strange, uncanny face, half concealed by a black beard that made the pallor of the upper part more striking. It was gone again instantly, but Cecil had only time to catch her breath and experience a thrill of alarm, when the long curtains that hung before the other half-open window stirred as if a hand grasped them, and through the narrow aperture between the folds the glitter of an eye was plainly visible. Fascinated by fear, the child sat motionless, longing to cry out, yet restrained by timidity and the hope that her companion would look up and see the intruder for himself.

He seemed absorbed in his book, and utterly unconscious of the hidden watcher, till an involuntary gesture caused another movement of the curtains, as if the hand loosened its grasp, for the eye vanished and Cecil covered her face with a long sigh of relief. Mr. Yorke glanced up, mistook the gesture for one of weariness, and evidently glad of an excuse to dispose of the child, he said abruptly, "You have come a long way today, and must be tired. Will you go to bed?"

"Oh, yes, I shall be glad to go," cried Cecil, eager to leave what to her was now a haunted room.

Taking a lamp, he led her along dimly lighted halls, up wide staircases, into a chamber that seemed immense to its small occupant, while the darkly curtained bed was so like a hearse she instantly decided that it would be impossible to sleep in it. Mr. Yorke glanced about as if desirous of making her comfortable, but quite ignorant how to set about it.

"The old woman who would have attended you is sick, but if you want anything, ring for Anthony. Good night."

Cecil was on the point of lifting her face for the good-night kiss she had been accustomed to receive from other lips, but remembering the careless pressure of his hand, the cold welcome he had given her, she restrained the impulse, and let him leave her with no answer but a quiet echo of his own "Good night."

The moment his steps died away, she opened the door again and watched the light mount higher and higher as he wound his way up a spiral flight of stairs that evidently led to the tower. Cecil longed to follow, for she was sleepless with the excitement of novelty and a lingering touch of fear (for the face still haunted her), and she now reproached herself for not having spoken to Mr. Yorke. She was about to make this an excuse for following him, when the sound of noises from above made her hesitate.

"I'll wait till he comes down, or till the person goes, for he ought to know about the man I saw, because it might be a thief," she thought.

After lingering on the threshold till she was tired, Cecil seated herself in an easy chair beside the door, and amused herself by examining the pictures on the wall. But she was more weary than she knew; the chair was luxuriously cushioned, the steady murmur of voices very soothing, and she soon lapsed away into a drowse.

The certainty that someone had touched her suddenly startled her wide awake. An instant's thought recalled her purpose, and fearing to be up too late, she ran into the upper hall, hoping to find Mr. Yorke descending. No one was in sight, however, yet so sure was she that a hand had touched her and a footstep sounded in the room that she looked over the balustrade, intending to call. Not a word left her lips, however, for neither Mr. Yorke nor Anthony appeared; but a man was going slowly down, wrapped in a cloak, with a shadowy hat drawn low over his brows. A slender hand shone white against the dark cloak, and as he reached the hall below he glanced over his shoulder, showing Cecil the same colorless face with its black beard and glittering eyes that had frightened her before, though he evidently did not see her now.

It alarmed her again, for it was a singularly sinister face in spite of its beauty. Never pausing to see what became of him, and conscious of nothing but an uncontrollable longing to be near Mr. Yorke, Cecil climbed the winding stairs without a pause till she reached an arched doorway, and seemed to see a gathering of ghosts beyond. The long, large room was filled with busts, statues, uncut blocks, tools, dust, and disorder, in the midst of which stood Mr. Yorke, dressed in a suit of gray linen, and intent on modeling something from a handful of clay. Many children would have been more alarmed at these inanimate figures than at the other, but Cecil found so much that was inviting, she forgot fear in delight, and boldly entered. A smiling woman seemed to beckon to her, a winged child to offer flowers, and all about the room pale gods and goddesses looked down upon her from their pedestals with what to her beauty-loving eye seemed varying expressions of welcome. Judas, the great dog, lay like a black statue on a tawny tiger skin, and the strong glow from a chandelier shone on his master as he worked with a swift dexterity that charmed Cecil.

Eager to ask questions, she began her explanations with a sudden "Bazil, I came up to—"

But got no further, for with a start that sent the model crumbling to the floor, he turned upon her almost angrily, demanding, "Who calls me by that name?"

"It's me; Mamma always said Bazil, and so I got used to it. What can I call you, sir?"

"Simply *Yorke,* as others do. I forbid that hateful name. Why are you here?"

"Indeed, I could not help it. I was so lonely and so frightened down there. I saw a face at the window, and wanted to tell you, but heard someone talking up here and I waited. But when I waked I saw the same face going down the stairs, and so I ran to you."

Yorke listened with curious intentness to her story, asked a question or two, mused a moment, then said, pointing to a half-finished athlete, "The man is my model for that. He is a strange person, and does odd things, but you need not fear him."

A quick-witted woman would have seen at a glance that dust lay thick on the clay figure, and have known that the slender hand grasping the cloak could never have belonged to the arm that served as a model for the brawny athlete. But Cecil's childish eyes saw no discrepancy between the two, and she believed the explanation at once. With a sigh

of mingled satisfaction and relief, she looked about her, and said beseech-
ingly, "Please let me stop and see your work. I like it so much, so very
much!"

"What do you know about it, child?" Yorke answered, wondering
at her interest and sudden animation.

"Why, I used to do it; Mamma taught me as you taught her, with
wax first, then pretty brown clay like this; and I was very happy doing it,
because I liked it best of all my plays."

"Your mother taught you! Why, Cecil?" And Yorke's grave face
kindled with an expression that won the child to franker speech at once.

"She liked it as well as I, and always called me little Bazil when
I made pretty things. She was fond of it because she used to be very
happy doing it a long time ago. She often told me about you when you
lived in her father's house; how you hated lessons, and loved to make
splendid things in wax and wood and clay; how you didn't care to eat
or sleep when you were busy, and how you made an image of her, but
broke it when she was unkind to you. She didn't tell me what she did,
but I wish you would, so that I may be careful not to do it while I'm
here."

He laughed such a bitter laugh, it both touched and troubled her,
as he answered harshly, "No fear of that; I never can be hurt again as
she hurt me thirteen years ago." Then with a sudden change in countenance and manner, he sat down on a block of marble with a half-finished
angel's head looking out of it, drew Cecil toward him, and looked at her
with hungry eyes as he said eagerly, "Tell me more. Did she talk of me?
Did she teach you to care for me? Child, speak fast—I vowed I would
ask no questions, but I must!"

His voice rose, his glance searched her face, his stern mouth grew
tremulous, and the whole man seemed to wake and glow with an unconquerable desire. Reassured by this sudden thaw in the frosty aspect
of her guardian, Cecil leaned confidingly against his knee and softly
answered, with her hand upon his shoulder, "Yes, Mamma often spoke
of you; she wished me to love you dearly—and the last thing she said was
that about the keepsake. I think she will be sorry if you send me away,
because she thought you'd care for me as you once did for her."

Some strange emotion rushed warm and tender over Bazil Yorke,
and as if the words, the gentle touch, had broken down some barrier
set up by pride or will, he took the child into his arms with an impetuous
gesture, saying brokenly, "She remembered me—and she sent me her all.
Surely I may keep the gift and put one drop of sweetness into this bitter
life of mine."

Bewildered, yet glad, Cecil clung to him, drawn by an attraction that she could not understand. For a moment Yorke hid his face in her long hair, then put her away as abruptly as he had embraced her, and returned to his work as if unused to such betrayals of feeling and ashamed of them. He merely said, as he took up his tools, "Amuse yourself as you please; I must work."

Quite contented, Cecil roved about the room till curiosity was satisfied; made timid advances toward the great dog, which were graciously received; and at length gathering up the crumbled clay that fell from Yorke's hand, she sat down beside Judas and began to mold as busily as the master.

Presently a little voice broke the silence, humming a song that Yorke remembered well. Softly as it was sung, Judas pricked up his ears, his master paused in his work, and leaning with folded arms, listened till the long hush recalled the singer from her happy reverie. She stopped instantly, but seeing no displeasure in the altered face above her, she held out her work, asking shyly, "Is it very bad, sir?"

It was a bunch of grapes deftly fashioned by small fingers that needed no other tool than their own skill, and though swiftly done, it was as graceful as if the gray cluster had just been broken from a vine. Yorke examined it critically, lifted the child's face and studied it intently for a moment, kissed it gravely on the forehead so like his own, and said, with an air of decision, "It is well done; I shall keep both it and you. Will you stay and work with me, Cecil, and be content with no friend but myself, no playmate but old Judas?"

Cecil read the yearning of the man's heart in his eyes with the quick instinct of a child, and answered it by exclaiming heartily, "Yes, I will; and be very happy here, for I like this place, I like Judas, and I love you already, because you make these lovely things, and are so kind to me now."

"Are you a discreet girl, Cecil? Can you see and hear things, and yet not ask questions or tell tales?" asked Yorke, somewhat anxiously.

"I think I am."

"So do I. Now I have a mind to keep you, for you are one of my sort; but I wish you to understand that nothing which goes on in my house is to be talked about outside of it. I let the world alone, and desire the world to do the same by me; so remember if you forget your promise, you march at once."

"I always keep my promises. But may I ask two questions now before I promise? Then I'll never do it anymore."

"Well, my inquisitive little person, what is it?"

"I want to know if I can sometimes see the pleasant boy who gave me this rose."

"And kissed you on the wall," added Yorke, with such a satirical look that Cecil colored high and involuntarily exclaimed, "Did you see us? I thought you couldn't from this high place."

"I see everything that happens on my premises. If you do not gossip you may see the boy occasionally. What is the other question?"

"Will that disagreeable man come here often—the model, I mean? He frightens me, and I don't want to see him unless you wish me to."

"You will not see him anymore. I shall not work at this figure for the present, so there will be no need of him. Make yourself easy; I shall never wish you to see or speak to him."

"You are very kind. I'll try to please you and not peep or ask questions. Can I wash my hands and look at this pretty book? I'll go quietly away to bed when I get sleepy."

With very much the air of a man who had undertaken the care of a butterfly, Yorke established her with the coveted portfolio on her lap, and soon entirely forgot her.

Accustomed to the deep reveries of a solitary life, hour after hour passed unheeded, and the city clocks tolled their warnings to deaf ears. After glancing once at the little chair and finding the child gone, he thought no more of her, till rising to rest his cramped limbs he saw her lying fast asleep on the tiger skin. One arm embraced the dog's shaggy neck, her long hair swept the dusty floor, and the rosy warmth of slumber made the childish face blooming and beautiful.

"Truly I am a fit guardian for a little creature like this," Yorke muttered, as he watched her a moment; then he covered her with a cloak and began to pace the room, busied with some absorbing thought. Once he paused and looked at the sleeper with an expression of grim determination, saying to himself as he eyed the group, "If I had power to kill the savage beast, skill to subdue the fierce dog, surely I can mold the child as I will, and make the daughter pay the mother's debt."

His face darkened as he spoke, the ruthless look deepened, and the sudden clenching of the hand boded ill for the young life he had taken into his keeping.

All night the child lay dreaming of her mother, all night the man sat pondering over an early wrong that had embittered a once noble nature, and dawn found them unchanged, except that Cecil had ceased to smile in her sleep, and Bazil Yorke had shaped a fugitive emotion into a relentless purpose.

✄ *Chapter II* ✄

THE BROKEN
CUPID

FIVE years later, a new statue stood in the studio; we might have
said two new statues, though one was a living creature. The marble
figure was a lovely, Psyche-bending form, and with her graceful
hand above her eyes, as if she watched her sleeping lover. Of all Bazil
Yorke's works this was the best, and he knew it, for, surrounded by new
influences, he had wrought at it with much of his youthful ardor—had
found much of the old happiness while so busied, and was so proud of
his success that no offer could tempt him to part with it—no certainty
of fame persuade him to exhibit it, except to a chosen few.

The human figure was Cecil, changed from a rosy child into a slender, deep-eyed girl. Colorless, like a plant deprived of sunshine, strangely
unyouthful in the quiet grace of her motions, the sweet seriousness of
her expression, but as beautiful as the Psyche and almost as cold. Her
dress heightened the resemblance, for the white folds draped her from
neck to ankle; not an ornament marred its severe simplicity, and the
wavy masses of her dark hair were gathered up with a fillet, giving her
the head of a young Hebe. It was a fancy of Yorke's, and as few eyes
but his beheld her, she dressed for him alone, unconscious that she
served as a model for his fairest work. Standing in the one ray of sunshine that shot athwart the subdued light of the studio, she seemed
intent upon a little Cupid exquisitely carved in the purest marble. She
was not working now, for the design was finished, but seemed to be
regarding it with mingled satisfaction and regret—satisfaction that it was
done so well, regret that it was done so soon. The little god was just
drawing an arrow from his quiver with an arch smile, and the girl

watched him with one almost as gay. A rare sight upon her lips, but some happy fancy seemed to bring it, and more than once she gave the graceful figure a caressing touch, as if she had learned to love it.

"Don't fire again, little Cupid, I surrender," suddenly exclaimed a blithe voice behind her, and, turning, Cecil saw her friend and neighbor, Alfred, now a tall young man, though much of the boyish frankness and impetuosity still remained.

"Do you like it, Alf?" she asked, with a quiet smile of welcome, and a repose of manner contrasting strongly with the eagerness of the newcomer's.

"You know I do, Cecil, for it has been my delight ever since you began it. The little god is perfect, and I must have him at any cost. Name your price, and let it be a high one."

"Yorke would not like that, neither should I. You have more than paid for it by friendly acts and words through these five years, so let me give it to you with all my heart."

She spoke tranquilly, and offered her hand as if transferring to him the lovely figure it had wrought. He took the white hand in both his own, and with a sudden glow on his cheek, a sudden ardor in his eye, said, in an impulsive voice, "With all your heart, Cecil? Let me take you at your word, let me claim, not only the image of love, but the reality, and keep this hand as mine."

A soft tinge of color touched the girl's cheek as she drew her hand away, but the quiet smile remained unchanged, and she still looked up at him with eyes as innocent and frank as any child's.

"I did not mean that, Alf; we are too young for such things yet, and I know nothing of love except in marble."

"Let me teach you then; we never are too young to learn that lesson," he urged eagerly. "I meant to wait another year before I spoke, for then I shall be my own master, and have a home to give you. But you grow so lovely and so dear, I must speak out and know my fate. Dear Cecil, what is it to be?"

"I cannot tell; this is so new and strange to me, I have no answer ready."

She looked troubled now, but more by his earnestness than by any maidenly doubts or fears of her own, and leaning her head upon her hand seemed to search for an answer, and search in vain. Alfred watched her a moment, then broke out indignantly, "No wonder it seems new and strange, for you have led a nun's life all these years, and know nothing of the world outside these walls. Yorke lets you read neither romance nor poetry, gives you no companions but marble men and women, no change but a twilight walk each day, or a new design to work out in this gloomy place. You never have been told you have a heart and a right to love like other women. Let me help you to know it, and find an answer for myself."

"Am I so different from other girls? Is my life strange and solitary? I've sometimes thought so, but I never felt quite sure. What *is* love, Alfred?"

"This!" And opening his arms her young lover would have answered her wistful question eloquently, but Cecil shrank a little, and put up her hand to check his impulse.

"Not so, tell me in words, Alf, how one feels when one truly loves."

"I only know how *I* feel, Cecil. I long for you day and night; think of you wherever I am; see no one half so beautiful, half so good as you; care for nothing but being here, and have no wish to live unless you will make life happy for me."

"And that is love?" She spoke low, to herself, for as he answered her face had slowly been averted, a soft trouble had dawned in her eyes, and a deeper color risen to her cheek, as if the quiet heart was waking suddenly.

"Yes; and you do love me, Cecil? Now I know it—now you will not deny it."

She looked up, pale but steady, for the child's expression was quite gone, and in her countenance was all a woman's pain and pity, as she said decidedly, "No, Alf, I do not love you. I know myself now, and feel that it is impossible."

But Alfred would not accept the hard word "impossible," and pleaded passionately, in spite of the quiet determination to end the matter, which made Cecil listen almost as coldly as if she did not hear. Anger succeeded surprise and hope, as the young man bitterly exclaimed, "You might make it possible, but you will not try!"

"No, I will not, and it is unkind of you to urge me. Let me be in peace—I'm happy with my work, and my nun's life was pleasant till you came to trouble it with foolish things."

She spoke impatiently, and the first glimpse of passion ever seen upon her face now disturbed its quietude, yet made it lovelier than ever.

"Well said, Cecil; my pupil does honor to her master."

Both started as the deep voice sounded behind them, and both turned to see Bazil Yorke leaning in the doorway with a satirical smile on his lips. Cecil made an involuntary motion to go to him, but checked herself as Alfred said hotly, "It is not well said! And but for the artful training you have given her, she would be glad to change this unnatural life, though she dare not say so, for you are a tyrant, in spite of your seeming kindness!"

"Do you fear me too much to tell the truth, Cecil?" asked Yorke, quite unmoved.

"No, master."

"Then decide between us two, now and forever, because I will not have your life or mine disturbed by such scenes as this. If you love Alfred, say so freely, and when my guardianship ends I will give you to his. If you prefer to stop with me, happy in the work you are wonderfully fitted to perform, content with the quiet life I deem best for you, and willing to be the friend and fellow laborer of the old master, then come to him and let us hear no more of lovers or of tyrants."

As he spoke Cecil had listened breathlessly, and when he paused, she went to him with such a glad and grateful face, such instant and entire willingness, that it touched him deeply, though he showed no sign of it except to draw her nearer, with a caressing gesture which he had not used since she ceased to be a child.

The words, the act, wounded the young lover to the heart, and he broke out, in a voice trembling with anger, sorrow, and reproach, "I might have known how it would be; I should have known if my own love had not blinded me. You have taught her something beside your art —have made too sure of her to fear any rival, and when the time comes you will change the guardian to a husband, and become her master in earnest."

"Not I! My day for such folly is long since past. Cecil will never be anything to me but my ward and pupil, unless some more successful lover than yourself should take her from me."

Yorke laughed scornfully at the young man's accusation, but looked down at the girl with an involuntary pressure of the arm that held her, for despite his careless manner, she was dearer to him than he knew.

"I will never leave you for any other—never, my dear master."

Alfred heard her soft whisper, saw her cling to Yorke, knew that there was no hope for him, and with a broken "Good-bye, Cecil, I shall not trouble you again," he was gone.

"Poor lad, he takes it hardly, but he'll soon forget. I should have warned him, had I not been sure it would have hastened what I desired to prevent. It is over at last, thank heaven, so look up, foolish child; there are no lovers here to frighten you now."

But Cecil did not look up, she hid her face and wept quietly, for Alfred had been her only young friend since the day he gave the rose and made the new home pleasant by his welcome.

Yorke let her tears flow unreproved for a few moments, then his patience seemed exhausted, and placing her in a seat, he turned away to examine the Cupid which Alfred had not accepted. As he looked at it he smiled, then frowned, as if some unwelcome fancy had been conjured up by it, and asked abruptly, "What suggested the idea of this, Cecil?"

"You did!" was the half-audible answer.

"I did? Never to my knowledge."

"Your making Psyche suggested Cupid, for though you did not tell me the pretty fable, Alf did, and told me how my image should be made. I could not do a large one, so I pleased myself with trying a little winged child with the bandage and the bow."

"Why would you not let me see it till it was done?"

"At first because I hoped to make it good enough to give you, then I thought it too full of faults to offer, so I gave it to Alf; but he would not have it without me, and now I don't care for it anymore."

Yorke smiled, as if well pleased at this proof of her indifference to the youth, then with a keen glance at the drooping face before him, he asked, "Are you quite sure that you do not care for Alfred?"

"Very sure, master."

"Then what has changed you so within a week or two? You sang yesterday like an uncaged bird, a thing you seldom do. You smile to yourself as you work, and when I wished to use your face as a model not an hour ago, you could not fix your eyes on me as I bade you, and cried when I chid you. What is it, Cecil? If you have anything upon your mind, tell me, and let nothing disturb us again if possible."

If the girl had been trained to repress all natural emotions and preserve an unvarying calmness of face, voice, and manner, she had also been taught to tell the truth, promptly and fearlessly. Now it was evident that she longed to escape the keen eye and searching questions of her master, as she loved to call him, but she dared not hesitate, and answered slowly, "I should have told you something before, only I did not like to, and I thought perhaps you knew it."

"Well, well, stop blushing and speak out; I know nothing but this boy's love and the change in you." Yorke spoke impatiently, and wore an anxious look, as if he dreaded more tender confessions, for Cecil never lifted her eyes as she rapidly went on:

"A week ago, as we came in from our evening walk, you stopped at the corner to call Judas, and I went on to open the door for you. Just as I put the key into the latch, a hand took mine, as if to slip something into it, but I was so startled I let the paper drop, and should have called to you if someone had not wrapped me in a cloak so closely that I could not speak, though I was kissed more than once and called 'my darling' in a very tender voice. It all happened in a minute, and before I knew what to do, the man was gone, and I ran in, too frightened to wait for you."

As she paused, Cecil looked up, and was amazed to see no wonder on Yorke's face, but an expression of pain and indignation that she could not understand. "Back again and I not know it," he muttered to himself, then aloud, almost sternly, "why did you not tell me this before?"

"You were busy that night, and when I'd thought of it a little I did not like to speak of it, because I remembered that you called me silly when I told you that people made me uncomfortable by looking at me as I walked in the day. I thought I'd wait, but it troubled me and made me seem unlike myself, I suppose."

"Are you sure it was not Alfred, playing some foolish prank in the twilight?" asked Yorke.

"I know it was not Alf; he wears no beard, and is not tall like this strange man."

"It could not have been Anthony?"

"Oh, no, that is impossible. Old Tony's hands are rough; these were soft though very strong, and the voice was too low and kind for his."

"Have you no suspicion who it might have been?" asked Yorke, searching her thoughtful face intently.

She blushed deeper than before, but answered steadily, "I did think of you, master, for you are tall and strong, you wear a beard and cloak, and your hand is soft. But your voice never is like that voice, and you never say 'my darling' in that tender way."

Yorke knit his brows, saying, a little bitterly, "You seem to have forgiven this insolent stranger already because of that, and to reproach me that I never use such sentimental phrases, or embrace my ward upon my doorstep. Shall I tell you who this interesting phantom probably was? The model, whom you disliked so much that I dismissed him when you came."

Cecil turned pale, for her childish terror had remained as fresh in her memory as the events that wakened it; and though she had merely caught glimpses of the man as he occasionally glided into Yorke's private room during the past five years, she still felt a curious mixture of interest and fear, and often longed to break her promise and ask questions concerning him and his peculiar ways.

"Why do you let him come?" she said, forgetting everything but surprise, as Yorke spoke as he had never done before.

"I wish I could prevent it!" he answered, eyeing her half sadly, half jealously. "I've bidden him to go, but he *will* come back to harass me. Now I'll end it at any cost."

"But why does he care for me?" asked Cecil, finding that her first question had received an answer.

"Because you are beautiful and—" There Yorke caught back the coming words, and after a pause said coldly, "Remember your promise— no more of this."

For several minutes he went to and fro, busied with anxious thoughts, while Cecil mused over the mystery, and grieved for Alfred's disappointment. Suddenly Yorke paused before her.

"Do you understand to what you pledge yourself when you say you will never leave me, Cecil?"

"I think I do" was the ready answer.

"Nothing is to be changed, you know."

"I hope not."

"No romances—no poetry to be allowed."

"I do not want them."

"No frivolities and follies like other women."

"I can be happy without."

"No more Cupids of any sort."

"Shall I break this one?"

"No, leave it as a warning, or send it to poor Alf."

"What else, master?" she asked wistfully.

"Only this: Can you be content year after year with study, solitude, steady progress, and in time fame for yourself, but never any knowledge of love as Alfred paints it?"

"*Never*, Yorke?"

"*Never*, Cecil!"

She shivered, as if the words fell cold upon her heart, all the glad light and color faded from her face, and she looked about her with longing eyes, as if the sunshine had gone out of her life forever. Yorke saw the change, and a momentary expression of pity softened the stern determination of his face.

"This never would have happened but for that romantic boy," he thought. "There shall be no more of it, and a little pain now shall spare us all misunderstanding hereafter."

"Cecil," he said aloud, "love makes half the misery of the world; it has been the bane of my life—it has made me what I am, a man without ambition, hope, or happiness—and out of my own bitter experience I warn you to beware of it. You know nothing of it yet, and if you are to stay with me you never will, unless this boy's folly has done more harm than I suspect. Carving Cupid has filled your head with fancies that will do you no good; banish them and be what I would have you."

"A marble woman like your Psyche, with no heart to love you, only grace and beauty to please your eye and bring you honor; is that what you would have me?"

He started, as if she had put some hidden purpose into words; his eye went from the gleaming statue to the pale girl, and saw that he had worked out his design in stone, but not yet in that finer material given him to mold well or ill. He did not see the pain and passion throbbing in her heart; he only saw her steady eyes; he only heard her low spoken question, and answered it, believing that he served her better than she knew.

"Yes, I would have you beautiful and passionless as Psyche, a creature to admire with no fear of disturbing its quiet heart, no fear of endangering one's own. I am kinder than I seem in saying this, for I desire to save you from the pain I have known. Stay with me always, if you can, but remember, Cecil, I am done with love."

"I shall remember, sir."

Yorke left her, glad to have the task over, for it had not been as easy as he fancied. Cecil listened and answered with her usual submission, stood motionless till the sound of a closing door assured her that he was gone, then a look of sharp anguish banished the composure of her face, and a woman's passionate pride trembled in her voice as she echoed his last words.

"I am done with love!" And lifting the little Cupid let it drop broken at her feet.

❧ *Chapter III* ❧

GERMAIN

FOR a week Cecil saw little of Yorke, as, contrary to his custom, he was out a greater part of each day, and when at home was so taciturn and absorbed that he was scarcely more than a shadow in the house. She asked no questions, appeared unconscious of any change, and worked busily upon a new design, thinking bitter thoughts the while. Alfred never came, and Cecil missed him; but Yorke was well satisfied, for the purpose formed so long ago had never changed; and though the young man's love endangered its fulfillment, that cloud had passed by, leaving the girl all his own again. She too seemed to cherish some purpose, that soon showed its influence over her; for her face daily grew more cold and colorless, her manner quieter, her smiles fewer, her words briefer, her life more nunlike than ever, till unexpected events changed the current of her thoughts, and gave her new mysteries to brood over.

One evening, as Cecil sat drawing, while Yorke paced restlessly up and down, he said suddenly, after watching her for several minutes, "Cecil, will you do me a great favor?"

"With pleasure, if I can and ought," she answered, without pausing in her work.

"I am sure you can, I think you ought, yet I cannot explain why I ask it, although it will annoy and perplex you. Will you have faith in me, and believe that what I do is done for the best?"

"I trust you, sir; you have taught me to bear in silence many things that perplex and annoy me, so I think I can promise to bear one more."

Something in her meek answer seemed to touch him like a reproach,

for his voice softened, as he said regretfully, "I know I am not all I might
be to you, but the day may come when you will see that I have spared
you greater troubles, and made my dull home a safer shelter than it
seems."

He took a turn or two, then stopped again, asking abruptly, "A
gentleman is to dine with me tomorrow; will you do the honors of the
house?"

It was impossible to conceal the surprise which this unusual request
produced, for during all the years they had been together, few strangers
had been admitted, and Cecil, being shy, had gladly absented herself
on these rare occasions. Now she laid down her pencil and looked up at
him, with mingled reluctance and astonishment in her face.

"How can I, when I know nothing of such things? Hester has
always suited you till now."

"I have neglected many womanly accomplishments which you
should have acquired, this among them; now you shall learn to be the
little mistress of the house, and leave Hester in her proper place. Will
you oblige me, Cecil?"

Yorke spoke as if discharging a painful duty which had been imposed upon him; Cecil was quick to see this; and any pleasure she might
have felt in the proposal was destroyed by his uneasy manner.

"As you please, sir" was all her answer.

"Thank you; now one thing more. Haven't you a plain gray gown?"
"Yes."

"Be kind enough to wear it tomorrow, instead of that white one,
which is more becoming, but too peculiar to appear in before strangers.
This, also, I want altered; let me show you how."

He untied the band that held her hair, and as it fell upon her
shoulders, he gathered the dark locks plainly back into a knot behind,
smoothing away the ripples on her forehead, and the curls that kept
breaking from his hold.

"Wear it so tomorrow. Look in the glass, and see how I mean," he
said, as he surveyed the change he had effected.

She looked, and smiled involuntarily, though a vainer girl would
have frowned, for the alteration added years to her age, apparently;
destroyed the beautiful outline of her face, and robbed her head of its
most graceful ornament.

"You wish me to look old and plain, I see. If you like it, I am
satisfied."

He looked annoyed at her quickness in divining his purpose, and
shook out the curls again, as he said hastily, "I do wish it, for my guest

worships beauty, and I have no desire for more love passages at present."

"No fear of that till poor Alf's forgotten."

She spoke proudly, and took up her pencil as if weary of the subject. Yorke stood for a moment, wondering if she found it hard to forget "poor Alf," but he said no more, and sat down as if a load were off his mind. Opening a book, he seemed to read, but Cecil heard no leaves turned, and a covert glance showed him regarding the page with absent eyes and a melancholy expression that troubled her. There had been a time when she would have gone to him with affectionate solicitude, but not now; and though her heart was full of sympathy, she dared not show it, so sat silent till the clock struck ten, then with a quiet "Good night" she was gone.

"We shall dine at six; I'll ring for you when Germain comes," said Yorke, as they came in from their walk the following day.

"I shall be ready, sir."

Cecil watched and waited for the stranger's arrival, in a flutter of expectation, which proved that in spite of Yorke's severe training, feminine curiosity was not yet dead. She heard Anthony admit the guest, heard Yorke receive him, and heard the old woman who came to help Hester on such occasions ejaculate from behind a door, "Bless me, what a handsome man!" But minute after minute passed, and no bell rang, no summons came for her. The clock was on the stroke of six, and she was thinking, sorrowfully, that he had forgotten her, when Yorke's voice was heard at the door, saying with unusual gentleness, "Come, Cecil; it is time."

"I thought you were to ring for me," she said, as they went down together.

"And I thought it more respectful to come and wait upon the little mistress, than to call her like a servant. How your heart beats! You need fear nothing. I shall be near you, child."

He took her by the hand with a protecting gesture that surprised her, but a moment later she understood both speech and action. A gentleman was standing at the far end of the room, and as they noiselessly approached, Cecil had time to mark the grace and strength of his tall figure, the ease of his attitude, the beauty of the hands loosely locked together behind him, before Yorke spoke.

"Germain, my ward, Miss Stein."

He turned quickly, and the eyes that Cecil was shyly averting, dilated with undisguised astonishment, for a single glance assured her that Germain was the mysterious model. Her hand closed over Yorke's, trembling visibly, as the stranger, in a singularly musical voice and with an unmistakably highbred air, paid his compliments to Miss Stein.

"Control yourself, and bear with this man for my sake, Cecil," whispered Yorke, as he led her to a seat, and placed himself so as to screen her for a moment.

She did control herself, for that had been her earliest lesson, and she had learned it well. She did bear with this man, for whom she felt such an aversion, and when he offered his arm to lead her in to dinner, she took it, though her eyes never met his, and she spoke not a word. It was long before she ventured to steal a look at him, and when she did so, it was long before she looked away again. The old woman was right, he *was* a handsome man; younger apparently than his host, and dressed with an elegance that Yorke had never attempted. Black hair and beard, carefully arranged, brilliant dark eyes, fine features, and that persuasive voice, all helped to make a most attractive person, for now the sinister expression was replaced by one of the serenest suavity, the stealthy gait and gestures exchanged for a graceful carriage, and some agreeable change seemed to have befallen both the man and his fortunes, as there was no longer any appearance of mystery or poverty about him. Cecil observed these things with a woman's quickness, and smiled to think she had ever feared the gay and gallant gentleman. Then she turned to examine Yorke, and saw that the accustomed gravity of his face was often disturbed by varying emotions; for sometimes it was sad, then stern, then tender, and more than once his eye met hers with a grateful look, as if he thanked her for granting him a greater favor than she knew.

Cecil performed her duties gracefully and well, but said little, and listened attentively to the conversation, which never strayed from general subjects. Though interested, she was not sorry when Yorke gave her the signal to withdraw, and went away into the drawing room. Here, leaning in an easy chair before the fire, she hoped to enjoy a quiet half hour at least, but was disappointed. Happening to lift her eyes to the mirror over the low chimneypiece, to study the effect of the plain bands of hair, she saw another face beside her own, and became aware that Mr. Germain was intently watching her in the glass, as he leaned upon the high back of her chair. Meeting her eyes, he came and stood upon the rug, which Judas yielded to him with a surly growl. Cecil arrested the dog, feeling a sense of security while he was by, for the childish dread was not yet quite gone, and despite his promise, Yorke did not appear. Germain seemed to understand the meaning of her hasty glance about the room, and answered it.

"Your guardian will follow presently, and sent me on to chat with you, meantime. Permit me."

As he spoke, Anthony entered, bringing coffee, but Germain brought Cecil's cup himself, and served her with an air of devotion that both confused and pleased her by its novelty. Drawing a chair to the other side of the tiny table between them, he sat down, and before she knew it, Cecil found herself talking to this dreaded person, shyly at first, then frankly and with pleasure.

"How was the great Rachel last night, Miss Stein?"

"I did not see her, sir."

"Ah, you prefer the opera, as I do, perhaps?"

"I never went."

"Then Yorke should take you, if you love music."

"I do next to my art, but I seldom hear any."

"Your art—then you are to be a sculptor?"

"I hope to be in time, but I have much to learn."

"You will go to Italy before long, I fancy? That's part of every artist's education."

"No, sir, I shall not go. Yorke has been, and can teach me all I need."

"You have no desire for it, then? Or do you wait till some younger guardian appears, who has not seen Italy, and can show it to you as it should be shown?"

"I shall never have any guardian but Yorke, we have already settled that—"

Here Cecil paused, for Germain looked at her keenly, smiled, and said significantly, "Pardon me, I had not learned that he intended to end his romance in the good old fashion, by making his fair ward his wife. I am an early friend, and have a right to take an interest in his future, so I offer my best wishes."

"You mistake me, sir; I should not have said that. Yorke is my guardian, nothing more, nor will he ever be. I have no father, and he tries to be one to me."

Cecil spoke with a bashful eagerness, burning cheeks, and downcast eyes, unconscious of the look of relief that passed over her companion's face as she explained.

"A thousand pardons; my mistake was natural, and may prove a prophecy. Now let me atone for it by asking how the Psyche prospers. Is it worthy of its maker and its model?"

"It is done, and very beautiful; everyone who sees it thinks it worthy of its maker, except me. I know he will do nobler things than that. He had no model but his own design; you have seen that, perhaps?"

"I see it now," he answered, bowing.

"Indeed, I am not; he never makes a model of me now, except for a moment. He has had none since you left."

A curious expression swept over Germain's face, and he exclaimed, with ill-disguised satisfaction, "You recognize me then? I was not sure that you had ever seen me, though I used to haunt the house like a restless spirit, as I am."

"Yes, I knew you at once, because I never could forget the fright you gave me years ago, peeping in, the night I came. Since then I've seen you several times, but never heard your name until yesterday."

"That is like Yorke. He hides his good deeds, and when I was most unfortunate, he befriended me, and more than once has kept me from what fate seems bent on making me, a solitary vagabond. The world goes better with me now, and one day I hope to take my proper place again; till then, I must wait to pay the debt I owe him."

This impulsive speech went straight to Cecil's heart, and banished the last trace of distrust. In the little pause that followed, she found time to wonder why Yorke did not come, and thinking of him, she asked if he would approve all she had been saying. A moment's recollection showed her that she had unconsciously given her companion many hints of the purpose, pursuits, and prospects of her life, during that seemingly careless conversation. She felt uncomfortable, and hoping Yorke had not heard her, sat silent until Germain spoke again.

"I see an instrument yonder. Let me lead you to it, for having owned that you love music, you cannot deny me the pleasure of listening to it."

Fearing to commit herself again, if she continued to talk, Cecil complied, but as they crossed the room together, she saw Yorke standing in the shadow of a curtained window. He made a warning sign, that caused her to hesitate an instant, trying to understand it; Germain's quick eye followed hers like a flash, and kindled with sudden fire; but before either could speak, Yorke advanced, saying gravely, "Will you venture, Cecil? Germain is a connoisseur in music."

"Then I dare not try; please let me refuse," she answered, drawing back, for now she comprehended that she was not to sing.

But Germain led her on, saying, with his most persuasive air, "You will not refuse me presently, when I have given you courage by doing my part first."

He sat down as he spoke, and began to sing; Cecil was stealing back to her seat, but paused in the act to listen; for a moment stood undecided, then turned, and slowly, step by step, drew nearer, like a fascinated bird, till she was again beside him, forgetful now of everything but the wonderful voice that filled the room with its mellow music. As it ceased, she gave a long sigh of pleasure, and exclaimed like a delighted child, "Oh! Sing again; it is so beautiful!"

Germain flashed a meaning glance over his shoulder at Yorke, who stood apart, gloomily watching them.

"Sit then, and let me do my best to earn a song from you." And placing a chair for her, he gave her music such as she had never dreamed of, as song after song poured from his lips, stirring her with varying emotions, as the airs were plaintive, passionate, or gay.

"Now may I claim my reward?" he said at length, and Cecil, without a thought of Yorke, gladly obeyed him.

Why she chose a little song her mother used to sing she could not tell; it came to her, and she sang it with all her heart, giving the tender words with unwonted spirit and sweetness. Sitting in his seat, Germain leaned his arm upon the instrument and watched her with absorbing interest. Unconsciously, she had pushed away the heavy bands that annoyed her, and now showed again the fair forehead with the delicate brow; her cheeks were rosy with excitement, her eyes shone, her lips smiled as she sang, and in spite of the gray gown with no ornament but a little knot of pansies, Cecil had never looked more beautiful than now. When she ended, she was surprised to see that this strange man's eyes were full of tears, and instead of compliments, he only pressed her hand, saying with lowered voice, "I cannot thank you as I would for this."

Yorke called the girl to him, and Germain slowly followed. At dinner he had led the conversation, now he left it to his host, saying little, but sitting with his eyes on Cecil, who, to her own surprise and Yorke's visible disquiet, did not feel abashed or offended by the pertinacious gaze. He lingered long, and went with evident reluctance, bidding Cecil good night in a tone so like the mysterious "my darling" that she retreated hastily, convinced that it must have been uttered by himself alone.

"How do you like this gentleman?" asked Yorke, returning from a somewhat protracted farewell in the hall.

"Very much. But why didn't you tell me who I was to see?"

"I had a fancy to test your powers of self-control, and I was satisfied."

"I will take care that you shall be, sir," she answered, with set lips and a flash of the eye.

"You seem to have quite outlived your old dislike, and quite forgotten his last offense," continued Yorke, as if ill pleased.

"I am no longer a silly child, and I have not forgotten his offense; but as you overlooked the insult, I could not refuse to meet your guest when you bade me to bear with him for your sake."

There was an air of dignity about her, and a touch of sarcasm in her tone, that was both new and becoming, yet it ruffled Yorke, though he disdained to show it.

"Of one thing I am satisfied. Seclude a woman as you may; when an opportunity comes, she will find her tongue. I did not know my silent girl tonight."

"You heard me, then? I am sorry, but I did not know what I was doing till it was done. You gave me a part to play, and I am no actress, as you see. Is the masquerade over now?"

"Yes, and it has not proved as successful as I hoped, yet I am glad it was no worse."

"So am I," and Cecil shook down her hair with an aspect of relief.

"Where are your pansies?" Yorke asked suddenly.

"They fell out as I was singing, they must have dropped just here," and she looked all about, but no pansies were visible.

"I thought so," muttered Yorke. "I shall repent this night's experiment, I fear, but God knows I did it for the best."

Cecil stood, thoughtfully coiling a dark lock around her finger for a moment, then she asked wistfully, "Will Mr. Germain come again? He said he hoped to do so, when he went."

"He will not, rest assured of that," answered Yorke grimly, adding, as if against his will, "he is a treacherous and dangerous man, in spite of his handsome face and charming manners. Beware of him, child, and shun him, if you would preserve your peace; mine is already lost."

"Then why do you—" There she checked herself, remembering that she was not to ask questions.

"Why do I bring him here? you would ask. That I shall never tell you, and it will never happen again, for the old spell is as strong as ever, I find."

He spoke bitterly, because in the girl's face he saw the first sign of distrust, and it wounded him deeply. It had been a hard evening for him, and he had hoped for a different result, but his failure was made manifest, as Cecil bowed her mute good-night, and went away more perplexed than ever.

❧ *Chapter IV* ❧

IN THE DARK

DAYS passed and Germain did not reappear, though Cecil strongly suspected that he had endeavored to do so more than once; for now the door was always locked. Anthony often mounted guard in the hall; Yorke seldom went out, and when they walked together chose a new route each day, while his face wore a vigilant expression as if he were perpetually on the watch. These changes kept the subject continually before the girl's mind, though not a word was spoken. More than once she caught glimpses of a familiar figure haunting the street, more than once she heard the mellow voice singing underneath her window, and more than once she longed to see this strange Germain again.

Standing at the window one somber afternoon, she thought of these things as she watched her guardian giving orders to Anthony, who was working in the garden. As Yorke turned to enter the house, she remembered that the studio was not lighted as he liked to find it, and hurried away to have it ready for his coming. Halfway up the first flight she stopped a moment, for a gust of fresh air blew up from below as if from some newly opened door or window. The hall was dusky with early twilight, and looking downward she saw nothing.

"Is that you, Yorke?" she asked, but no one answered, and she went on her way. At the top of the second flight she paused again, fancying that she heard steps behind her. The sound ceased as she stopped, and thinking to herself, "It's Judas," she ran up the spiral stairs leading to the tower. These were uncarpeted, and in a moment the sound of steps was distinctly audible behind her; neither the slow tread of Yorke, nor the quick patter of the dog, but soft and stealthy footfalls as of someone anxious to follow unsuspected. She paused, and the steps paused also; she went on and the quick sound began again; she peered downward through the gloom, but the stairs wound abruptly round and round, and nothing could be seen. She called to Yorke and the dog again, but there was no reply except the rustle of garments brushing against the wall, and the rapid breathing of a human creature. A nervous thrill passed over her; the thought of Germain flashed into her mind, and the early terror woke again, for time and place suggested the forbidding figure she had seen lurking there so long ago. Fearing to descend and meet him, she sprang on, hoping to reach the studio in time to call Yorke from the window and lock the door. As she darted upward, the quick tread of a man's foot was plainly heard, and when she flung the door behind her, a strong hand prevented it from closing, a tall figure entered, the key was turned, and Germain's well-remembered voice exclaimed:

"Do not cry out. I have risked my life by entering at a window, for I must speak to you, and Yorke guards you like a dragon."

"Why do you come if he forbids it, following and frightening me in the dark?" cried Cecil, grasping vainly for a lamp as Germain placed himself between her and the window.

"Because he keeps you from me, and he has no right to do it. I love you as he never can, yet though I plead day and night, and promise anything, he will not let me see you, even for an hour. Do not fear or shun me, but come to me, little Cecil, come to me, and let me feel that you are mine."

With voice and gesture of intensest love and longing, he advanced as if to claim her, but Cecil, terrified by this impetuous wooing, fled before him to an inner room, bolted the door, and rang the bell until it broke. Vainly Germain shook the door and implored her to hear him; she neither answered nor listened, but called for help till the room rang again.

Soon, very soon, Yorke's familiar step came leaping up the stairs, and his voice demanded, in tones of wonder and alarm, "Cecil, where are you? Speak to me, and open instantly."

"I cannot come—it is Germain—"

More she could not say, for with the arrival of help her strength deserted her, and she dropped down upon the floor, faint but not unconscious. Lying thus, she heard the outer door give way, heard a wrathful exclamation from Yorke, an exultant laugh from Germain, then hurried conversation too low for her to catch a word, till suddenly both voices rose, one defiant, the other determined.

"I tell you, Bazil, I *will* see her!"

"Not if I can prevent it."

"Then I swear I will use force!"

"I swear you shall not!"

A quick movement followed, and the terrified listener heard unmistakable sounds of a fierce but brief struggle in the darkened room, the stamp of feet, the hard breathing of men wrestling near at hand, the crash of a falling statue and a human body, a low groan, then sudden silence. In that silence Cecil lost her consciousness, for her quiet life had ill prepared her for such scenes. Only for a moment, however; the sound of retreating footsteps recalled her, and trying to control the frightened flutter of her heart, she listened breathlessly. What had happened? Where was Yorke? These questions roused her, and the longing to answer them gave her courage to venture from her refuge.

Softly drawing the bolt, she looked out. Nothing could be seen but the pale glimmer of stars through the western window; all near at hand was hidden by the deep shadow of a tall screen that divided the studio. A moment she stood trembling with apprehension lest Germain had not gone, then stole a few steps forward, whispering, "Yorke, are you here?"

There was no answer, but as the words left her lips she stumbled over something at her feet, something that stirred and faintly sighed. Losing fear in an all-absorbing anxiety, Cecil sprang boldly forward, groped for a match, lighted the lamp with trembling hands, and looked about her. The beautiful Psyche lay headless on the ground, but the girl scarcely saw it, for half underneath it lay Yorke, pale and senseless. How she dragged him out she never knew; superhuman strength seemed given her, and self-possession to think and do her best for him. Throwing up the window, she called to Anthony still busy in the garden, then bathed the white face, fanned the breathless lips, chafed the cold hands, and soon had the joy of seeing Yorke's eyes open with a conscious look.

"It is I. Where are you hurt? What shall I do for you, dear master?"

"Tell them the Psyche fell, nothing more," he answered, painfully, but with a clear mind and a commanding glance.

She understood and obeyed him when the old man arrived. With many exclamations of concern and much wonderment as to how the accident could have occurred, Anthony laid his master on the couch, gave him such restoratives as were at hand, and then went to fetch a surgeon and find Hester, who was gossiping in a neighbor's kitchen, according to her wont.

"Tell me what happened, my poor child," whispered Yorke when they were alone, and Cecil sat beside him with a face almost as pallid as his own.

"Not now, you are not fit. Wait awhile," she began.

But he interrupted her, saying with a look she dared not disobey, "No, tell me now—I must know it!"

She told him, but he seemed too weak for indignation, and looked up at her with a faint glimmer of his old sarcastic smile.

"Another lover, Cecil, and a strange one; but you need not fear him, for though as rash and headstrong as a boy, he will not harm you." Then Yorke's face changed and darkened as he said, earnestly, "Promise me that you will never listen to him, never meet him, or countenance his mad pursuit of you. No good can come of it to you, and only the bitterest disappointment to me. Promise me this, I implore you, Cecil."

She hesitated, but his face grew haggard with suspense, and something in her own heart pleaded for him more persuasively than his anxious eyes or urgent words.

"I promise this. Now rest and let me fan you, for your lips are white with pain."

He did not speak again till steps and voices were heard approaching; then he drew her down to him, whispering, "Not a word of Germain to anyone; keep near me till I am up again, then I will take measures to prevent the recurrence of a scene like this."

For several days Yorke saw no one but the doctor and his servants, for the fall and the heavy weight upon his chest had seriously injured him. He rebelled against the order to be still, finding a single week's confinement very irksome with no society but Hester, no occupation but a book or his own thoughts. Cecil did not come to nurse him as she used to do when slighter indispositions kept him in his rooms. She sent no little gifts to tempt his appetite or enliven his solitude; she made daily inquiries for his health, but nothing more. He missed his familiar spirit and her gentle ministrations, but would not send for her, thinking, with a mixture of satisfaction and regret, "She takes me at my word, and perhaps it's better so, for absence will soon cure any girlish pique my frankness may have caused her."

But though he would not call her, he left his room sooner than was wise, and went to find her in the studio. Everything was in its accustomed order, Cecil at her place, and his first exclamation one of pleasant surprise.

"Why, here's my Psyche mended and mounted again! Many thanks, my little girl."

She went to take the hand he offered, saying very quietly, "I am glad to see you, master, and to find you like what I have done."

"I never thought my Psyche would cause me so much suffering, but I forgive her for her beauty's sake," answered Yorke, laughing, for an unusual cheerfulness possessed him, and it was pleasant to be back in his old haunt again. "Well, what do you see in it?" he asked, observing that the girl stood with her eyes fixed on the statue.

"I see my model."

He remembered his own words, and was glad to change the conversation by a question or two.

"How have you got on through these days that have been so wearisome to me? Have you missed the old master?"

"I have been busily at work, and I have missed you, for I often want help, and Tony cannot always walk with me."

Yorke felt slightly disappointed both at the answer and her welcome, but showed no sign of it as he said, "Nothing has been seen of Germain since his last freak, I fancy?"

"He has been here."

"The deuce he has!" ejaculated Yorke, looking amazed. "Did you see him, Cecil?"

"Yes; I could not help it. I was watching for the doctor one day, and hearing a ring, I opened the door, for Tony and Hester were with you. Germain stepped quickly in and asked, 'Is Yorke alive?' I said yes. 'I thank God for that!' he cried. 'Tell him to get well in peace; I'll not disturb him if I can keep away—' Then Anthony appeared and he was gone as quickly as he came."

"That was like him, reckless and generous, fierce and gentle by turns. Pity that so fine a nature should be so early wrecked."

Yorke mused a moment, and Cecil, as if anxiety or pity made her forget her promise, asked suddenly, "Shall you let him go unmolested after such an outrage as this?"

"Yes, even if he had half murdered me or maimed me for life, I would not lift a finger against him. God knows I have my faults, and plenty of them, but I can forgive blows like his easier than some that gentler hands have dealt me."

Cecil made no answer, but seemed lost in wonderment, till Yorke, observing how pale and heavy-eyed she looked, said kindly, "Have you, too, been ill? I asked for you every day, and Hester always gave a good report. Is anything amiss? Tell me, child."

"I am not ill, and nothing is amiss except that I do not sleep, owing to want of exercise, perhaps."

"This must be mended; I'll give you sleep tonight, and tomorrow we will have a long drive together."

Going to an ancient cabinet, he took from it a quaint flask, poured a few drops of some dark liquid into a tiny glass, and mingling it with water, brought it to her.

"It is bitter, but it will bring you deep and dreamless sleep. Drink, little wakeful spirit, drink and rest."

Without offering to take the glass, she bent and drank, not the first bitter draft his hand had given her.

"I think you would drink hemlock without a question if I gave it to you," he said, smiling at her mute obedience.

"I think I should. But I asked no questions now because I knew that this was laudanum. Mamma used it when in pain, and I have often tasted it, playing that I made it sweet for her."

Yorke turned hastily away as if to replace the flask and cup, and when he spoke again he was his gravest self. "Go now, and sleep, Cecil. Tomorrow the old quiet life shall begin again."

It did begin again, and week after week, month after month passed in the same monotonous seclusion. They went nowhere, saw scarcely anyone; Yorke's genius was almost unknown, Cecil's beauty blooming unseen; and so the year rolled slowly by.

≫ *Chapter V* ≪

GOSSIP

PUTTING his head into the studio where Cecil was at work as usual, and Yorke lounged on the sofa in a most unwonted fit of indolence, "Mrs. Norton's compliments, and can she see the master for a few minutes?" said Anthony.

"Alfred's mother! What next? I'll come, Tony," answered the master, turning to observe the effect of this announcement upon the girl.

But she scarcely seemed to have heard the question or answer, and went on smoothing the rounded limbs of a slender Faun, with an aspect of entire absorption.

"What an artist I have made of her, if a lump of clay is more interesting than the news of her first lover," thought her guardian, as he left the room with a satisfied smile.

Since Alfred's disappointment, there had been a breach between the neighbors, and his mother discontinued the friendly calls she had been wont to make since Cecil came. She was a gray-haired, gracious lady, with much of her son's frankness and warmth of manner. After a few moments spent in general inquiries, she said, with some embarrassment but with her usual directness, "Mr. Yorke, I have felt it my duty to come and tell you certain things, of which I think you should be informed without delay. You lead such a secluded life that you are not likely to hear any of the injurious rumors that are rife concerning Cecil and yourself. They are but natural, for any appearance of mystery or peculiarity always excites curiosity and gossip, and as a woman and a neighbor, I venture to warn you of them, because I take a deep interest in the girl, both for her own sake and my son's."

"I thank you, Mrs. Norton, and I beg you will speak freely. I am entirely ignorant of these rumors, though I know that tattling tongues find food for scandal in the simplest affairs."

The guest saw that the subject was distasteful to her host, but steadily continued, "While she was a child, the relationship of guardian and ward was all sufficient; but now that she is a woman, and so beautiful a woman, it strikes outside observers that you are too young a man to be her sole companion. It is known that you live here together with no society, few friends, and those chiefly gentlemen; that you have neither governess nor housekeeper, only an old female servant. Cecil goes nowhere, and never walks without yourself or Anthony; while her beauty attracts so much attention that interest and curiosity are unavoidably aroused and increased by the peculiarity of her life. It would be a trying task to repeat the reports and remarks that have come to me; you can imagine them, and feel how much pain they cause me, although I know them to be utterly groundless and unjust."

Intense annoyance was visible in Yorke's face, as he listened and answered haughtily, "Those who know me will need no denial of these absurd rumors. I care nothing for the idle gossip of strangers, nor does Cecil, being too innocent to dream that such things exist."

"But you know it, sir, and you know that a man may defy public opinion, and pass scatheless, a woman must submit and walk warily, if she would keep her name unsullied by the breath of slander. A time may come when she will learn this, and reproach you with unfaithfulness to your charge, if you neglect to surround her with the safeguards which she is, as yet, too innocent to know that she needs."

Mrs. Norton spoke earnestly, and her maternal solicitude for the motherless girl touched Yorke's heart, for he *had* one, though he had done his best to starve and freeze it. His manner softened, his eye grew anxious, and he asked, with the air of one convinced in spite of himself, "What would you have me do? I sincerely desire to be faithful to my duty, but I begin to fear that I have undertaken more than I can perform."

"May I suggest that the presence of a respectable gentlewoman in your house would most effectually silence busy tongues, and might be a great advantage to Miss Stein, who must suffer for the want of female society?"

"I have tried that plan and it failed too entirely to make me willing to repeat the experiment."

A slight flush on Yorke's dark cheek and a disdainful curl of the lips told the keen-eyed lady as plainly as words that the cause of the dismissal of a former governess had been too much devotion to the guardian, too little to the ward. Mrs. Norton was silent a moment, and then said, with some hesitation, "May I ask you a very frank question, Mr. Yorke?"

"Your interest in Cecil gives you a right to ask anything, madam," he replied, bowing with the grace of manner which he could assume at will.

"Then let me inquire if you intend to make this girl your wife, at some future time?"

"Nothing can be further from my intentions" was the brief but decided reply.

"Pardon me; Alfred received an impression that you were educating her for that purpose, and I hoped it might be so. I can suggest nothing else, unless some other gentleman is permitted to give the protection of his name and home. My poor boy still loves her, in spite of absence, time, and efforts to forget; he is still eager to win her, and I would gladly be a mother to the sweet girl. Is there no hope for him?"

"None, I assure you. She loves nothing but her art, as I just had an excellent proof; for when you were announced, and your son's name mentioned, she seemed to hear nothing, remember nothing, but worked on, undisturbed."

Mrs. Norton rose, disappointed and disheartened by the failure of her mission.

"I have ventured too far, perhaps, but it seemed a duty, and I have performed it as best I could. I shall not intrude again, but I earnestly entreat you to think of this, for the girl's sake, and take immediate steps to contradict these injurious rumors. Call upon me freely, if I can aid you in any way, and assure Cecil that I am still her friend, although I may have seemed estranged since Alfred's rejection."

Yorke thanked her warmly, promised to give the matter his serious consideration, and bade her adieu, with a grateful respect that won her heart, in spite of sundry prejudices against him.

As the door closed behind her, he struck his hands impatiently together, saying to himself, "I might have known it would be so! Why did I keep the child until I cannot do without her, forgetting that she would become a woman, and bring trouble as inevitably as before? I'll not have another companion to beset me with the romantic folly I've forsworn; neither will I marry Cecil to silence these malicious gossips; I'll take her away from here, and in some quiet place we will find the old peace, if possible."

In pursuance of this purpose, he announced that he was going away upon business that might detain him several days, and after many directions, warnings, and misgivings, he went. He was gone a week, for the quiet place was not easily found, and while he looked, he saw and heard enough to convince him that Mrs. Norton was right. He took pains to gather, from various sources, the reports to which she had alluded, and was soon in a fever of indignation and disgust. Her words haunted him; he soon saw clearly the wrong he had been doing Cecil, felt that his present plan would but increase it, and was assured that one of two things must be done without delay, either provide her with a chaperon or marry her himself, for he rebelled against the idea of giving her to any other. The chaperon was the wisest but most disagreeable expedient, for well he knew that a third person, however discreet and excellent, would destroy the seclusion and freedom which he loved so well, and had enjoyed so long. It was in every respect repugnant to him, and he believed it would be to Cecil also. The other plan to his own surprise did not seem so impossible or distasteful, and the more he thought of it, the more attractive it became. Nothing need be changed except her name, slander would be silenced, and her society secured to him for life. But would she consent to such a marriage? He recalled with pleasure the expression of her face when she went to him, saying, "I will never leave you, my dear master, never"; and half regretted that he had checked the growth of the softer sentiment, which seemed about to take the place of her childish affection. He did not love her as a husband should, but he felt how sweet it was to be beloved, knew that she was happy with him, and longed to keep his little ward, at any cost, to himself.

Still undecided, but full of new and not unpleasurable fancies, he hurried home, feeling a strong curiosity to know how Cecil would regard this proposition should he make it. No one ran to meet him, as he entered, no one called out a glad welcome, and the young face that used to brighten when he came was nowhere visible.

"Where is Miss Cecil?" he asked of Hester.

"In the garden, master," she answered, with a significant nod, that sent him to the nearest window that opened on the garden.

Cecil was walking here with Alfred, and Yorke's face darkened ominously, as a jealous fear assailed him that she was about to solve the question for herself. He eyed her keenly, but her face was half averted, and he could see that she listened intently to her companion, who talked rapidly, and with an expression that made his handsome face more eloquent than his ardent voice.

"Cecil!" called Yorke sharply, unwilling to prolong a scene that angered him, more than he would confess even to himself.

Alfred looked up, bowed with a haughty, half-defiant air, said a few words to Cecil, and leaped the wall again. But she, after one glance upward, went in so slowly that her guardian chafed at the delay, and when at length she came to him with a cold handclasp, and a tranquil "Home so soon?" he answered, almost harshly, "Too soon, perhaps. Why do I find that boy here? I thought he was away again."

"He is going soon, and came because he could not keep away, he said. Poor Alf, I wish he did not care for me so much."

While she was speaking, Yorke examined her with a troubled look, for that brief absence made him quick to see the changes a year had wrought, unobserved till now. Something was gone that once made her beauty a delight to heart as well as eye; some nameless but potent charm that gave warmth, grace, and tenderness to her dawning womanhood. He felt it, and for the first time found a flaw in what he had thought faultless until now. There was no time to analyze the feeling, for drawing away the hand he had detained, she brought him from her desk three letters, directed to herself, in a man's bold writing.

"Germain!" exclaimed Yorke, as his eye fell on them. "Has he dared to write, when he swore he would not? Have you read them?"

She turned them in his hand, and showed the seals unbroken. A flash of pleasure banished the disquiet from his face, and there was no harshness in his voice as he asked, "How did they come? I forbade Tony to receive any communication he might venture to make."

"Tony knows nothing of them. One came in a bouquet, which was tossed over the wall the very day you went; one was brought by a carrier dove soon afterward; the bird came pecking at my window, and thinking it was hurt, I took it in; the third was thrust into my hand by someone whom I did not see, as I was walking with Hester yesterday. I suspected who they were from, and did not open them, because I promised not to listen to this man."

"Rare obedience in a woman! Have you no wish to see them? Will you give me leave to look at them before I burn them?"

"Do what you like, I care nothing for them now."

She spoke so confidingly, and smiled so contentedly, as she stood folding up his gloves, that Yorke felt his purpose strengthening every instant. The letters confirmed it, for as he flung the last into the fire, he said to himself, "There is no way but this; there will be peace for neither of us while Alfred and Germain have hopes of her. Once mine, and I shall have a legal right to defy and banish both."

Turning with decision, he drew her down to a seat beside him, saying, in a tone he had not used since the Cupid was broken, "Sit here and listen, for I've many things to tell you, my little girl. You are eighteen tomorrow, and according to your mother's desire may choose what guardian you will. I leave you free, having no right to influence you, but while I have a home it always will be yours, if you are happy here."

She turned her face away, and for an instant some inward agitation marred its habitual repose, but she answered steadily, though there was an undertone of pain in her voice, "I know it, Yorke, and you are very kind. I am happy here, but I cannot stay, because hard things are said of us, things that wrong you and wound me, more than tongue can tell."

"Who told you this?" he demanded, angrily.

"Alfred; he said I ought to know it, and if you would not follow his mother's advice, I should choose another guardian."

"And will you, Cecil?"

"Yes, for your sake as well as my own."

The tone of resolution made her soft voice jar upon his ear, and convinced him that she would keep her word.

"Whom will you choose?" he gravely asked.

"It is hard to tell; I have made no friends in all these years, and now I have nowhere to go, unless I turn to Mrs. Norton. She will be a mother to me, Alfred a very gentle guardian, and in time I may learn to love him."

Yorke felt both reproached and satisfied; reproached, because it was his fault that the girl had made no friends, and satisfied because there was as much regret as resolution in her voice, and his task grew easier as he thought of Alfred, whom she should never learn to love.

"But you promised to stay with me, and I want you, Cecil."

"I did promise, but then I knew nothing of all this. I want to stay, but now I cannot, unless you do something to make it safe and best."

"Something shall be done. Will you have another governess or an elderly companion?" he asked, wishing to assure himself of her real feeling before he spoke more plainly.

She sighed, and looked all the repugnance that she felt, but answered sorrowfully, "I dread it more than you do, but there is no other way."

"One other way. Shall I name it?"

"Oh, yes, anything is better than another Miss Ulster."

"If my ward becomes my wife, gossip will be silenced, and we may still keep together all our lives."

He spoke very quietly, lest he should startle her, but his voice was eager, and his glance wistful in spite of himself. The eager eyes that had been lifted to his own fell slowly, a faint color came up to her cheek, and she answered with a slight shake of the head, as if more perplexed than startled, "How can I, when we don't care for one another?"

"But we do care for one another. I love you as if you were a child of my own, and I think if nothing had disturbed us that you would have chosen me to be your guardian for another year, at least, would you not?"

"Yes, you are my one friend, and this is home."

"Then stay, Cecil, and keep both. Nothing need be changed between us; to the world we can be husband and wife, here guardian and ward, as we have been for six pleasant years. No one can reproach or misjudge us then; I shall have the right to protect my little pupil, she to cling to her teacher and her friend. We are both solitary in the world. Why can we not go on together in the old way, with the work we love and live for?"

"It sounds very pleasant, but I am so ignorant I cannot tell if it is best. Perhaps you will regret it if I stay, perhaps I shall become a burden when it is too late to put me away, and you may tire of the old life, with no one but a girl to share it with you."

Her face was downcast, and he did not see her eyes fill, her lips tremble, or the folded hands, pressed tight together, as she listened to the proposition which gave her a husband's name, but not a husband's heart. He saw that she thought only of him, forgetful of herself—knew that he offered very little in exchange for the liberty of this young life, and began to think that he had been mistaken in supposing that she loved him, because she showed so little emotion now; but in spite of all this, the purpose formed so long ago was still indomitable, and though forced by circumstances to modify it, he would not relinquish his design. The relentless look replaced all others, as he rose to leave her, though he said, "Do not answer yet, think well of this, be assured that I desire it, shall be happy in it, and see no other course open, unless you choose to leave me. Decide for yourself, my child, and when we meet tomorrow morning, tell me which guardian you have chosen."

"I will."

Cecil was usually earliest down, but when the morrow came, Yorke waited for her with an impatience that he could not control, and when she entered, he went to meet her, with an inquiring eye, an extended hand. She put her own into it without a word, and he grasped the little hand with a thrill of joy that surprised him as much as did the sudden impulse which caused him to stoop and kiss the beautiful, uplifted face that made the sunshine of his life.

Ashamed of this betrayal of his satisfaction, he controlled himself, and said, with as much of his usual composure as he could assume, "Thank you, Cecil; now all is decided, and you never shall regret this step, if I can help it. We will be married privately, and at once, then let the gossips tattle as they please."

"Are you quite satisfied with me for choosing as I have done?" she asked, as he led her to her place.

"Quite satisfied, quite proud and happy that my ward is to be mine forever. Is she content?"

"Yes, I chose what was pleasantest, and will do my best to be all you would have me, to thank you for giving me so much."

No more was said, and very soon all trace of any unusual emotion had vanished from Cecil's face; not so with Yorke. A secret unrest possessed him, and did not pass away. He thought it was doubt, anxiety, remorse, perhaps, for what he was about to do, but try as he would, the inward excitement kept him from his usual pursuits, and made him long to have all over without delay. Feeling that he owed Mrs. Norton some explanation of his seeming caprice, he went to her, frankly stated his reasons for the change, and took counsel with her upon many matters. With the readiness of a generous nature, she put aside her own disappointment, and freely did her best for her peculiar neighbor, glad that she had served the girl so well.

She soon convinced him that it would be better not to have a private wedding, but openly to marry and give the young wife a gay welcome home, that nothing mysterious or hasty should give fresh food for remark. He yielded, for Cecil's sake, and the good lady, with a true woman's love of such affairs, soon had everything her own way, much to Yorke's annoyance, and Cecil's bewilderment. Alfred was gone, and his mother wisely left him in ignorance of the approaching marriage, and stifled many a sigh, as she gave her orders and prepared the little bride.

Great was the stir and intense the surprise among the sculptor's few friends when it was known what was afloat, and Yorke was driven half wild with questions, congratulations, and praises of his betrothed. So much interest and goodwill pleased even while it fretted him; and bent on righting both himself and Cecil, in a manner that should preclude all further misconception, he asked friends and neighbors from far and near to his wedding, thinking, with a half-sad, half-scornful smile, "Let them come, they will see that she is lovely, will think that I am happy, and never guess what a mockery it is to me."

They did come, did think the bride beautiful, the bridegroom happy; and would have had no suspicion of the mockery, but for one little incident that had undue effect upon the eager-eyed observers. Among the guests was one whom none of the others knew; a singularly handsome man, who glided in unannounced, just before the ceremony, and placed himself in the shadow of the draperies that hung before a deep window in the drawing room. Two or three of the neighbors whispered together, and nodded their heads significantly, as if they had suspicions; but the entrance of the bridal pair hushed the whispers, and suspended the nods for a time at least. As they took their places, Cecil was seen to start and change color when her eye fell on the stranger, leaning in the purple gloom of the recess; Yorke did the same, then he frowned; she drew her veil about her, and stern bridegroom and pale bride appeared to compose themselves for the task before them.

The instant the ceremony was over, one gossip whispered to another, "I told you so, it is the same person who used to sing under her window, and watch the house for hours. A lover, without doubt, and why she preferred this gloomy Mr. Yorke to that devoted creature passes my comprehension."

"It's my opinion that she didn't prefer him, but was persuaded into it. He's far too old and grave for such a young thing, and I suspect she agrees with me. Did you see her turn as pale as her dress when she saw that fine-looking man in the recess? Poor thing, it's plain to see that she is marrying from gratitude, or fear, or something of that sort."

This romantic fancy soon took wing, and flew from ear to ear, although the stranger vanished as suddenly as he came. Yorke caught a hint of it, but only smiled disdainfully, and watched Cecil with a keen sense of satisfaction, in the knowledge that she was all his own. Not only was his eye gratified by her beauty that day, but his pride also, for the admiration she excited would have satisfied the most enamored bridegroom. She seemed to have grown a woman suddenly, for gentle dignity replaced her former shyness, and she bore herself like a queen; pale as the flowers in her bosom, calm as the marble Psyche that adorned an alcove, and so like it that more than one enthusiastic gentleman begged Yorke to part with the statue, now that he possessed the beautiful model. All this flattered his pride as man and artist, enhanced his pleasure in the events of the day, roused his ambition that had slept so long, and banished his last doubt regarding the step he had so hastily taken.

When all was over, and the house quiet again, he roamed through the empty rooms, still odorous and bright with bridal decorations, looking for his wife, and smiling, as he spoke the word low to himself, for the pleasant excitement of the day was not yet gone. But nowhere did he see the slender white figure in the misty veil; her little glove lay where she dropped it when the ring was put on, her bouquet of roses and orange flowers was fading in the seat she left, and an array of glittering gifts still stood unexamined by their new mistress. Thinking she was worn out and had gone to rest, he went slowly toward the studio, wondering if he should not feel more like his old self in that familiar place. Passing Cecil's room, he saw that the door was open, and no one within but the newly hired maid, who was busy folding up the silvery gown.

"Where is Miss Cecil?" he asked.

"Mrs. Yorke is in the tower, sir," answered the woman, with a simper at his mistake.

He bit his lip, and went on; but as he climbed the winding stairs, he passed his hand across his eyes, remembering a happy time, nineteen years ago, when that name had almost been another and a dearer woman's. Dressed in the plain gray gown, and with no change about her but the ring on the hand that caressed the dog's shaggy head, Cecil sat reading as if nothing had disturbed the usual quiet routine of her day. If she had looked up with a word of welcome or a smile of pleasure, it would have pleased him well, for his heart was very tender just then, and she was very like her mother. But she seemed unconscious of his presence till he stood before her, regarding her with the expression that was so attractive and so rare.

"Are you worn out with the bustle of the day, and so come here to rest and find yourself, as I do?" he asked, stroking the soft waves of her hair.

"Yes, I am tired, but I was never more myself than I have been today," she answered, turning a leaf, as if waiting to read on.

"What did it all seem like, Cecil?"

"A pretty play, but I was glad to have it over."

"It was a pretty play, though Germain might have spoiled it if I had not warned him away. But it is not quite over, as I was reminded on my way up. We must remember that before others I am your husband, and you my little wife, else I shall call you 'Miss Cecil' again, and you say 'master,' as you did half an hour ago."

"What would you have me do? I know I shall forget, for there is nothing to remind me but this," and she turned the ring to and fro upon her finger, adding, as he thought, regretfully, "It begins to make a difference already, and you said nothing would be changed."

"Nothing shall be changed, except that," he answered, chilled by her coldness, and turning sharply round, he seized chisel and mallet, and fell to work, regardless of bridal broadcloth and fine linen.

≫ Chapter VI ≪

CECIL'S SECRET

IT was easy to say that nothing should be changed, but they soon found it very hard to prevent decided alterations in the lives of both. Yorke's friends, rejoicing in the new tie that seemed about to give him back to the world he had shunned so long, did everything in their power to help on the restoration by all manner of festivities after the wedding. Having yielded once or twice by Mrs. Norton's advice, Yorke found it both difficult and irksome to seclude himself again, for it seemed as if a taste of the social pleasures neglected for so many years had effectually roused him from his gloom and given him back his youth again. But the chief cause of the change was Cecil. Wherever she went she won such admiration that his pride was fostered by the praise it fed on, and regarding her as his best work, he could not deny himself the satisfaction of beholding the homage paid his beautiful young wife. She submitted with her usual docility, yet expressed so little interest in anything but her art that he soon grew jealous of it, and often urged her to go pleasuring lest she should grow old and gray before her time, as he had done.

"Look your loveliest tonight, Cecil, for there will be many strangers at Coventry's, and I have promised him that my handsome wife would come," he said, as he came into the drawing room one tempestuous afternoon and found her looking out into the deserted street where the rain fell in torrents and the wind blew gustily.

"It is so stormy, need we go?"

"We must. The wind will fall at dark, and one does not mind rain in a closed carriage. You wonder at me, I dare say, and so do I at myself;

but I think I'm waking up and growing young again. Now I shall be old Yorke and read studiously for an hour."

He laughed as he spoke and laid himself on the couch, book in hand. But he read little, for Cecil's unusual restlessness distracted his attention, and he had fallen into a way of observing her lately while she worked or studied and he sat idle. She too opened a book, but soon put it down; she made a sketch, but seemed ill pleased with it, and threw it in the fire; she worked half a flower at her embroidery frame, turned over two or three portfolios with a listless air, then began to wander up and down the room so noiselessly that it would not have disturbed him had he been as absorbed as he seemed. Watching her covertly, he saw her steps grow rapid, her eyes wistful, her whole face and figure betray impatience and an intense desire for something beyond her reach. Several times she seemed about to follow an almost uncontrollable impulse, but checked herself on the way to the door and resumed her restless march, pausing with each turn to look out into the storm.

"What is it, Cecil? You want something. Can I get it for you?" he said at last, unable to restrain the question.

"I do want something, but you cannot get it for me," she answered, pausing with an expression of mingled doubt and desire infinitely more becoming than her usual immobility.

"Come here and tell me what it is; you so seldom ask anything of me I am curious to know what this may be."

Drawing her down upon the couch where he still lay, he waited for her request with an amused smile, expecting some girlish demand. But she delayed so long that he turned her face to his, saying, as he studied its new aspect, "Is it to stay at home tonight, little girl?"

"No, it is to go out now, and alone."

"Alone, and in this raging storm? You are crazy, child."

"I like the storm; I'm tired of the house. Please let me go for just half an hour."

"Why do you wish to be alone, and where are you so eager to go?"

"I cannot tell you. Be kind and don't ask me, Yorke."

"A secret from me! That's something new. When shall I know it?"

"Never, if I can help it."

He lay looking at her with a curious feeling of wonder and admiration, for this sudden earnestness made her very charming, and he found it extremely pleasant to while away an idle hour discovering the cause of this new waywardness in Cecil.

"I think you will tell me like an obedient little wife, and ask me prettily to go with or for you."

"I cannot tell you, and you must not come with me. Dear Yorke, let me go, please let me go!"

She folded her hands, dropped on her knees before him, and pleaded so earnestly with voice, and eyes, and outstretched hands, that he sat up amazed.

"What does it mean, Cecil? You have no right to keep a secret from me, and I cannot let you go out in such a storm on such a mysterious errand as this. A month ago you promised to obey me. Will you rebel so soon, and risk your health if nothing else by this strange freak?"

There was a sudden kindling of the eye as she rose and turned away with a resolute, white face, saying, in a tone that startled him, "I have the same right to my secret as you have to yours, and I shall keep it as carefully. A month ago I did promise to love, honor, and obey; but the promises meant nothing, and your will is not my law, because though my husband before the world, you are only my guardian here. I harm no one but myself in doing this, and I *must* go."

"Will you go if I forbid it?" he asked, rising in real perplexity and astonishment.

"Yes," she answered, steadily.

"How if I follow you?"

"I shall do something desperate, I'm afraid."

She looked as if she might, and he dared not insist. Entreaties and commands had failed; perhaps submission might succeed, and he tried it.

"Go, then; I shall not follow. I trust you in this, as you have trusted me more than once, and hope you will be as worthy of confidence as I try to be."

He thought he had conquered, for as he spoke, gravely yet kindly, she covered up her face as if subdued, and expecting a few tears, an explanation, and penitence, he stood waiting and recalling scenes of childish waywardness which had always ended so. No, not so; for to his unspeakable surprise Cecil left the room without a word. Five minutes later the hall door closed, and he saw her fighting her way against wind and rain with the same intense longing, the same fixed resolution in her face.

For an hour he watched and waited, racking his brain to discover some clue to this mysterious outbreak. Several trifling events now returned to his memory and deepened his perplexity. Just before they were married he brought her home a pretty bonbonnière to hold the comfits for which she still had a childish fancy. Having filled it for her, he was about to drop it into one of the ornamented pockets of the little apron she wore, but as he touched it a paper rustled, and as if the sound recalled some forgotten secret, she had clutched the pocket in a sudden panic and begged him to stop. He had accused her of having love letters from Alfred hidden there, and she had indignantly denied it, but hurried away as if to put her secret under lock and key. Later she had ventured out alone once or twice, always asking pardon when reproved for these short flights, but repeating them till strictly forbidden. Since then she had grown more taciturn than ever, and often went away to her own room to read or rest, she said. How she did spend the long hours passed there, Yorke was too proud to ask either mistress or maid, though he had felt much curiosity to know. The present mystery recalled these lesser ones, but gave no help in explaining anything, and he could only roam about the room and watch the storm more restlessly than Cecil.

Another hour passed and he began to feel anxious, for twilight gathered fast and still she did not come. A third hour rolled slowly by; the streetlamps glimmered through the mist, but among the passing figures no familiar one appeared, and he was fast reaching that state of excitement which makes passive waiting impossible when, as he stood peering out into the wild, wet night, a slight rustle was heard behind him, and a soft voice broke the long silence.

"I am ready, Yorke."

Turning with a start, he saw that all his fears had been in vain, for no storm-beaten figure stood before him, but Cecil shining in festival array.

"Thank heaven you are safe! I've been watching for you, but I did not see you come," he said, eyeing her with renewed wonder.

"No, I took care that you should not, and have been busy for an hour making myself pretty, as you bade me. Are you satisfied?"

He would have been hard to please if he was not satisfied with the fair apparition standing in the light of the newly kindled chandelier. A rosy cloud seemed to envelop her, bridal pearls gathered up the dark hair, shone on graceful neck and arms, and glimmered here and there among the soft-hued drapery. A plumy fan stirred in her hand, and a white down-trimmed cloak half covered shoulders almost as fair, for Yorke adorned his living statue with a prodigal hand. He could not but smile delightedly and forgive her, though she asked no pardon, for he was too glad to have her back to think of questions or reproaches.

"I am more than satisfied. Now come and let me play hostess among the teapots, for you are too splendid for anything but to be looked at, and you must need refreshment after your wild walk."

"No, I want nothing; let Hester fill my place. I'll wait for you here, and enjoy the pleasant fire you have made for me."

She knelt down before it, and he went slowly away, looking backward at the pretty picture the firelight showed him. When he rejoined her after tea and toilet, she was lying in a deep chair looking straight before her with a singular expression, dreamy, yet intense, blissfully calm, yet full of a mysterious brightness that made her face strangely beautiful. He examined her keenly, but she did not see him, he spoke, but she did not hear him, and not until he touched her did she seem conscious of his presence. Then the rapt look passed away, and she roused herself with an effort.

But Yorke could not forget it, and later in the evening when Coventry's rooms were full of friends and strangers, he stepped aside into a corner to observe Cecil from a distance and receive the compliments that now were so welcome to him. Two gentlemen paused nearby and, unconscious who was overhearing them, spoke freely of his ward.

"Where is Yorke's statue as they call her? A dozen people are waiting for my opinion, and I must not disappoint them," said the elder of the two, with the air of an experienced connoisseur.

"She is sitting yonder. Do you see her, Dent? The dark-haired angel with the splendid eyes," returned the younger, speaking with artistic enthusiasm.

Dent took a survey, and Yorke waited for his opinion, feeling sure that it would be one of entire and flattering approval.

"As a work of art she is exquisite, but as a woman she is a dead failure. Why in heaven's name didn't Yorke marry one of his marble goddesses and done with it?"

"They say he has," laughed Ascot, as Dent put down his glass with a shake of the head. "He fell in love with her beauty, and is as proud of it as if he had carved the fine curves of her figure and cut the clear outline of her face. If it were not for color and costume, she might be mounted on a pedestal as a mate for that serenely classical Pallas just behind her."

"Now to my eye," said Dent, "that rosy, sweet-faced little woman sitting near her is far lovelier than this expressionless, heartless-looking beauty. See how young Mrs. Vivian kindles and glows with every passing emotion; look at her smile, hear her laugh, see her meet her husband's eye with a world of love in her own, and then contrast her with your statuesque Mrs. Yorke."

"Every man to his taste. I admire the sculptor's, but I don't envy him his handsome wife unless he possesses the art of warming and waking his Galatea. I doubt it, however, for he hasn't the look of a Pygmalion, though a very personable man. Come and introduce me to charming Mrs. Vivian; I've looked at the snow image till I'm positively chilled."

They passed on, and Yorke sent a glance after them that might have
hastened their going had they met it. He had heard nothing but praise
before, and this was quite a revelation to him. He was hurt and angry,
yet ashamed of being so, and drawing back into his corner, began to
contrast Cecil with her neighbor. The gentlemen were right; that in-
definable something which she had once possessed was gone now, and
her beauty had lost its magic. The woman near her was all they had said,
young, blooming, blithe, and tender, with her new happiness shining
in her face, and making her far more winsome than her fairer neighbor.
He watched her look up at her husband with her heart in her eyes, and
felt a sense of wrong because he had never met a glance like that in the
dark eyes he knew so well. He saw the young pair dance together, and
as they floated by, forgetful of everything but one another, he sighed
involuntarily, remembering that he had done with love. He looked long
at Cecil, and began to wonder if he did possess the power to animate
his statue. For the first time he forgot his purpose, and yielding to the
impulse of the moment, crossed the room, bent over her, and asked,
"Cecil, can you waltz?"

"Yes; poor Alf taught me."

The tone in which the name was uttered roused the old jealous
feeling, for she never spoke *his* name in that softened voice.

"Come, then, and waltz with me," he said, with a masterful air as
novel as the request.

"With you? I thought you never danced."

"I will show you that I do. Lean on my arm, and let me see if I
can bring some color into those white cheeks of yours."

She glanced up at him with a curious smile, for he looked both
melancholy and excited; the next minute she forgot his face to wonder
at his skill, for with a strong arm and steady foot he bore her round and
round with a delightsome sense of ease and motion as the music rose
and fell and their flying feet kept time. Yorke often looked down to mark
the effect of this on Cecil, and was satisfied, for soon she glowed with
the soft excitement of exercise and pleasure; the mysterious brightness
returned to her eyes again and shone upon her face. Once he paused
purposely before Dent and Ascot, and as he waited as if to catch the
time, he heard the young man whisper, "Look at her now and own that
she is beautiful."

"That she is, for this is nature and not art. The man *can* animate
his statue and I envy him," returned the other, drawing nearer to watch
the brilliant creature swaying on her husband's arm as Yorke swept her
away, wearing an expression that caused more than one friend to smile
and rejoice.

"Rest a little, then we will dance again," he said, when he seated her, and leaning on her chair began to ply the fan, still bent on trying his power, for the test interested him.

"Do you see Mrs. Vivian yonder, Cecil? Tell me what you think of her."

"I think she is very pretty, and that her husband loves her very much."

"Don't you envy her?"

"No."

"Now that you have seen something of the world, and tasted many of its pleasures, do you never regret that you tied yourself to me so young, never reproach me for asking you to do it?" He leaned nearer as he spoke and looked deep into her eyes; they looked back at him as if they read his heart, and something in their lustrous depths stirred him strangely; but he saw no love there, and she answered in that undemonstrative voice of hers, "I am contented, Yorke."

"Call me Bazil; I am tired of the other, and it is too ugly for your lips."

She smiled to herself, remembering a time when Bazil was forbidden, and asked a question in her turn.

"Who are the gentlemen just passing?"

"Dent and Ascot, artists, I believe. Why do you ask?"

"I thought they were friends of yours, they seem to take so much interest in us."

"They are no friends of mine. Shall I tell you what they say of us?"

"Yes, Bazil, if you like."

He did not answer for a moment, because the long unused name came very sweetly from her lips, and he paused to enjoy it. Then he told her; but she only smoothed the ruffled plumage of the fan he had been using, and looked about her undisturbed.

"Mrs. Vivian tries to please her husband by being fond and gay; I try to please mine by being calm and cool. If both are satisfied, why care for what people say?"

"But I do care, and it displeases me to have you criticized in that way. Be what you like at home, but in public try to look as if you cared for me a little, because I will not have it said that I married you for your beauty alone."

"Shall I imitate Mrs. Vivian? You are hard to please, but I can try."

He laughed a sudden and irrepressible laugh, partly at her suggestion, partly at his own request, and she smiled for sympathy, so blithe and pleasant was the sound.

"What a capricious fool I am becoming," he said. "I no longer know myself, and shall begin to think my gray hairs have come too soon if this goes on. *Am* I very old and grave, Cecil?"

"Eight-and-thirty is not old, Bazil, and if you always dressed as carefully as tonight, and looked as happy, no one would call you my old husband, as a lady did just now."

Yorke glanced at a mirror opposite and fancied she was right; then his face clouded over, and he shook his head as if reproaching himself for a young man's folly. But the reflection he saw was that of a stately-looking man, with fine eyes and a thoughtful countenance which just then wore a smile that made it singularly attractive. Here their host was seen approaching with the strangers, and Yorke whispered suddenly, "Imitate Mrs. Vivian if you can; I want to try the effect upon these gentlemen."

She bowed and held the fan above her eyes a moment, as if to screen them from the light. When it dropped, as the newcomers were presented, they saw a blooming, blushing face, with smiles on the lips, light in the eyes, and happiness in every tone of the youthful voice. Amazed at the rapidity of the change, yet touched by her obedience and charmed with her address, her husband could only look and listen for the first few minutes, wondering what spirit possessed the girl. So well did she act her part that he soon entered heartily into his own, and taking young Vivian for his model, played the devoted husband so successfully that Dent and Ascot lingered long, and went away at last to report that Mrs. Yorke was the most charming woman in the room, and the sculptor the happiest man.

"Was my imitation a good one? Is that what you wish me to be in public?" asked Cecil, dropping back into her accustomed manner the instant they were alone, though her face still wore its newly acquired charm.

"It was done to the life, and you quite took my breath away with your 'loves' and 'dears,' and all manner of small fascinations. Where did you learn them? What possesses you tonight, Cecil?"

"An evil spirit. I have called it up, and now I cannot lay it."

She laid her hands against her cheeks, where a color like the deep heart of a rose burned steadily, while her eyes glittered and the flowers on her bosom trembled with the rapid beating of her heart, and some inward excitement seemed to kindle her into a life and loveliness that startled Yorke and half frightened herself. She saw that her words bewildered him still more than her actions, and, as if anxious to make him forget both, she rose, saying with an imperious little gesture, "We have sat apart in this nook too long; it is ill-bred. Come and dance with me."

He obeyed as if they had changed places, and for an hour Cecil danced like a devotee, delighting and surprising those about by the gaiety and grace with which she bore her part in the brilliant scene. When not with her, Yorke lingered nearby, longing to take her home, for her spirits seemed unnatural to him, and a half-painful, half-pleasurable sentiment of tender anxiety replaced his former pride in her. She had blossomed so suddenly he scarcely knew his quiet pupil, and while her secret perplexed him, this new change both charmed and troubled him, and kept him hovering about her till she came to him flushed and breathless, saying in the same excited manner as before, "Take me home, Bazil, or I shall dance myself to death. I want to be quiet now, for my head aches and burns, and I'm so tired I shall fall asleep before I know it."

Making their adieus, he took her to a quiet anteroom and left her to rest while he went to find his carriage. He was absent many minutes, being detained by the way, and when he returned it was to find Cecil fast asleep. Her fan and gloves had fallen from her hands, and she lay with her disordered hair scattered on the pillow, her white arms folded under her head, looking as if an unconquerable drowsiness had overpowered her. Wrapping her in her cloak Yorke took her away half awake, let her sleep undisturbed on his shoulder during the drive, and reluctantly gave her into the hands of her maid when they reached home.

Very little sleep did he get that night, for Cecil's figure was continually dancing before his eyes, sometimes as he first saw it that evening in the firelight, then as it looked when she played Mrs. Vivian with such spirit, or when she answered with that strange expression, "An evil spirit. I have called it up, and now I cannot lay it." But oftenest as he watched it by the light of the streetlamps, with a soft cheek against his own, and recollections of that other Cecil curiously blended with thoughts of the one sleeping on his shoulder. Calling himself a fool, with various adjectives attached, and resolutely fixing his mind on other things, having failed to bring repose, he lighted both lamp and meerschaum and read till dawn.

His first question when he met Victorine in the morning was "How is Mrs. Yorke?"

"Still asleep, sir, and I haven't called her, for the only thing she said last night was to bid me let her rest all day unless she woke."

"Very well, let her be quiet, and tell me when she rises."

He went to his studio, but could settle to nothing, and found the day wearisomely long, for Cecil did not rise. He asked for her at dinner, but she was still asleep, and hoping for a long evening with her, he resigned himself to a solitary afternoon. The clock was on the stroke of six when Victorine came in, looking frightened.

"I think Mrs. Yorke is ill, sir."

"Is she awake?" he asked, starting up.

"I've tried to wake her, but I can't. Perhaps you could, sir, for something must be amiss—she looks so strangely and hasn't stirred since morning."

Before the last sentence was out of her mouth Yorke was halfway upstairs, and in another minute at Cecil's bedside. A great change had come over her since he saw her last, a change that alarmed him terribly. The restless sleep had deepened into a deathlike immobility; the feverish flush was gone, and violet shadows gave her closed eyes a sunken look; through her pale lips slow breaths came and went; and when he felt her pulse her hand dropped heavily as he relinquished it. Stooping, he whispered gently yet urgently, "Cecil, wake up, it is time."

But there was no sign of waking, and nothing stirred but the faint flutter of her breath. He raised her, brushed the damp hair from her forehead, and cried in a voice tremulous with fear, "My darling, speak to me!"

But she lay mute and motionless. With a desperate sort of energy he flung up the window, rolled the bed where a fresh wind blew in, laid her high on the pillows, bathed her head and face, held pungent salts to her nostrils, and chafed her hands. Still all in vain; not a sound or motion answered him, and all his appeals, now tender, now commanding, could not break the trance that held her. Desisting suddenly from his fruitless efforts, he sent Victorine for a physician, and till he came suffered the most terrible suspense. Before Dr. Home could open his lips Yorke explained hurriedly, and bade him do something for heaven's sake.

The old gentleman took a long survey, touched pulse and temples, listened to her breathing, and then asked, though his own medicine case was in his hand, "Do you keep laudanum in the house?"

"I have some that I've had a long time. I'll get it for you." And Yorke was gone in spite of Victorine's offer of assistance. But he returned with a fresh anxiety, for the little flask was empty.

"It was half full two days ago; no one goes to that cabinet but myself. I don't understand it," he began.

"I do."

And there was something in the doctor's tone that caused the bottle to drop from Yorke's hand as he whispered, with a look of incredulity and dismay, "Do you think she has taken it?"

"I have no doubt of it."

Yorke seized the old man's arm with a painful grip, asking in a terror-stricken tone, "Do you mean she tried to destroy herself?"

"Nothing of the sort; she has only taken an overdose and must sleep it off."

"Doctor, you deceive me! I know enough of this perilous stuff to know that the bottle under my feet contained enough to kill a man."

"Perhaps so, but not your wife; and the fact that she is still alive proves that I am right."

Terror changed to intense relief as Yorke asked with an appeasing gesture, "Can you do nothing for her? Will she not sleep herself to death?"

"I assure you there is no danger; she will wake in a few hours, weak and languid, but all the better for the lesson she has unintentionally given herself. It's a dangerous habit, and I advise you to put a stop to it."

"To what? I don't understand you, sir."

The doctor looked up from the powder he was preparing, saw Yorke's perplexity, and answered with a significant nod, "I see you don't, but you shall, for she is too young for such things yet. Your wife eats opium, I suspect."

For a moment Yorke stared at him blankly, then said impetuously, "I'll not believe it!"

"Ask the maid," returned the doctor, but Victorine spoke for herself.

"Upon my word, sir, I know nothing of it. Mrs. Yorke sleeps a deal some days and is very quiet, but I never saw her take anything but the little comfits."

"Hum! She is more careful than I suspected. I'm sure of it, however, and perhaps you can satisfy yourself if you choose to look."

The doctor cast a suggestive glance about the room. Yorke understood it, and taking Cecil's keys began his search, saying sternly, "I have a right to satisfy myself and save her from further danger if it is so."

He did not look long, for in a corner of the drawer where certain treasures were kept he found a paper which had evidently been a wrapper for something that left a faintly acrid odor behind. A few grayish crumbs were shaken from the folds, and Dr. Home tasted them with a satisfied "I thought so."

Yorke crushed the paper in his hand, asking in a tone of mingled pain and perplexity, "Why should she do it?"

"A whim, perhaps, ennui, wakefulness; a woman's reasons for such freaks are many. You must ask her and put a stop to it, though I think this may break up the habit."

"What led you to suspect her of it?" asked Yorke, trying to find his way out of the mystery.

"I detected laudanum in her breath; that explained the unnatural sleep. The fact that it had not already killed her assured me that she was used to it, for, as you said, a dose like that would kill a man, but not a woman who had been taking opium for months. I can do nothing now; keep the room cool, let her wake naturally, then give her this, and if she is not comfortable tomorrow, let me know."

With that the doctor left him, Victorine began her watch beside the pale sleeper, and Yorke went away to wander through the silent house haunted by thoughts that would not let him rest.

❧ *Chapter VII* ❧

HEART FOR HEART

DR. Home was right; Cecil's heavy sleep gradually passed into a natural one, and in the morning she woke, wan and nerveless, but entirely ignorant that she had lost a day. A misty recollection of some past excitement remained, but brought no explanation of her present lassitude, except a suspicion that she had taken more opium than was prudent. Finding herself alone when she woke, she did not ring for Victorine, but made her toilet hastily, rubbed a transient color into her pale cheeks, drew her hair low on her temples to conceal her heavy eyes, and went down fearing that it was very late.

Yorke sat in his place with a newspaper in his hand, but he was not reading, and there was something in his face that made Cecil pause involuntarily to examine it. It seemed as if years had been added to his age since she saw him last; his mouth was grave, his eye sad; a weary yet resolute expression was visible, but also the traces of some past suffering that touched the girl and caused her to lay her hand upon his shoulder, saying in her gentlest tone, "Good morning, Bazil; forgive me for being so wilful yesterday. I am punished for my fault by finding you so grave and tired now."

"I am only tired of waiting for my breakfast" was all the answer she got, but she felt him start and saw the paper rustle in his hand as she spoke, though whether surprise or displeasure caused these demonstrations she could not tell, and fancying him in one of his moody fits, took her place in silence. His coffee stood untouched till it was cold before he looked up and said, with a keen glance which made her eyes falter and fall, "Are you quite rested, Cecil?"

"Not quite; I danced too much last night."

"The night before last, you mean."

"We were at Coventry's last evening, Bazil."

"No, on Monday evening."

"Yes, and today is Tuesday."

He turned the paper toward her and Wednesday stared her full in the face. She looked incredulous, then bewildered, and putting her hand to her forehead seemed trying to recollect, while a foreboding fear came over her.

"Then what became of yesterday? I remember nothing of it," she asked with a troubled look.

"You slept it away."

"What! All day?"

"For six-and-thirty hours, without a word, almost without a motion."

His eye was still upon her, his voice was ominously quiet, and as he spoke her wandering glance fell on an open book that lay beside him. She read its title—*Confessions of an Opium-Eater*—and overcome by a painful blending of shame and fear, she covered up her face without a word.

"Is it true, Cecil?"

"Yes, Bazil."

"How long has it been?"

"A year."

"What tempted you to try such a dangerous cure, or pleasure?"

"Yourself."

"I! How? When?"

"You gave me laudanum when I could not sleep. I liked its influence, and after that I tried it whenever I was sad or tired."

"Was this the secret I nearly discovered once, the cause of your solitary walks, the evil spirit that possessed you at Coventry's?"

"Yes; I had opium in my pocket that day, and was so frightened when I thought you would discover it, because I knew you would be angry. I went out those times to get it, for I dared not trust anyone. Last night, no, Monday night, I had none, and I longed for it so intensely I could not wait. I disobeyed you, but the storm was too much for me, and I was just turning back in despair, when I remembered the little flask. You seldom go to the cabinet, never use the laudanum, and I thought I could replace it by-and-by."

"But, child, had you no fear of consequences when playing such perilous pranks with yourself? You might have killed yourself, as you came near doing just now."

"I was used to it because Mamma often had it, and at first I was very careful; but the habit grew upon me unconsciously, and became so fascinating I could not resist it. In my hurry I took too much, and was frightened afterward, for everything seemed strange. I don't know what I did, but nothing seemed impossible to me, and it was a splendid hour; I wish it had been my last."

Tears fell between her fingers, and for a moment she was shaken by some uncontrollable emotion. Yorke half rose as if to go to her, but checked the impulse and sat down again with the air of a man bent on subduing himself at any cost. Cecil was herself again almost immediately, and wiping away her tears, seemed to await his reproof with her accustomed meekness.

But none came, for very gently he said, "Was this kind to yourself or me?"

"No; forgive me, Bazil. I will amend my fault."

"And promise never to repeat it?"

"I promise, but you cannot know how hard a thing it is to give up when I need it so much."

"Why, Cecil?"

"Because—" she stopped an instant, as if to restrain some impetuous word, and added, in an altered tone, "because I find it hard to tame myself to the quiet, lonely life you wish me to lead. I am so young, so full of foolish hopes and fancies, that it will take time to change me entirely, and what I have seen of the world lately makes it still more difficult. Have patience with me, and I shall be wiser and more contented soon."

He had left the table as if to throw up a window, and lingered for a moment to enjoy the balmy air, perhaps to conceal or conquer some pang of self-reproach, some late regret for what he had done. When he returned, it was to say, with an undertone of satisfaction in his grave voice, "Yes, it is too soon to ask so much of you, and if you give up this dangerous comforter, surely I can give up a little of the seclusion that I love. It is hard to break off such a habit. I will help you, and for a time we will forget these troubles in new scenes and employments. Will you go to the seashore for a month, Cecil, and so make home pleasanter by absence?"

"Oh, so gladly! I love the sea, and it will do me good. You are very kind to think of it, and I thank you so much, Bazil!"

She did thank him, with eyes as well as lips, for her face brightened like a prisoner's when the key turns in the lock and sunshine streams into his cell. Yorke saw the joy, heard the tone of gratitude, and stifled a sigh, for they showed him what a captive he had made of her, and betrayed how much she had suffered silently.

"Shall I go with you?" he asked, in a curiously unauthoritative tone, but with a longing look that might have changed her reply had she seen it.

"If you care to, I shall feel safer; but do not unless it is pleasant to you."

"It *is* pleasant. We will go tomorrow," he said decidedly. "Rest and prepare today; take Victorine with you, and leave your troubles all behind, and in a month we will come back our happy selves again."

"I hope so" was all her answer, and the change was settled without more words.

"The charm does not work," sighed Yorke within himself, as he looked down at Cecil leaning on his arm while they went pacing along the smooth beach seven days later, with the great waves rolling up before them, a fresh wind blowing inward from the sea, and summer sunshine brooding over the green islands of the bay. The week had brought no change to Cecil; air and bathing, exercise and change of scene, thoughtful care and daily devotion on her husband's part, all seemed to have failed, and she walked beside him with the old quietude and coldness intensified instead of lightened.

"What shall I do with you, Cecil? You don't get strong and rosy as I hoped you would, and you often have a longing look as if you wanted your opium again; but you know I dare not give it to you."

"I shall learn to do without it in time, or find something else to take its place. Hark!"

As the words left her lips, her hand arrested him, her eyes kindled, a smile broke over her face, and her whole figure seemed to start into life. He stood still wondering, but instantly he learned what magic had wrought the spell, for on the wings of the wind came the fitful music of a song from a solitary boatman whose skiff lay rocking far out in the bay. Both recognized the voice, both watched the white sail gliding nearer, and both faces altered rapidly; Cecil's warmed and brightened as she listened with head erect and detaining hand, but Yorke's darkened with the blackest frown it had ever worn as he drew her away with an impatient gesture and peremptory "Come in; it is too warm to linger here for a fisherman's song!"

The smile broke into a laugh as she said, following with evident reluctance, "Do fishermen sing Italian and go fishing in costumes like that?"

"Your ears and eyes must be keener than mine if you can discover what I neither hear nor see," he answered almost petulantly. But still smiling, she looked backward as she began to sing like a soft echo of the stranger's voice, and let him lead her where he would. Till sunset he kept her in their rooms, busy with pencil, book, or needle, blind to the wistful glances she often sent seaward, and deaf to hints that they were losing the hours best suited for sketching. Victorine came in at last, bringing Cecil's hat and mantle, and, as if the nod she gave him was a preconcerted signal, Yorke rose at once, saying promptly, "Yes, now we can go, without fear of sun or—"

"Fishermen," added Cecil, with a slightly scornful smile.

"Exactly." And Yorke put on her mantle without a sign of displeasure at her interruption. She seemed upon the point of refusing the stroll that now had no charm for her, but yielded, and they went out together, leaving Victorine to lift her hands and wonder afresh at the strange behavior of her master and mistress.

"I have a fancy to walk upon the rocks; can I, Bazil?" were the first words Cecil uttered, as they came into the splendor of the evening hour that bathed sea and sky within its ruddy glow.

A single sail was skimming down the bay, and not a figure sat or stood among the rocks. Yorke saw this, and answered with a gracious smile, "Walk where you will; I leave the path to you."

She climbed the cliffs and stood watching the lonely boat until it vanished round the rocky point where the lighthouse tower showed its newly kindled spark. Then she turned and said wearily, "Let us go home. I find it chilly here."

He led her down another path than that by which they came, but stopped suddenly, and she felt his hand tighten its hold as he exclaimed, "Go back; it is not safe. Go, I beg of you!"

It was too late, for she had seen a figure lying on a smooth ledge of the cliff, had recognized it, and glided on with a willful look, a smile of satisfaction. He set his teeth and sprang after her, but neither spoke, for Germain lay asleep, and the entire repose of his fine face not only restrained their tongues, but riveted their beauty-loving eyes. Cecil was touched to see how changed he was; for all the red glow shining over him, his face was very pale; the wind blew back the hair from his temples, showing how hollow they had grown; and stooping to brush an insect from his forehead, she saw many gray hairs among the dark locks scattered on the stone. His mouth was half hidden by the black beard, but the lips smiled as if some happy dream haunted his sleep, and in the hands folded on his broad chest, she saw a little knot of ribbon that had dropped from her dress that morning as she listened to his song.

Yorke saw it, also, and made an involuntary gesture to pluck it from the sleeper's hold, but Cecil caught his arm, whispering sharply, "Let him keep it! You care nothing for it, and he needs something to comfort him, if I read his face aright."

Yorke stood motionless an instant, then seemed to take some sudden resolution, for drawing her gently aside, he said with a mildness that was as new as winning, "You are right; he does need comfort, and he shall have it. Go on alone, Cecil; I will follow soon."

She obeyed him, but glancing backward as she went, she saw him turn his face to the cliff behind him, and lay his head down on his arm in an attitude of deep dejection or of doubt. He stood so till the last sound of her light step died away, then he stopped and touched the sleeper, with a low-spoken "August, it is I."

Germain leaped to his feet as if the slight touch had been a blow, the quiet call a pistol shot, and his hand went to his breast with an instinctive motion that half revealed a hidden weapon. A single glance seemed to reassure him, for though his heart beat audibly, and his very lips were white, he laughed and offered the hand that had just been ready to deal death to some imaginary captor. Yorke did not take it, and, as if the discourtesy reminded him of something, Germain drew back, bowed with the grace that was habitual to him, and said coolly, "Pardon me; your sudden waking makes me forgetful. I was dreaming of you, and in the dream we were friends as of old."

"Never again, August; it is impossible. But I will do my best for you now, as before, if I may trust you."

"Have I not kept my word this time? Have I not left you in peace for nearly a year? Did I not obey you today when you bade me shun you, though the merest accident betrayed your presence to me?"

"You have done well for one so tempted and so impetuous; but you forget the letters written to Cecil in my absence, and lying down to sleep in our very path is not putting the bay between us as I bade you."

"Forgive the letters; they did no harm, for she never read them, I suspect. Ah, you smile! Then I am right. As for finding me here, it was no plot of mine. I thought you always walked on the beach, so I crept up to catch one glimpse of her unseen, before I went away for another year, perhaps. Be generous, Bazil. You have made her all your own; do not deny me this poor boon."

"I will not. Promise me to keep our secret sacredly, and you shall see her when you will. But you must control yourself, eye, tongue, voice, and manner, else I must banish you again. Remember your life is in my hands, and I will give you up rather than let harm come to her."

"I swear it, Bazil. You may safely indulge me now, for I shall not haunt you long; my wanderings are almost over, and you may hear Death knocking at my heart."

Real solicitude appeared in Yorke's face as the other spoke with a melancholy smile, and obeying a kindly impulse, he laid his hand on Germain's shoulder.

"I hope not, for it is a very tender heart, in spite of all its wayward-ness and past offenses. But if it be so, you shall not be denied the one happiness that I can give you. Come home with me, and for an hour sun yourself in Cecil's presence. I do not fear you in this mood, and there is no danger of disturbing her; I wish there was!"

"God bless you, Bazil! Trust me freely. The wild devil is cast out, and all I ask is a quiet time in which to repent before I die. Take me to her; I will not mar her peace or yours. May I keep this? It is my only relic."

He showed the ribbon with a beseeching look, and remembering Cecil's words, Yorke bowed a mute assent as he led the way down the rude path and along the beach where slender footprints were still visible in the damp sand.

She was waiting in the softly lighted room, with no sign of impa-tience as she sat singing at the instrument. It was the air Germain had sung, and pausing behind her, he blended the music of his voice with hers in the last strains of the song. She turned then, and put out her hand, but caught it back and glanced at Yorke, for the recollection of the struggle in the dark returned to check the impulse that prompted her to welcome this man whom she could not dislike, in spite of mystery, violence, and unmistakable traces of a turbulent life. Yorke saw her doubt and answered it instantly.

"Give him your hand, Cecil, and forgive the past; there is no ill will between us now, and he will not forget himself again."

Germain bowed low over the little hand, saying in the tone that always won its way, "Rest assured of that, Mrs. Yorke, and permit me to offer my best wishes, now that my prophecy has been fulfilled."

In half an hour Yorke saw the desired change, for Germain worked the miracle, and Cecil began to look as she had done a year ago. Sitting a little apart, he watched them intently, as if longing to learn the secret, for he had failed to animate his statue since the night when for a time he believed he had some power over her, but soon learned that it was to opium, not to love, that he owed his brief success. Cecil paid no heed to him, but seemed forgetful of his presence, as Germain entertained her with an animation that increased the fascination of his manner. An irresistible mingling of interest, curiosity, and compassion attracted her to him. Yorke's assurance, as well as his own altered demeanor, soon removed all misgivings from her mind, and the indescribable charm of his presence made the interview delightful, for he was both gay and gentle, devoted and respectful. The moment the hour struck, he rose and went, with a grateful glance at Yorke, a regretful one at Cecil. She did not ask now as before, "Will he come again?" but her eyes looked the question.

"Yes, he will come tomorrow, if you like. He is ill and lonely, and not long for this world; so do your best for him while you may."

"I will, with all my heart, for indeed I pity him. It is very generous of you to forget his wrongdoing, and give me this pleasure."

"Then come and thank me for it a la Mrs. Vivian."

He spoke impulsively and held his hands to her, but she drew back, swept him a stately little curtsy, and answered with her coolest air, "We are not in public now, so, thank you, guardian, and good night."

She smiled as she spoke, but he turned as if he had been struck, and springing out of the low window, paced the sands until the young moon set.

They had come to the seaside before the season had begun, but now the great hotel was filling fast, and solitude was at an end. Cecil regretted this, and so did Yorke, for the admiration which she always excited no longer pleased but pained him, because pride had changed to a jealous longing to keep her to himself. In public she was the brilliant, winning wife, in private, the cold, quiet ward, and nothing but Germain's presence had power to warm her then. He came daily, seeming to grow calmer and better in the friendly atmosphere about him. Cecil enjoyed his society with unabated pleasure, and Yorke left them free after being absent for hours and apparently intent upon some purpose of his own. Of course, there were many eyes to watch, many tongues to comment upon the actions of the peculiar sculptor and his lovely wife. Germain was known to be a friend; it was evident that he was an invalid, and no longer young; but flirting young ladies and gossiping old ones would make romances, while the idle gentlemen listened and looked on. Cecil soon felt that something was amiss, for though her secluded life had made her singularly childlike in some things, she was fast learning to know herself, and understand her relations to the world. She wondered if Yorke heard what was said, and hoped he would speak if anything displeased him; but till he did, she went on her way as if untroubled, walking, sailing, singing, and driving with Germain, who never forgot his promise, and who daily won from her fresh confidence and regard. So the days passed till the month was gone, and with a heavy heart Cecil heard her husband give orders to prepare for home.

"Are you ready?" he asked, coming in as she stood recalling the pleasant hours spent with Germain, and wondering if he would come to say farewell.

"Yes, Bazil, I am ready."

"But not glad to go?"

"No, for I have been very happy here."

"And home is not made pleasanter by absence?"

"I shall try to think it is pleasanter."

"And I shall try to make it so. Here is the carriage. Shall we go?"

As they rolled away, Cecil looked back, half suspecting to see some signal of adieu from window, cliff, or shore, but there was none, and Yorke said, interpreting the look aright, "It is in vain to look for him; he has already gone."

"It is much better so. I am glad of it," she said decidedly, as she drew down her veil, and leaning back, seemed to decline all further conversation. Her companion consoled himself with Judas, but something evidently filled him with a pleasant excitement, for often he smiled unconsciously, and several times sang softly to himself, as if well pleased at some fancy of his own. Cecil thought her disappointment amused him, and much offended, sat with her eyes closed behind her veil, careless of all about her, till the sudden stopping of the carriage roused her, and looking up, she saw Yorke waiting to hand her out.

"Why stop here? This is not home," she said, looking at the lovely scene about with wondering eyes.

"Yes, this is home," he answered, as leading her between blooming parterres and up the wide steps, he brought her into a place so beautiful that she stood like one bewildered. A long, lofty hall, softly lighted by the sunshine that crept in through screens of flowers and vines. A carpet, green and thick as forest moss, lay underfoot; warm-hued pictures leaned from the walls, and all about in graceful alcoves stood Yorke's fairest statues, like fit inhabitants of this artist's home. Before three wide windows airy draperies swayed in the wind, showing glimpses of a balcony that overhung the sea, whose ever-varying loveliness was a perpetual joy, and on this balcony a man sat, singing.

"Does it please you, Cecil? I have done my best to make home more attractive by bringing to it all that you most love."

Yorke spoke with repressed eagerness, for his heart was full, and try as he might, he could not quite conceal it. Cecil saw this, and a little tremor of delight went through her; but she only took his hand in both her own, exclaiming gratefully, "It is too beautiful for me! How shall I thank you? This is the work you have been doing secretly, and this is why you sent Germain before us to give me a sweet welcome. How thoughtful, and how beautiful it was of you."

He looked pleased but not satisfied, and led her up and down, showing all the wonders of the little summer palace by the sea. Everywhere she found her tastes remembered, her comfort consulted, her least whim gratified, and sometimes felt as if she had found something dearer than all these. Still no words passed her lips warmer than gratitude, and when they returned to the hall of statues, she only pressed the generous hand that gave so much, and said again, "It is too beautiful for me. How can I thank you for such kindness to your little ward?"

"Say wife, Cecil, and I am satisfied."

"Pardon me, I forgot that, and like the other best because it is truer. Now let me go and thank Germain."

She went on before him, and coming out into the wide balcony, saw nothing for a moment but the scene before her. Below, the waves broke musically on the shore, the green islands slept in the sunshine, the bay was white with sails, the city spires glittered in the distance, and beyond, the blue sea rolled to meet the far horizon.

"Has he not done well? Is it not a charming home to live and die in?" said Germain, as she turned to greet him, with both hands extended, and something more than gratitude in her face. That look, so confiding and affectionate, was too much for Germain; he took the hands and bent to give her a tenderer greeting, remembering his promise just in time, and with a half-audible apology, hurried away, as if fearing to trust himself.

Cecil looked after him sorrowfully, but when Yorke approached, asking in some surprise, "Where is Germain?" she answered reproachfully, "He is gone, and he must not come again."

"Why not?"

"Because he cannot forget, and others see it as well as I. You might have spared him this, and for my sake have remembered that it is not always wise to be kind."

"Ah, they gossip again, do they? Let them; I've done one rash and foolish thing to appease Mrs. Grundy, and now I shall trouble myself no further about her or her tongue."

Leaning on the balustrade, he did not look at her, though he held his breath to catch her reply, but seemed intent on watching leaf after leaf float downward to the sea. His careless tone, his negligent attitude wounded Cecil as deeply as his words; her eyes kindled, and real resentment trembled in her voice.

"Who should care, if not you? Do you know what is said of us?"

"Only what is said of every pretty woman at a watering place." And he leaned over to watch the last leaf fall.

"You do not care, then? It gives you no pain to have it said that I am happier with Germain than with you?"

He clenched the hand she could not see, but shrugged his shoulders and looked far off at sea, as if watching a distant sail.

"For once, rumor tells the truth, and why should I deny it? My pride may be a little hurt, but I'm not jealous of poor Germain."

If he had seen her hold her lips together with almost as grim a look as his own often wore, and heard her say within herself, "I will prove that," he would have carried his experiment no further. But he never turned his head, and Cecil asked, with a touch of contempt in her voice that made him wince, "Do you wish this mysterious friend of yours to go and come as freely as he has done of late?"

"Why not, if he is happy? He has not long to enjoy either life or love."

"And I am to receive him as before, am I?"

"As you please. If his society is agreeable to you, I have no desire to deprive you of it, since mine is burdensome and Alfred away."

Something in the emphasis unconsciously put upon the last name caused a smile to flit over Cecil's face, but it was gone instantly, and her voice was cold as ice.

"Thank you; and you have no fear of the consequences of this unparalleled generosity of yours?"

"None for myself or my snow image. Has she for herself?"

"I fear nothing for myself; I have no heart, you know."

She laughed a sudden laugh that made him start, and as she vanished behind the floating curtains, he struck his hand on the iron bar before him with a force that brought blood, saying, in an accent of despair, "And she will never know that I have one, till she has broken it!"

≥ *Chapter VIII* ≤

MASKS

"CECIL, the world begins to wonder why Mrs. Yorke does not admit it to a glimpse of her new home."

"Mrs. Yorke is supremely indifferent to the world's wonder or its wishes."

She certainly looked so, as she sat in the couch corner singing to herself, and playing with a useless fan—for the room was breezy with sea airs, though an August sun blazed without. Yorke was strolling from alcove to alcove, as if studying the effects among his statues, and Germain lounged on the wide step of the balcony window, with a guitar across his knee, for he still came daily, as neither master nor mistress had forbidden him.

"I think I have proved my indifference, but people annoy me with questions, and I suspect we shall have no peace till we give some sort of an entertainment, and purchase freedom hereafter by the sacrifice of one evening now."

"You are right, Yorke; I, too, have been beset by curious inquirers, and I suggest that you end their suspense at once. Why not have a masquerade? These rooms are admirably fitted for it, there has been none this season, and the moon is at the full next week. What does 'my lady' say?"

Germain spoke in his persuasive voice, and Cecil looked interested now.

"If we must have anything let it be that. I like such things, and it is pleasant to forget oneself sometimes. Does the fancy suit you, Bazil?"

"Anything you please, or nothing at all. I only spoke of it, thinking you might find some pleasure in pleasing others," he returned, still busy with the piping Faun that had a place among the finer works of his own hands.

"I used to do so, and tried very hard to please, but no good came of it, so now I enjoy myself, and leave others to do likewise. What characters shall we assume, Germain?"

As she asked the question, her voice changed as abruptly as her manner, and languid indifference was replaced by lively interest.

"I shall assume none, I have not spirits enough for it, but in a domino can glide about and collect compliments for you. Your husband must take the brilliant part, as a host should."

"He had better personate Othello; the costume would be becoming, and the character an easy one for him to play, he is such a jealous soul."

She spoke ironically, and he answered in the same tone.

"No, thank you, I prefer Hamlet, but you would succeed well as the princess in the fairy tale, who turned to stone whenever her husband approached her, though a very charming woman to all others. Perhaps, however, you would prefer to personate some goddess; I can recommend Diana, as a cool character for a sultry summer evening."

"I hate goddesses, having lived with them all my life. Everyone will expect me to be some classical creature or other, so I shall disappoint them, and enjoy myself like a mortal woman. I'll imitate the French marquise whom we saw last winter at the theater; she was very charming, and the dress is easily prepared, if one has jewels enough."

Germain laughed involuntarily at the idea of Cecil in such a character, and she laughed also, a lighthearted laugh, pleasant to hear.

"You think I cannot do it? Wait and see. I am a better actress than you think; I've had daily practice since I was married, and Bazil will testify that I do my part well."

"So well that sometimes it is impossible not to mistake art for nature. When shall this fete take place, Madame la Marquise?"

"Next week; four days are enough for preparation, and if we wait longer, I shall get tired of the fancy, and give it up."

"Next week it shall be then."

Yorke stood looking down the long room at the pretty tableau at the end, for Germain was leaning on the back of the couch now, dropping odorous English violets into the white hands lifted to catch them, and Cecil looked as if she was already enjoying herself as a mortal woman. Standing apart among the statues, he wondered if she remembered the time when his will was law, and it was herself who obeyed with a weakness he had not yet learned. Now this was changed, and he called himself a fool for losing his old power, yet gaining no new hold upon her. She ruled him, but seemed not to know it, and keeping her smiles for others, showed her darkest side to him, being as lovely and as thorny as any brier rose. Presently she sprang up, saying with unusual animation, "I will go and consult with Victorine, and then we will drive to town and give our orders. You must come with me, Germain. I want your taste in my selection; Bazil has none, except in stones."

"One cannot doubt that, with such proofs all about one," answered Germain, as he followed her toward the door. "When shall we have another statue, Yorke? You have been idle of late."

"Never busier in my life; I have a new design in my mind, but it takes time to work it out. Wait a few weeks longer, and I will show you something that shall surpass all these."

"Unless you have lost your skill."

Yorke's face had kindled as he spoke, but it fell again when Cecil whispered these words in passing, with a glance that seemed to prophesy a failure for the new design, whatever it might be. A flush of passionate pain passed across his face, and he lifted his arms as if to hurl poor Psyche down again, but the sight of the bruised hand seemed to recall some purpose, and calm him by its spell.

For four days there was much driving to and fro between the city and the beach; the great hotel was all astir, and the villas along the shore were full of busy tongues and needles, for summer is the time for pleasure, and the Yorkes' masquerade was the event of the season. On the appointed evening all things were propitious, the night was balmy, the sky cloudless, the moon lent her enchantment to the scene, and the lonely home beside the sea wore its most inviting aspect, for the hall of statues was brilliant with lights, blooming with flowers, and haunted by the fitful music of a band concealed among the shrubbery without. Yorke, looking stately and somber as the melancholy Dane, and Germain in a plain black silk domino, stood waiting for Cecil, mask in hand. Presently she came rustling down, in a costume both becoming and piquant, for the powdered hair made her fair skin dazzling, and the sweeping brocades of violet and silver set off her slender figure. She wore no ornaments, but a profusion of rich lace upon the dress, white plumes in her hair, and a cluster of roses on her bosom. With the costume she seemed to have assumed the coquetry of the French marquise, and greeted her companions in broken English, spoken with a charming accent and sprightly grace that caused Germain to compliment her on her skill, and Yorke to survey her with undisguised pride, as he said, with a significant smile, "Let me put the last touch to this ravishing toilet of yours, and prove that you were right in saying I had some taste in stones."

Cecil bent her beautiful neck to let him clasp a diamond necklace about it, and held out a pair of lovely arms to receive their glittering fetters, with a little cry of pleasure, and a characteristic *"Merci, monsieur!* You are too gallant in so revenging yourself upon me for my idle words. These are superb, I kiss your munificent hands," and as he essayed to fasten in the brooch, she touched his hand with her lips. The pin dropped, Germain took it up, and turning to him, she said, in her own voice, "Put it in my hair just here, there is no room for it below; diamonds are best on the head, and roses on the heart."

As he deftly fastened it above her white forehead, she drew out a flower broken by Yorke's unskillful hand, and tying it to the ribbon of Germain's domino, she said, "Wear this, else among so many black dominoes I shall not know my friend, and make my confidences to wrong ears."

"Now I am prouder of my rose than you of your jewels, madame, and thank you for it heartily," he replied, surveying it with delight.

"Shall I wear not your favor, also?" asked Yorke, with extended hand.

"Oh, yes, but not that one, because it does not suit you. There's rue for you; and here's some for me, but we may wear our rue with a difference."

As she quoted poor Ophelia's words, from a vase nearby she gathered a flowerless sprig, and gave it to him with a glance that cut him to the heart. He took it silently, and instantly resuming her gay manner, she exclaimed, as the roll of a carriage was heard, "It is the Coventrys, they come early, because I asked them to play the host and hostess for an hour to increase the bewilderment of our guests, and give us greater freedom. She is to be Juno, and while she is masked, no one will suspect that it is not I. Come, Germain, let us slip away, and return later."

The rooms filled rapidly, and the mock host and hostess did the honors so well that the guests had no doubt of their identity, while the real master of the house moved among them unsuspected, watching impatiently for the arrival of the marquise and her friend. He waited long, but at last the white plumes were seen approaching, and many eyes followed the brilliant figure that entered, not on the arm of a black domino, but a young courtier in the picturesque costume of Elizabeth's time. Yorke saw at a glance that this was not Germain; who was it then? Alfred flashed into his mind, but he was across the water, and not expected to return for months. No new-made acquaintance of Cecil's carried himself with such a gay and gallant air; for the disguise seemed to sit easily upon him, and he wore doublet and hose, velvet cloak and lovelocks, ruff and sword with none of the awkwardness that most men exhibit when in costume. Nor was this all he saw to disturb him; the charming marquise leaned upon the arm of this debonair Sir Walter Raleigh, talking with an animation that attracted attention, while the devotion of her escort, and the grace of both, roused much curiosity concerning this striking young couple. Hamlet followed them like a shadow, but their conversation was in whispers, and they went their way as if unconscious of anything but themselves. Yorke soon met the black domino with the white rose dangling on his breast, and drew him apart to ask eagerly, "Who is that with Cecil?"

"I have no idea."

"Where did she meet him?"

"I cannot tell you."

"But you went away together, and were to return together. When and how did you part?"

"We went to the music room to wait a little, but soon she sent me for her fan, which had been forgotten. I was gone some time, for the maid was busy with the ladies; when I returned Madame had disappeared, and I saw no more of her till she came in with Sir Walter."

"Rude to you, that is not like her!"

"I was to blame, if anyone; she grew tired of waiting, doubtless, and finding some friend, left me to follow her. I am glad she did, for he is a fitter escort for youth and beauty than I. They look like a prince and princess out of a fairy tale, and it does one's heart good to watch them."

Yorke made no reply, but stood motionless beside Germain, looking where *he* looked, for the dancing had begun, and the young pair were slowly circling round the room to the sound of music, inspiring enough to stir the coldest blood. Twice the marquise floated by, with a glance over her shoulder as she passed; but the third time she looked in vain, for the two dark figures were gone, and a splendid Cleopatra held her court in the deserted recess.

"I am out of breath; let us stroll about and hear people's comments on me and mine; that will be amusing," she said, pausing, and her escort obeyed.

It was amusing, and something more, for as they passed through the glittering throng, or mingled with the groups gathered about each statue-haunted alcove, Cecil saw and heard the wonder, admiration, and reverence her husband's genius inspired. This was the first time his works had been exhibited, and there was something so romantic in the fact that these fine statues had stood unknown, unseen, till they were brought to decorate his wife's home, as if love alone could make him care for fame, that their beauty seemed increased fourfold in the spectators' eyes; and so warm were the commendations bestowed upon the marbles, so varied and beautiful the tributes paid the man, that Cecil glowed behind the mask, and was glad of that screen to hide her smiles and tears. From many lips she heard the same story, sorrow, love, and fame, with endless embellishments, but always the same contrast between romance and reality for her. If he loved her, why so careless about Germain? What was the mystery that bound the two so closely together, with such a strange mingling of dislike and gratitude, forbearance and submission? Had she not a right to solve the secret if she could, now that her happiness depended on it? These thoughts saddened and silenced her so visibly that her companion soon perceived it.

"Where are all your spirits gone? Have I really offended you by coming? Or do these chattering people weary you? Tell me, Cecil, and let me do my best to make you gay again," he whispered, bending till his curling locks touched her shoulder.

"Neither, Sir Walter; the heat oppresses me, so take me out into the garden, and leave me to rest, while you play the cavalier to some other lady, lest your devotion to one should give offense."

"If I submit now, I may join you when I've done penance in a single dance, may I not? Remember how short my time is, and how much I have to say."

"You may come if you will forget the past, and think only of the future."

"I can safely promise that, for it is now the desire of my heart," and with a curious blending of joy and regret in his voice, Sir Walter left the marquise on the broad steps that led down into the garden. Moonlight flooded the terrace, grove, and flowery paths where changing figures wandered to and fro, or sat in the green nooks, each group making a graceful picture in that magic light. Here a troubadour sang to his guitar, as knights and ladies listened to his lay; there glided a monk or nun, somber and silent, as if blind and deaf to the gaiety about them; elves glittered in the grove; Mephistopheles followed a blond Margaret; Louis Fourteenth and Marie Stuart promenaded with stately pace along the terrace; and Rebecca the Jewess was flirting violently with Cardinal Wolsey on the steps. Enjoying the mirth and mystery with a divided mind, Cecil wandered on, declining all courteous offers of companionship from fellow wanderers, and came at last to a retired nook, where a rustic seat stood under a leafy arch before the little fountain that sparkled in the moonlight. Scarcely was she seated, however, before a long shadow fell across the path, and turning, she saw a black domino behind her.

"Does Madame recognize me?"

The voice was feigned, nothing but the outline of the figure was visible, and no badge distinguished this domino from a dozen others, but after a moment's pause and a brief scrutiny, Cecil seemed satisfied, and removing her mask, exclaimed with an air of perfect confidence, "It is Germain; you cannot hide yourself from me."

"Is Madame sure?"

"Yes, I know you by the rapid beating of your heart. You forget that, *mon ami*."

"Does no other heart beat fast when it approaches you, lovely marquise?"

"None but yours, I fancy. You have been dancing, and I bade you not, it is dangerous. Come now, and rest with me; the music is delicious from this distance, and the night too beautiful to waste in crowded rooms."

With an inviting gesture she swept her silken train aside, that he might share the little seat, and as he took it, put up her hand to remove his mask, with the smile still shining on her face, the friendly tone still softening her voice.

"Take off that ugly thing, it impedes your breathing, and is bad for you."

But he caught the hand, and imprisoned it in both his own, while the heartbeats grew more audible, and some inward agitation evidently made it difficult to speak quietly.

"No, permit me to keep it on; I cannot show as calm a face as you tonight, so let me hide it."

Something in the touch and tone caused Cecil to look closer at the mask, which showed nothing but glittering eyes and glimpses of a black beard.

"Where is the sign that will assure me you are Germain?" she demanded.

"Here," and turning to a fold of the black domino she saw the rose still hanging as she had tied it.

"No wonder you did not care to show your badge, it is so faded. Break a fresh one from the trellis yonder, and I will place it better for you."

"Give me one from your bouquet, that is fresher and sweeter to me than any other in the garden or the world."

"Moonlight and masquerading make you romantic; I feel so too, and will make a little bargain with you, since you prize my rose so highly. You shall take your choice of these I wear, if you will answer a few questions."

"Ask anything—" he began eagerly, but caught back the words, adding, "put your questions, and if I can answer them without forfeiting my word, I will, truly and gladly."

"Ah, I thought that would follow. If I forfeit my word in asking, surely you may do the same in answering. I promised Bazil to control my curiosity; I have kept my promise till he broke his, now I am free to satisfy myself."

"What promise has he broken?"

"I will answer that when you have earned the rose. Come, grant my wish, and then you may question in return."

"Speak, I will do my best."

"Tell me then what tie binds you to Yorke?"

"The closest, yet most inexplicable."

"You are his brother?"

"No."

"He cannot be your father, that is impossible?"

"Decidedly, as there are but a few years difference between our ages."

She heard a short laugh as this answer came, and smiled at her own foolish question.

"Then you must be akin to me, and so bound to him in some way. Is that it?"

"I am not akin to you, yet I am bound to you both, and thank God for it."

"What is the mystery? Why do you haunt me? Why does Yorke let you come? And why do I trust you in spite of everything?"

"The only key I can give you to all this is the one word, love."

She drew back, as he bent to whisper it, and put up her hand as if to forbid the continuance of the subject, but Germain said warmly, "It is because I love you that I haunt you. Yorke permits it, because he cannot prevent it, and you trust me, because your heart is empty and you long to fill it. Is not this true? I have answered your questions, now answer mine, I beg of you."

"No, it is not true."

"Then you do love?"

"Yes."

"Whom, Cecil, whom?"

"Not you, Germain, believe that, and ask no more."

"Is it a younger, comelier man than I?"

"Yes."

"And you have loved him long?"

"For years."

"He is here tonight?"

"He is. Now let us go in, I am tired of this."

"Not yet, stay and answer me once more. You shall not go till I am satisfied. Tell me, have you no love for Yorke?"

His sudden violence terrified her, for, as she endeavored to rise, he held her firmly, speaking vehemently, and waiting her reply, with eyes that flashed behind the mask. Remembering his wild nature, and fearing some harm to Bazil, she dared not answer truly, and hoping to soothe him, she laid her hand upon his arm, saying, with well-feigned coldness, "How can I love him, when I have been taught for years only to respect and obey him? He has been a stern master, and I never can forget my lesson. Now release me, Germain, and never let this happen again. It was my fault, so I forgive you, but there must be no more of it."

There was no need to bid him release her, for as the words left her lips, like one in a paroxysm of speechless repentance, grief, or tenderness, he covered her hands with passionate tears and kisses, and was gone as suddenly as he had come. Cecil lingered a moment to recover herself and readjust her mask, and hardly had she done so when down the path came Hamlet, as if in search of her. The difference between the two had never been more strongly marked than now, for Germain had been in his most impetuous mood, and Yorke seemed unusually mild and calm, as Cecil hurried toward him, with a pleasant sense of safety as she took his arm, and listened to his quiet question.

"What has frightened you, my child?"

"Germain, he is so violent, so strange, that I can neither control nor understand him, and he must be banished, though it is hard to do it."

"Poor Germain, he suffers for the sins of others as well as for his own. But if he makes you unhappy, he shall go, and go at once. Why did you not tell me so before?"

"I did, but you said, let him stay. Have you forgotten that so soon?"

Yorke laughed low to himself.

"It seems that I have forgotten. It was kind of me, however, to let him stay where he was the happiest; did you not think so, Cecil?"

"No, I thought it very unwise. I was hurt at your indifference, and tried to show you your mistake; but I have done harm to Germain, and he must go, although in him I lose my dearest friend, my pleasantest companion. I am very proud, but I humble myself to ask this favor of you, Bazil."

"Gentle heart, how can he ever thank you for your compassion and affection? Be easy, he shall go; but as a last boon, give him one more happy day, and I will make sure that he shall not offend again, as he seems to have done tonight. I, too, am proud, but I humble myself, Cecil, to ask this favor of you."

So gently he spoke, so entirely changed he seemed, that Cecil's eyes filled, for her heart felt very tender, and before she could restrain it, an impulsive exclamation escaped her.

"Ah, Bazil, if you were always as kind as now, how different my life would be."

"So would mine, if I dared be kind." The answer was impulsive as the exclamation, and he made a gesture as if to take her to himself; but something restrained him, and with a heavy sigh he walked in silence.

"Dared to be kind?" she echoed, in a grieved and wondering tone. "Are you afraid to show that you care for me a little?"

"Mortally afraid, because I cannot tell you all. But, thank heaven, there will come a time when I may speak, and for that hour I long, though it will be my last."

"O Bazil, what do you mean by such strange words?"

"I mean that when I lie dying, I can tell my miserable mystery, and you will pity and pardon me at last."

"But you once said you would never tell me."

"Did I? Well, then Germain shall tell you when he dies. You'll not have long to wait."

Cecil shivered at the ominous words, and started with a faint cry, for they seemed confirmed, as her eye fell on a dark figure lying with hidden face among the grass, not far from the solitary path they had unconsciously chosen. There was something so pathetic about the prostrate figure, flung down as if in the abandonment of despair, that Cecil was on the point of going to offer comfort, when her companion detained her, whispering earnestly, "Leave him to me, and go on alone. It is time for the unmasking, and we shall be missed. I'll follow soon, and bring him with me."

She obeyed, and went on, more heavyhearted than when she came. Within, the gaiety was at its height, and as she entered, Sir Walter was instantly at her side, leading her away for the last dance before the masks were removed. Presently silence fell upon the motley throng, and all stood ready to reveal themselves, when a signal came. A single horn sounded a mellow blast, and in a moment the room brightened with smiling faces, as the black masks fell, while a general peal of laughter filled the air. Cecil glanced about her for her husband and Germain. They were standing together near the door, both unmasked now, and both more mysterious to her than ever. Neither looked as she expected to see them; Yorke was grim and pale, with smileless lips and gloomy eyes; Germain leaned near him, smiling his enchanting smile, and wearing the indescribable air of romance which always attached to him, and even now, rendered him a more striking figure than many of the gayer ones about him.

"Shall I ever understand them?" she sighed to herself, as her eyes turned from them to Sir Walter, standing beside her, one hand on his sword hilt, the other still holding the half-mask before his face, as if anxious to preserve his incognito as long as possible. Yorke's eye was upon him, also, as he waited with intense impatience to see his suspicion confirmed; but in the confusion of the moment, he lost sight of the marquise and her attendant before this desire was gratified. Making his way through the crowd as fast as frequent salutations, compliments, and jests permitted, he came at last to the balcony. A single glance assured him that his search was ended, and stepping into the deep shadow of the projecting wall, he eyed the group before him with an eye that boded ill to the unconscious pair.

Cecil's face was toward him, and it wore a look of happiness that had long been a stranger to it, as she spoke earnestly but in so low a tone that not a word was audible. Her companion listened intently, and made brief replies; he was unmasked now, but the long plume of his hat drooping between his face and the observer still prolonged his suspense. Only a few moments did they stand so, for, as if bidding him adieu, Cecil waved her hand to him, and reentered the hall through the nearest window. Sir Walter seated himself on the wide railing of the balcony, flung his hat at his feet, and turned his face full to the light, as if enjoying the coolness of the sea breeze. One instant he sat humming a blithe cavalier song to himself, the next, a strong hand clutched and swung him over the low balustrade, as a face pale with passion came between him and the moon, and Yorke's voice demanded fiercely, "What brings you here? Answer me truly, or I will let go my hold, and nothing but my hand keeps you from instant death."

It was true, for though Alfred's feet still clung to the bars, his only support was the arm, inflexible as iron, that held him over the rocky precipice, below which rolled the sea. But he was brave, and though his face whitened, his eye was steady, his voice firm, as he replied unhesitatingly, "I came to see Cecil."

"I thought so! Are you satisfied?"

"Fully satisfied."

"That she loves you as you would have her love?"

"Yes, as I would have her love."

"You dare say this to me!" and Yorke's grip tightened, as a savage light shot into his black eyes, and his voice shook with fury.

"I dare anything. If you doubt it, try me."

Alfred's blood was up now, and he forgot himself in the satisfaction it gave him to inflict a pang of jealousy as sharp as his own had been.

"What was she saying to you as she left?" demanded Yorke, under his breath.

"I shall answer no questions, and destroy no confidences" was the brief reply.

"Then I swear I will let go my hold!"

"Do it, and tell Cecil I was true to the end."

With a defiant smile, Alfred took his hands from the other's arm, and hung there only by that desperate clutch. The smile, the words, drove Yorke beyond himself; a mad devil seemed to possess him, and in the drawing of a breath, the young man would have been dashed upon the jagged cliffs below, had not Germain saved them both. Where he came from, neither saw, nor what he did, for with inconceivable rapidity Yorke was flung back, Alfred drawn over the balustrade, and planted firmly on his feet again. Then the three looked at one another: Yorke was speechless with the mingled rage, shame, and grief warring within him; Alfred still smiling disdainfully; Germain pale and panting with the shock of surprise at such a sight, and the sudden exertion which had spared the gay evening a tragic close. He spoke first, and as one having authority, drawing the young man with him, as he slowly retreated toward the steep steps that wound from the balcony to the cliff that partially supported it.

"Go, Bazil, and keep this from Cecil; I have a right to ask it, for half the debt to you is canceled by saving you from this act, that would have made your life as sad a failure as my own. I shall return tomorrow for the last time; till then I shall guard this boy, for you are beside yourself."

With that they left him, and he let them go without a word, feeling that indeed he was beside himself. How long he stood there, he did not know; a stir within recalled him to the necessity of assuming composure, and fighting down the agitation that must be controlled, he went in to play the courteous host at his own table, and answer to the toasts drunk to the health and happiness of himself and his fair wife. He went through with his duties with a desperate sort of gaiety that deceived careless observers, but not Cecil. She too was feverishly restless for Alfred did not appear, and Germain was gone also; but she hid her disquiet better than Yorke, and the effort made her so brilliantly beautiful and blithe that the old fancy of "Yorke's statue" was forgotten, and "Yorke's wife" became "the star of the goodly companie."

The evening came to an end at last, and Yorke's long torment was over. Early birds were beginning to twitter, and the short summer night was nearly past, as the latest guest departed, leaving the weary host and hostess alone. Cecil's first act was to unclasp the diamonds, and offer to restore them to the giver, saying gratefully, yet with gravity, "I thank you for your generous thought of me, and have tried to do honor to your gift, but please take them back now, they are too costly ornaments for me."

"Too heavy chains, you mean," and with a sudden gesture, he sent the glittering handful to the ground, adding, in a tone that made her start, "Did you bring that boy here?"

"Do you mean the gallant Sir Walter?"

"I mean Alfred Norton."

"No, I did not ask him."

"You knew he was coming?"

"I only hoped so."

The dark veins rose on Yorke's forehead, he locked his hands tightly together behind him, and fixed on her a look that she never could forget, as he said slowly, as if every word was wrung from him, "You must see him no more. I warn you, harm will come of it if you persist."

A smile broke over her face, and with a shrug of her white shoulders, and an accent of merry malice that almost drove him frantic, she answered nonchalantly, "Why mind him more than poor Germain? If he comes, I cannot shun him, unless my lord and master has turned jealous, and forbids it; does he?"

"Yes."

Yorke left the room, as he uttered the one word that was both an answer and a confession; had he looked backward, he would have seen Cecil down upon her knees gathering up the scattered diamonds, with that inexplicable smile quenched in tears, and on her face that tender expression he so longed to see.

⤙ *Chapter IX* ⤚

ON THE RACK

T HE house was not astir till very late next day, for master and
mistress breakfasted in their own rooms at noon, and seemed in
no haste to meet. A more miserable man than Yorke the sun did
not shine on. Oppressed with remorse for last night's violence, shame at
last night's betrayal of jealousy, and bitter sorrow for last night's defeat,
he longed yet dreaded to see Cecil, feeling that all hope of winning her
heart was lost, and nothing but the resignation of despair remained
for him.

Fearing that Alfred might venture back, he haunted house and
garden like a restless ghost, despising himself the while, yet utterly
unable to resist the power that controlled him. No one came, however;
not even Germain, and the afternoon was half over before Cecil appeared. He knew the instant she left her room, for not a sound escaped
him; he saw her come down into her boudoir looking so fresh and fair
he found it hard to feign unconsciousness of her presence, till he was
composed enough to meet her as he would. The windows of her room
opened on the shady terrace where he had been walking for an hour.
After passing and repassing several times, in hopes that she would
speak to him, he pulled his hat low over his brows, and looking in, bade
her "Good morning." She answered with unusual animation, but her eye
did not meet his, and she bent assiduously over her work as if to hide
her varying color. Yorke was quick to see these signs of disquiet, but
the thought of Alfred made him interpret them in his own way, and
find fresh cause of suffering in them.

Both seemed glad to ignore last night, for neither spoke of it, though conversation flagged, and long pauses were frequent, till Yorke, in sheer desperation, took up a book, offering to read aloud to her. She thanked him, and leaning on the window ledge he opened at random and began to read. Of late, poems and romances had found their way into the house, apparently introduced by Germain, and to her surprise Yorke allowed Cecil to read them, which she did with diligence, but no visible effect as yet. In five minutes Yorke wished she had refused his offer, for the lines he had unwittingly chosen were of the tenderest sort, and he found it very hard to read the tuneful raptures of a happy lover, when his own heart was heaviest. He hurried through it as best he could, and not till the closing line was safely delivered did he venture to look at Cecil. For the first time she seemed affected by the magic of poetry; her hands lay idle, her head was averted, and her quickened breath stirred the long curls that half hid her face.

"She thinks of Alfred," groaned Yorke, within himself, and throwing down the book, he abruptly left her for another aimless saunter through the garden and the grove. He did not trust himself near her again, but lying in the grass where he could see her window, he watched her unobserved. Still seated at her embroidery frame, she worked at intervals, but often dropped her needle to look out as if longing for someone who did not come. "She waits for Alfred," sighed Yorke, and laying his head down on his arm, he fell to imagining how different all might have been had he not marred his own happiness by blindly trying to atone for one wrong with another. The air was sultry, the soft chirp of insects very soothing; the weariness of a wakeful night weighed down his eyelids, and before he was aware of its approach, a deep sleep fell upon him, bringing happier dreams to comfort him than any his waking thoughts could fashion.

A peal of thunder startled him wide awake, and glancing at his watch, he found he had lost an hour. Springing up, he went to look for Cecil, as he no longer saw her at her window. But nowhere did he find her, and after a vain search he returned to the boudoir, thinking some clue to her whereabouts might be discovered there. He did discover a clue, but one that drove him half mad with suspense and fear. Turning over the papers on her writing table, hoping to find some little message such as she often left for him, he came upon a card bearing Alfred's name, and below it a single line in French.

"At five, on the beach. Do not fail."

Yorke's face was terrible as he read the words that to his eyes seemed a sentence of lifelong desolation, for, glancing despairingly about the room, he saw that Cecil's hat was gone, and understood her absence now. A moment he stood staring at the line like one suddenly gone blind; then all the pain and passion passed into an unnatural calmness as he thrust the card into his pocket and rang like a man who has work to do that will not brook delay.

"Where is Mrs. Yorke?" was the brief question that greeted Anthony when he appeared.

"Gone to the beach, I think, sir."

"How long ago?"

"Nearly an hour, I should say. It was half past four when I came home; she was here then, for I gave her the note; but she went out soon after, and now it's half past five."

"What note was that?"

"An answer to one I carried to the hotel, sir."

"To Mr. Alfred, was it not?"

"Yes, sir."

"Did you see him, Anthony?"

"Gave it into his own hand, sir, as Mistress bade me, for it was important, she said."

"Very important! He answered it, you say?"

"Yes, sir. I met him on the lawn, and when he'd read the note, he just wrote something outlandish on his card and told me to hurry back. Is anything wrong, master?"

"Mrs. Yorke has gone boating with him, I believe, and I am anxious about her, for a storm is blowing up and Mr. Alfred is no sailor. Are you sure she went that way?"

"Very sure, sir; she had her boat cloak with her, and went down the beach path. I thought she spoke to you lying under the pine, but I suppose you were asleep, so she didn't wake you."

"She stopped, did she?"

"Yes, sir, several minutes, and stooped down as if speaking to you."

"You were watching her, it seems. Why was that?"

"Beg pardon, sir, but I couldn't help it; she looked so gay and pretty it did my old eyes good to look at her."

"You may go."

The instant he was alone, Yorke caught up a delicate lace handkerchief that lay on a chair, and calling Judas, showed it to him with a commanding "Find her." The dog eyed his master intelligently, smelled the bit of cambric, and with nose to the ground, dashed out of the house, while Yorke followed, wearing the vigilant, restless look of an Indian on the war trail. Under the pine Judas paused, snuffed here and there, hurried down the path, and set off across the beach, till coming to a little cove, he seemed at fault, ran to and fro a minute, then turned his face seaward and gave a long howl as if disappointed that he could not follow his mistress by water as by land. Yorke came up breathless, looked keenly all about him, and discovered several proofs of the dog's sagacity. Cecil's veil lay on a rocky seat, large and small footprints were visible in the damp sand, and a boat had been lately drawn up in the cove, for the receding tide had not washed the mark of the keel away.

"She could not be so treacherous—she has gone with Germain— I will not doubt her yet." But as the just and generous emotion rose, his eye fell on an object which plainly proved that Alfred *had* been there. A gold sleeve button lay shining at his feet; he seized it, saw the initials *A. N.* upon it, and doubted no longer, as the hand that held it closed with a gesture full of ominous significance, and turning sharply, he went back more rapidly than he came. Straight home he hurried, and calling Anthony, alarmed the old man as much by his appearance as by the singular orders he gave.

"If Germain comes, tell him to wait here for me; if young Norton comes, do not admit him; if Mrs. Yorke comes, put a light in the little turret window. I am going to look for her, and shall not return till I find her, unless the light recalls me."

"Lord bless us, sir! If you're scared about Mistress, let someone go with you. I'll be ready in a jiffy."

"No; I shall go alone. Get me the key of the boathouse, and do as I tell you."

"But, master, they'll put in somewhere when they see the squall coming on. Better send down to the hotel, or ride round to the Point. It's going to be a wild night, and you don't look fit to face it."

But Yorke was deaf to warnings or suggestions, and hastily preparing himself for the expedition, he repeated his orders, and left Anthony shaking his head over "Master's recklessness."

As he unmoored the boat, Judas leaped in, and standing in the bow, looked into the dim distance with an alert, intent expression, as if he shared the excitement of his companion. Up went the sail, and away flew the *Sea Gull*, leaving a track of foam behind, and carrying with it a heart more unquiet than stormy sea or sky. Across the bay skimmed the boat, and landing on the now deserted beach, Yorke went up to the hotel, so calm externally that few would have suspected the fire that raged within.

"Is young Norton here?" he asked of a clerk lounging in the office.

"Left this afternoon, sir."

"Rather sudden, wasn't it? Are you sure he's gone?"

"Don't know about the suddenness, Mr. Yorke, but I do know that he paid his bill, sent his baggage by the four-thirty train, and said he should follow in the next."

"Did he say anything about coming over to the Cliffs? I expected him today."

"I heard nothing of it, and the last I saw of him he was going toward the beach to bid the ladies good-bye, I supposed."

"Thank you, Gay. I had a message for him, but I can send it by mail." And Yorke sauntered away as if his disappointment was a very trifling one. But the instant he was out of sight his pace quickened to a stride, and he made straight for the depot, cursing his ill-timed sleep as he went. Another official was soon found and questioned, but no young gentleman answering to Alfred's description had purchased a ticket; of this the man was quite sure, as very few persons had left by either of the last trains.

"Well planned for so young a head, but Judas and his master will outwit him yet," muttered Yorke between his teeth, concentrating all his wrath on Alfred, for he dared not think of Cecil.

Stopping at Germain's lodging, he was told that his friend had gone to town at noon, and had not yet returned. This intelligence settled one point in his mind and confirmed his worst fear. Regardless of the gathering storm, he put off again, shaping his course for the city, led by a conviction that the lovers would endeavor to conceal themselves there for a time at least. A strange pair of voyagers went scudding down the harbor that afternoon: the great black hound, erect and motionless at the bow, though the spray dashed over him, and the boat dipped and bounded as it drove before the wind; the man erect and motionless at the helm, one hand on the rudder and one on the sail, his mouth grimly set, and his fiery eye fixed on the desired haven with an expression which proved that an indomitable will defied both danger and defeat. Craft of all sorts were hurrying into port, and more than one belated pleasure boat crossed Yorke's track. The occupants of each were scanned with a scrutinizing glance, and once or twice he shouted an inquiry as they passed. But in none appeared the faces he sought, no answer brought either contradiction or confirmation of his fear, and no backward look showed him the welcome light burning in the little turret window. Coming at last to the wharf where they always landed, he questioned the waterman to whose care he gave his boat.

"Aye, aye, sir; this squall line sent more than one philandering young couple home in a hurry. The last came in twenty minutes ago, just in time to save the crew from more water than they bargained for."

"Did you observe them? Was the lady beautiful? The gentleman young? Did you catch the name of either? Where—"

"Drop anchor there, sir, till I overhaul the first cargo of questions," broke in the man, for Yorke was hurrying one inquiry upon the heels of another without waiting for an answer to any. "Did I observe 'em? No, I didn't, particularly. Was the lady pretty? Don't know; she was wrapped up and scared. Was the gentleman young? Not more than three-and-twenty, I should say. Did I catch their names? Not a name, being busy with the boats."

"Did they seem fond of one another? Were they in a hurry? Which way did they go?"

"Uncommon fond, and in a devil of a hurry. Which way they went I can't tell; it was no business of mine, so I didn't look. Anything more, sir?" said the man good-humoredly.

"Yes; take this for your trouble, and show me the boat they came in."

"Thanky, sir; that's it over yonder. The lad must have been half-seas over with love or liquor, to bring his sweetheart all the way from the Point in a cockleshell like that."

"From the Point? It is a hotel boat, then?"

"Aye, sir; I know 'em all, and the *Water Witch* is the worst of the lot, but her smart rigging gives her a rakish look to them that don't know a mud scow from a wherry."

"Did the young man give you any orders about the boat?"

"Only to keep her till she was called for."

"And you have no idea which way they went?"

"No, sir; they steered straight ahead as far as the corners, but what course they took then I can't say."

Yorke was gone before the man had finished his sentence, and with Judas at his heels, turned toward his old home, feeling little doubt but he should find the fugitives at Mrs. Norton's close by; for though she was absent for the summer, her house was accessible to her son. Admitting himself without noise, he searched his own premises, and from the garden reconnoitered the adjoining ones. Every window was closely shuttered; no light anywhere appeared, and the house was evidently unoccupied. Hester, when called, had heard and seen nothing of Mr. Alfred for months, and was much surprised at her master's sudden appearance, though he fabricated a plausible excuse for it. Out he went again into the storm that now raged furiously, and for several hours searched every place where there was the least possibility of finding those he sought. He looked also for Germain, hoping he might lend some help; but he was in none of his usual haunts, and no clue to the lost wife was found.

Drenched, despairing, and exhausted with his fruitless quest, he stepped into a lighted doorway for shelter, while he took a moment's thought what course to pursue next. As he stood there, Ascot, the young artist, came from the billiard room within; he had been Yorke's guest the night before, and recognizing his host in the haggard, weatherbeaten man standing in the light, he greeted him gaily.

"Good evening, ancient mariner; you look as if your last voyage had not been a prosperous one. I can sympathize with you, for thanks to that confounded *Water Witch,* we nearly went to the bottom in the squall this afternoon."

"The *Water Witch?*" cried Yorke, checking himself in the act of abruptly quitting Ascot, whose gaiety was unbearable just then.

"Yes, I warn you against her. We came over from the Point in her, and had a narrow escape of being made 'demd, damp, moist, unpleasant bodies,' as Manteline says."

"This afternoon, Ascot? At what time?"

"Between five and six."

"Did you leave the boat at the lower wharf where we usually land?"

"Yes; and there she may stay till doomsday, though we ought to be grateful to her, after all."

"We? Then you were not alone?"

"No, my Grace was with me—" There Ascot stopped, looking half embarrassed, half relieved, but added, with a frank laugh, "I never could keep a secret, and as I have betrayed myself, I may as well confess that I took advantage of the storm and danger to make myself a very happy man. Give me joy, Yorke; Grace Coventry is mine."

"Joy! Your torment has but just begun," with which gloomy answer Yorke left the astonished young gentleman to console himself with love dreams and a cigar.

"Have I lost my senses as well as my heart, that I go chasing shadows, and deluding myself with jealous fears and fancies, when perhaps there is no mystery or wrong but what I conjure up?" mused Yorke, as he crossed the deserted park, intent upon a new and hopeful thought. Having made one mistake, he began to believe that he had made another, and wasted time and strength in looking for what never had been lost. Weariness calmed him now, the rain beating on his uncovered head cooled the fever of his blood, and the new hope seemed to brighten as he cherished it.

"I'll go back and wait; perhaps she has already come, or tidings of her. Anything is better than this terrible suspense," he said, and set about executing his design in spite of all obstacles.

It was nearly midnight now, too dark and wild to attempt returning by water, and the last train had left; but only a few miles lay between him and home, and neither weariness nor tempest could deter him. Soon mounted on a powerful horse, he was riding swiftly through the night, recalling legends of the Wild Huntsman to the few belated travelers who saw the dark horseman dash by them, with the dark hound following noiselessly behind. The storm was in accordance with his mood, and he liked it better than a summer night, though the gusts buffeted him and the rain poured down with unabated violence. At the first point where the Cliffs were visible, he reined up and strained his eyes to catch a glimpse of the light that should assure him of Cecil's safety. But a thick mist obscured land and sea, and no cheering ray could pierce the darkness. A mile nearer his eye was gladdened by the sight of a pale gleam high above the lower lights that glimmered along the shore. Brighter and brighter it grew as he approached, and soon, with a thrill of joy that made his heart leap, he saw that it shone clear and strong from the little turret window. An irrepressible shout broke from his lips as he galloped up the steep road, leaped the gate, and burst into the hall before man or maid could open for him.

"Where is she?" he cried, in a voice that would have assured the wanderer of a tender welcome had she been there to hear and answer it.

Anthony started from a restless doze in his chair, and shook his gray head as he eyed his master pitifully.

"She ain't here, sir, but we've had news of her; so I lit the lamp to bring you home."

Yorke dropped into a seat as if he had been shot, for with the loss of his one hope, all strength seemed to desert him, and he could only look at Anthony with such imploring yet despairing eyes that the old man's hard face began to work as he said below his breath, "After you'd gone, sir, I went down to the Point and stayed round there till dark. Just as I was coming away, old Joe came in bringing a sail he'd picked up halfway down the harbor. There were several of us standing about the pier, and naturally we asked questions. Then it come out from one and another that the sail belonged to the boat Mr. Alfred took this afternoon. He left there alone, but one of the men saw him with a lady afterward, and by his description I knew it was Mistress."

Yorke covered up his face as if he knew what was coming and had not courage to meet it; but soon he said, brokenly, "Go on," and Anthony obeyed.

"The man wasn't quite sure about Mr. Alfred, as he don't know him, and didn't mind him much; but he was sure of Mistress, and could swear to the boat and sail, for he helped rig it, and his sweetheart made the streamer. I'd like to think he was wrong, but as Mr. Alfred hired the boat, and the dear lady was seen in it, I'm awfully afraid they were wrecked in the squall."

How still the house seemed as the words dropped slowly from Anthony's lips. Nothing stirred but poor Judas panting on his mat, and nothing broke the silence but the soft tick of a clock and the sobbing of the wind without. Yorke had laid down his head as if he never cared to lift it up again, and sat motionless in an attitude of utter despair, while the old servant stood respectfully silent, with tears rolling down his withered cheeks, for his gentle mistress had won his heart, and he mourned for her as for a child of his own.

Suddenly Yorke looked up and spoke.

"Have you sent anyone to look for them?"

"Yes, master, long ago, and—"

"What is it? You keep something back. Out with it, man; I can bear anything but suspense."

"They found the boat, and it was empty, master."

"Where was it? Tell me all, Anthony."

"Just outside the little bay, where the gale would blow hardest and the tide run strongest. The mast was broken short off, the boat half full of water, and one broken oar still hung in the rowlock, but there was no signs of anyone except this."

Turning his face away, Anthony offered a little silken scarf, wet, torn, and stained, but too familiar to be mistaken. Yorke took it, looked at it with eyes out of which light and life seemed to have died, then put it in his breast, and turning to the faithful hound, said in a tone the more pathetic for its calmness: "Come, Judas; we went together to look for her alive, now let us go together and look for her dead."

Before Anthony could detain him he had flung himself into the saddle and was gone. All that night he haunted the shores, looking long after others had relinquished the vain search, and morning found him back in the city, inquiring along the wharves for tidings of the lost.

Taking his own boat, he turned homeward at last, feeling that he could do no more, for the reaction had begun, and he was utterly spent. The storm had passed, and dawn was breaking beautifully in the east; the sea was calm, the sky cloudless; the wind blew balmily, and the sea gull floated along a path of gold as the sun sent its first shaft of light over the blue waste. A strange sense of peace came to the lonely man after that wild night of tempest and despair. The thought of Cecil quiet underneath the sea was more bearable than the thought of Cecil happy with another, for in spite of repentance and remorse, he could not accept his punishment from Alfred's hand, and clung to the belief that she was dead, trying to find some poor consolation for his loss in the thought that life was made desolate by death, not by treachery. So sailing slowly through the rosy splendor of a summer dawn, he came among the cluster of small islands that lay midway between the city and the little bay. Some were green and fair, some were piles of barren rocks; none were inhabited, but on one still stood a rude hut, used as a temporary shelter for pleasure parties or such fishermen as frequented the neighborhood. Yorke saw nothing of the beauty all about him; his eyes were fixed upon the white villa that once was home; his mind was busy with memories of the past, and he was conscious of nothing but the love that had gone down into that shining sea. Judas was more alert, for, though sitting with his head on his master's knee, as if trying to comfort him by demonstrations of mute affection, he caught sight of a little white flag fluttering from the low roof of the hut, and leaped up with a bound that nearly took him overboard. The motion roused Yorke, and following the direction of the dog's keen eye, he saw the signal—saw, also, a woman wrapped in a dark cloak sitting in the doorway, with her head upon her knees, as if asleep.

In an instant both dog and man were trembling with excitement, for there was something strangely familiar about the cloak, the bent head with its falling hair, the slender hands folded one upon another. Like one inspired with sudden life, Yorke plied his oars with such energy that a few vigorous strokes sent the boat high upon the pebbly shore, and leaping up the bank, while Judas followed baying with delight, he saw the figure start to its feet, and found himself face to face with Cecil.

❧ *Chapter X* ❧

AT LAST

WHILE Yorke slept, on the previous afternoon, Cecil met Alfred on the beach, talked with him for half an hour, and when he left her, hastily, she stood waving her hand till he was out of sight; then she looked about her, as if in search of someone, and her face brightened as she saw Germain approaching.

"I am glad you are come," she said, "for I was just trying to find a man to take this boat home, and here I find a gentleman. Alfred came in it, but delayed so long that he had only time to run across the cliffs and catch the train. Will you ferry me over to the Point, and add another favor to the many I already owe you?"

"Nothing would please me better, but instead of landing so soon, let me take you down below the lighthouse, as I promised you I would. This will be my only opportunity, for I go away tomorrow, and you know you said I should have one more happy day."

"Did Bazil tell you that?" asked Cecil, looking disturbed, as his words recalled last night's adventure.

"No, but I am well aware that I trouble you—that you wish me gone, and I shall obey; but give me this last pleasure, for I may never come again."

The smile he gave her was both melancholy and submissive; she longed to bid him stay but dared not, yet remembering Bazil's wish that she should bear with him a little longer, she was glad to grant it, for she felt her power over this man, and feared nothing for herself. A moment's hesitation, then she went toward the boat, saying, in her friendliest tone, "I trust you, and you shall have your pleasure; but, believe me, if I wish you gone it is for your own sake, not mine."

"I know it—I am grateful for your pity, and I will not disturb your confidence by any violence. Indeed, I think I'm done with my old self, and grow quieter as the end approaches."

Cecil doubted that, as she remembered the scene before the fountain, but Germain was certainly his gentlest self now, and as they sailed across the bay before the freshening wind she found the hour full of real rest and enjoyment despite her care. Absorbed in animated conversation, and unconscious of the lapse of time, they glided past the Point, the pleasant islands, the city with its cloud of smoke, the lighthouse on its lonely rock, and were floating far down the harbor, when the growling of distant thunder recalled them from the delights of a musical discussion to the dangers of an impending storm. A bank of black clouds was piled up in the west, the wind came in strong gusts, the waves rolled in long swells, and sea and sky portended a summer squall.

"How careless I have been," exclaimed Germain, looking anxiously about him. "But I fancy we need fear nothing except a drenching, for it will take some time to return in the teeth of this gale. Wrap your cloak about you, and enjoy the fine sight, while I do my best to atone for my forgetfulness."

Cecil had no fear, for Germain was a skillful boatman, and she loved to watch the grand effects of light and shade as the thunderous clouds swept across the sky, blotting out the blue and making the water somber with their shadows. An occasional flash seemed to rend the dark wall, but no rain fell, and by frequent tacking Germain was rapidly decreasing the distance between them and home. Safely past the city they went, for Cecil would not land there lest Yorke should be alarmed at her long absence, and as the storm still delayed, she hoped to reach shelter before it broke.

"Once past the islands and we are quite safe, for the little bay is quiet, and we can land at any point if the rain begins. A few minutes more of this rough work, and we can laugh at the gale. Bend your head, please, I must tack again else—"

The rest of the sentence was lost in a crash of thunder like the report of cannon, as a fierce gust swept down upon them, snapping the slender mast like a bulrush, and carrying Germain overboard wrapped in the falling sail. With a cry of horror Cecil sprang up, eager yet impotent to save either herself or him; but in a moment he appeared, swimming strongly, cleared away the wreck of the sail, righted the boat, and climbed in, dripping but unhurt.

"Only another of my narrow escapes. I'm surely born to die quietly in my bed, for nothing kills me," he said coolly, as he brushed the wet hair from his eyes and took breath.

"Thank heaven! You are safe. Land anywhere, for now the sail is gone we must not think of reaching home," cried Cecil, looking about her for the nearest shore.

"We will make for the lower island; the storm will not last long, and we can find shelter there. Unfortunate that I am, to make my last day one of danger and discomfort for you."

"I like it, and shall enjoy relating my adventures when we are at home. Let me row, it is too violent exercise for you," she said, as he drew out the oars and took off his coat.

"It will not hurt me—or if it does what matter? I would gladly give my life to see you safe."

"No, no, you must not do it. Let the boat drift, or give me an oar; I am strong; I fear nothing; let me help you, Germain."

"Take the rudder then and steer for the island; that will help me, and the sight of you will give me strength for a short tussle with the elements."

Cecil changed her seat, and with her hand upon the helm, her steady eyes upon the green spot before them, sat smiling at the storm, so fair and fearless that the sight would have put power into any arm, courage into any heart. For a time it seemed to inspire Germain, and he pulled stoutly against wind and tide; but soon, to his dismay, he felt his strength deserting him, each stroke cost a greater effort, each heart-beat was a pang of pain. Cecil watched the drops gather on his forehead, heard his labored breathing, and saw him loosen the ribbon at his throat, and more than once dash water over his face, alternately deeply flushed and deadly pale. Again and again she implored him to desist, to let her take his place, or trust to chance for help, rather than harm himself by such dangerous exertion. But to all entreaties, suggestions, and commands, he answered with a gentle but inflexible denial, an utter disregard of self, and looks of silent love that Cecil never could forget.

The rain fell now in torrents, the gale steadily increased, and the waves were white with foam as they dashed high against the rocky shore of the island which the little boat was struggling to reach. Nearer and nearer it crept, as Germain urged it on with the strength of desperation, till, taking advantage of a coming billow, they were carried up and left upon the sand, with a violence that nearly threw them on their faces. Cecil sprang out at once; Germain leaned over the broken oars panting heavily, as if conscious of nothing but the suffering that racked him.

Her voice roused him, but only to fresh exertion, for seizing her hand he staggered up the bank, flung open the door of the hut, and dropped down at her feet as if in truth he had given his life to save her. For a moment she was in despair; she ran out into the storm, called, waved her handkerchief, and looked far and near, hoping some passing boat might bring help. But nothing human was in sight; the nearest point of land was inaccessible, for an ebbing wave had washed the boat away, and she was utterly alone with the unconscious man upon the barren island. She had a brave spirit, a quick wit, and these were her supporters now, as, forgetting her own fears, she devoted herself to her suffering comrade. Fortunately, her vinaigrette was in her pocket, and water plentiful; using these simple remedies with skill, the deathlike swoon yielded at last, and Germain revived.

With the return of consciousness he seemed to remember her situation before his own, and exert himself to lighten its discomforts by feeble efforts to resume his place as protector. As soon as he had breath enough to speak, he whispered, with a reassuring glance, "Do not be afraid, I will take care of you. The pain has gone for this time, and I shall be better soon."

"Think of yourself, not me. If I only had a fire to dry and warm you I should be quite happy and content," answered Cecil, looking round the gloomy place that darkened momentarily.

With the courtesy as native to him as his impetuosity, Germain tried to rise as he took out a little case and pointed toward a corner of the hut.

"You need fire more than I; here are matches, there is wood; help me a little and you shall be 'quite happy and content.'"

But as he spoke the case dropped from his hand, and he fell back with a sharp pang that warned him to submit.

"Lie still and let me care for you; I like to do it, and the exercise will keep me warm. Here is wood enough to last all night, and with light and heat we shall be very comfortable till morning and help comes."

With the heartiness of a true woman when compassion stirs her, Cecil fell to work, and soon the dark hut glowed with a cheery blaze, the wooden shutter was closed, excluding wind and rain, the straw scattered here and there was gathered into a bed for Germain, and with her cloak over him, he lay regarding her with an expression that both touched and troubled her, so humble, grateful, and tender was it. When all was done, she stepped to the door, thinking she heard the sound of passing oars; nothing appeared, however, but as she listened on the threshold Germain's voice called her with an accent of the intensest longing.

"Do not leave me! Come back to me, my darling, and let nothing part us anymore."

She thought he was wandering, and gave no answer but a soothing "Hush, rest now, poor Germain."

"Never that again; call me Father, and let me die happy in my daughter's arms."

"Father?" echoed Cecil, as a thrill of wonder, joy, and blind belief shook her from head to foot.

"Yes, I may claim you at last, for I am dying. Let our heart speak; come to me, my little Cecil, for as God lives I am your father."

He struggled up, spread wide his arms, and called her in a tone of tenderness that would have carried conviction to the most careless listener. Cecil's heart did speak; instinct was quicker than memory or reason. In an instant she understood the attraction that led her to him, owned the tender tie that bound them, and was gathered to her father's bosom, untroubled by a doubt or fear. For a time there were only broken exclamations, happy tears, and demonstrations of delight, as father and daughter forgot everything but the reunion that gave them back to one another. Soon Cecil calmed herself for his sake, made him lie down again, and while she dried his hair and warmed his cold hands in her own, she began to question eagerly.

"Why was I never told of this before?" she sorrowfully said, regretting the long years of ignorance that had deferred the happiness which made that hour so bright, in spite of darkness and danger.

"My life depended upon secrecy, and this knowledge would have been no joy, but a shame and sorrow to you, my poor child."

"Mamma always told me that you died when I was a baby; did she believe it?"

"No, she knew I was alive, but in one sense I did die to her, and all the world, for a convict has no country, home, or friends."

"A convict!" And Cecil shrank involuntarily.

He saw it, but clung to her, saying imploringly, "Hear me before you cast me off. Try to pity and forgive me, for with all his sins your father loves you better than his life."

"I do not cast you off—I will love, pity, and forgive; believe this, and trust your daughter, now that she is yours again."

Cecil spoke tenderly, and tried to reassure him with every affectionate demonstration she could devise, for the one word "father" had unlocked her heart, and all its pent-up passion flowed freely now that a natural vent was found. Lying with her hand in his, August Stein told the story of the past, and Cecil learned the secret of her father's and her husband's life.

"Dear, nineteen years ago Bazil and your mother were betrothed. The gifted young man was a fit mate for the beautiful girl, and but for me they might have been a happy pair this day. In an evil hour I saw her, loved her, and resolved to win her in spite of every obstacle, for my passions ruled me, and opposition only made me the more resolute and reckless. I used every art to dazzle, captivate, and win her, even against her will, and I succeeded; but the brief infatuation was not love, and though she fled with me, she soon discovered that her heart still clung to Bazil. Well it might, for though we had wronged him deeply he took no revenge, and would have helped us in our sorest strait. We were not happy, for I led a wild life, and your mother longed for home. Her father disowned her, when our secret marriage was discovered, her friends deserted her, and for a year we wandered from place to place, growing poorer and more wretched as hope after hope failed. I had squandered my own fortune, and had no means of earning a livelihood except my voice. That had won me my wife, and I tried to sing my way to competence for her sake. To do this, I was obliged to leave her; I always did so reluctantly, for the birth of my little daughter made the mother dearer than before. Cecil, always remember that I loved you both with all the fervor of an undisciplined nature, and let that fact lighten your condemnation of what follows."

"I shall remember, Father."

"Coming home unexpectedly one day, I found Bazil there. He had discovered us and, seeing our poverty, generously offered help. I should have thanked and honored him for that, but knowing that he did it for Cecilia's sake I hated and distrusted him, refused his kindness, and forbade him the house. He bore with me, promised your mother that he would befriend her, and went away, hoping I would relent when I was calmer. His nobleness made my own conduct seem more base; the knowledge that my wife reproached me for destroying her happiness wounded me deeply; and the thought that Bazil saw my failure and pitied me rankled in my heart and made me miserable. I had been brooding darkly over these things as I returned from my distasteful work a night or two later, and was in a desperate mood. As I entered quietly, I saw a man bending over the cradle where my baby lay; I thought it was Bazil, my wrath rose hot against him, some devil goaded me to it, and I felled him with a single blow. But when the light shone on his dead face I saw that it was not Bazil but the young surgeon who had saved both wife and child for me."

There was a long pause, broken only by Stein's fluttering breath and Cecil's whisper.

"Do not go on; be quiet and forget."

"I cannot forget or be quiet till I tell you everything. I was tried, sentenced to imprisonment for life, and for ten years was as dead to the world as if I had lain in my grave. I raged and pined like a savage creature in my prison, made many desperate attempts to escape, and at last succeeded. I left Australia, and after wandering east and west, a homeless vagabond for two weary years, I ventured back to England, hoping to learn something of my wife, as no tidings of her had reached me all those years. I could not find her, and dared not openly inquire; Yorke tells me she concealed herself from everyone, accepted nothing even from him, but devoted herself to you, and waited patiently till it pleased heaven to release her."

"Poor Mamma! Now I know how heavy her burden must have been, and why she longed to lay it down."

"Child, she did not find it half so heavy as I found mine, nor long to lay it down as bitterly as I have longed for eighteen years. If she had loved me it would have saved us both, for affection can win and hold me as nothing else has power to do. It has done much for me already, because, since I knew you, my darling, I have learned to repent and, for your sake, to atone, as far as may be, for my wasted life."

"It is very sweet to hear you say that, Father, and to feel that I have helped you, even unconsciously. Now leave the sorrowful past, and tell me how you found Bazil and myself."

"Growing bold, after two years of safety, I ventured to inquire for Yorke, thinking that he could tell me something of your mother. He had left Germany, where we first met, and had gone home to America. I followed, and found him leading the solitary life you know so well. He was so changed I hardly recognized him; I was still more altered, and trusting to the disguise which had baffled keener eyes than his, I offered myself as a model, feeling curiously drawn to him as the one link between Cecilia and myself. He accepted my services, and paid me well, for I was very poor; he pitied me, knowing only that I was a lonely creature like himself, and so generously befriended me that I could not harden my heart against him; but overpowered by remorse and gratitude I betrayed myself, and put my life into his hands, only asking to see or hear of my wife. He knew nothing of her then, but with a magnanimity that bound me to him forever, he kept my secret, and endeavored to forgive the wrong which he never could entirely forget."

"O Basil, so generous, so gentle, why did I not know this sooner, and thank you as I ought?"

The tender words were drowned in sudden tears, as Cecil hid her face, weeping with mingled self-reproach and joy over each revelation that showed her something more to love and honor in her husband. But she soon dried her tears to listen, for her father hurried on as if anxious to be done.

"I saw you, my child, the night you came, and was sure you were mine, you were so like your mother. I implored Basil to let me have you, when I knew that she was gone, but he would not, having promised to guard you from me, and never let your life be saddened by the knowledge of your convict father. He has kept that promise sacredly, and bound me to an equal silence, under penalty of betrayal if I break it, except as I do now, when I have nothing more to fear. He let me see you secretly, when you slept, or walked, or were busy at your work, for he had not the heart to deny me that. Ah, Cecil, you never knew how near I often was to you—never guessed what right I had to love you, or how much I longed to tell you who I was. More than once I forgot myself, and would have broken my word at any cost, but something always checked me in time, and Basil's patience was long-suffering. The night he let me see and sing to you did me more good than years of prison life, for you unconsciously touched all that was best in me, and by the innocent affection that you could not control made that hour more beautiful and precious than I can tell you. Since then, whether near or absent, gloomy or gay, I have regarded you as my saving angel, and tried in my poor way to be more worthy of you, and earn a place in your memory when I am gone."

Such love and gratitude shone in his altered face that Cecil could only lay her head upon his shoulder, praying that he might be spared for a longer, better life, and a calmer death at last. Soon her father spoke again, smiling the old sweet smile, as he caressed the beautiful head that leaned against him as if its place were there.

"Did my little girl think me a desperate lover, with my strange devices to attract and win her? Basil told me that I frightened you, and I tried to control myself; but it was so hard to stand aside and see my own child pass me like a stranger, that I continually forgot your ignorance and betrayed how dear you were to me. What did you think of that mysterious Germain?"

"What could I think but that he loved me? How could I dream that you were my father when all my life I had believed you dead? Even now I almost doubt it, you are so young, so charming and lighthearted when you please."

"I am past forty, Cecil, and what I am is only the shadow of what I was, a man endowed with many good gifts; but all have been wasted or misused, owing to a neglected education, a wayward will, an impetuous nature, and a sanguine spirit, which has outlived disgrace and desolation, suffering and time."

"And this is the mystery that has perplexed me for so long. I think you might have told me as well as Bazil, and let me do my part to make you happy, Father."

"I longed to do so, and assured him that we might trust you; but he would not break his promise to your mother. It was wise, though very hard to bear. I was not a fit guardian for a beautiful young girl like mine, and I knew it, yet I wanted you, and made his life a burden to him by my importunity. Love him, Cecil, love him faithfully, for he has spared you much sorrow, and through you has saved your father."

She did not answer, but looking into her face, he was satisfied. Thus opening their hearts to one another, the night wore on, yet neither found it long, and when at last Stein slept, exhausted, Cecil sat beside him, thinking happy thoughts, while the wind raved without, the rain beat on the low roof, the sea thundered round the island, and Yorke went searching for her far and wide.

Morning dawned at last, and as her father still slept, she opened the little window, that the balmy air might refresh him, put up her signal of distress, and sat down to watch and wait. The sound of hurrying feet roused her from her reverie, and looking up, she saw her husband coming toward her, so changed and haggard that her joy turned to fear. Dreading to excite her father, she instantly glanced over her shoulder, and barred the entrance with her extended arm. Her gesture, her expression, instantly arrested Yorke, and while Judas fawned delightedly about her feet, he stood apart, with the sad certainty that she was not alone, to mar his joy at finding her.

"Is he there?" was his first question, sternly put.

"Yes; he is ill and sleeping; you must not disturb him. Blame me if you will, but he shall be left in peace."

She spoke resolutely, and closed the door between them and the sleeper, keeping her place upon the threshold, as if ready to defend him, for Yorke's manner alarmed her even more than his wild appearance. The action seemed to affect him like an insult; he seized her arm, and holding it in a painful grasp, eyed her almost fiercely, as he said, with a glance that made her tremble, "Then you did leave me sleeping, and go away with this man, to be wrecked here, and so be discovered?"

"Yes; why should I deny it?"

"And you love him, Cecil?"

"With all my heart and soul, and you can never part us anymore."

As she answered, with a brave, bright smile, and a glad voice, she felt Yorke quiver as if he had received a blow, saw his face whiten, and heard an accent of despair in his voice, when he said slowly, "You will leave him, if I command it?"

"No—he has borne enough. I can make him happy, and I shall cling to him through everything, for you have no right to take me from him."

"No right?" ejaculated Yorke, loosening his hold, with a bewildered look.

"None that I will submit to, if it parts us. You let me know him, let me learn to love him, and now, when he needs me most, you would take me from him. Bazil, you have been very generous, very kind to both of us, and I am truly grateful, but while he lives, I must stay with him, because I have promised."

He looked at her with a strange expression, at first as if he felt his senses going, then he seemed to find a clue to her persistency. A bitter laugh escaped him, but his voice betrayed wounded pride and poignant sorrow.

"I understand now; you intend to hold me to my bond, and see in me nothing but your guardian. You are as ignorant as headstrong, if you think this possible. I gave up that foolish delusion long ago, and tried to show you a truer, happier tie. But you were blind and would not see, deaf and would not hear, hardhearted and would not relent."

"You bade me be a marble woman, with no heart to love you, only grace and beauty, to please your eye and do you honor. Have I not obeyed you to the letter?"

Coldly and quietly she spoke, yet kept her eyes on the ground, her hand on her breast, as if to hold some rebellious emotion in check. As the soft voice reechoed the words spoken long ago, all that scene came back to Yorke, and made the present moment doubly hard to bear.

"You have, you have! God forgive me for the wrong I did you. I tried to atone for it, but I have failed, and this is my punishment."

He spoke humbly, despairingly, and his proud eyes filled as he turned his face to hide the grief he was ashamed to show. Cecil stood with bent head, and face half hidden by her falling hair, but though she trembled, she compelled voice and features to obey her with the ease which long practice had made second nature.

"If you had cared to teach me a gentler lesson, I would have gladly learned it; but you did not, and having done your best to kill love in my heart, you should not reproach me if you are disappointed now, or wonder that I turn to others for the affection without which none of us can live."

"I will not reproach; I do not wonder, but I cannot give you up. Cecil, there is still time to relent, and to return; let me tell you how hard I have tried to make you love me, in spite of my own decree, and perhaps my patience, my penitence, may touch your heart. I will not urge my right as husband, but plead as lover. Will you listen?"

"Yes."

Cecil stole a glance at him as she spoke, and a curious smile touched her lips, though she listened with beating heart to words poured out with the rapidity of strong emotion.

"When you came to me, I kept you because you were like your mother, whom I loved, and who deserted me. That loss embittered my whole nature, and I resolved to make your life as loveless as my own. It seemed a small atonement for a great wrong, and believing that it was just to visit the sins of the parents upon the children, I carried out my purpose with a blind persistency that looks like madness to me now. But the sentiment I had forsworn revenged itself upon me, and while trying to cheat you of love, it crept into my own heart, and ruled me like a tyrant. Unconsciously, I loved you long before I knew it; that was why I disliked Alfred, why I was so willing to marry you, and why I was so disappointed when others found in you the same want that I felt yet would not own. The night I watched beside you, fearing you would never wake, I found the key to my own actions, saw my delusion, and resolved to conquer it."

He paused for breath, but Cecil did not speak, though the hidden face brightened, and the heart fluttered like a caged bird.

"I could not conquer it, for it was my master. You can never know how hard I tried, how rebellious my pride was, or how firm my purpose, but all failed, and I was forced to own that my happiness, my peace, depended upon you. Then I determined to undo my six years' work, to teach you how to love, and make my wife mine in heart as in name. I gave myself wholly to the task of winning you; I studied your tastes, gratified your whims, and tried every art that can attract a woman. You were tired of the old home, and I gave you a new one; you enjoyed Germain's society, and I let him come, in defiance of my better judgment; you had some pride in my talent, for your sake I displayed it; you loved pleasure, and I labored to supply it freely; I even tried to lure you with splendor and bribe you with diamonds. But I had lost my skill, and all my efforts were in vain, for no veritable marble woman could have received my gifts more coldly, or ignored my unspoken love more utterly than you. One smile like those you daily gave Germain would have repaid me, but you never shed it over me; one frank word or affectionate look would have brought me to your feet; but all the compassion, confidence, and tenderness were given to others—for me you had only indifference, gratitude, and respect. Cecil, I have suffered one long torment since I married you, longing for my true place, yet not daring to claim it, lest I should rouse aversion and not love."

Still with her head bent, her face hidden, and her hand upon her heart, she stood, and Yorke went on, more passionately than before.

"I know that I have forfeited my right to expect affection or demand obedience, but I implore you to forget this infatuation, and retrieve this rash step. You do not know what you are doing, for this will mar your whole life, and make mine worthless. Cecil, come back to me, and let me try again to win you! I will work and wait for years, will be your servant, not your master, will bear and suffer anything if I may hope to touch your heart at last. Is this impossible? Do you love Alfred more than reputation, home, or husband?"

"I never have loved Alfred."

"Then who, in God's name, is this man to whom you will cling through everything?"

"My father."

She looked up now, and turned on him a face so full of hope and joy, that he stood dumb with astonishment as she drew nearer and nearer, with outstretched hands, beaming eyes, and tender voice.

"O Bazil! I know all; the past is forgiven, your long labor and atonement are over, and there is no need for you to work or wait, because my heart always has been yours."

If the dead Cecilia had come to him in the youthful guise she used to wear, it would not have more amazed and startled him than did these words from his wife's lips, and not till he felt her clinging to him so trustfully, so tenderly, did he fully realize his happiness.

"What does it mean? Why keep this from me so long? Did you not see I loved you, Cecil?"

"It means that I, too, tried to conquer myself, and failed. Till very lately, I was not sure you loved me, and I could not bear to be repulsed again."

"Ah, there is the thorn that has vexed you! You are a true woman, in spite of all my training, and you could not forget that hour, so I had to suffer till you were appeased. Is it possible that my innocent, artless girl could lay such plots, and wear a mask so long, that she might subdue her guardian's proud heart?"

"Everything is possible to a woman when she loves, and you were only conquered with your own weapons, Bazil. Let me make my confession now, and you shall see that you have not suffered, worked, and waited all alone. When you bade me renounce love, I found it very hard to kill the affection that had grown warmer than you chose to have it. But I did my best to seem what you desired me to be, and your lessons of self-control stood me in good stead. I chilled and hardened myself rigorously; I forced myself to be meek, cold, and undemonstrative to you, whatever I might be to others; I took opium, that I might forget my pain, and feign the quietude I could not feel, and I succeeded beyond my hopes. When you asked me to marry you, I was half prepared for it, because Alfred insisted that you loved me. I wished to believe it; I wanted to stay, and would have frankly owned how dear you were to me, if you had not insisted upon offering me protection, but no love. That night I resolved to show you your mistake, to prove to you that you had a heart, and teach you a better lesson than any you had taught your pupil."

"You have done so, little dearest, and I am your scholar henceforth. Teach me gently, and I will study all my days. What more, Cecil?"

"I found it very hard to resist when you grew so kind, and should have been sure you loved me, but for Germain. Why you let him come, and showed no displeasure at my delight in his society, was so inexplicable to me that I would not yield till I was satisfied. Last night my father told me all, and if anything could make you dearer, it would be the knowledge of the great debt we owe you. My generous, patient husband, how can I thank you as I ought?"

He showed her how, and for several minutes they stood in the sunshine, very silent, very happy, while the waves broke softly on the shore, as if all storms had passed away forever. Yorke spoke first.

"One thing more, Cecil, lest I forget it, for this sudden happiness has turned my brain, I think, and nothing is clear to me but that you are mine. What does this mean?" And drawing out the card, he held it before her eyes, with some anxiety dimming the brightness of his own.

She took it, tore it up, and as the white shreds went flying away on the wind, she said smiling, "Let all your jealous fears go with them, never to come back again. What a miserable night you must have had, if you believed that I had left you for Alf."

"An awful night, Cecil," and he told her all the wanderings and his fears.

"I will not say that you deserved it for harboring such a thought, because you have suffered enough, and it is so much sweeter to forgive than to reproach. But you must promise never to be jealous anymore, not even of 'poor Alf.'"

The happy-hearted laugh he had so longed to hear gladdened his ear, as she looked up at him with the arch expression that made her charming.

"I'll try," he answered meekly, "but keep him away till I am very sure you love me, else I shall surely fling him into the sea, as I nearly did the night Sir Walter and the marquise tormented me. Why did he come? And why did you meet him yesterday?"

"He came to tell me that he had replaced my image with a more gracious one, for when he heard that I was married, he cast me off, and found consolation in his pretty cousin's smiles. His was a boyish love, ardent but short-lived, and he is happy now, with one who loves him as I never could have loved. Hearing of our masque, he planned to come in disguise, and tell his story as a stranger, that he might the better watch its effect on me. But I knew him instantly, and we enjoyed mystifying those about us, till I forgot him in my own mystification. You did not wish him to come again, so I wrote to him, saying good-bye, and begging him to go at once. The disobedient boy had more to tell me, and sent word he should be on the beach at five. I knew he would come to the house unless I met him, and fearing a scene—for you have grown very tragic, dear—I went. He delayed so long that he had only time to hurry across to the lower depot for the last train, leaving his boat to Father and myself."

"What misery the knowledge of this would have spared me! Why did you not tell me, when we were together yesterday, that Alfred had forgotten you?"

"I meant to do so, but you gave me no opportunity, for you were so restless and strange I was half afraid of you. Besides, since you had confessed jealousy, I hoped you would confess love also, and I waited, thinking it would come."

"How could I own it, when *you* had confessed you loved a younger man than I, and my eyes were blinded by Alfred's silence and your own?"

"I did not tell you that it was my father. Did he betray me?"

She looked perplexed, and Yorke half ashamed, as he confessed another proof of his affection.

"It was I, Cecil, who came to you in the garden, who questioned you, and was stabbed to the heart by your answers. Good heavens, how blind I've been!"

"Never reproach me with treachery, after that. Why did you change dresses? To try me?"

"Yes; and as you sat there so near me, so gentle, frank, and beautiful, I found it almost impossible to sustain my character; but I knew if I revealed myself, you would freeze again, and all the charm be gone. Heaven knows I was a miserable man that night, for you disappointed me, and Alfred drove me half mad; but your father saw my folly, and saved me from myself. God bless him for that!"

"Yes, God bless him for that, and for saving me to be your happy wife. Come now and wake him; he has been very ill, and needs care."

They went, and kneeling by him, Cecil called him gently, but he did not answer; and taking her into his arms, her husband whispered tenderly, "Dear, he will never wake again."

Never again in this world, for the restless heart was still at last, and the sunshine fell upon a face of such reposeful beauty that it was evident the long sleep had painlessly deepened into death.

The Skeleton
in the Closet

"LOUIS, to whom does that château belong?" I asked, as we checked our horses under the antique gateway, and my eye, following the sweep of the lawn, caught a glimpse of the mansion embosomed in a blooming paradise of flowers and grand old trees.

"To Mme. Arnheim, the loveliest widow in all France," Louis answered, with a sigh.

"And the cruelest, I fancy, or you would have been master here," I replied, interpreting the sigh aright, for my friend was a frequent captive to the gentle sex.

"Never its master, Gustave—I should always have remained a slave while Mathilde was there," he answered, with a moody glance through the iron gates that seemed to bar him from the heaven of his desire.

"Nay, Louis, come down from the clouds and tell me something of the Circe whose spells have ensnared you; come hither and sit on this little knoll where we have a better view of the château, and while our horses rest, you shall tell the story of your love, as the romances have it." And dismounting as I spoke, I threw myself upon the green sward opposite the flowery lawn that sloped up to the terraces whereon the château stood.

Louis flung himself beside me, saying abruptly, "There is no tale to tell, Gustave. I met Mathilde at the general's a year ago—loved her, of course, and of course without success. I say of course, for I am not the only one that has laid siege to her cold heart, and got frostbitten in the attempt. She is a marble image, beautiful and cold, though there are rare flashes of warmth that win, a softness that enchants, which make her doubly dangerous. She lives yonder with her old duenna, Mlle. D'Aubigny, caring little for the world, and seldom blessing it with her presence. She has made an Eden, but desires no Adam, and is content to dwell year after year solitary in her flowery nook like the English poet's Lady of Shalott."

"And trust me, like that mysterious lady, she, too, will one day see—

> *"A bow-shot from her bower-eaves,*
> *Riding 'mong the barley-sheaves,*
> *The sunlight dazzling thro' the leaves,*
> *And flashing on his greaves*
> *   A bold Sir Lancelot.*
> *She'll leave her web, and leave her loom,*
> *She'll make three paces thro' the room,*
> *She'll see the water-lilies bloom,*
> *She'll see the helmet and the plume,*
> *   And follow down to Camelot,"*

chanted I, making a free translation of the lines to suit my jest.

"There she is! Look, Gustave, look!" cried Louis, springing to his feet, with an eager gesture toward the lawn.

I looked, almost expecting to behold the shadowy lady of the poet's song, so fully had the beauty of the spot enchanted me. A female figure was passing slowly down the broad steps that led from terrace to terrace into the shaded avenue. Silently I drew Louis into the deep shadow of the gateway, where we could look unperceived.

The slender, white-robed figure came slowly on, pausing now and then to gather a flower, or caress the Italian greyhound tripping daintily beside her. My interest was excited by my friend's words, and I looked eagerly for the beauty he extolled. She *was* beautiful—and when she paused in the shadow of a drooping acacia, and stood looking thoughtfully toward the blue lake shining in the distance, I longed to be an artist, that I might catch and keep the picture.

The sunshine fell upon her through the leaves, turning her hair to gold, touching the soft bloom of her cheek, and rendering more fair the graceful arms half bared by the fresh wind tossing the acacia boughs. A black lace scarf was thrown about her, one end drawn over her blond hair, as the Spanish women wear their veils; a few brilliant flowers filled her hands, and gave coloring to her unornamented dress. But the chief charm of her delicate face was the eyes, so lustrous and dark, so filled with the soft gloom of a patient grief that they touched and won my heart by their mute loveliness.

We stood gazing eagerly, forgetting in our admiration the discourtesy of the act, till a shrill neigh from my horse startled us, and woke Mme. Arnheim from her reverie. She cast a quick glance down the avenue, and turning, was soon lost to us in the shelter of a winding path.

"Come, Louis, come away before we are discovered; it was a rude act, and I am ashamed of it," I cried, drawing him away, though my eye still watched the lover, hoping for another glance.

Louis lingered, saying bitterly, "Gustave, I envy that dog the touch of her hand, the music of her voice, and proud as I am, would follow her like a hound, even though she chid me like one, for I love her as I never loved before, and I have no hope."

Wondering no longer at the passion of my friend, I made no reply to his gloomy words, but turning away, we mounted, and with a lingering look behind, departed silently. Louis returned to Paris; I to my friend General Moreau, at whose hospitable home I was visiting to recruit my health, shattered by long illness.

The general's kind lady, even amid her cares as hostess to a mansion full of friends, found time to seek amusement for her feeble guest, and when I had exhausted her husband's stock of literature, as if prompted by some good angel she proposed a visit to Mme. Arnheim to bespeak for me admission to her well-stored library.

Concealing my delight, I cheerfully accompanied Mme. Moreau, asking sundry questions as we drove along, concerning the fair recluse. There was a slight reserve in Madame's manner as she answered me.

"Mathilde has known much sorrow in her short life, *mon ami*, and seeks to forget the past in the calmness of the present. She seldom visits us except we are alone—then she comes often, for the general regards her with a fatherly affection; and in her society I feel no want of other friends."

"Has she been long a widow?" I asked, impelled by a most unmasculine curiosity to learn yet more.

"Seven years," replied Madame. "Her husband was a German—but I know little of her past life, for she seldom speaks of it, and I have only gathered from the few allusions she has made to it, that she married very young, and knew but little happiness as a wife."

I longed to ask yet more, and though courtesy restrained my tongue, my eyes betrayed me; Mme. Moreau, who had taken the invalid to her motherly heart, could not resist that mute appeal, for, as she drew up the window to shield me from the freshening breeze, she said smilingly:

"Ah, my child, I may repent this visit if I lead you into temptation, for boy as you seem to me, there is a man's heart in this slight frame of yours and a love of beauty shining in these hollow eyes. I cannot satisfy you, Gustave—she came hither but two years ago, and has lived secluded from the world, regardless of many solicitations to quit her solitude and widowhood. Your friend Louis was one of her most earnest suitors, but, like the rest, only procured his own banishment, for Mathilde only desires friends and not lovers. Therefore, let me warn you, if you desire the friendship of this charming woman, beware of love. But see, we have arrived, so bid adieu to ennui for a while at least."

Up the wide steps and over the green terraces we passed into a room whose chief charm was its simplicity; no costly furniture encumbered it, no tasteless decorations marred it; a few rare pictures enriched its walls, and a few graceful statues looked out from flowery nooks. Light draperies swayed to and fro before the open casements, giving brief glimpses of bloom and verdure just without. Leafy shadows flickered on the marble floor, and the blithe notes of birds were the only sounds that broke the sunny silence brooding over the whole scene.

Well as I fancied I remembered Mme. Arnheim, I was struck anew with the serene beauty of her face as she greeted us with cordial courtesy.

A rapt pity seemed to fill the pensive eyes as Madame spoke of my long illness, and her whole manner was full of interest, and a friendly wish to serve that captivated me and made me bless the pallid face that wore so sweet a pity for me.

We visited the library, a fascinating place to me, full of rare old books, and the soft gloom of shade and silence so dear to a student's heart. A few graceful words made me welcome here, and I promised myself many blissful hours in a spot so suited to my taste and fancy.

"Come now to the chapel, where M. Novaire will find another friend whose sweet discourse may have power to beguile some hours of their slow flight," said Mme. Arnheim, as she led the way into a little chapel rich in Gothic arches and stained windows, full of saintly legends that recalled the past.

"Ah, yes, here is indeed a treasure for you, Gustave—I had forgotten this," said Mme. Moreau, as our hostess led me to a fine organ, and with a smile invited me to touch its tempting keys.

With a desire to excel never experienced before, I obeyed, and filled the air with surges of sweet sound that came and went like billows breaking melodiously on the strand. Mme. Arnheim listened with drooping eyes and folded hands; and as I watched her standing in the gloom with one mellow ray of sunlight falling on her golden hair, she seemed to my excited fancy a white-robed spirit with the light of heaven shining on its gentle head.

The beautiful eyes were full of tender dew as they met mine in thanking me, and a certain deference seemed to mark her manner, as if the music I had power to create were a part of myself, and still lingered about me when the organ keys were mute.

Returning toward the château, we found a dainty little feast spread on a rustic table in the shadow of a group of foreign trees. No servants appeared, but Mme. Arnheim served us herself with a cordial ease that rendered doubly sweet the light wines she poured for us, and the nectarines she gathered from the sunny wall.

It was a new and wonderfully winning thing to me to see a creature beautiful and gifted—so free from affectation, so unconscious of self, so childlike, yet so full of all the nameless charms of gracious womanhood. To an imaginative temperament like mine it was doubly dangerous, and I dreaded to depart.

I sat apparently listening to the low dash of the fountain, but eye, ear, and mind were all intent on her; watching the pliant grace of her slender form, listening to the silvery music of her voice, and musing on the changeful beauty of her countenance. As I thus regarded her, my eye was caught by the sole ornament she wore, an ornament so peculiar and so ill-suited to its gentle wearer that my attention was arrested by it.

As she refilled my glass, a bracelet slipped from her arm to her wrist, and in that brief moment I had examined it attentively. It was of steel, delicately wrought, clasped by a golden lock, the tiny key of which hung by a golden chain. A strange expression stirred the sweet composure of her face as she saw the direction of my glance, and with a sudden gesture she thrust the trinket out of sight.

But as her hands moved daintily among the fruit in serving us, the bracelet often fell with a soft clash about her slender wrist, and each time she thrust it back, till her white arm was reddened with the marks of its slight links.

It seemed a most unfitting ornament, and as I watched her closely, I fancied some sad memory was connected with it, for the sight of it seemed painful, and all notice irksome to her. Ah, I little knew to what a fate it fettered her!

As we stood upon the terrace, awaiting the carriage, I turned from the château with its airy balconies without, and its inviting apartments within, to the blooming scene before me, exclaiming with enthusiasm, "This is the loveliest spot in France! A perfect picture of a peaceful, happy home. Ah, madame, many must envy you this tranquil retreat from the cares and sorrows of the world."

Mme. Arnheim's dark eyes wandered over the fair home I admired, and again I saw that strange expression flit across her face, but now more vividly than before. Pain, abhorrence, and despair seemed to sit for an instant on those lovely features; a swift paroxysm of mute anguish seemed to thrill through her whole figure; and I saw the half-hidden hands clenched as if controlling some wild impulse with an iron will. Like a flash it came and went, and with a long, deep sigh she answered slowly, "Do not envy me, for you have all the world before, free to choose a home where fancy leads. This is my world, and is often wearisome for all its loveliness."

There was a mournful cadence in her voice that saddened me, and a black shadow seemed to fall across the sunny landscape as I listened. The carriage came, and when she turned to say adieu, no trace of gloom marred the sweet serenity of her pale countenance.

"Come often and come freely, Monsieur Novaire," she said, adding, with a smile that would have won from me any boon I had the power to bestow, "My books, my organ, and my gardens are most sincerely at your service, and I only claim the right to listen when you fill my little chapel with the melody I love so well."

I could only thank her in words that sounded very poor and cold, remembering the sweetness of her own, and we drove away, leaving her in the shadow of the hall, still smiling her adieu.

Frankly as the favor had been granted, I accepted it, and went often to the château which soon became a "Castle Dangerous," and its fair mistress the one beloved object in the world to me. Day after day I went to muse in the quiet library, or to soothe my restless spirit with the music of the chapel organ. Mme. Arnheim I but seldom saw until I learned the spell which had power to lure her to my longing eyes. At the château she was the stately hostess, always courteous and calm, but when I sat alone in the chapel, filling the air with the plaintive or triumphal melody, I never failed to see a shadow gliding past the open door, or hear the light fall of a step along the echoing aisles, and with an altered mien she came to listen as I spoke to her in the tenderest strains heart could devise or hand execute.

This filled me with a sense of power I exulted in, for, remembering Mme. Moreau's warning words, "If you desire Mathilde's friendship, beware of love," I concealed my growing passion, and only gave it vent in the music that lured her to my side, and spoke to her in accents that never could offend. Slowly the coldness of her manner vanished, and though still chary of her presence, she came at last to treat me as a friend. At rare intervals some sudden interest in the book I read, some softened mood produced by the song I sang, the strain I played, gave me glimpses of a nature so frank and innocent, and a heart so deep and tender, that the hope of winning it seemed vain, and I reproached myself with treachery in accepting thus the hospitalities of her home and the blessing of her friendship, while so strong a love burned like a hidden fire in my breast.

Calmly the days flowed by, and nothing marred my peace till a slight incident filled me with restless doubts and fears. Wandering one day among the gardens, led by the desire of meeting Mathilde, I struck into an unfrequented path which wound homeward round a wing of the château which I had never visited and which I had believed unused. Pausing on the hillside to examine it, my eye fell on an open window opposite the spot where I was standing, and just within it I beheld Mathilde sitting with bent head and averted face. Eager to catch a glimpse of that beloved countenance, I stood motionless, screened by a drooping tree. As I peered further into the shaded room a jealous pang shot through me and my heart stood still, for in the high carved chair beside Mathilde I saw the arm and shoulder of a man. With straining eyes I watched it, and set my teeth fiercely when I saw the arm encircle her graceful neck, while the hand played idly with a tress of sunny hair I would have given worlds to touch. The arm was clothed in the sleeve of a damask robe de chambre, somber yet rich, and the hand seemed delicate and white; its motions were languid and I heard the murmur of a low voice often broken by faint laughter.

I could not move, but stood rooted to the spot till Mathilde dropped the curtain, and a moment after her voice rose soft and sweet, singing to that unknown guest, then I turned and dashed into the wood like one possessed.

From that day my peace was gone, for though Mathilde was unchanged, between us there always seemed to rise the specter of that hidden friend or lover, and I could not banish the jealous fears that tortured me. I knew from Mme. Moreau that Mathilde had no relatives in France, and few friends beside the general and his wife. The unknown was no cousin, no brother then, and I brooded over the mystery in vain. A careless inquiry of a servant if there were any guests at the château received a negative reply, given with respectful brevity and a quick, scrutinizing glance—while, as he spoke, down through hall and corridor floated the sound of Mathilde's voice singing in that far-off room.

Once more, and only once, I watched that window, waiting long in vain, but the curtain was thrown back at length, and then I saw

Mathilde pacing to and fro with clasped hands and streaming eyes, as if full of some passionate despair; while the low laughter, I remember well, seemed mocking her great sorrow.

She came to the casement and flung it wide, leaning far out, as if to seek consolation in the caressing breath of the balmy air and the soft sighing of the pines. As she stood thus, I saw her strike her fettered arm a cruel blow upon the strong stone balcony enclosing the window—a blow which left it bruised; though she never heeded it, but turned again into the room, as if in answer to some quick command.

I never looked again—for whatever secret sin or sorrow was there concealed, I had no right to know it, for by no look or word did Mathilde ever seek my sympathy or aid; but with a growing paleness on her cheek, a deepening sadness in her eye, she met me with unaltered kindness, and listened when I played as if she found her only solace there.

So the summer passed, and silently the hidden passion that possessed me did its work, till the wan shadow that once mocked me from my mirror was changed into the likeness of an ardent, healthful man, clear of eye, strong of arm, and light of foot. They said it was the fresh air of the hills; I knew it was the healing power of a beloved presence and the magic of an earnest love.

One soft September day, I had wandered with Mathilde into the deep ravine that cleft a green hill not far from the château. We had sat listening to the music of the waterfall as it mingled pleasantly with our conversation, till a sudden peal of thunder warned us home. Shut in by the steep cliffs, the gathering clouds had been unobserved until the tempest was close at hand. We hastily wound our way up from below, and paused a moment to look out upon the wildly beautiful scene.

Standing thus, there came a sudden glare before my eyes, followed by a deafening crash that brought me faint and dizzy to the ground. A flood of rain revived me, and on recovering I was conscious that Mathilde's arms encircled me, and my head was pillowed on her bosom; I felt the rapid beating of her heart, and heard the prayers she was murmuring as she held me thus. Her mantle was thrown about me, as if to shield me from the storm, and shrouded in its silken folds I lay as if in a dream, with no fear of thunderbolt or lightning flash—conscious only of the soft arms enfolding me, the faint perfume of her falling hair, and the face so near my own that every whispered word fell clearly on my ear.

How long I should have remained thus I cannot tell, for warmer drops than rain fell on my cheek and recalled me to myself. Putting aside the frail screen she had placed between me and the sudden danger, I staggered to my feet, unmindful of my dizzy brain and still half-blinded eyes.

"Not dead! Not dead! Thank God for that" was the glad cry that broke from Mathilde's lips, as I stood wild-eyed and pale before her. "O Gustave, are you unscathed by that awful bolt which I thought had murdered you before me?"

I reassured her, and felt that it was now my turn to shelter and protect, for she clung to me trembling and tearful, so changed that the calm, cold Mme. Arnheim of the fair château and the brave, tenderhearted creature on the cliff seemed two different women, but both lovely and beloved.

Swiftly and silently we hurried home, and when I would have quitted her she detained me with gentle force, saying, "You must remain my guest tonight, I cannot suffer you to leave my roof in such a storm as this."

Old Mlle. D'Aubigny bustled to and fro, and after refreshment and repose left us together by the cheerful firelight on the library hearth.

Mathilde sat silent, as if wrapped in thought, her head bent on her hand. I sat and looked at her till I forgot all but my love, and casting prudence to the winds, spoke out fervently and fast.

"Mathilde," I said, "deal frankly with me, and tell me was it *fear* or *love* that stirred this quiet heart of yours, and spoke in words of prayerful tenderness when you believed me dead? Forgive me if I pain you, but remembering that moment of unlooked-for bliss, I can no longer keep the stern silence I have imposed upon myself so long. I have loved you very truly all these months of seeming coldness, have haunted this house not in search of selfish ease, but to be near you, to breathe the air you breathed, to tread the ground you trod, and to sun myself in the light of your beloved presence. I should have been silent still, knowing my unworthiness, but as I lay pillowed on your bosom, through the tumult of the storm, a low voice from your heart seemed to speak to mine, saying 'I love you.' Tell me, dearest Mathilde, did I hear aright?"

An unwonted color dawned upon her cheek, a world of love and longing shone upon me in her glance, while a change as beautiful as it was brief passed over her, leaving in the stately woman's place a tender girl, whose heart looked from her eyes, and made her broken words more full of music than the sweetest song.

"Gustave, you heard aright; it was not fear that spoke." She stretched her hand to me, and clasping it in both my own I bent to kiss it with a lover's ardor—when between my eager lips and that fair hand dropped the *steel bracelet* with a sharp metallic sound.

With a bitter cry, Mathilde tore herself from my hold, and covering up her face shrank away, as if between us there had risen up a barrier visible to her alone.

"Mathilde, what is it? What power has this bauble, to work such a change as this? See! It is off and gone forever; for this hand is mine now, and shall wear no fetter but the golden one I give it," I cried, as kneeling on the cushion at her feet I repossessed myself of her passive hand, and unlocking the hateful bracelet, flung it far away across the room.

Apparently unconscious of my presence, Mathilde sat with such mute anguish and despair in every line of her drooping figure that a keen sense of coming evil held me silent at her feet, waiting some look or word from her.

A sharp struggle must have passed within her, for when she lifted up her face, all light and color had died out, and the whole countenance was full of some stern resolve, that seemed to have chilled its beauty into stone. Silently she motioned me to rise, and with a statelier mien than I had ever seen her wear, she passed down the long room to where the ominous steel bracelet glittered in the light. Silently she raised it, reclasped it on her arm, then with rapid motion rent away the tiny key and flung it into the red embers glowing on the hearth.

A long, shuddering sigh heaved her bosom as it vanished, a sound more eloquent of patient despair than the bitterest tears that ever fell. Coming to my side, she looked into my eyes with such love and pity shining through the pale determination of her face that I would have folded her to my breast, but with a swift gesture of that fettered arm she restrained me, saying slowly as if each word wrung her heart:

"God forgive me that I could forget the solemn duty this frail chain binds me to. Gustave, I never meant to wrong you thus, and will atone for it by giving you the confidence never bestowed on any human being. Come and see the secret anguish of my life, the haunting specter of my home, the stern fate which makes all love a bitter mockery, and leaves me desolate."

Like a shadow she flitted from me, beckoning me to follow. The storm still raged without, but all was bright and still within as we passed through gallery and hall into that distant wing of the château. The radiance of shaded lamps fell on the marble floors—graceful statues gleamed among the flowers, and the air was full of perfume, but I saw no beauty anywhere, for between me and the woman whom I loved an unknown phantom seemed to stand, and its black shadow darkened all the world to me.

Mathilde paused in a silent corridor at length, and looking back at me, whispered imploringly, "Gustave, do not judge me till I have told you all." Then before I could reply, she passed before me into a dimly lighted room, still beckoning me to follow.

Bernhardt, an old servant whom I had seldom seen, rose as she entered, and at a motion from Mathilde bade me be seated. Mechanically I obeyed, for all strength seemed to desert me as I looked upon the scene before me.

On the floor, clothed in the dress I well remembered, sat a man playing with the childish toys that lay around him. The face would have been a young and comely one, were it not for the awful blight which had fallen on it; the vacant gaze of his hollow eyes, the aimless movements of his feeble hands, and the unmeaning words he muttered to himself, all told the fearful loss of that divine gift—reason.

Mathilde pointed to the mournful wreck, saying, with a look of desolation which few human faces wear, "Gustave, am I not a widow?"

Then I knew that I saw the husband of my Mathilde—and he an idiot!

A brief sensation of mingled disgust, despair, and rage possessed me, for I knew how powerless I was to free the heart I coveted from this long slavery; one thought of Mathilde recalled me, one glance into those eyes so full of pain and passion banished every feeling but a tender pity for her cruel lot, and a redoubled love and admiration for the patient strength which had borne this heavy weight of care all those years. I could not speak, I only took that fettered hand and kissed it reverently.

The imbecile (I cannot say husband) rose, when he saw Mathilde, and creeping to her side filled her hands with toys, still smiling that vacant smile, so pitiful to see in eyes that have shone unclouded upon such a wife, still muttering those senseless words so dreadful to hear, from lips that should have spoken with a man's wisdom and a husband's tenderness to her.

My heart ached, as I saw that young, fair woman sit near that wreck of manhood, soothing his restless spirit with the music of her voice, while his wandering hands played with the one ornament she wore, that bracelet whose slight links were so strong a chain to bind her to a bitter duty, so sorrowful a badge of slavery to a proud soul like hers.

Sleep fell suddenly on that poor, wandering mind, and with a few words to old Bernhardt, Mathilde led me back into the quiet room we left.

I sank into a chair, and dropping my head upon my folded arms, sat silent, knowing now what lay before us.

The storm rolled and crashed above our heads, but in the silence of the room, the voice I loved so well spoke softly at my side, as Mathilde told the story of her life.

"Gustave, I was an orphan, and my stern guardian found his ward an irksome charge. He looked about him for some means of relief, and but two appeared, marriage or a convent. I was but sixteen then, blithe of heart, and full of happy dreams; the convent seemed a tomb to me, and any fate a blessed one that saved me from it. I had a friend—heaven forgive her the wrong she did me!—and this friend influenced my guardian's choice, and won for me the husband you have seen. She knew the fearful malady that cursed him even then, but bade him conceal it from my guardian and me. He loved me, and obeyed her, and thus she led me into that dark web of woe where I have struggled all these years.

"I had innocently won a heart that she coveted, and though I did not listen to that lover's suit, he was lost to her, and for that she hated me. I knew nothing of her passion then, and trusted her implicitly. We were in Germany, and I, a stranger in a strange land, followed where she pointed, and so walked smilingly to my doom. Reinhold Arnheim was a gentle but weakhearted man, guided by his cousin Gertrude, my false friend. He loved me with all the ardor of his feeble nature, and I, seeing a free future before me, thought I gave him my heart, when it was but a girlish affection for the man who saved me from the fate I dreaded.

"My guardian's last illness coming suddenly upon him, he desired to see me safe in a husband's home, before he left me forever. I was married, and he died, believing me a happy wife—I, a child, betrothed one little month.

"Nine years ago, that marriage mockery took place, but to me it seems a lifetime full of pain. Ah! I should have been a happier woman in a nun's narrow cell than a wife worse than widowed, with a secret grief like this!" Mathilde paused, and for a moment nothing broke the silence but the wind, as it swept moaning away across the lake.

"Let me pass lightly over the two years that followed that unhappy bridal," she continued hurriedly. "I was frantic with indignation and dismay when I learned the secret Gertrude's wickedness and Reinhold's weakness had withheld from me. I had no friends to flee to, no home but my husband's, and too proud to proclaim the wrongs for which I knew no redress, I struggled to conceal my anguish, and accept my fate.

"My husband pleaded with me to spare him, the victim of a hereditary curse. I knew he loved me, and pity for his misfortune kept me silent. For years, no one knew the secret of his malady but Gertrude, his physician, Bernhardt, and myself.

"We seemed a happy pair, for Reinhold was truly kind, and I played my part well, proud to show my false friend that her cruel blow had failed to crush me.

"Gustave, tongue can never tell how I suffered—how I prayed for strength and patience; love would have made it easier to bear, but when those years of trial made a woman of the careless girl, and looking into my heart for some affection to sustain me, I found only pity and aversion, then I saw the error I had committed in my ignorance—I never loved him, and this long suffering has been my punishment for that great sin. Heaven grant it may atone!

"Gustave, I tried to be a patient wife—I tried to be a cheerful companion to poor Reinhold in his daily life, a brave comforter in those paroxysms of sharp agony which tortured him in secret—but all in vain. I could not love him, and I came at length to see my future as it stretched before me black and barren.

"Tied for life, to a man whose feeble mind left no hope of comforting companionship in our long pilgrimage, and with whom duty, unsweetened by affection, grew to a loathsome slavery—what wonder that I longed to break away and flee from my prison by the only outlet left to my despair?

"I wavered long, but resolved at length to end the life now grown too burdensome to bear. I wrote a letter to my husband, asking forgiveness for the grief I caused him, and freely pardoning the great wrong he had done me. No reproaches embittered my last words, but tenderly and truthfully I showed him all my heart, and said farewell forever.

"But before I could consummate my sinful purpose, I was seized with what I fondly hoped would prove a mortal illness, and while lying unconscious of all grief and care, Reinhold found and read that letter. He never told me the discovery he had made, but hid the wound and loved me still—never kinder than when he watched beside me with a woman's patient tenderness, as I slowly and reluctantly came back to life and health again.

"Then when he deemed me strong enough to bear the shock, he kissed me fondly one sad day, and going out with dogs and gun, as if to his favorite sport, at nightfall was brought home a ghastly spectacle.

"To all but his old servant it seemed a most unhappy accident, but in the silence of the night, as we watched beside what we believed to be his dying bed, old Bernhardt told me, that from broken words and preparations made in secret, he felt sure his master had gone out that day intending never to return alive—choosing to conceal his real design under the appearance of a sad mischance, that no remorse might poison my returning peace.

"With tears the old man told his fears, and when I learned that Reinhold had read that fatal letter, I could no longer doubt. It was a sad and solemn sight to me—for sitting in the shadow of death, I looked back upon my life, and seeing clearly where I had failed in wifely duty and in Christian patience, I prayerfully devoted my whole future to the atonement of the wrong I had committed against God, my husband, and myself.

"Reinhold lived, but never knew me again, never heard my entreaties for pardon, or my tender assurances of pity and affection—all I could truly offer even then. The grief my desperate resolve had caused him and the shock of that rash act were too much for his weak body and weak brain, and he rose up from that bed of suffering the mournful wreck you see him now.

"Gustave, I have kept my vow, and for seven long years have watched and guarded him most faithfully. I could not bear the pity of those German friends, and after wandering far and wide in search of health for my unhappy husband, I came hither unknown and friendless, bringing my poor husband to a quiet home, where no rude sound could disturb, no strange face make afraid. I was a widow in the saddest sense of that sad word, and as such I resolved henceforward to be known.

"The few who knew of the existence of the shadow you have seen believe him to be my brother, and I have held my peace, making a secret sorrow of my past, rather than confess the weakness and wickedness of those most near to me; I may have erred in this, but wronging no one, I hoped to win a little brightness to my life, to find a brief oblivion of my grief.

"I fled from the world; seeking to satisfy the hunger of my heart with friendship, and believing myself strong to resist temptation, I welcomed you and tasted happiness again, unconscious of love's subtle power, till it was too late to recall the heart you made your own. Gustave, I shunned you, I seemed cold and calm, when longing to reply to the unspoken passion shining in your glance; I felt my unseen fetters growing too heavy to be borne, and my life of seeming peace a mockery whose gloom appalled and tortured me.

"Heaven knows I struggled to be firm, and but for that unguarded moment of today, when death seemed to have bereft me of the one joy I possessed, I should still have the power to see you go unsaddened by a hopeless love, unburdened by a tale of grief like this. O my friend, forgive and pity me! Help me to bear my burden as I should, and patiently accept the fate heaven sends."

We had sat motionless, looking into each other's eyes as the last words fell from Mathilde's lips; but as she ceased and bent her head as if in meek submission, my heart overflowed. I threw myself before her, and striving to express the sympathy that mingled with my love, could only lay my throbbing forehead on her knee, and weep as I had not wept for years.

I felt her light touch on my head, and seemed to gather calmness from its soothing pressure.

"Do not banish me, Mathilde," I said, "let me still be near you with a glance of tenderness, a word of comfort for your cheer. There is a heavy shadow on your home. Let me stay and lighten it with the love that shall be warm and silent as the summer sunshine on your flowers."

But to my prayer there came a resolute reply, though the face that looked into my own was eloquent with love and grief.

"Gustave, we must part at once, for while my husband lives I shall guard his honorable name from the lightest breath. You were my friend, and I welcomed you—you are my lover, and henceforth are banished. Pardon me, and let us part unpledged by any vow. You are free to love whenever you shall weary of the passion that now rules your heart. I am bound by a tie which death alone can sever; till then I wear this fetter, placed here by a husband's hand nine years ago; it is a symbol of my life, a mute monitor of duty, strong and bright as the hope and patience which now come to strengthen me. I have thrown away the key, and its place is here till this arm lies powerless, or is stretched free and fetterless to clasp and hold you mine forever!"

"Give me some charm, some talisman, to keep my spirit brave and cheerful through the separation now before us, and then I will go," I cried, as the chapel clock tolled one, and the last glimmer died upon the hearth.

Mathilde brushed the hair back from my eager face, and gazed long and earnestly into my eyes, then bent and left a kiss upon my forehead, saying, as she rose, "It is a frank, true countenance, Gustave, and I trust the silent pledge it gives me. God keep you, dearest friend, and grant us a little happiness together in the years to come!"

I held her close for one moment, and with a fervent blessing turned to go, but pausing on the threshold, I looked back. The storm had died, and through the black clouds broke the moon with sudden radiance. A silvery beam lit that beloved face, and seemed to lure me back. I

started to return, but Mathilde's clear voice cried farewell; and on the
arm that waved a last adieu, the steel bracelet glittered like a warning
light. Seeing that, I knew there was no return. I went out into the night
a better and a happier man for having known the blessedness and pain
of love.

Three years went by, but my hidden passion never wavered, never
died—and although I wandered far and wide over the earth, I found no
spot so beautiful to me as the sunny château in its paradise of flowers,
and no joy so deep as the memory of Mathilde.

I never heard from her, for, though I wrote as one friend to another,
no reply was returned. I lamented this, but could not doubt the wisdom
of her silence, and waited patiently for my recall.

A letter came at length, not to welcome, but to banish me forever.
Mathilde had been a widow, and was a wife again. Kindly she told me
this, speaking of my love as a boyish passion, of her own as a brief delusion—asking pardon for the pain she feared to give, and wishing for me
a happiness like that she had now won.

It almost murdered me, for this hope was my life. Alone in the
Far East, I suffered, fought, and conquered, coming out from that sharp
conflict with no faith, no hope, no joy, nothing but a secret love and
sorrow locked up in my wounded heart to haunt me like a sad ghost, till
some spell to banish it was found.

Aimlessly, I journeyed to and fro, till led by the longing to again
see familiar faces, I returned to Paris and sought out my old friend
Moreau. He had not left the city for his summer home, and desiring to
give him a glad surprise, I sprang up the stairs unannounced and entered
his saloon.

A lady stood alone in the deep window, gazing thoughtfully upon
the busy scene below. I knew the slender figure draped in white, the
golden hair, the soft dark eyes, and with a sharp pang at my heart, I
recognized Mathilde—more lovely and serene than ever.

She turned, but in the bronzed and bearded man did not recognize
the youth she parted from, and with a glance of quiet wonder waited
for me to speak. I could not, and in a moment it was needless, for eye
spoke to eye, heart yearned to heart, and she remembered. A sudden
color flushed her cheek as she leaned toward me with dilated eyes; the
knot of Parmese violets upon her bosom rose and fell with her quickened
breath, and her whole frame thrilled with eagerness as she cried joyfully,
"Gustave! Come back to meet me at last!"

I stirred to meet her, but on the arms outstretched to greet me no steel bracelet glittered, and recollecting all my loss I clasped my hands before my face, crying mournfully, "O Mathilde, how can you welcome me, when such a gulf has parted us forever? How smile upon the friend whose love you have so wronged, whose life you have made so desolate?"

A short silence ensued, and then Mathilde's low voice replied, still tenderly, but full of pain, "Gustave, there is some mystery in this; deal frankly with me, and explain how I have wronged, how made you desolate?"

"Are you not married, and am I not bereft of the one dear gift I coveted? Did not your own hand part us and give the wound that still bleeds in my faithful heart, Mathilde?" I asked, with a glance of keen inquiry.

"Gustave, I never doubted your truth, though years passed, and I received no answer to the words of cheer I sent to comfort your long exile—then why doubt mine? Some idle rumor has deceived you, for I am now free—free to bestow the gift you covet, free to reward your patient love, if it still glows as warmly as mine."

Doubt, fear, and sorrow fled at once; I cared for nothing, remembered nothing, desired nothing, for Mathilde was free to love me still. That was rapture enough for me, and I drank freely of the cup of joy offered, heedless of unanswered doubts, unraveled mysteries and fears.

A single hour lifted me from gloom and desolation to blessedness again, and in the light of that returning confidence and peace all that seemed dark grew clear before our eyes. Mathilde had written often, but not one word from her had reached me, and not one line of mine had gladdened her. The letter telling of her marriage she had never penned, but knew now to whom she owed the wrong; and pale with womanly indignation told me that the enemy who had schemed to rob us of our happiness was Louis my friend.

He had met her again in Paris, and the passion, smothered for a long time, blazed up afresh. He never spoke of it in words lest he should again be banished, but seemed content to be her friend, though it was evident he hoped to win a warmer return in time.

Poor Reinhold died the year we parted, and was laid to rest in the quiet chapel where sunlight and silence brooded over his last sleep. Mathilde had written often to recall me, but when no reply to those fond missives came, she ceased, and waited hopefully for my return. Louis knew of my friendship with Mathilde, and must have guessed our love, for by some secret means he had thus intercepted letters, which would have shortened my long exile, and spared us both much misery and doubt.

More fully to estrange us he had artfully conveyed through other lips the tidings of my falsehood to Mathilde, hoping to destroy her faith in me and in her sorrow play the comforter and win her to himself. But she would not listen to the rumors of my marriage, would not doubt my truth, or accept the friendship of a man who could traduce a friend.

But for that well-counterfeited letter I too had never doubted, never suffered, and my ireful contempt rose fiercely as I listened to these proofs of Louis's treachery and fraud.

He was absent on some sudden journey, and ere he could return I won Mathilde to give me the dear right to make her joys and griefs my own. One soft, spring morning we went quietly away into a neighboring church, and returned one in heart and name forever.

No one but our old friends the general and his wife knew the happy truth, for Mathilde dreaded the gossip of the world, and besought me not to proclaim my happiness till we were safe in our quiet home, and I obeyed, content to know her mine.

The crimson light of evening bathed the tranquil face beside me as we sat together a week after our marriage, full of that content which comes to loving mortals in those midsummer days of life—when suddenly a voice we both remembered roused us from our happy reverie. Mathilde's eye lit, her slender figure rose erect, and as I started with a wrathful exclamation on my lips, she held me fast, saying, in the tones that never failed to sway me to her will, "Let me deal with him, for he is not worthy of your sword, Gustave; let me avenge the wrong he did us, for a woman's pity will wound deeper than your keenest thrust; promise me, dearest Gustave, that you will control yourself for love of me, remembering all the misery you might bring down upon us both!"

She clung to me with such fond entreaty that I promised, and standing at her side endeavored to be calm, though burning with an indignation nothing but the clasp of that soft hand had power to restrain.

Singing a blithe song Louis entered, but with arrested step and half-uttered greeting paused upon the threshold, eyeing us with a glance of fire, and struggling to conceal the swift dismay that drove the color from his cheek, the power from his limbs.

Mathilde did not speak, and with an effort painful to behold, Louis regained composure; for some sudden purpose seemed to give him courage and sent a glance of triumph to his eye, as with a mocking smile he bowed to the stately woman at my side, saying with malicious emphasis, "I come to present my compliments to Mme. Arnheim on my return from Germany, from Frankfort, her old home—and I bear to her the tenderest greetings from our fair friend Mme. Gertrude Steinburg. Will Madame accept as gladly as I offer them?"

"A fit messenger from such a friend?" icily replied Mathilde.

With a quick perception of her meaning, and a warning pressure of my clenched hand, Louis threw himself into a seat, and with an assumption of friendly ease, belied by the pallor of his countenance and the fierce glitter of the eye, continued with feigned sympathy—determined to leave no bitter word unsaid:

"She is a charming woman, and confided much to me that filled me with surprise and grief. What desolation will be carried to the hearts of Madame's many lovers when they learn that she is no lovely widow, but a miserable wife bound to an idiotic husband—how eagerly will they shun the fair château where Madame guards the secret shame and sorrow of her life, and how enviable must be the feelings of my friend when he discovers the deception practiced upon him and the utter hopelessness of his grand passion."

His keen eye was upon me as he spoke, and seeing the conflict which raged within me, mistook it for dismay and fear. A sardonic laugh broke from his lips, and before Mathilde could reply, he said, "I little thought, when listening to the cheerful story Mme. Steinburg told with such grace, how speedy and agreeable a use I should have power to make of it. Believe me, madame, I sympathize with your misfortunes, and admire the art which renders you all ice to one lover, and all fire to another."

Mathilde dropped my hand, and stood with folded arms, lofty pride in her mien, calm pity in her eye, and cool contempt upon her lips, as she replied in clear, cold tones:

"I am not what you think me, sir, and your generous sympathy comes too late. I was a widow; for the husband whose misfortune should have made his name sacred even to you died three years ago—I am a wife, happy in the love doubt could not estrange or time destroy. Your dark designs have failed, and for every year of needless separation we forgive you, since it renders our affection doubly strong, our union doubly blessed. Your absence at Mme. Steinburg's side removed the only barrier that could have kept us still asunder. Let me thank both of those false friends for the one kind deed that crowned our happiness. Gustave has left your punishment to me. See! It is this."

With a gesture of impassioned grace she threw herself upon my breast, and looking out from that fond shelter with a countenance all radiant with love, and pride, and joy, she cried, "Go! We pity you, and from the fullness of our bliss we pardon all."

She had avenged us well, for in the glance my proud eyes met, I read passion, humiliation, and despair, as Louis gazed upon us for a moment, and then vanished, the last cloud that dimmed our sky.

Paris lay behind us, and we stood on the green terrace looking over the fair domain now so full of peace and promise to our eyes.

Remembering the look of hopeless anguish that had stirred the face I loved in that same spot so long ago, I looked down to read its lineaments afresh.

It was there, close beside me, bright with happiness, and beautiful with the returning bloom that banished its former pensive charm. Trust spoke in the clinging touch upon my arm, joy beamed in the blithe smile of her lips, and love sat like a glory in her tender eyes.

She met my glance, and with a sudden impulse folded her hands, saying softly, "The shadow has departed, Gustave, never to return, and I am free at last. May I be truly grateful for my happy lot."

"No, dearest Mathilde, you are a captive still, not to duty, but to love, whose thralldom shall be to you as light as the fetter I now bind you with." And as I spoke I clasped a slender chain of gold upon the fair arm where for nine bitter years lay the weight of that steel bracelet.

A Whisper
in the Dark

AS we rolled along, I scanned my companion covertly, and saw much to interest a girl of seventeen. My uncle was a handsome man, with all the polish of foreign life fresh upon him; yet it was neither comeliness nor graceful ease which most attracted me; for even my inexperienced eye caught glimpses of something stern and somber below these external charms, and my long scrutiny showed me the keenest eye, the hardest mouth, the subtlest smile I ever saw—a face which in repose wore the look that comes to those who have led lives of pleasure and learned their emptiness. He seemed intent on some thought that absorbed him, and for a time rendered him forgetful of my presence, as he sat with folded arms, fixed eyes, and restless lips. While I looked, my own mind was full of deeper thought than it had ever been before; for I was recalling, word for word, a paragraph in that half-read letter:

> At eighteen Sybil is to marry her cousin, the compact having been made between my brother and myself in their childhood. My son is with me now, and I wish them to be together during the next few months, therefore my niece must leave you sooner than I at first intended. Oblige me by preparing her for an immediate and final separation, but leave all disclosures to me, as I prefer the girl to remain ignorant of the matter for the present.

That displeased me. Why was I to remain ignorant of so important an affair? Then I smiled to myself, remembering that I did know, thanks to the willful curiosity that prompted me to steal a peep into the letter that Mme. Bernard had pored over with such an anxious face. I saw only

a single paragraph, for my own name arrested my eye; and, though wild
to read all, I had scarcely time to whisk the paper back into the reticule
the forgetful old soul had left hanging on the arm of her chair. It was
enough, however, to set my girlish brain in a ferment, and keep me
gazing wistfully at my uncle, conscious that my future now lay in his
hands; for I was an orphan and he my guardian, though I had seen him
but seldom since I was confided to Madame a six years' child.

Presently my uncle became cognizant of my steady stare, and returned it with one as steady for a moment, then said, in a low, smooth
tone, that ill accorded with the satirical smile that touched his lips, "I am
a dull companion for my little niece. How shall I provide her with
pleasanter amusement than counting my wrinkles or guessing my
thoughts?"

I was a frank, fearless creature, quick to feel, speak, and act, so I
answered readily, "Tell me about my cousin Guy. Is he as handsome,
brave, and clever as Madame says his father was when a boy?"

My uncle laughed a short laugh, touched with scorn, whether for
Madame, himself, or me I could not tell, for his countenance was hard
to read.

"A girl's question and artfully put; nevertheless I shall not answer
it, but let you judge for yourself."

"But, sir, it will amuse me and beguile the way. I feel a little
strange and forlorn at leaving Madame, and talking of my new home
and friends will help me to know and love them sooner. Please tell me,
for I've had my own way all my life, and can't bear to be crossed."

My petulance seemed to amuse him, and I became aware that he
was observing me with a scrutiny as keen as my own had been; but I
smilingly sustained it, for my vanity was pleased by the approbation his
eye betrayed. The evident interest he now took in all I said and did was
sufficient flattery for a young thing, who felt her charms and longed to
try their power.

"I, too, have had my own way all my life; and as the life is double
the length, the will is double the strength of yours, and again I say no.
What next, mademoiselle?"

He was blander than ever as he spoke, but I was piqued, and resolved to try coaxing, eager to gain my point, lest a too early submission
now should mar my freedom in the future.

"But that is ungallant, Uncle, and I still have hopes of a kinder
answer, both because you are too generous to refuse so small a favor to
your 'little niece,' and because she can be charmingly wheedlesome when
she likes. Won't you say yes now, Uncle?" And pleased with the daring

of the thing, I put my arm about his neck, kissed him daintily, and perched myself upon his knee with most audacious ease.

He regarded me mutely for an instant, then, holding me fast, deliberately returned my salute on lips, cheeks, and forehead, with such warmth that I turned scarlet and struggled to free myself, while he laughed that mirthless laugh of his till my shame turned to anger, and I imperiously commanded him to let me go.

"Not yet, young lady. You came here for your own pleasure, but shall stay for mine, till I tame you as I see you must be tamed. It is a short process with me, and I possess experience in the work; for Guy, though by nature as wild as a hawk, has learned to come at my call as meekly as a dove. Chut! What a little fury it is!"

I was just then; for exasperated at his coolness, and quite beside myself, I had suddenly stooped and bitten the shapely white hand that held both my own. I had better have submitted; for slight as the foolish action was, it had an influence on my afterlife as many another such has had. My uncle stopped laughing, his hand tightened its grasp, for a moment his cold eye glittered and a grim look settled round the mouth, giving to his whole face a ruthless expression that entirely altered it. I felt perfectly powerless. All my little arts had failed, and for the first time I was mastered. Yet only physically; my spirit was rebellious still. He saw it in the glance that met his own, as I sat erect and pale, with something more than childish anger. I think it pleased him, for swiftly as it had come the dark look passed, and quietly, as if we were the best of friends, he began to relate certain exciting adventures he had known abroad, lending to the picturesque narration the charm of that peculiarly melodious voice, which soothed and won me in spite of myself, holding me intent till I forgot the past; and when he paused I found that I was leaning confidentially on his shoulder, asking for more, yet conscious of an instinctive distrust of this man whom I had so soon learned to fear yet fancy.

As I was recalled to myself, I endeavored to leave him; but he still detained me, and, with a curious expression, produced a case so quaintly fashioned that I cried out in admiration, while he selected two cigarettes, mildly aromatic with the herbs they were composed of, lit them, offered me one, dropped the window, and leaning back surveyed me with an air of extreme enjoyment, as I sat meekly puffing and wondering what prank I should play a part in next. Slowly the narcotic influence of the herbs diffused itself like a pleasant haze over all my senses; sleep, the most grateful, fell upon my eyelids, and the last thing I remember was my uncle's face dreamily regarding me through a cloud of fragrant smoke. Twilight wrapped us in its shadows when I woke, with the night wind blowing on my forehead, the muffled roll of wheels sounding in my ear, and my cheek pillowed upon my uncle's arm. He was humming a French *chanson* about "love and wine, and the Seine tomorrow!" I listened till I caught the air, and presently joined him, mingling my girlish treble with his flutelike tenor. He stopped at once and, in the coolly courteous tone I had always heard in our few interviews, asked if I was ready for lights and home.

"Are we there?" I cried; and looking out saw that we were ascending an avenue which swept up to a pile of buildings that rose tall and dark against the sky, with here and there a gleam along its gray front.

"Home at last, thank heaven!" And springing out with the agility of a young man, my uncle led me over a terrace into a long hall, light and warm, and odorous with the breath of flowers blossoming here and there in graceful groups. A civil, middle-aged maid received and took me to my room, a bijou of a place, which increased my wonder when told that my uncle had chosen all its decorations and superintended their arrangement. "He understands women," I thought, handling the toilet ornaments, trying luxurious chair and lounge, and ending by slipping my feet into the scarlet-and-white Turkish slippers, coquettishly turning up their toes before the fire. A few moments I gave to examination, and, having expressed my satisfaction, was asked by my maid if I would be pleased to dress, as "the master" never allowed dinner to wait for anyone. This recalled to me the fact that I was doubtless to meet my future husband at that meal, and in a moment every faculty was intent upon achieving a grand toilette for this first interview. The maid possessed skill and taste, and I a wardrobe lately embellished with Parisian gifts from my uncle which I was eager to display in his honor.

When ready, I surveyed myself in the long mirror as I had never done before, and saw there a little figure, slender, yet stately, in a dress of foreign fashion, ornamented with lace and carnation ribbons which enhanced the fairness of neck and arms, while blond hair, wavy and golden, was gathered into an antique knot of curls behind, with a carnation fillet, and below a blooming dark-eyed face, just then radiant with girlish vanity and eagerness and hope.

"I'm glad I'm pretty!"

"So am I, Sybil."

I had unconsciously spoken aloud, and the echo came from the doorway where stood my uncle, carefully dressed, looking comelier and cooler than ever. The disagreeable smile flitted over his lips as he spoke, and I started, then stood abashed, till beckoning, he added in his most courtly manner, "You were so absorbed in the contemplation of your charming self that Janet answered my tap and took herself away unheard. You are mistress of my table now. It waits; will you come down?"

With a last touch to that unruly hair of mine, a last, comprehensive glance and shake, I took the offered arm and rustled down the wide staircase, feeling that the romance of my life was about to begin. Three covers were laid, three chairs set, but only two were occupied, for no Guy appeared. I asked no questions, showed no surprise, but tried to devour my chagrin with my dinner, and exerted myself to charm my uncle into the belief that I had forgotten my cousin. It was a failure, however, for that empty seat had an irresistible fascination for me, and more than once, as my eye returned from its furtive scrutiny of napkin, plate, and trio of colored glasses, it met my uncle's and fell before his penetrative glance. When I gladly rose to leave him to his wine—for he did not ask me to remain—he also rose, and, as he held the door for me, he said, "You asked me to describe your cousin. You have seen one trait of his character tonight; does it please you?"

I knew he was as much vexed as I at Guy's absence, so quoting his own words, I answered saucily, "Yes, for I'd rather see the hawk free than coming tamely at your call, Uncle."

He frowned slightly, as if unused to such liberty of speech, yet bowed when I swept him a stately little curtsy and sailed away to the drawing room, wondering if my uncle was as angry with me as I was with my cousin. In solitary grandeur I amused myself by strolling through the suite of handsome rooms henceforth to be my realm, looked at myself in the long mirrors, as every woman is apt to do when alone and in costume, danced over the mossy carpets, touched the grand piano, smelled the flowers, fingered the ornaments on étagère and table, and was just giving my handkerchief a second drench of some refreshing perfume from a filigree flask that had captivated me when the hall door was flung wide, a quick step went running upstairs, boots tramped overhead, drawers seemed hastily opened and shut, and a bold, blithe voice broke out into a hunting song in a tone so like my uncle's that I involuntarily flew to the door, crying, "Guy is come!"

Fortunately for my dignity, no one heard me, and hurrying back I stood ready to skim into a chair and assume propriety at a minute's notice, conscious, meanwhile, of the new influence which seemed suddenly to gift the silent house with vitality, and add the one charm it needed—that of cheerful companionship. "How will he meet me? And how shall I meet him?" I thought, looking up at the bright-faced boy, whose portrait looked back at me with a mirthful light in the painted eyes and a trace of his father's disdainful smile in the curves of the firm-set lips. Presently the quick steps came flying down again, past the door, straight to the dining room opposite, and, as I stood listening with a strange flutter at my heart, I heard an imperious young voice say rapidly, "Beg pardon, sir, unavoidably detained. Has she come? Is she bearable?"

"I find her so. Dinner is over, and I can offer you nothing but a glass of wine."

My uncle's voice was frostily polite, making a curious contrast to the other, so impetuous and frank, as if used to command or win all but one.

"Never mind the dinner! I'm glad to be rid of it; so I'll drink your health, Father, and then inspect our new ornament."

"Impertinent boy!" I muttered, yet at the same moment resolved to deserve his appellation, and immediately grouped myself as effectively as possible, laughing at my folly as I did so. I possessed a pretty foot, therefore one little slipper appeared quite naturally below the last flounce of my dress; a bracelet glittered on my arm as it emerged from among the lace and carnation knots; that arm supported my head. My profile was well cut, my eyelashes long, therefore I read with face half averted from the door. The light showered down, turning my hair to gold; so I smoothed my curls, retied my snood, and, after a satisfied survey, composed myself with an absorbed aspect and a quickened pulse to await the arrival of the gentlemen.

Soon they came. I knew they paused on the threshold, but never stirred till an irrepressible "You are right, sir!" escaped the younger.

Then I rose prepared to give him the coldest greeting, yet I did not. I had almost expected to meet the boyish face and figure of the picture; I saw instead a man comely and tall. A dark moustache half hid the proud mouth; the vivacious eyes were far kinder, though quite as keen as his father's; and the freshness of unspoiled youth lent a charm which the older man had lost forever. Guy's glance of pleased surprise was flatteringly frank, his smile so cordial, his "Welcome, cousin!" such a hearty sound that my coldness melted in a breath, my dignity was all forgotten, and before I could restrain myself I had offered both hands with the impulsive exclamation "Cousin Guy, I know I shall be very happy here! Are you glad I have come?"

"Glad as I am to see the sun after a November fog."

And bending his tall head, he kissed my hand in the graceful foreign fashion he had learned abroad. It pleased me mightily, for it was both affectionate and respectful. Involuntarily I contrasted it with my uncle's manner, and flashed a significant glance at him as I did so. He understood it, but only nodded with the satirical look I hated, shook out his paper, and began to read. I sat down again, careless of myself now; and Guy stood on the rug, surveying me with an expression of surprise that rather nettled my pride.

"He is only a boy, after all; so I need not be daunted by his inches or his airs. I wonder if he knows I am to be his wife, and likes it."

The thought sent the color to my forehead, my eyes fell, and despite my valiant resolution I sat like any bashful child before my handsome cousin. Guy laughed a boyish laugh as he sat down on his father's footstool, saying, while he warmed his slender brown hands, "I beg your pardon, Sybil. (We won't be formal, will we?) But I haven't seen a lady for a month, so I stare like a boor at sight of a silk gown and highbred face. Are those people coming, sir?"

"If Sybil likes, ask her."

"Shall we have a flock of people here to make it gay for you, Cousin, or do you prefer our quiet style better; just riding, driving, lounging, and enjoying life, each in his own way? Henceforth it is to be as you command in such matters."

"Let things go on as they have done then. I don't care for society, and strangers wouldn't make it gay to me, for I like freedom; so do you, I think."

"Ah, don't I!"

A cloud flitted over his smiling face, and he punched the fire, as if some vent were necessary for the sudden gust of petulance that knit his black brows into a frown, and caused his father to tap him on the shoulder with the bland request, as he rose to leave the room, "Bring the portfolios and entertain your cousin; I have letters to write, and Sybil is too tired to care for music tonight."

Guy obeyed with a shrug of the shoulder his father touched, but lingered in the recess till my uncle, having made his apologies to me, had left the room; then my cousin rejoined me, wearing the same cordial aspect I first beheld. Some restraint was evidently removed, and his natural self appeared. A very winsome self it was, courteous, gay, and frank, with an undertone of deeper feeling than I thought to find. I watched him covertly, and soon owned to myself that he was all I most admired in the ideal hero every girl creates in her romantic fancy; for I no longer looked upon this young man as my cousin, but my lover, and through all our future intercourse this thought was always uppermost, full of a charm that never lost its power.

Before the evening ended Guy was kneeling on the rug beside me,

our two heads close together, while he turned the contents of the great
portfolio spread before us, looking each other freely in the face, as I
listened and he described, both breaking into frequent peals of laughter
at some odd adventure or comical mishap in his own travels, suggested
by the pictured scenes before us. Guy was very charming, I my blithest,
sweetest self, and when we parted late, my cousin watched me up the
stairs with still another "Good night, Sybil," as if both sight and sound
were pleasant to him.

"Is that your horse Sultan?" I called from my window next morning, as I looked down upon my cousin, who was coming up the drive
from an early gallop on the moors.

"Yes, bonny Sybil; come and admire him," he called back, hat in
hand, and a quick smile rippling over his face.

I went, and standing on the terrace, caressed the handsome creature,
while Guy said, glancing up at his father's undrawn curtains, "If your
saddle had come, we would take a turn before 'my lord' is ready for
breakfast. This autumn air is the wine you women need."

I yearned to go, and when I willed the way soon appeared; so
careless of bonnetless head and cambric gown, I stretched my hands to
him, saying boldly, "Play young Lochinvar, Guy; I am little and light;
take me up before you and show me the sea."

He liked the daring feat, held out his hand, I stepped on his boot
toe, sprang up, and away we went over the wide moor, where ·the sun
shone in a cloudless heaven, the lark soared singing from the green grass
at our feet, and the September wind blew freshly from the sea. As we
paused on the upland slope, that gave us a free view of the country
for miles, Guy dismounted, and standing with his arm about the saddle
to steady me in my precarious seat, began to talk.

"Do you like your new home, Cousin?"

"More than I can tell you!"

"And my father, Sybil?"

"Both yes and no to that question, Guy; I hardly know him yet."

"True, but you must not expect to find him as indulgent and fond
as many guardians would be to such as you. It's not his nature. Yet you
can win his heart by obedience, and soon grow quite at ease with him."

"Bless you! I'm that already, for I fear no one. Why, I sat on his
knee yesterday and smoked a cigarette of his own offering, though
Madame would have fainted if she had seen me; then I slept on his
arm an hour, and he was fatherly kind, though I teased him like a gnat."

"The deuce he was!"

With which energetic expression Guy frowned at the landscape and harshly checked Sultan's attempt to browse, while I wondered what was amiss between father and son, and resolved to discover; but finding the conversation at an end, started it afresh by asking, "Is any of my property in this part of the country, Guy? Do you know I am as ignorant as a baby about my own affairs; for, as long as every whim was gratified and my purse full, I left the rest to Madame and Uncle, though the first hadn't a bit of judgment, and the last I scarcely knew. I never cared to ask questions before, but now I am intensely curious to know how matters stand."

"All you see is yours, Sybil" was the brief answer.

"What, that great house, the lovely gardens, these moors, and the forest stretching to the sea? I'm glad! I'm glad! But where, then, is your home, Guy?"

"Nowhere."

At this I looked so amazed that his gloom vanished in a laugh, as he explained, but briefly, as if this subject were no pleasanter than the first, "By your father's will you were desired to take possession of the old place at eighteen. You will be that soon; therefore, as your guardian, my father has prepared things for you, and is to share your home until you marry."

"When will that be, I wonder?" And I stole a glance from under my lashes, wild to discover if Guy knew of the compact and was a willing party to it.

His face was half averted, but over his dark cheek I saw a deep flush rise, as he answered, stooping to pull a bit of heather, "Soon, I hope, or the gentleman sleeping there below will be tempted to remain a fixture with you on his knee as 'Madame my wife.' He is not your own uncle, you know."

I smiled at the idea, but Guy did not see it; and seized with a whim to try my skill with the hawk that seemed inclined to peck at its master, I said demurely, "Well, why not? I might be very happy if I learned to love him, as I should, if he were always in that kindest mood of his. Would you like me for a little mamma, Guy?"

"No!" short and sharp as a pistol shot.

"Then you must marry and have a home of your own, my son."

"Don't, Sybil! I'd rather you didn't see me in a rage, for I'm not a pleasant sight, I assure you; and I'm afraid I shall be in one if you go on. I early lost my mother, but I love her tenderly, because my father is not much to me, and I know if she had lived I should not be what I am."

Bitter was his voice, moody his mien, and all the sunshine gone
at once. I looked down and touched his black hair with a shy caress,
feeling both penitent and pitiful.

"Dear Guy, forgive me if I pained you. I'm a thoughtless creature,
but I'm not malicious, and a word will restrain me if kindly spoken. My
home is always yours, and when my fortune is mine you shall never
want, if you are not too proud to accept help from your own kin. You
are a little proud, aren't you?"

"As Lucifer, to most people. I think I should not be to you, for
you understand me, Sybil, and with you I hope to grow a better man."

He turned then, and through the lineaments his father had bequeathed him I saw a look that must have been his mother's, for it was
womanly, sweet, and soft, and lent new beauty to the dark eyes, always
kind, and just then very tender. He had checked his words suddenly,
like one who has gone too far, and with that hasty look into my face had
bent his own upon the ground, as if to hide the unwonted feeling that
had mastered him. It lasted but a moment, then his old manner returned, as he said gaily, "There drops your slipper. I've been wondering
what kept it on. Pretty thing! They say it is a foot like this that oftenest
tramples on men's hearts. Are you cruel to your lovers, Sybil?"

"I never had one, for Madame guarded me like a dragon, and I
led the life of a nun; but when I do find one I shall try his mettle well
before I give up my liberty."

"Poets say it is sweet to give up liberty for love, and they ought to
know," answered Guy, with a sidelong glance.

I liked that little speech, and recollecting the wistful look he had
given me, the significant words that had escaped him, and the variations
of tone and manner constantly succeeding one another, I felt assured
that my cousin was cognizant of the family league, and accepted it, yet
with the shyness of a young lover, knew not how to woo. This pleased
me, and quite satisfied with my morning's work, I mentally resolved to
charm my cousin slowly, and enjoy the romance of a genuine wooing,
without which no woman's life seems complete—in her own eyes at
least. He had gathered me a knot of purple heather, and as he gave it
I smiled my sweetest on him, saying, "I commission you to supply me
with nosegays, for you have taste, and I love wild flowers. I shall wear
this at dinner in honor of its giver. Now take me home; for my moors,
though beautiful, are chilly, and I have no wrapper but this microscopic
handkerchief."

Off went his riding jacket, and I was half smothered in it. The hat
followed next, and as he sprang up behind I took the reins, and felt

a thrill of delight in sweeping down the slope with that mettlesome creature tugging at the bit, that strong arm around me, and the happy hope that the heart I leaned on might yet learn to love me.

The day so began passed pleasantly, spent in roving over house and grounds with my cousin, setting my possessions in order, and writing to dear old Madame. Twilight found me in my bravest attire, with Guy's heather in my hair, listening for his step, and longing to run and meet him when he came. Punctual to the instant he appeared, and this dinner was a far different one from that of yesterday, for both father and son seemed in their gayest and most gallant mood, and I enjoyed the hour heartily. The world seemed all in tune now, and when I went to the drawing room I was moved to play my most stirring marches, sing my blithest songs, hoping to bring one at least of the gentlemen to join me. It brought both, and my first glance showed me a curious change in each. My uncle looked harassed and yet amused; Guy looked sullen and eyed his father with covert glances.

The morning's chat flashed into my mind, and I asked myself, "Is Guy jealous so soon?" It looked a little like it, for he threw himself upon a couch and lay there silent and morose; while my uncle paced to and fro, thinking deeply, while apparently listening to the song he bade me finish. I did so, then followed the whim that now possessed me, for I wanted to try my power over them both, to see if I could restore that gentler mood of my uncle's, and assure myself that Guy cared whether I was friendliest with him or not.

"Uncle, come and sing with me; I like that voice of yours."

"Tut, I am too old for that; take this indolent lad instead. His voice is fresh and young, and will chord well with yours."

"Do you know that pretty *chanson* about 'love and wine, and the Seine tomorrow,' cousin Guy?" I asked, stealing a sly glance at my uncle.

"Who taught you that?" And Guy eyed me over the top of the couch with an astonished expression which greatly amused me.

"No one; Uncle sang a bit of it in the carriage yesterday. I like the air, so come and teach me the rest."

"It is no song for you, Sybil. You choose strange entertainment for a lady, sir."

A look of unmistakable contempt was in the son's eye, of momentary annoyance in the father's, yet his voice betrayed none as he answered, still pacing placidly along the room, "I thought she was asleep, and unconsciously began it to beguile a silent drive. Sing on, Sybil; that Bacchanalian snatch will do you no harm."

But I was tired of music now they had come, so I went to him, and passing my arm through his, walked beside him, saying with my most persuasive aspect, "Tell me about Paris, Uncle; I intend to go there as soon as I'm of age, if you will let me. Does your guardianship extend beyond that time?"

"Only till you marry."

"I shall be in no haste, then, for I begin to feel quite homelike and happy here with you, and shall be content without other society; only you'll soon tire of me, and leave me to some dismal governess, while you and Guy go pleasuring."

"No fear of that, Sybil; I shall hold you fast till some younger guardian comes to rob me of my merry ward."

As he spoke, he took the hand that lay upon his arm into a grasp so firm, and turned on me a look so keen, that I involuntarily dropped my eyes lest he should read my secret there. Eager to turn the conversation, I asked, pointing to a little miniature hanging underneath the portrait of his son, before which he had paused, "Was that Guy's mother, sir?"

"No, your own."

I looked again, and saw a face delicate yet spirited, with dark eyes, a passionate mouth, and a head crowned with hair as plenteous and golden as my own; but the whole seemed dimmed by age, the ivory was stained, the glass cracked, and a faded ribbon fastened it. My eyes filled as I looked, and a strong desire seized me to know what had defaced this little picture of the mother whom I never knew.

"Tell me about her, Uncle; I know so little, and often long for her so much. Am I like her, sir?"

Why did my uncle avert his eyes as he answered, "You are a youthful image of her, Sybil"?

"Go on, please, tell me more; tell me why this is so stained and worn; you know all, and surely I am old enough now to hear any history of pain and loss."

Something caused my uncle to knit his brows, but his bland voice never varied a tone as he placed the picture in my hand and gave me this brief explanation:

"Just before your birth your father was obliged to cross the Channel, to receive the last wishes of a dying friend. There was an accident; the vessel foundered, and many lives were lost. He escaped, but by some mistake his name appeared in the list of missing passengers; your mother saw it, the shock destroyed her, and when your father returned he found only a motherless little daughter to welcome him. This miniature, which he always carried with him, was saved with his papers at the last moment; but though the seawater ruined it he would never have it copied or retouched, and gave it to me when he died in memory of the woman I had loved for his sake. It is yours now, my child; keep it, and never feel that you are fatherless or motherless while I remain."

Kind as was both act and speech, neither touched me, for something seemed wanting. I felt yet could not define it, for then I believed in the sincerity of all I met.

"Where was she buried, Uncle? It may be foolish, but I should like to see my mother's grave."

"You shall someday, Sybil," and a curious change came over my uncle's face as he averted it.

"I have made him melancholy, talking of Guy's mother and my own; now I'll make him gay again if possible, and pique that negligent boy," I thought, and drew my uncle to a lounging chair, established myself on the arm thereof, and kept him laughing with my merriest gossip, both of us apparently unconscious of the long dark figure stretched just opposite, feigning sleep, but watching us through half-closed lids, and never stirring except to bow silently to my careless "Good night."

As I reached the stairhead, I remembered that my letter to Madame, full of the frankest criticisms upon people and things, was lying unsealed on the table in the little room my uncle had set apart for my boudoir; fearing servants' eyes and tongues, I slipped down again to get it. The room adjoined the parlors, and just then was lit only by a ray from the hall lamp.

I had secured the letter, and was turning to retreat, when I heard Guy say petulantly, as if thwarted yet submissive, "I *am* civil when you leave me alone; I *do* agree to marry her, but I won't be hurried or go a-wooing except in my own way. You know I never liked the bargain, for it's nothing else; yet I can reconcile myself to being sold, if it relieves you and gives us both a home. But, Father, mind this, if you tie me to that girl's sash too tightly I shall break away entirely, and then where are we?"

"I should be in prison and you a houseless vagabond. Trust me, my boy, and take the good fortune which I secured for you in your cradle. Look in pretty Sybil's face, and resignation will grow easy; but remember time presses, that this is our forlorn hope, and for God's sake be cautious, for she is a headstrong creature, and may refuse to fulfill her part·if she learns that the contract is not binding against her will."

"I think she'll not refuse, sir; she likes me already. I see it in her eyes; she has never had a lover, she says, and according to your account a girl's first sweetheart is apt to fare the best. Besides, she likes the place, for I told her it was hers, as you bade me, and she said she could be very happy here, if my father was always kind."

"She said that, did she? Little hypocrite! For your father, read yourself, and tell me what else she babbled about in that early *tête-à-tête* of yours."

"You are as curious as a woman, sir, and always make me tell you all I do and say, yet never tell me anything in return, except this business, which I hate, because my liberty is the price, and my poor little cousin is kept in the dark. I'll tell her all, before I marry her, Father."

"As you please, hothead. I am waiting for an account of the first love passage, so leave blushing to Sybil and begin."

I knew what was coming and stayed no longer, but caught one glimpse of the pair. Guy in his favorite place, erect upon the rug, half laughing, half frowning as he delayed to speak, my uncle serenely smoking on the couch; then I sped away to my own room, thinking, as I sat down in a towering passion, "So he does know of the baby betrothal and hates it, yet submits to please his father, who covets my fortune—mercenary creatures! I can annul the contract, can I? I'm glad to know that, for it makes me mistress of them both. I like you already, do I, and you see it in my eyes? Coxcomb! I'll be the thornier for that. Yet I do like him; I do wish he cared for me, I'm so lonely in the world, and he can be so kind."

So I cried a little, brushed my hair a good deal, and went to bed, resolving to learn all I could when, where, and how I pleased, to render myself as charming and valuable as possible, to make Guy love me in spite of himself, and then say yes or no, as my heart prompted me.

That day was a sample of those that followed, for my cousin was by turns attracted or repelled by the capricious moods that ruled me. Though conscious of a secret distrust of my uncle, I could not resist the fascination of his manner when he chose to exert its influence over me; this made my little plot easier of execution, for jealousy seemed the most effectual means to bring my wayward cousin to subjection. Full of this fancy, I seemed to tire of his society, grew thorny as a brier rose to him, affectionate as a daughter to my uncle, who surveyed us both with that inscrutable glance of his, and slowly yielded to my dominion as if he had divined my purpose and desired to aid it. Guy turned cold and gloomy, yet still lingered near me as if ready for a relenting look or word. I liked that, and took a wanton pleasure in prolonging the humiliation of the warm heart I had learned to love, yet not to value as I ought, until it was too late.

One dull November evening as I went wandering up and down the hall, pretending to enjoy the flowers, yet in reality waiting for Guy, who had left me alone all day, my uncle came from his room, where he had sat for many hours with the harassed and anxious look he always wore when certain foreign letters came.

"Sybil, I have something to show and tell you," he said, as I garnished his buttonhole with a spray of heliotrope, meant for the laggard, who would understand its significance, I hoped. Leading me to the drawing room, my uncle put a paper into my hands, with the request "This is a copy of your father's will; oblige me by reading it."

He stood watching my face as I read, no doubt wondering at my composure while I waded through the dry details of the will, curbing my impatience to reach the one important passage. There it was, but no word concerning my power to dissolve the engagement if I pleased; and, as I realized the fact, a sudden bewilderment and sense of helplessness came over me, for the strange law terms seemed to make inexorable the paternal decree which I had not seen before. I forgot my studied calmness, and asked several questions eagerly.

"Uncle, did my father really command that I should marry Guy, whether we loved each other or not?"

"You see what he there set down as his desire; and I have taken measures that you *should* love one another, knowing that few cousins, young, comely, and congenial, could live three months together without finding themselves ready to mate for their own sakes, if not for the sake of the dead and living fathers to whom they owe obedience."

"You said I need not, if I didn't choose; why is it not here?"

"I said that? Never, Sybil!" and I met a look of such entire surprise and incredulity it staggered my belief in my own senses, yet also roused my spirit, and, careless of consequences, I spoke out at once.

"I heard you say it myself the night after I came, when you told Guy to be cautious, because I could refuse to fulfill the engagement, if I knew that it was not binding against my will."

This discovery evidently destroyed some plan, and for a moment threw him off his guard; for, crumpling the paper in his hand, he sternly demanded, "You turned eavesdropper early; how often since?"

"Never, Uncle; I did not mean it then, but going for a letter in the dark, I heard your voices, and listened for an instant. It was dishonorable, but irresistible; and if you force Guy's confidence, why should not I steal yours? All is fair in war, sir, and I forgive as I hope to be forgiven."

"You have a quick wit and a reticence I did not expect to find under that frank manner. So you have known your future destiny all these

months then, and have a purpose in your treatment of your cousin and
myself?"

"Yes, Uncle."

"May I ask what?"

I was ashamed to tell; and in the little pause before my answer
came, my pique at Guy's desertion was augmented by anger at my
uncle's denial of his own words the ungenerous hopes he cherished, and
a strong desire to perplex and thwart him took possession of me, for I
saw his anxiety concerning the success of this interview, though he
endeavored to repress and conceal it. Assuming my coldest mien, I said,
"No, sir, I think not; only I can assure you that my little plot has
succeeded better than your own."

"But you intend to obey your father's wish, I hope, and fulfill your
part of the compact, Sybil?"

"Why should I? It is not binding, you know, and I'm too young to
lose my liberty just yet; besides, such compacts are unjust, unwise. What
right had my father to mate me in my cradle? How did he know what I
should become, or Guy? How could he tell that I should not love someone else better? No! I'll not be bargained away like a piece of mer-
chandise, but love and marry when I please!"

At this declaration of independence my uncle's face darkened ominously, some new suspicion lurked in his eye, some new anxiety beset
him; but his manner was calm, his voice blander than ever as he asked,
"Is there then someone whom you love? Confide in me, my girl."

"And if there were, what then?"

"All would be changed at once, Sybil. But who is it? Some young
lover left behind at Madame's?"

"No, sir."

"Who, then? You have led a recluse life here. Guy has no friends
who visit him, and mine are all old, yet you say you love."

"With all my heart, Uncle."

"Is this affection returned, Sybil?"

"I think so."

"And it is not Guy?"

I was wicked enough to enjoy the bitter disappointment he could
not conceal at my decided words, for I thought he deserved that momentary pang; but I could not as decidedly answer that last question,
for I would not lie, neither would I confess just yet; so, with a little
gesture of impatience, I silently turned away, lest he should see the
telltale color in my cheeks. My uncle stood an instant in deep thought,
a slow smile crept to his lips, content returned to his mien, and something

like a flash of triumph glittered for a moment in his eye, then vanished, leaving his countenance earnestly expectant. Much as this change surprised me, his words did more, for, taking both my hands in his, he gravely said, "Do you know that I am your uncle by adoption and not blood, Sybil?"

"Yes, sir; I heard so, but forgot about it," and I looked up at him, my anger quite lost in astonishment.

"Let me tell you then. Your grandfather was childless for many years, my mother was an early friend, and when her death left me an orphan, he took me for his son and heir. But two years from that time your father was born. I was too young to realize the entire change this might make in my life. The old man was too just and generous to let me feel it, and the two lads grew up together like brothers. Both married young, and when you were born a few years later than my son, your father said to me, 'Your boy shall have my girl, and the fortune I have innocently robbed you of shall make us happy in our children.' Then the family league was made, renewed at his death, and now destroyed by his daughter, unless—Sybil, I am forty-five, you not eighteen, yet you once said you could be very happy with me, if I were always kind to you. I can promise that I will be, for I love you. My darling, you reject the son, will you accept the father?"

If he had struck me, it would scarcely have dismayed me more. I started up, and snatching away my hands, hid my face in them, for after the first tingle of surprise an almost irresistible desire to laugh came over me, but I dared not, and gravely, gently he went on.

"I am a bold man to say this, yet I mean it most sincerely. I never meant to betray the affection I believed you never could return, and would only laugh at as a weakness; but your past acts, your present words, give me courage to confess that I desire to keep my ward mine forever. Shall it be so?"

He evidently mistook my surprise for maidenly emotion, and the suddenness of this unforeseen catastrophe seemed to deprive me of words. All thought of merriment or ridicule was forgotten in a sense of guilt, for if he feigned the love he offered it was well done, and I believed it then. I saw at once the natural impression conveyed by my conduct; my half confession and the folly of it all oppressed me with a regret and shame I could not master. My mind was in dire confusion, yet a decided "No" was rapidly emerging from the chaos, but was not uttered; for just at this crisis, as I stood with my uncle's arm about me, my hand again in his, and his head bent down to catch my answer, Guy swung himself gaily into the room.

A glance seemed to explain all, and in an instant his face assumed that expression of pale wrath so much more terrible to witness than the fiercest outbreak; his eye grew fiery, his voice bitterly sarcastic, as he said, "Ah, I see; the play goes on, but the actors change parts. I congratulate you, sir, on your success, and Sybil on her choice. Henceforth I am *de trop,* but before I go allow me to offer my wedding gift. You have taken the bride, let me supply the ring."

He threw a jewel box upon the table, adding, in that unnaturally calm tone that made my heart stand still:

"A little candor would have spared me much pain, Sybil; yet I hope you will enjoy your bonds as heartily as I shall my escape from them. A little confidence would have made me your ally, not your rival, Father. I have not your address; therefore I lose, you win. Let it be so. I had rather be the vagabond this makes me than sell myself, that you may gamble away that girl's fortune as you have your own and mine. You need not ask me to the wedding, I will not come. Oh, Sybil, I so loved, so trusted you!"

And with that broken exclamation he was gone.

The stormy scene had passed so rapidly, been so strange and sudden, Guy's anger so scornful and abrupt, I could not understand it, and felt like a puppet in the grasp of some power I could not resist; but as my lover left the room I broke out of the bewilderment that held me, imploring him to stay and hear me.

It was too late, he was gone, and Sultan's tramp was already tearing down the avenue. I listened till the sound died, then my hot temper rose past control, and womanlike asserted itself in vehement and voluble speech. I was angry with my uncle, my cousin, and myself, and for several minutes poured forth a torrent of explanations, reproaches, and regrets, such as only a passionate girl could utter.

My uncle stood where I had left him when I flew to the door with my vain cry; he now looked baffled, yet sternly resolved, and as I paused for breath his only answer was "Sybil, you ask me to bring back that headstrong boy; I cannot; he will never come. This marriage was distasteful to him, yet he submitted for my sake, because I have been unfortunate, and we are poor. Let him go, forget the past, and be to me what I desire, for I loved your father and will be a faithful guardian to his daughter all my life. Child, it must be—come, I implore, I command you."

He beckoned imperiously as if to awe me, and held up the glittering betrothal ring as if to tempt me. The tone, the act, the look put me quite beside myself. I did go to him, did take the ring, but said as resolutely as himself, "Guy rejects me, and I have done with love. Uncle, you would have deceived me, used me as a means to your own selfish ends. I will accept neither yourself nor your gifts, for now I despise both you and your commands." And as the most energetic emphasis I could give to my defiance, I flung the ring, case and all, across the room; it struck the great mirror, shivered it just in the middle, and sent several loosened fragments crashing to the floor.

"Great heavens! Is the young lady mad?" exclaimed a voice behind us. Both turned and saw Dr. Karnac, a stealthy, sallow-faced Spaniard, for whom I had an invincible aversion. He was my uncle's physician, had been visiting a sick servant in the upper regions, and my adverse fate sent him to the door just at that moment with that unfortunate exclamation on his lips.

"What do you say?"

My uncle wheeled about and eyed the newcomer intently as he repeated his words. I have no doubt I looked like one demented, for I was desperately angry, pale and trembling with excitement, and as they fronted me with a curious expression of alarm on their faces, a sudden sense of the absurdity of the spectacle came over me; I laughed hysterically a moment, then broke into a passion of regretful tears, remembering that Guy was gone. As I sobbed behind my hands, I knew the gentlemen were whispering together and of me, but I never heeded them, for as I wept myself calmer a comforting thought occurred to me. Guy could not have gone far, for Sultan had been out all day, and though reckless of himself he was not of his horse, which he loved like a human being; therefore he was doubtless at the house of a humble friend nearby. If I could slip away unseen, I might undo my miserable work, or at least see him again before he went away into the world, perhaps never to return. This hope gave me courage for anything, and dashing away my tears, I took a covert survey. Dr. Karnac and my uncle still stood before the fire, deep in their low-toned conversation; their backs were toward me; and hushing the rustle of my dress, I stole away with noiseless steps into the hall, seized Guy's plaid, and, opening the great door unseen, darted down the avenue.

Not far, however; the wind buffeted me to and fro, the rain blinded me, the mud clogged my feet and soon robbed me of a slipper; groping for it in despair, I saw a light flash into the outer darkness; heard voices calling, and soon the swift tramp of steps behind me. Feeling like a hunted doe, I ran on, but before I had gained a dozen yards my shoeless foot struck a sharp stone, and I fell half stunned upon the wet grass of the wayside bank. Dr. Karnac reached me first, took me up as if I were a naughty child, and carried me back through a group of staring servants to the drawing room, my uncle following with breathless entreaties that I would be calm, and a most uncharacteristic display of bustle.

I was horribly ashamed; my head ached with the shock of the fall, my foot bled, my heart fluttered, and when the doctor put me down the crisis came, for as my uncle bent over me with the strange question "My poor girl, do you know me?" an irresistible impulse impelled me to push him from me, crying passionately, "Yes, I know and hate you; let me go! Let me go, or it will be too late!" Then, quite spent with the varying emotions of the last hour, for the first time in my life I swooned away.

Coming to myself, I found I was in my own room, with my uncle, the doctor, Janet, and Mrs. Best, the housekeeper, gathered about me, the latter saying, as she bathed my temples, "She's a sad sight, poor thing, so young, so bonny, and so unfortunate. Did you ever see her so before, Janet?"

"Bless you, no, ma'am; there was no signs of such a tantrum when I dressed her for dinner."

"What do they mean? Did they never see anyone angry before?" I dimly wondered, and presently, through the fast disappearing stupor that had held me, Dr. Karnac's deep voice came distinctly, saying, "If it continues, you are perfectly justified in doing so."

"Doing what?" I demanded sharply, for the sound both roused and irritated me, I disliked the man so intensely.

"Nothing, my dear, nothing," purred Mrs. Best, supporting me as I sat up, feeling weak and dazed, yet resolved to know what was going on. I was "a sad sight" indeed: my drenched hair hung about my shoulders, my dress was streaked with mud, one shoeless foot was red with blood, the other splashed and stained, and a white, wild-eyed face completed the ruinous image the opposite mirror showed me. Everything looked blurred and strange, and a feverish unrest possessed me, for I was not one to subside easily after such a mental storm. Leaning on my arm, I scanned the room and its occupants with all the composure I could collect. The two women eyed me curiously yet pitifully; Dr. Karnac stood glancing at me furtively as he listened to my uncle, who spoke rapidly in Spanish as he showed the little scar upon his hand.

That sight did more to restore me than the cordial just administered, and I rose erect, saying abruptly, "Please, everybody, go away; my head aches, and I want to be alone."

"Let Janet stay and help you, dear; you are not fit," began Mrs. Best; but I peremptorily stopped her.

"No, go yourself, and take her with you; I'm tired of so much stir about such foolish things as a broken glass and a girl in a pet."

"You will be good enough to take this quieting draft before I go, Miss Sybil."

"I shall do nothing of the sort, for I need only solitude and sleep to be perfectly well," and I emptied the glass the doctor offered into the fire.

He shrugged his shoulders with a disagreeable smile, and quietly began to prepare another draft, saying, "You are mistaken, my dear young lady; you need much care, and should obey, that your uncle may be spared further apprehension and anxiety."

My patience gave out at this assumption of authority; and I determined to carry matters with a high hand, for they all stood watching me in a way which seemed the height of impertinent curiosity.

"He is not my uncle! Never has been, and deserves neither respect nor obedience from me! I am the best judge of my own health, and you are not bettering it by contradiction and unnecessary fuss. This is my house, and you will oblige me by leaving it, Dr. Karnac; this is my room, and I insist on being left in peace immediately."

I pointed to the door as I spoke; the women hurried out with scared faces; the doctor bowed and followed, but paused on the threshold, while my uncle approached me, asking in a tone inaudible to those still hovering round the door, "Do you still persist in your refusal, Sybil?"

"How dare you ask me that again? I tell you I had rather die than marry you!"

"The Lord be merciful to us! Just hear how she's going on now about marrying Master. Ain't it awful, Jane?" ejaculated Mrs. Best, bobbing her head in for a last look.

"Hold your tongue, you impertinent creature!" I called out; and the fat old soul bundled away in such comical haste I laughed, in spite of languor and vexation.

My uncle left me, and I heard him say as he passed the doctor, "You see how it is."

"Nothing uncommon; but that virulence is a bad symptom," answered the Spaniard, and closing the door locked it, having dexterously removed the key from within.

I had never been subjected to restraint of any kind; it made me reckless at once, for this last indignity was not to be endured.

"Open this instantly!" I commanded, shaking the door. No one answered, and after a few ineffectual attempts to break the lock I left it, threw up the window and looked out; the ground was too far off for a leap, but the trellis where summer vines had clung was strong and high, a step would place me on it, a moment's agility bring me to the terrace below. I was now in just the state to attempt any rash exploit, for the cordial had both strengthened and excited me; my foot was bandaged, my clothes still wet; I could suffer no new damage, and have my own way at small cost. Out I crept, climbed safely down, and made my way to the lodge as I had at first intended. But Guy was not there; and returning, I boldly went in at the great door, straight to the room where my uncle and the doctor were still talking.

"I wish the key of my room" was my brief command.

Both started as if I had been a ghost, and my uncle exclaimed, "You here! How in heaven's name came you out?"

"By the window. I am no child to be confined for a fit of anger. I will not submit to it; tomorrow I shall go to Madame; till then I will be mistress in my own house. Give me the key, sir."

"Shall I?" asked the doctor of my uncle, who nodded with a whispered "Yes, yes; don't excite her again."

It was restored, and without another word I went loftily up to my room, locked myself in, and spent a restless, miserable night. When morning came, I breakfasted abovestairs, and then busied myself packing trunks, burning papers, and collecting every trifle Guy had ever given me. No one annoyed me, and I saw only Janet, who had evidently received some order that kept her silent and respectful, though her face still betrayed the same curiosity and pitiful interest as the night before. Lunch was brought up, but I could not eat, and began to feel that the exposure, the fall, and excitement of the evening had left me weak and nervous, so I gave up the idea of going to Madame till the morrow; and as the afternoon waned, tried to sleep, yet could not, for I had sent a note to several of Guy's haunts, imploring him to see me; but my messenger brought word that he was not to be found, and my heart was too heavy to rest.

When summoned to dinner, I still refused to go down; for I heard Dr. Karnac's voice, and would not meet him, so I sent word that I wished the carriage early the following morning, and to be left alone till then. In a few minutes, back came Janet, with a glass of wine set forth on a silver salver, and a card with these words: "Forgive, forget, for your father's sake, and drink with me, 'Oblivion to the past.'"

It touched and softened me. I knew my uncle's pride, and saw in this an entire relinquishment of the hopes I had so thoughtlessly fostered in his mind. I was passionate, but not vindictive. He had been kind, I very willful. His mistake was natural, my resentment ungenerous. Though my resolution to go remained unchanged, I was sorry for my part in the affair; and remembering that through me his son was lost to him, I accepted his apology, drank his toast, and sent him back a dutiful "Good night."

I was unused to wine. The draft I had taken was powerful with age, and, though warm and racy to the palate, proved too potent for me. Still sitting before my fire, I slowly fell into a restless drowse, haunted by a dim dream that I was seeking Guy in a ship, whose motion gradually lulled me into perfect unconsciousness.

Waking at length, I was surprised to find myself in bed, with a shimmer of daylight peeping through the curtains. Recollecting that I was to leave early, I sprang up, took one step, and remained transfixed with dismay, for the room was not my own! Utterly unfamiliar was every object on which my eyes fell. The place was small, plainly furnished, and close, as if long unused. My trunks stood against the wall, my clothes lay on a chair, and on the bed I had left trailed a fur-lined cloak I had often seen on my uncle's shoulders. A moment I stared about me bewildered, then hurried to the window. It was grated!

A lawn, sere and sodden, lay without, and a line of somber firs hid the landscape beyond the high wall which encompassed the dreary plot. More and more alarmed, I flew to the door and found it locked. No bell was visible, no sound audible, no human presence near me, and an ominous foreboding thrilled cold through nerves and blood, as, for the first time, I felt the paralyzing touch of fear. Not long, however. My native courage soon returned, indignation took the place of terror, and excitement gave me strength. My temples throbbed with a dull pain, my eyes were heavy, my limbs weighed down by an unwonted lassitude, and my memory seemed strangely confused; but one thing was clear to me: I must see somebody, ask questions, demand explanations, and get away to Madame without delay.

With trembling hands I dressed, stopping suddenly with a cry; for lifting my hands to my head, I discovered that my hair, my beautiful, abundant hair, was gone! There was no mirror in the room, but I could feel that it had been shorn away close about face and neck. This outrage was more than I could bear, and the first tears I shed fell for my lost charm. It was weak, perhaps, but I felt better for it, clearer in mind and readier to confront whatever lay before me. I knocked and called. Then, losing patience, shook and screamed; but no one came or answered me; and wearied out at last, I sat down and cried again in impotent despair.

An hour passed, then a step approached, the key turned, and a hard-faced woman entered with a tray in her hand. I had resolved to be patient, if possible, and controlled myself to ask quietly, though my eyes kindled, and my voice trembled with resentment, "Where am I, and why am I here against my will?"

"This is your breakfast, miss; you must be sadly hungry" was the only reply I got.

"I will never eat till you tell me what I ask."

"Will you be quiet, and mind me if I do, miss?"

"You have no right to exact obedience from me, but I'll try."

"That's right. Now all I know is that you are twenty miles from the Moors, and came because you are ill. Do you like sugar in your coffee?"

"When did I come? I don't remember it."

"Early this morning; you don't remember because you were put to sleep before being fetched, to save trouble."

"Ah, that wine! Who brought me here?"

"Dr. Karnac, miss."

"Alone?"

"Yes, miss; you were easier to manage asleep than awake, he said."

I shook with anger, yet still restrained myself, hoping to fathom the mystery of this nocturnal journey.

"What is your name, please?" I meekly asked.

"You can call me Hannah."

"Well, Hannah, there is a strange mistake somewhere. I am not ill—you see I am not—and I wish to go away at once to the friend I was to meet today. Get me a carriage and have my baggage taken out."

"It can't be done, miss. We are a mile from town, and have no carriages here; besides, you couldn't go if I had a dozen. I have my orders, and shall obey 'em."

"But Dr. Karnac has no right to bring or keep me here."

"Your uncle sent you. The doctor has the care of you, and that is all I know about it. Now I have kept my promise, do you keep yours, miss, and eat your breakfast, else I can't trust you again."

"But what is the matter with me? How can I be ill and not know or feel it?" I demanded, more and more bewildered.

"You look it, and that's enough for them as is wise in such matters. You'd have had a fever, if it hadn't been seen to in time."

"Who cut my hair off?"

"I did; the doctor ordered it."

"How dared he? I hate that man, and never will obey him."

"Hush, miss, don't clench your hands and look in that way, for I shall have to report everything you say and do to him, and it won't be pleasant to tell that sort of thing."

The woman was civil, but grim and cool. Her eye was unsympathetic, her manner businesslike, her tone such as one uses to a refractory child, half soothing, half commanding. I conceived a dislike to her at once, and resolved to escape at all hazards, for my uncle's inexplicable movements filled me with alarm. Hannah had left my door open, a quick glance showed me another door also ajar at the end of a wide hall, a glimpse of green, and a gate. My plan was desperately simple, and I executed it without delay. Affecting to eat, I presently asked the woman for my handkerchief from the bed. She crossed the room to get it. I darted out, down the passage, along the walk, and tugged vigorously at the great bolt of the gate, but it was also locked. In despair I flew into the garden, but a high wall enclosed it on every side; and as I ran round and round, vainly looking for some outlet, I saw Hannah, accompanied by a man as gray and grim as herself, coming leisurely toward me, with no appearance of excitement or displeasure. Back I would not go; and inspired with a sudden hope, swung myself into one of the firs that grew close against the wall. The branches snapped under me, the slender tree swayed perilously, but up I struggled, till the wide coping of the wall was gained. There I paused and looked back. The woman was hurrying through the gate to intercept my descent on the other side, and close behind me the man, sternly calling me to stop. I looked down; a stony ditch was below, but I would rather risk my life than tamely lose my liberty, and with a flying leap tried to reach the bank; failed, fell heavily among the stones, felt an awful crash, and then came an utter blank.

For many weeks I lay burning in a fever, fitfully conscious of Dr. Karnac and the woman's presence; once I fancied I saw my uncle, but was never sure, and rose at last a shadow of my former self, feeling pitifully broken, both mentally and physically. I was in a better room now, wintry winds howled without, but a generous fire glowed behind the high closed fender, and books lay on my table.

I saw no one but Hannah, yet could wring no intelligence from her beyond what she had already told, and no sign of interest reached me from the outer world. I seemed utterly deserted and forlorn, my spirit was crushed, my strength gone, my freedom lost, and for a time I suc-

cumbed to despair, letting one day follow another without energy or
hope. It is hard to live with no object to give zest to life, especially for
those still blessed with youth, and even in my prison house I soon found
one quite in keeping with the mystery that surrounded me.

As I sat reading by day or lay awake at night, I became aware that
the room above my own was occupied by some inmate whom I never
saw. A peculiar person it seemed to be; for I heard steps going to and
fro, hour after hour, in a tireless march that wore upon my nerves, as
many a harsher sound would not have done. I could neither tease nor
surprise Hannah into any explanation of the thing, and day after day
I listened to it, till I longed to cover up my ears and implore the unknown
walker to stop, for heaven's sake. Other sounds I heard and fretted over:
a low monotonous murmur, as of someone singing a lullaby; a fitful tap-
ping, like a cradle rocked on a carpetless floor; and at rare intervals cries
of suffering, sharp but brief, as if forcibly suppressed. These sounds,
combined with the solitude, the confinement, and the books I read, a collection of ghostly tales and weird fancies, soon wrought my nerves to a
state of terrible irritability, and wore upon my health so visibly that I was
allowed at last to leave my room.

The house was so well guarded that I soon relinquished all hope
of escape, and listlessly amused myself by roaming through the unfur-
nished rooms and echoing halls, seldom venturing into Hannah's domain; for there her husband sat, surrounded by chemical apparatus,
poring over crucibles and retorts. He never spoke to me, and I dreaded
the glance of his cold eye, for it looked unsoftened by a ray of pity at
the little figure that sometimes paused a moment on his threshold, wan
and wasted as the ghost of departed hope.

The chief interest of these dreary walks centered in the door of
the room above my own, for a great hound lay before it, eyeing me sav-
agely as he rejected all advances, and uttering his deep bay if I approached too near. To me this room possessed an irresistible fascination.
I could not keep away from it by day, I dreamed of it by night, it haunted
me continually, and soon became a sort of monomania, which I con-
demned, yet could not control, till at length I found myself pacing to
and fro as those invisible feet paced overhead. Hannah came and stopped
me, and a few hours later Dr. Karnac appeared. I was so changed that
I feared him with a deadly fear. He seemed to enjoy it; for in the pride
of youth and beauty I had shown him contempt and defiance at my
uncle's, and he took an ungenerous satisfaction in annoying me by a
display of power. He never answered my questions or entreaties, regarded
me as being without sense or will, insisted on my trying various mixtures

and experiments in diet, gave me strange books to read, and weekly received Hannah's report of all that passed. That day he came, looked at me, said, "Let her walk," and went away, smiling that hateful smile of his.

Soon after this I took to walking in my sleep, and more than once woke to find myself roving lampless through that haunted house in the dead of night. I concealed these unconscious wanderings for a time, but an ominous event broke them up at last and betrayed them to Hannah.

I had followed the steps one day for several hours, walking below as they walked above; had peopled that mysterious room with every mournful shape my disordered fancy could conjure up; had woven tragical romances about it, and brooded over the one subject of interest my unnatural life possessed with the intensity of a mind upon which its uncanny influence was telling with perilous rapidity. At midnight I woke to find myself standing in a streak of moonlight, opposite the door whose threshold I had never crossed. The April night was warm, a single pane of glass high up in that closed door was drawn aside, as if for air; and as I stood dreamily collecting my sleep-drunken senses, I saw a ghostly hand emerge and beckon, as if to me. It startled me broad awake, with a faint exclamation and a shudder from head to foot. A cloud swept over the moon, and when it passed the hand was gone, but shrill through the keyhole came a whisper that chilled me to the marrow of my bones, so terribly distinct and imploring was it.

"Find it! For God's sake find it before it is too late!"

The hound sprang up with an angry growl; I heard Hannah leave her bed nearby; and with an inspiration strange as the moment, I paced slowly on with open eyes and lips apart, as I had seen *Amina* in the happy days when kind old Madame took me to the theater, whose mimic horrors I had never thought to equal with such veritable ones. Hannah appeared at her door with a light, but on I went in a trance of fear; for I was only kept from dropping in a swoon by the blind longing to fly from that spectral voice and hand. Past Hannah I went, she following; and as I slowly laid myself in bed, I heard her say to her husband, who just then came up, "Sleepwalking, John; it's getting worse and worse, as the doctor foretold; she'll settle down like the other presently, but she must be locked up at night, else the dog will do her a mischief."

The man yawned and grumbled; then they went, leaving me to spend hours of unspeakable suffering, which aged me more than years. What was I to find? Where was I to look? And when would it be too late? These questions tormented me; for I could find no answers to them,

divine no meaning, see no course to pursue. Why was I here? What
motive induced my uncle to commit such an act? And when should I be
liberated? were equally unanswerable, equally tormenting, and they
haunted me like ghosts. I had no power to exorcise or forget. After that
I walked no more, because I slept no more; sleep seemed scared away,
and waking dreams harassed me with their terrors. Night after night I
paced my room in utter darkness—for I was allowed no lamp—night after
night I wept bitter tears wrung from me by anguish, for which I had
no name; and night after night the steps kept time to mine, and the faint
lullaby came down to me as if to soothe and comfort my distress. I felt
that my health was going, my mind growing confused and weak; my
thoughts wandered vaguely, memory began to fail, and idiocy or madness
seemed my inevitable fate; but through it all my heart clung to Guy,
yearning for him with a hunger that would not be appeased.

At rare intervals I was allowed to walk in the neglected garden,
where no flowers bloomed, no birds sang, no companion came to me but
surly John, who followed with his book or pipe, stopping when I stopped,
walking when I walked, keeping a vigilant eye upon me, yet seldom
speaking except to decline answering my questions. These walks did me
no good, for the air was damp and heavy with vapors from the marsh; for
the house stood near a half-dried lake, and hills shut it in on every side.
No fresh winds from upland moor or distant ocean ever blew across the
narrow valley; no human creature visited the place, and nothing but a
vague hope that my birthday might bring some change, some help, sustained me. It did bring help, but of such an unexpected sort that its
effects remained through all my afterlife. My birthday came, and with it
my uncle. I was in my room, walking restlessly—for the habit was a confirmed one now—when the door opened, and Hannah, Dr. Karnac, my
uncle, and a gentleman whom I knew to be his lawyer entered, and
surveyed me as if I were a spectacle. I saw my uncle start and turn pale;
I had never seen myself since I came, but if I had not suspected that I
was a melancholy wreck of my former self, I should have known it then,
such sudden pain and pity softened his ruthless countenance for a single
instant. Dr. Karnac's eye had a magnetic power over me; I had always
felt it, but in my present feeble state I dreaded, yet submitted to it with
a helpless fear that should have touched his heart—it was on me then,
I could not resist it, and paused fixed and fascinated by that repellent
yet potent glance.

Hannah pointed to the carpet worn to shreds by my weary march,
to the walls which I had covered with weird, grotesque, or tragic figures

to while away the heavy hours, lastly to myself, mute, motionless, and scared, saying, as if in confirmation of some previous assertion, "You see, gentlemen, she is, as I said, quiet, but quite hopeless."

I thought she was interceding for me; and breaking from the bewilderment and fear that held me, I stretched my hands to them, crying with an imploring cry, "Yes, I *am* quiet! I *am* hopeless! Oh, have pity on me before this dreadful life kills me or drives me mad!"

Dr. Karnac came to me at once with a black frown, which I alone could see; I evaded him, and clung to Hannah, still crying frantically—for this seemed my last hope—"Uncle, let me go! I will give you all I have, will never ask for Guy, will be obedient and meek if I may only go to Madame and never hear the feet again, or see the sights that terrify me in this dreadful room. Take me out! For God's sake take me out!"

My uncle did not answer me, but covered up his face with a despairing gesture, and hurried from the room; the lawyer followed, muttering pitifully, "Poor thing! Poor thing!" and Dr. Karnac laughed the first laugh I had ever heard him utter as he wrenched Hannah from my grasp and locked me in alone. My one hope died then, and I resolved to kill myself rather than endure this life another month; for now it grew clear to me that they believed me mad, and death of the body was far more preferable than that of the mind. I think I *was* a little mad just then, but remember well the sense of peace that came to me as I tore strips from my clothing, braided them into a cord, hid it beneath my mattress, and serenely waited for the night. Sitting in the last twilight I thought to see in this unhappy world, I recollected that I had not heard the feet all day, and fell to pondering over the unusual omission. But if the steps had been silent in that room, voices had not, for I heard a continuous murmur at one time: the tones of one voice were abrupt and broken, the other low, yet resonant, and that, I felt assured, belonged to my uncle. Who was he speaking to? What were they saying? Should I ever know? And even then, with death before me, the intense desire to possess the secret filled me with its old unrest.

Night came at last; I heard the clock strike one, and listening to discover if John still lingered up, I heard through the deep hush a soft grating in the room above, a stealthy sound that would have escaped ears less preternaturally alert than mine. Like a flash came the thought, "Someone is filing bars or picking locks: will the unknown remember me and let me share her flight?" The fatal noose hung ready, but I no longer cared to use it, for hope had come to nerve me with the strength and courage I had lost. Breathlessly I listened; the sound went on, stopped; a dead silence reigned; then something brushed against my door, and with a suddenness that made me tingle from head to foot like an electric shock, through the keyhole came again that whisper, urgent, imploring, and mysterious, "Find it! For God's sake find it before it is too late!" Then fainter, as if breath failed, came the broken words, "The dog—a lock of hair—there is yet time."

Eagerness rendered me forgetful of the secrecy I should preserve, and I cried aloud, "What shall I find? Where shall I look?" My voice, sharpened by fear, rang shrilly through the house; Hannah's quick tread rushed down the hall; something fell; then loud and long rose a cry that made my heart stand still, so helpless, so hopeless was its wild lament. I had betrayed and I could not save or comfort the kind soul who had lost liberty through me. I was frantic to get out, and beat upon my door in a paroxysm of impatience, but no one came; and all night long those awful cries went on above, cries of mortal anguish, as if soul and body were being torn asunder. Till dawn I listened, pent in that room which now possessed an added terror; till dawn I called, wept, and prayed, with mingled pity, fear, and penitence; and till dawn the agony of that unknown sufferer continued unabated. I heard John hurry to and fro, heard Hannah issue orders with an accent of human sympathy in her hard voice; heard Dr. Karnac pass and repass my door; and all the sounds of confusion and alarm in that once quiet house. With daylight all was still, a stillness more terrible than the stir; for it fell so suddenly, remained so utterly unbroken, that there seemed no explanation of it but the dread word death.

At noon Hannah, a shade paler but grim as ever, brought me some food, saying she forgot my breakfast, and when I refused to eat, yet asked no questions, she bade me go into the garden and not fret myself over last night's flurry. I went, and passing down the corridor, glanced furtively at the door I never saw without a thrill; but I experienced a new sensation then, for the hound was gone, the door was open, and with an impulse past control, I crept in and looked about me. It was a room like mine, the carpet worn like mine, the windows barred like mine; there the resemblance ended, for an empty cradle stood beside the bed, and on that bed, below a sweeping cover, stark and still a lifeless body lay. I was inured to fear now, and an unwholesome craving for new terrors seemed to have grown by what it fed on: an irresistible desire led me close, nerved me to lift the cover and look below—a single glance—then with a cry as panic-stricken as that which rent the silence of the night, I fled away, for the face I saw was a pale image of my own. Sharpened by suffering, pallid with death, the features were familiar as those I used to see; the hair, beautiful and blond as mine had been, streamed long over the pulseless breast, and on the hand, still clenched in that last struggle, shone the likeness of a ring I wore, a ring bequeathed me by my father. An awesome fancy that it was myself assailed me; I had plotted death, and with the waywardness of a shattered mind, I recalled legends of spirits returning to behold the bodies they had left.

Glad now to seek the garden, I hurried down, but on the threshold of the great hall door was arrested by the sharp crack of a pistol; and as a little cloud of smoke dispersed, I saw John drop the weapon and approach the hound, who lay writhing on the bloody grass. Moved by compassion for the faithful brute whose long vigilance was so cruelly repaid, I went to him, and kneeling there, caressed the great head that never yielded to my touch before. John assumed his watch at once, and leaning against a tree, cleaned the pistol, content that I should amuse myself with the dying creature, who looked into my face with eyes of almost human pathos and reproach. The brass collar seemed to choke him as he gasped for breath, and leaning nearer to undo it, I saw, half hidden in his own black hair, a golden lock wound tightly round the collar, and so near its color as to be unobservable, except upon a close inspection. No accident could have placed it there; no head but mine in that house wore hair of that sunny hue—yes, one other, and my heart gave a sudden leap as I remembered the shining locks just seen on that still bosom.

"Find it—the dog—the lock of hair," rang in my ears, and swift as light came the conviction that the unknown help was found at last. The little band was woven close. I had no knife, delay was fatal. I bent my head as if lamenting over the poor beast and bit the knot apart, drew out a folded paper, hid it in my hand, and rising, strolled leisurely back to my own room, saying I did not care to walk till it was warmer. With eager eyes I examined my strange treasure trove. It consisted of two strips of thinnest paper, without address or signature, one almost illegible, worn at the edges and stained with the green rust of the collar; the other fresher, yet more feebly written, both abrupt and disjointed, but terribly significant to me. This was the first:

> I have never seen you, never heard your name, yet I know that you are young, that you are suffering, and I try to help you in my poor way. I think you are not crazed yet, as I often am; for your voice is sane, your plaintive singing not like mine, your walking only caught from me, I hope. I sing to lull the baby whom I never saw; I walk to lessen the long journey that will bring me to the husband I have lost—stop! I must not think of those things or I shall forget. If you are not already mad, you will be; I suspect you were sent here to be made so; for the air is poison, the solitude is fatal, and Karnac remorseless in his mania for prying

into the mysteries of human minds. What devil sent you I may never know, but I long to warn you. I can devise no way but this; the dog comes into my room sometimes, you sometimes pause at my door and talk to him; you may find the paper I shall hide about his collar. Read, destroy, but obey it. I implore you to leave this house before it is too late.

The other paper was as follows:

I have watched you, tried to tell you where to look, for you have not found my warning yet, though I often tie it there and hope. You fear the dog, perhaps, and my plot fails; yet I know by your altered step and voice that you are fast reaching my unhappy state; for I am fitfully mad, and shall be till I die. Today I have seen a familiar face; it seems to have calmed and strengthened me, and though he would not help you, I shall make one desperate attempt. I may not find you, so leave my warning to the hound, yet hope to breathe a word into your sleepless ear that shall send you back into the world the happy thing you should be. Child! Woman! Whatever you are, leave this accursed house while you have power to do it.

That was all. I did not destroy the papers, but I obeyed them, and for a week watched and waited till the propitious instant came. I saw my uncle, the doctor, and two others follow the poor body to its grave beside the lake, saw all depart but Dr. Karnac, and felt redoubled hatred and contempt for the men who could repay my girlish slights with such a horrible revenge. On the seventh day, as I went down for my daily walk, I saw John and Dr. Karnac so deep in some uncanny experiment that I passed out unguarded. Hoping to profit by this unexpected chance, I sprang down the steps, but the next moment dropped half stunned upon the grass; for behind me rose a crash, a shriek, a sudden blaze that flashed up and spread, sending a noisome vapor rolling out with clouds of smoke and flame.

Aghast, I was just gathering myself up when Hannah fled out of the house, dragging her husband senseless and bleeding, while her own face was ashy with affright. She dropped her burden beside me, saying, with white lips and a vain look for help where help was not, "Something they were at has burst, killed the doctor, and fired the house! Watch John till I get help, and leave him at your peril." Then flinging open the gate she sped away.

"Now is my time," I thought, and only waiting till she vanished, I boldly followed her example, running rapidly along the road in an op- posite direction, careless of bonnetless head and trembling limbs, intent only upon leaving that prison house far behind me. For several hours,

I hurried along that solitary road; the spring sun shone, birds sang in the blooming hedges, green nooks invited me to pause and rest; but I heeded none of them, steadily continuing my flight, till spent and footsore I was forced to stop a moment by a wayside spring. As I stooped to drink, I saw my face for the first time in many months, and started to see how like that dead one it had grown, in all but the eternal peace which made that beautiful in spite of suffering and age. Standing thus and wondering if Guy would know me, should we ever meet, the sound of wheels disturbed me. Believing them to be coming from the place I had left, I ran desperately down the hill, turned a sharp corner, and before I could check myself passed a carriage slowly ascending. A face sprang to the window, a voice cried "Stop!" but on I flew, hoping the traveler would let me go unpursued. Not so, however; soon I heard fleet steps following, gaining rapidly, then a hand seized me, a voice rang in my ears, and with a vain struggle I lay panting in my captor's hold, fearing to look up and meet a brutal glance. But the hand that had seized me tenderly drew me close, the voice that had alarmed cried joyfully, "Sybil, it is Guy: Lie still, poor child, you are safe at last."

Then I knew that my surest refuge was gained, and too weak for words, clung to him in an agony of happiness, which brought to his kind eyes the tears I could not shed.

The carriage returned; Guy took me in, and for a time cared only to soothe and sustain my worn soul and body with the cordial of his presence, as we rolled homeward through a blooming world, whose beauty I had never truly felt before. When the first tumult of emotion had subsided, I told the story of my captivity and my escape, ending with a passionate entreaty not to be returned to my uncle's keeping, for henceforth there could be neither affection nor respect between us.

"Fear nothing, Sybil; Madame is waiting for you at the Moors, and my father's unfaithful guardianship has ended with his life."

Then with averted face and broken voice Guy went on to tell his father's purposes, and what had caused this unexpected meeting. The facts were briefly these: The knowledge that my father had come between him and a princely fortune had always rankled in my uncle's heart, chilling the ambitious hopes he cherished even in his boyhood, and making life an eager search for pleasure in which to drown his vain regrets. This secret was suspected by my father, and the household league was formed as some atonement for the innocent offense. It seemed to soothe my uncle's resentful nature, and as years went on he lived freely, assured that ample means would be his through his son. Luxurious, self-indulgent, fond of all excitements, and reckless in their pursuit, he took

no thought for the morrow till a few months before his return. A gay
winter in Paris reduced him to those straits of which women know so
little; creditors were oppressive, summer friends failed him, gambling
debts harassed him, his son reproached him, and but one resource remained—Guy's speedy marriage with the half-forgotten heiress. The boy
had been educated to regard this fate as a fixed fact, and submitted, believing the time to be far distant; but the sudden summons came, and
he rebelled against it, preferring liberty to love. My uncle pacified the
claimants by promises to be fulfilled at my expense, and hurried home
to press on the marriage, which now seemed imperative. I was taken to
my future home, approved by my uncle, beloved by my cousin, and, but
for my own folly, might have been a happy wife on that May morning
when I listened to the unveiling of the past. My mother had been melancholy mad since that unhappy rumor of my father's death; this affliction had been well concealed from me, lest the knowledge should prey
upon my excitable nature and perhaps induce a like misfortune. I believed her dead, yet I had seen her, knew where her solitary grave was
made, and still carried in my bosom the warning she had sent me,
prompted by the unerring instinct of a mother's heart. In my father's will
a clause was added just below the one confirming my betrothal, a clause
decreeing that, if it should appear that I inherited my mother's malady,
the fortune should revert to my cousin, with myself a mournful legacy,
to be cherished by him whether his wife or not. This passage, and that
relating to my freedom of choice, had been omitted in the copy shown
me on the night when my seeming refusal of Guy had induced his father
to believe that I loved him, to make a last attempt to keep the prize by
offering himself, and, when that failed, to harbor a design that changed
my little comedy into the tragical experience I have told.

Dr. Karnac's exclamation had caused the recollection of that clause
respecting my insanity to flash into my uncle's mind—a mind as quick to
conceive as fearless to execute. I unconsciously abetted the stratagem,
and Dr. Karnac was an unscrupulous ally, for love of gain was as strong
as love of science; both were amply gratified, and I, poor victim, was
given up to be experimented upon, till by subtle means I was driven
to the insanity which would give my uncle full control of my fortune
and my fate. How the black plot prospered has been told; but retribution
speedily overtook them both, for Dr. Karnac paid his penalty by the sudden death that left his ashes among the blackened ruins of that house
of horrors, and my uncle had preceded him. For before the change of
heirs could be effected my mother died, and the hours spent in that
unhealthful spot insinuated the subtle poison of the marsh into his blood;

years of pleasure left little vigor to withstand the fever, and a week of suffering ended a life of generous impulses perverted, fine endowments wasted, and opportunities forever lost. When death drew near, he sent for Guy (who, through the hard discipline of poverty and honest labor, was becoming a manlier man), confessed all, and implored him to save me before it was too late. He did, and when all was told, when each saw the other by the light of this strange and sad experience—Guy poor again, I free, the old bond still existing, the barrier of misunderstanding gone— it was easy to see our way, easy to submit, to forgive, forget, and begin anew the life these clouds had darkened for a time.

Home received me, kind Madame welcomed me, Guy married me, and I was happy; but over all these years, serenely prosperous, still hangs for me the shadow of the past, still rises that dead image of my mother, still echoes that spectral whisper in the dark.

Perilous Play

"IF someone does not propose a new and interesting amusement, I shall die of ennui!" said pretty Belle Daventry, in a tone of despair. "I have read all my books, used up all my Berlin wools, and it's too warm to go to town for more. No one can go sailing yet, as the tide is out; we are all nearly tired to death of cards, croquet, and gossip, so what shall we do to while away this endless afternoon? Dr. Meredith, I command you to invent and propose a new game in five minutes."

"To hear is to obey," replied the young man, who lay in the grass at her feet, as he submissively slapped his forehead, and fell a-thinking with all his might.

Holding up her finger to preserve silence, Belle pulled out her watch and waited with an expectant smile. The rest of the young party, who were indolently scattered about under the elms, drew nearer, and brightened visibly, for Dr. Meredith's inventive powers were well-known, and something refreshingly novel might be expected from him. One gentleman did not stir, but then he lay within earshot, and merely turned his fine eyes from the sea to the group before him. His glance rested a moment on Belle's piquant figure, for she looked very pretty with her bright hair blowing in the wind, one plump white arm extended to keep order, and one little foot, in a distracting slipper, just visible below the voluminous folds of her dress. Then the glance passed to another figure, sitting somewhat apart in a cloud of white muslin, for an airy burnoose floated from head and shoulders, showing only a singularly charming face. Pale and yet brilliant, for the Southern eyes were magnificent, the clear olive cheeks contrasted well with darkest hair; lips like a pomegranate flower, and delicate, straight brows, as mobile as the lips. A cluster of crimson flowers, half falling from the loose black braids, and a golden bracelet of Arabian coins on the slender wrist were the only ornaments she wore, and became her better than the fashionable frippery of her companions. A book lay on her lap, but her eyes, full of a passionate melancholy, were fixed on the sea, which glittered round an island green and flowery as a summer paradise. Rose St. Just was as beautiful as her Spanish mother, but had inherited the pride and reserve of her English father; and this pride was the thorn which repelled lovers from the human flower. Mark Done sighed as he looked, and as if the sigh, low as it was, roused her from her reverie, Rose flashed a quick glance at him, took up her book, and went on reading the legend of "The Lotus Eaters."

"Time is up now, Doctor," cried Belle, pocketing her watch with a flourish.

"Ready to report," answered Meredith, sitting up and producing a little box of tortoiseshell and gold.

"How mysterious! What is it? Let me see, first!" And Belle removed the cover, looking like an inquisitive child. "Only bonbons; how stupid! That won't do, sir. We don't want to be fed with sugarplums. We demand to be amused."

"Eat six of these despised bonbons, and you *will* be amused in a new, delicious, and wonderful manner," said the young doctor, laying half a dozen on a green leaf and offering them to her.

"Why, what are they?" she asked, looking at him askance.

"Hashish; did you never hear of it?"

"Oh, yes; it's that Indian stuff which brings one fantastic visions, isn't it? I've always wanted to see and taste it, and now I will," cried Belle, nibbling at one of the bean-shaped comfits with its green heart.

"I advise you not to try it. People do all sorts of queer things when they take it. I wouldn't for the world," said a prudent young lady warningly, as all examined the box and its contents.

"Six can do no harm, I give you my word. I take twenty before I can enjoy myself, and some people even more. I've tried many experiments, both on the sick and the well, and nothing ever happened amiss, though the demonstrations were immensely interesting," said Meredith, eating his sugarplums with a tranquil air, which was very convincing to others.

"How shall I feel?" asked Belle, beginning on her second comfit.

"A heavenly dreaminess comes over one, in which they move as if on air. Everything is calm and lovely to them: no pain, no care, no fear of anything, and while it lasts one feels like an angel half asleep."

"But if one takes too much, how then?" said a deep voice behind the doctor.

"Hum! Well, that's not so pleasant, unless one likes phantoms, frenzies, and a touch of nightmare, which seems to last a thousand years. Ever try it, Done?" replied Meredith, turning toward the speaker, who was now leaning on his arm and looking interested.

"Never. I'm not a good subject for experiments. Too nervous a temperament to play pranks with."

"I should say ten would be about your number. Less than that seldom affects men. Ladies go off sooner, and don't need so many. Miss St. Just, may I offer you a taste of Elysium? I owe my success to you," said the doctor, approaching her deferentially.

"To me! And how?" she asked, lifting her large eyes with a slight smile.

"I was in the depths of despair when my eye caught the title of your book, and I was saved. For I remembered that I had hashish in my pocket."

"Are you a lotus-eater?" she said, permitting him to lay the six charmed bonbons on the page.

"My faith, no! I use it for my patients. It is very efficacious in nervous disorders, and is getting to be quite a pet remedy with us."

"I do not want to forget the past, but to read the future. Will hashish help me to do that?" asked Rose with an eager look, which made the young man flush, wondering if he bore any part in her hopes of that veiled future.

"Alas, no. I wish it could, for I, too, long to know my fate," he answered, very low, as he looked into the lovely face before him.

The soft glance changed to one of cool indifference and Rose gently brushed the hashish off her book, saying, with a little gesture of dismissal, "Then I have no desire to taste Elysium."

The white morsels dropped into the grass at her feet; but Dr. Meredith let them lie, and turning sharply, went back to sun himself in Belle's smiles.

"I've eaten all mine, and so has Evelyn. Mr. Norton will see goblins, I know, for he has taken quantities. I'm glad of it, for he don't believe in it, and I want to have him convinced by making a spectacle of himself for our amusement," said Belle, in great spirits at the new plan.

"When does the trance come on?" asked Evelyn, a shy girl, already rather alarmed at what she had done.

"About three hours after you take your dose, though the time varies with different people. Your pulse will rise, heart beat quickly, eyes darken and dilate, and an uplifted sensation will pervade you generally. Then these symptoms change, and the bliss begins. I've seen people sit or lie in one position for hours, rapt in a delicious dream, and wake from it as tranquil as if they had not a nerve in their bodies."

"How charming! I'll take some every time I'm worried. Let me see. It's now four, so our trances will come about seven, and we will devote the evening to manifestations," said Belle.

"Come, Done, try it. We are all going in for the fun. Here's your dose," and Meredith tossed him a dozen bonbons, twisted up in a bit of paper.

"No, thank you; I know myself too well to risk it. If you are all going to turn hashish-eaters, you'll need someone to take care of you, so I'll keep sober," tossing the little parcel back.

It fell short, and the doctor, too lazy to pick it up, let it lie, merely saying, with a laugh, "Well, I advise any bashful man to take hashish when he wants to offer his heart to any fair lady, for it will give him the courage of a hero, the eloquence of a poet, and the ardor of an Italian. Remember that, gentlemen, and come to me when the crisis approaches."

"Does it conquer the pride, rouse the pity, and soften the hard hearts of the fair sex?" asked Done.

"I dare say now is your time to settle the fact, for here are two ladies who have imbibed, and in three hours will be in such a seraphic state of mind that 'No' will be an impossibility to them."

"Oh, mercy on us; what *have* we done? If that's the case, I shall shut myself up till my foolish fit is over. Rose, you haven't taken any; I beg you to mount guard over me, and see that I don't disgrace myself by any nonsense. Promise me you will," cried Belle, in half-real, half-feigned alarm at the consequences of her prank.

"I promise," said Rose, and floated down the green path as noiselessly as a white cloud, with a curious smile on her lips.

"Don't tell any of the rest what we have done, but after tea let us go into the grove and compare notes," said Norton, as Done strolled away to the beach, and the voices of approaching friends broke the summer quiet.

At tea, the initiated glanced covertly at one another, and saw, or fancied they saw, the effects of the hashish, in a certain suppressed excitement of manner, and unusually brilliant eyes. Belle laughed often, a silvery ringing laugh, pleasant to hear; but when complimented on her good spirits, she looked distressed, and said she could not help her merriment; Meredith was quite calm, but rather dreamy; Evelyn was pale, and her next neighbor heard her heart beat; Norton talked incessantly, but as he talked uncommonly well, no one suspected anything. Done and Miss St. Just watched the others with interest, and were very quiet, especially Rose, who scarcely spoke, but smiled her sweetest, and looked very lovely.

The moon rose early, and the experimenters slipped away to the grove, leaving the outsiders on the lawn as usual. Some bold spirit asked Rose to sing, and she at once complied, pouring out Spanish airs in a voice that melted the hearts of her audience, so full of fiery sweetness or tragic pathos was it. Done seemed quite carried away, and lay with his face in the grass, to hide the tears that would come; till, afraid of openly disgracing himself, he started up and hurried down to the little wharf, where he sat alone, listening to the music with a countenance which plainly revealed to the stars the passion which possessed him. The sound of loud laughter from the grove, followed by entire silence, caused him to wonder what demonstrations were taking place, and half resolve to go and see. But that enchanting voice held him captive, even when a boat put off mysteriously from a point nearby, and sailed away like a phantom through the twilight.

Half an hour afterward, a white figure came down the path, and Rose's voice broke in on his midsummer night's dream. The moon shone clearly now, and showed him the anxiety in her face as she said hurriedly, "Where is Belle?"

"Gone sailing, I believe."

"How could you let her go? She was not fit to take care of herself!"

"I forgot that."

"So did I, but I promised to watch over her, and I must. Which way did they go?" demanded Rose, wrapping the white mantle about her, and running her eye over the little boats moored below.

"You will follow her?"

"Yes."

"I'll be your guide then. They went toward the lighthouse; it is too far to row; I am at your service. Oh, say yes," cried Done, leaping into his own skiff and offering his hand persuasively.

She hesitated an instant and looked at him. He was always pale, and the moonlight seemed to increase this pallor, but his hat brim hid his eyes, and his voice was very quiet. A loud peal of laughter floated over the water, and as if the sound decided her, she gave him her hand and entered the boat. Done smiled triumphantly as he shook out the sail, which caught the freshening wind, and sent the boat dancing along a path of light.

How lovely it was! All the indescribable allurements of a perfect summer night surrounded them: balmy airs, enchanting moonlight, distant music, and, close at hand, the delicious atmosphere of love, which made itself felt in the eloquent silences that fell between them. Rose seemed to yield to the subtle charm, and leaned back on the cushioned seat with her beautiful head uncovered, her face full of dreamy softness, and her hands lying loosely clasped before her. She seldom spoke, showed no further anxiety for Belle, and soon seemed to forget the object of her search, so absorbed was she in some delicious thought which wrapped her in its peace.

Done sat opposite, flushed now, restless, and excited, for his eyes glittered; the hand on the rudder shook, and his voice sounded intense and passionate, even in the utterance of the simplest words. He talked continually and with unusual brilliancy, for, though a man of many accomplishments, he was too indolent or too fastidious to exert himself, except among his peers. Rose seemed to look without seeing, to listen without hearing, and though she smiled blissfully, the smiles were evidently not for him.

On they sailed, scarcely heeding the bank of black cloud piled up in the horizon, the rising wind, or the silence which proved their solitude. Rose moved once or twice, and lifted her hand as if to speak, but sank back mutely, and the hand fell again as if it had not energy enough to enforce her wish. A cloud sweeping over the moon, a distant growl of thunder, and the slight gust that struck the sail seemed to rouse her. Done was singing now like one inspired, his hat at his feet, hair in disorder, and a strangely rapturous expression in his eyes, which were fixed on her. She started, shivered, and seemed to recover herself with an effort.

"Where are they?" she asked, looking vainly for the island heights and the other boat.

"They have gone to the beach, I fancy, but we will follow." As Done leaned forward to speak, she saw his face and shrank back with a sudden flush, for in it she read clearly what she had felt, yet doubted until now. He saw the telltale blush and gesture, and said impetuously, "You know it now; you cannot deceive me longer, or daunt me with your pride! Rose, I love you, and dare tell you so tonight!"

"Not now—not here—I will not listen. Turn back, and be silent, I entreat you, Mr. Done," she said hurriedly.

He laughed a defiant laugh and took her hand in his, which was burning and throbbing with the rapid heat of his pulse.

"No, I *will* have my answer here, and now, and never turn back till you give it; you have been a thorny Rose, and given me many wounds.

I'll be paid for my heartache with sweet words, tender looks, and frank confessions of love, for proud as you are, you do love me, and dare not deny it."

Something in his tone terrified her; she snatched her hand away and drew beyond his reach, trying to speak calmly, and to meet coldly the ardent glances of the eyes which were strangely darkened and dilated with uncontrollable emotion.

"You forget yourself. I shall give no answer to an avowal made in such terms. Take me home instantly," she said in a tone of command.

"Confess you love me, Rose."

"Never!"

"Ah! I'll have a kinder answer, or—" Done half rose and put out his hand to grasp and draw her to him, but the cry she uttered seemed to arrest him with a sort of shock. He dropped into his seat, passed his hand over his eyes, and shivered nervously as he muttered in an altered tone, "I meant nothing; it's the moonlight; sit down, I'll control myself—upon my soul I will!"

"If you do not, I shall go overboard. Are you mad, sir?" cried Rose, trembling with indignation.

"Then I shall follow you, for I *am* mad, Rose, with love—hashish!"

His voice sank to a whisper, but the last word thrilled along her nerves, as no sound of fear had ever done before. An instant she regarded him with a look which took in every sign of unnatural excitement, then she clasped her hands with an imploring gesture, saying, in a tone of despair, "Why did I come! How will it end? Oh, Mark, take me home before it is too late!"

"Hush! Be calm; don't thwart me, or I may get wild again. My thoughts are not clear, but I understand you. There, take my knife, and if I forget myself, kill me. Don't go overboard; you are too beautiful to die, my Rose!"

He threw her the slender hunting knife he wore, looked at her a moment with a far-off look, and trimmed the sail like one moving in a dream. Rose took the weapon, wrapped her cloak closely about her, and crouching as far away as possible, kept her eye on him, with a face in which watchful terror contended with some secret trouble and bewilderment more powerful than her fear.

The boat moved round and began to beat up against wind and tide; spray flew from her bow; the sail bent and strained in the gusts that struck it with perilous fitfulness. The moon was nearly hidden by scudding clouds, and one-half the sky was black with the gathering storm. Rose looked from threatening heavens to treacherous sea, and tried to be ready for any danger, but her calm had been sadly broken, and she could not recover it. Done sat motionless, uttering no word of encouragement, though the frequent flaws almost tore the rope from his hand, and the water often dashed over him.

"Are we in any danger?" asked Rose at last, unable to bear the silence, for he looked like a ghostly helmsman seen by the fitful light, pale now, wild-eyed, and speechless.

"Yes, great danger."

"I thought you were a skillful boatman."

"I am when I am myself; now I am rapidly losing the control of my will, and the strange quiet is coming over me. If I had been alone I should have given up sooner, but for your sake I've kept on."

"Can't you work the boat?" asked Rose, terror-struck by the changed tone of his voice, the slow, uncertain movements of his hands.

"No. I see everything through a thick cloud; your voice sounds far away, and my one desire is to lay my head down and sleep."

"Let me steer—I can, I must!" she cried, springing toward him and laying her hand on the rudder.

He smiled and kissed the little hand, saying dreamily, "You could not hold it a minute; sit by me, love; let us turn the boat again, and drift away together—anywhere, anywhere out of the world."

"Oh, heaven, what will become of us!" and Rose wrung her hands in real despair. "Mr. Done—Mark—dear Mark, rouse yourself and listen to me. Turn, as you say, for it is certain death to go on so. Turn, and let us drift down to the lighthouse; they will hear and help us. Quick, take down the sail, get out the oars, and let us try to reach there before the storm breaks."

As Rose spoke, he obeyed her like a dumb animal; love for her was stronger even than the instinct of self-preservation, and for her sake he fought against the treacherous lethargy which was swiftly overpowering him. The sail was lowered, the boat brought round, and with little help from the ill-pulled oars it drifted rapidly out to sea with the ebbing tide.

As she caught her breath after this dangerous maneuver was accomplished, Rose asked, in a quiet tone she vainly tried to render natural, "How much hashish did you take?"

"All that Meredith threw me. Too much; but I was possessed to do it, so I hid the roll and tried it," he answered, peering at her with a weird laugh.

"Let us talk; our safety lies in keeping awake, and I dare not let you sleep," continued Rose, dashing water on her own hot forehead with a sort of desperation.

"Say you love me; that would wake me from my lost sleep, I think.

I have hoped and feared, waited and suffered so long. Be pitiful, and answer, Rose."

"I do; but I should not own it now."

So low was the soft reply he scarcely heard it, but he felt it and made a strong effort to break from the hateful spell that bound him. Leaning forward, he tried to read her face in a ray of moonlight breaking through the clouds; he saw a new and tender warmth in it, for all the pride was gone, and no fear marred the eloquence of those soft, Southern eyes.

"Kiss me, Rose, then I shall believe it. I feel lost in a dream, and you, so changed, so kind, may be only a fair phantom. Kiss me, love, and make it real."

As if swayed by a power more potent than her will, Rose bent to meet his lips. But the ardent pressure seemed to startle her from a momentary oblivion of everything but love. She covered up her face and sank down, as if overwhelmed with shame, sobbing through passionate tears, "Oh, what am I doing? I am mad, for I, too, have taken hashish."

What he answered she never heard, for a rattling peal of thunder drowned his voice, and then the storm broke loose. Rain fell in torrents, the wind blew fiercely, sky and sea were black as ink, and the boat tossed from wave to wave almost at their mercy. Giving herself up for lost, Rose crept to her lover's side and clung there, conscious only that they would bide together through the perils their own folly brought them. Done's excitement was quite gone now; he sat like a statue, shielding the frail creature whom he loved with a smile on his face, which looked awfully emotionless when the lightning gave her glimpses of its white immobility. Drenched, exhausted, and half senseless with danger, fear, and exposure, Rose saw at last a welcome glimmer through the gloom, and roused herself to cry for help.

"Mark, wake and help me! Shout, for God's sake—shout and call them, for we are lost if we drift by!" she cried, lifting his head from his breast, and forcing him to see the brilliant beacons streaming far across the troubled water.

He understood her, and springing up, uttered shout after shout like one demented. Fortunately, the storm had lulled a little; the lighthouse keeper heard and answered. Rose seized the helm, Done the oars, and with one frantic effort guided the boat into quieter waters, where it was met by the keeper, who towed it to the rocky nook which served as harbor.

The moment a strong, steady face met her eyes, and a gruff, cheery voice hailed her, Rose gave way, and was carried up to the house, looking more like a beautiful drowned Ophelia than a living woman.

"Here, Sally, see to the poor thing; she's had a rough time on't. I'll take care of her sweetheart—and a nice job I'll have, I reckon, for if he ain't mad or drunk, he's had a stroke of lightnin', and looks as if he wouldn't get his hearin' in a hurry," said the old man as he housed his unexpected guests and stood staring at Done, who looked about him like one dazed. "You jest turn in yonder and sleep it off, mate. We'll see to the lady, and right up your boat in the morning," the old man added.

"Be kind to Rose. I frightened her. I'll not forget you. Yes, let me sleep and get over this cursed folly as soon as possible," muttered this strange visitor.

Done threw himself down on the rough couch and tried to sleep, but every nerve was overstrained, every pulse beating like a trip-hammer, and everything about him was intensified and exaggerated with awful power. The thundershower seemed a wild hurricane, the quaint room a wilderness peopled with tormenting phantoms, and all the events of his life passed before him in an endless procession, which nearly maddened him. The old man looked weird and gigantic, his own voice sounded shrill and discordant, and the ceaseless murmur of Rose's incoherent wanderings haunted him like parts of a grotesque but dreadful dream.

All night he lay motionless, with staring eyes, feverish lips, and a mind on the rack, for the delicate machinery which had been tampered with revenged the wrong by torturing the foolish experimenter. All night Rose wept and sang, talked and cried for help in a piteous state of nervous excitement, for with her the trance came first, and the after-agitation was increased by the events of the evening. She slept at last, lulled by the old woman's motherly care, and Done was spared one tormenting fear, for he dreaded the consequences of this folly on her, more than upon himself.

As day dawned he rose, haggard and faint, and staggered out. At the door he met the keeper, who stopped him to report that the boat was in order, and a fair day coming. Seeing doubt and perplexity in the old man's eye, Done told him the truth, and added that he was going to the beach for a plunge, hoping by that simple tonic to restore his unstrung nerves.

He came back feeling like himself again, except for a dull headache, and a heavy sense of remorse weighing on his spirits, for he distinctly recollected all the events of the night. The old woman made him eat and drink, and in an hour he felt ready for the homeward trip.

Rose slept late, and when she woke soon recovered herself, for her dose had been a small one. When she had breakfasted and made a hasty toilet, she professed herself anxious to return at once. She dreaded yet longed to see Done, and when the time came armed herself with pride, feeling all a woman's shame at what had passed, and resolving to feign forgetfulness of the incidents of the previous night. Pale and cold as a statue she met him, but the moment he began to say humbly, "Forgive me, Rose," she silenced him with an imperious gesture and the command "Don't speak of it; I only remember that it was very horrible, and wish to forget it all as soon as possible."

"All, Rose?" he asked, significantly.

"Yes, *all*. No one would care to recall the follies of a hashish dream," she answered, turning hastily to hide the scarlet flush that would rise, and the eyes that would fall before his own.

"*I* never can forget, but I will be silent if you bid me."

"I do. Let us go. What will they think at the island? Mr. Done, give me your promise to tell no one, now or ever, that I tried that dangerous experiment. I will guard your secret also." She spoke eagerly and looked up imploringly.

"I promise," and he gave her his hand, holding her own with a wistful glance, till she drew it away and begged him to take her home.

Leaving hearty thanks and a generous token of their gratitude, they sailed away with a fair wind, finding in the freshness of the morning a speedy cure for tired bodies and excited minds. They said little, but it was impossible for Rose to preserve her coldness. The memory of the past night broke down her pride, and Done's tender glances touched her heart. She half hid her face behind her hand, and tried to compose herself for the scene to come, for as she approached the island, she saw Belle and her party waiting for them on the shore.

"Oh, Mr. Done, screen me from their eyes and questions as much as you can! I'm so worn out and nervous, I shall betray myself. You will help me?" And she turned to him with a confiding look, strangely at variance with her usual calm self-possession.

"I'll shield you with my life, if you will tell me why you took the hashish," he said, bent on knowing his fate.

"I hoped it would make me soft and lovable, like other women. I'm tired of being a lonely statue," she faltered, as if the truth was wrung from her by a power stronger than her will.

"And I took it to gain courage to tell my love. Rose, we have been near death together; let us share life together, and neither of us be any more lonely or afraid?"

He stretched his hand to her with his heart in his face, and she gave him hers with a look of tender submission, as he said ardently, "Heaven bless hashish, if its dreams end like this!"

TITLE	CENTRAL THEME(S)
"Pauline's Passion and Punishment" Anonymous	Manipulating Heroine
"A Whisper in the Dark" Anonymous	Mind Control
"V. V.: or, Plots and Counterplots" By A Well Known Author	Manipulating Heroine
"A Marble Woman: or, The Mysterious Model" By A. M. Barnard	Manipulating Hero Opium Addiction
"Behind a Mask: or, A Woman's Power" By A. M. Barnard	Manipulating Heroine

FIRST PUBLICATION	REPRINT HISTORY
Frank Leslie's Illustrated Newspaper, Vol. XV, Nos. 379 & 380 (January 3 & 10, 1863). Stern 27 *	*Behind a Mask* (From file of *Leslie's* at New York Public Library and New York Historical Society)
Frank Leslie's Illustrated Newspaper, Vol. XVI, Nos. 401 & 402 (June 6 & 13, 1863). Stern 30	*A Modern Mephistopheles and A Whisper in the Dark* (Boston: Roberts Brothers, 1889). BAL 219 †
	Plots and Counterplots ** (From Stern copy of *A Modern Mephistopheles and A Whisper in the Dark*)
The Flag of Our Union, Vol. XX, Nos. 5, 6, 7, 8 (February 4, 11, 18, 25, 1865). Stern 47	*Ten Cent Novelette,* No. 80, By A. M. Barnard (Boston: Thomes & Talbot, *ca.* 1870). BAL 165
	Plots and Counterplots (From copy of *Ten Cent Novelette* at New York Public Library, Rare Book Division)
The Flag of Our Union, Vol. XX, Nos. 20, 21, 22, 23 (May 20, 27, June 3, 10, 1865). Stern 51	*Plots and Counterplots* (From issues of *The Flag of Our Union* at Houghton Library, Harvard University)
The Flag of Our Union, Vol. XXI, Nos. 41, 42, 43, 44 (October 13, 20, 27, November 3, 1866). Stern 53	*Behind a Mask* (From issues of *The Flag of Our Union* at American Antiquarian Society)

* Stern numbers refer to numbered items in the Alcott Bibliography appended to Madeleine B. Stern, ed., *Louisa's Wonder Book: A Newly Discovered Alcott Juvenile* (Mount Pleasant, Michigan: Clarke Historical Library, Central Michigan University, 1975).

† BAL numbers refer to *Bibliography of American Literature,* compiled by Jacob Blanck (New Haven: Yale University Press, 1955) Vol. I.

** *Plots and Counterplots* refers to the original hardcover title of this book, *A Marble Woman.*

TITLE	CENTRAL THEME(S)
"The Abbot's Ghost: or, Maurice Treherne's Temptation" By A. M. Barnard	Gothic Romance
"The Skeleton in the Closet" By L. M. Alcott	Madness
"The Mysterious Key, and What It Opened" By L. M. Alcott	Italianate Englishman Gothic Devices
"Perilous Play" By L. M. A.	Hashish Experimentation

FIRST PUBLICATION	REPRINT HISTORY
The Flag of Our Union, Vol. XXII, Nos. 1, 2, 3, 4 (January 5, 12, 19, 26, 1867). Stern 55	*Behind a Mask* (From issues of *The Flag of Our Union* in Rare Book Division, Library of Congress)
Ten Cent Novelette, No. 49 (Boston: Elliott, Thomes & Talbot [1867]). Trailer to *The Foundling* by Perley Parker. Stern 60; BAL 151	*Plots and Counterplots* (From copy in Alderman Library, University of Virginia)
Ten Cent Novelette, No. 50 (Boston: Elliott, Thomes & Talbot [1867]. Stern 64; BAL 152	*The Leisure Hour Library*, No. 382 (New York: F. M. Lupton, *ca.* 1900).
	Behind a Mask (From copy of *Ten Cent Novelette* in Alderman Library, University of Virginia, previously owned by Carroll A. Wilson)
Frank Leslie's Chimney Corner, Vol. VIII, No. 194 (February 13, 1869). Stern 94	*Frank Leslie's Popular Monthly*, Vol. II, No. 5 (November, 1876).
	Plots and Counterplots (From issue of *Frank Leslie's Chimney Corner* in New York Public Library)

NOTES

[1] Louisa May Alcott, *Little Women* (New York and London, [1975]), pp. 382, 385.

[2] Ednah D. Cheney, ed., *Louisa May Alcott: Her Life, Letters, and Journals* (Boston, 1889), p. 193 [hereinafter Cheney].

[3] *Behind a Mask: The Unknown Thrillers of Louisa May Alcott. Edited and with an Introduction by Madeleine Stern* (New York: William Morrow & Company, 1975).

[4] Alcott, *Little Women*, pp. 385–386.

[5] *Comic Tragedies Written by "Jo" and "Meg" and Acted by the "Little Women"* (Boston, 1893); Madeleine B. Stern, *Louisa May Alcott* (Norman, Oklahoma, 1971), p. 54.

[6] Cheney, pp. 97–98, 111; Stern, *Louisa May Alcott*, p. 95.

[7] Bronson Alcott to Anna, Concord, January 29, 1863, in Richard L. Herrnstadt, ed., *The Letters of A. Bronson Alcott* (Ames, Iowa, [1969]), p. 334; Cheney, pp. 137, 145–147; Stern, *Louisa May Alcott*, pp. 129–132; Madeleine B. Stern, "Louisa M. Alcott, Civil War Nurse," *Americana*, XXXVII: 2 (April, 1943), pp. 296–325.

[8] Bronson Alcott to Louisa, Concord, December 17, 1865, in Herrnstadt, *op. cit.*, p. 379.

[9] Cheney, pp. 109, 130, 132, 161, 197.

[10] Alcott, *Little Women*, p. 383.

[11] "V. V.: or, Plots and Counterplots," *The Flag of Our Union*, XX: 5, 6, 7, 8 (February 4, 11, 18, 25, 1865). Reprinted as No. 80 in the *Ten Cent Novelettes* of *Standard American Authors* series *ca.* 1870, under the pseudonym of A. M. Barnard. Now reprinted from the *Novel-*

ette in the New York Public Library, Rare Book Division, through the courtesy of Mrs. Maud Cole, Chief.

[12] Cheney, p. 165.

[13] Alcott, *Little Women*, p. 302.

[14] James R. Elliott to Louisa M. Alcott, Boston, January 7, 1865 (Houghton Library, Harvard University).

[15] Cheney, p. 165.

[16] "A Marble Woman: or, The Mysterious Model," *The Flag of Our Union*, XX: 20, 21, 22, 23 (May 20, 27, June 3, 10, 1865). Published under the pseudonym of A. M. Barnard. Now reprinted from the issues at Houghton Library, Harvard University, through the courtesy of Miss Carolyn Jakeman.

[17] Stern, *Lousia May Alcott*, pp. 138–139, 184.

[18] John Rublowsky, *The Stoned Age: A History of Drugs in America* (New York, [1974]), pp. 35, 117–130.

[19] Madeleine B. Stern, *Imprints on History: Book Publishers and American Frontiers* (Bloomington, Indiana, 1956), p. 208.

[20] Stern, *Louisa May Alcott*, p. 147.

[21] James R. Elliott to Louisa M. Alcott, Boston, June 15, 1865 (Houghton Library, Harvard University).

[22] Bronson Alcott to Louisa, Concord, March 25, 1866, in Herrnstadt, *op. cit.*, p. 391.

[23] Cheney, p. 184; Stern, *Louisa May Alcott*, p. 167.

[24] L. M. Alcott, *The Skeleton in the Closet*. Published with Perley Parker, *The Foundling* (Boston: Elliott, Thomes & Talbot [1867]) as No. 49 in the *Ten Cent Novelettes* of *Standard American Authors* series. Now reprinted through the courtesy of Dr. Julius P. Barclay and Miss Joan Crane, Alderman Library, University of Virginia. For date of deposit, see Jacob Blanck, *Bibliography of American Literature* (New Haven, 1955), I, No. 151.

[25] "Pauline's Passion and Punishment," *Frank Leslie's Illustrated Newspaper*, XV: 379 and 380 (January 3 and 10, 1863). Reprinted in *Behind a Mask*.

[26] "A Whisper in the Dark," *Frank Leslie's Illustrated Newspaper*, XVI: 401 and 402 (June 6 and 13, 1863). Reprinted in *A Modern Mephistopheles and A Whisper in the Dark* (Boston, 1889). Now reprinted from the copy of the latter owned by Madeleine B. Stern. In the periodical version the horse is named Satan, not Sultan. The illustrations are from *Frank Leslie's Illustrated Newspaper* (June 6 and 13, 1863), courtesy New York Historical Society.

[27] "Perilous Play," *Frank Leslie's Chimney Corner*, VIII: 194 (Feb-

ruary 3, 1869). Reprinted in *Frank Leslie's Popular Monthly*, II: 5 (November, 1876). Now reprinted from the periodical *Frank Leslie's Chimney Corner* in the New York Public Library.

[28] Cheney, p. 165.

[29] Madeleine B. Stern, *Purple Passage: The Life of Mrs. Frank Leslie* (Norman, Oklahoma, 1970), pp. 44–46.

[30] Rublowsky, *The Stoned Age*, pp. 35, 94–99.

[31] L. M. Alcott, *The Mysterious Key, and What It Opened* (Boston: Elliott, Thomes & Talbot [1867]). Issued as No. 50 in the *Ten Cent Novelettes* of *Standard American Authors* series. Reprinted as No. 382 in The Leisure Hour Library by F. M. Lupton of New York, *ca.* 1900. Reprinted in *Behind a Mask*.

[32] Stern, *Imprints on History*, pp. 211–214.

[33] Cheney, pp. 379–382.

[34] *A Modern Mephistopheles* (Boston, 1877). Published anonymously. Reprinted as Louisa M. Alcott, *A Modern Mephistopheles and A Whisper in the Dark* (Boston, 1889).

[35] See *Behind a Mask*, p. *xxvi*.

[36] Cheney, p. 297.

[37] Louisa M. Alcott, *A Modern Mephistopheles and A Whisper in the Dark* (Boston, 1889), advertisement at end, quoting from review in *The New Age*.

AVON BOOKS TRADE PAPERBACKS

___ **The Brave Cowboy** $11.00 US/$15.00 Can   71459-0
      by Edward Abbey

___ **Fire on the Mountain** $10.00 US/$12.00 Can   71460-4
      by Edward Abbey

___ **The Fool's Progress:** $12.00 US/$15.00 Can   70856-6
      An Honest Novel
      by Edward Abbey

___ **The Monkey Wrench Gang** $12.50 US/$15.00 Can   71339-X
      by Edward Abbey

___ **Durable Goods** $9.00 US/$11.00 Can   72308-5
      by Elizabeth Berg

___ **An American Romance** $12.50 US/$15.00 Can   71240-7
      by John Casey

___ **Spartina** $11.00 US/$13.00 Can   71104-4
      by John Casey

___ **A Model World and Other Stories** $10.00 US/$12.00 Can   71099-4
      by Michael Chabon

___ **Rumor Has It** $9.00 US/$11.00 Can   71346-2
      by Charles Dickinson

___ **Charms for the Easy Life** $10.00 US/$12.00 Can   72557-6
      by Kaye Gibbons

___ **Foreign Affairs** by Alison Lurie $11.00 US/$15.00 Can   70990-2

___ **Imaginary Friends** $8.95 US/$10.95 Can   71136-2
      by Alison Lurie

___ **Only Children** by Alison Lurie $7.95 US/$9.95 Can   70875-2

___ **The Truth About Lorin Jones** $11.00 US   70807-8
      by Alison Lurie

___ **The War Between the Tates** $8.95 US/$10.95 Can   71135-4
      by Alison Lurie

___ **Afterlife** by Paul Monette $10.00 US/$12.00 Can   71197-4

___ **Halfway Home** by Paul Monette $11.00 US/$15.00 Can   71797-2

___ **Coffee Will Make You Black** $10.00 US/$12.00 Can   72459-6
      by April Sinclair

___ **The Lady at Liberty** $9.95 US/$11.95 Can   76427-X
      by Hudson Talbott

___ **The Fugitive** $8.95 US/$10.95 Can   71496-5
      by Pramoedya Ananta Toer

Buy these books at your local bookstore or use this coupon for ordering:

··

Mail to: Avon Books, Dept BP, Box 767, Rte 2, Dresden, TN 38225   D
Please send me the book(s) I have checked above.
❏ My check or money order—no cash or CODs please—for $_____is enclosed (please
add $1.50 to cover postage and handling for each book ordered—Canadian residents add 7%
GST).
❏ Charge my VISA/MC Acct#_____Exp Date_____
Minimum credit card order is two books or $7.50 (please add postage and handling
charge of $1.50 per book—Canadian residents add 7% GST). For faster service, call
1-800-762-0779. Residents of Tennessee, please call 1-800-633-1607. Prices and numbers are
subject to change without notice. Please allow six to eight weeks for delivery.

Name_____
Address_____
City_____State/Zip_____
Telephone No._____   TRF 0595